England through Colonial Eyes in Twentieth-Century Fiction

Also by Ann Blake

CHRISTINA STEAD'S POLITICS OF PLACE

Also by Leela Gandhi

MEASURES OF HOME: Poems
POSTCOLONIAL THEORY: A Critical Introduction
SHAKESPEARE: Canon and Critique

Also by Sue Thomas

ELIZABETH ROBINS (1862–1952): A Bibliography
THE WORLDING OF JEAN RHYS

England through Colonial Eyes in Twentieth-Century Fiction

Ann Blake
Honorary Associate
La Trobe University
Bundoora
Melbourne
Australia

Leela Gandhi
Senior Lecturer in English
La Trobe University
Bundoora
Melbourne
Australia

and

Sue Thomas
Reader in English
La Trobe University
Bundoora
Melbourne
Australia

823. 91093242
eng

First published 2001 by
PALGRAVE
Houndmills, Basingstoke, Hampshire RG21 6XS and
175 Fifth Avenue, New York, N. Y. 10010
Companies and representatives throughout the world

PALGRAVE is the new global academic imprint of
St. Martin's Press LLC Scholarly and Reference Division and
Palgrave Publishers Ltd (formerly Macmillan Press Ltd).

ISBN 0–333–73744–X

This book is printed on paper suitable for recycling and
made from fully managed and sustained forest sources.

A catalogue record for this book is available
from the British Library.

Library of Congress Cataloging-in-Publication Data
Blake, Ann, 1941–
    England through colonial eyes in twentieth-century fiction /
    Ann Blake, Leela Gandhi, and Sue Thomas.
        p. cm.
    Includes bibliographical references and index.
    ISBN 0–333–73744–X (cloth)
    1. Commonwealth fiction (English)—History and criticism.
    2. English fiction—20th century—History and criticism.
    3. England—Foreign public opinion, Commonwealth. 4. England–
    –Relations—Commonwealth countries. 5. Commonwealth
    countries—Relations—England. 6. Postcolonialism–
    –Commonwealth countries. 7. England—In literature. I. Gandhi,
    Leela, 1966– II. Thomas, Sue, 1955– III. Title.
    PR9084 .B58 2001
    823'.91093242—dc21
                                                    00–054206

10   9   8   7   6   5   4   3   2   1
10   09 08 07 06 05 04 03 02 01

Printed in Great Britain by Antony Rowe Ltd, Chippenham, Wiltshire

To Derick (A. B.),
Pauline (L. G.),
and Hazel and Ray (S. T.)

Contents

List of Abbreviations

F-G City	*The Four-Gated City*	Doris Lessing
HL	*The Housing Lark*	Samuel Selvon
Letters	*The Collected Letters of Katherine Mansfield*	
LL	*The Lonely Londoners*	Samuel Selvon
MM	*The Mimic Men*	V. S. Naipaul
Notebooks	*The Katherine Mansfield Notebooks*	
Stories	*The Stories of Katherine Mansfield*	

Jean Rhys often uses ellipses as a stylistic device. We distinguish between her use of ellipses and ours in quoting from her work. Our ellipses are indicated with square brackets: [. . .].

Acknowledgements

The writing of this book was crucially supported by an Australian Research Council small grant in 1999. Ann Blake wishes also to acknowledge grants in 1999 from the La Trobe University Faculty of Humanities and Social Sciences Research and Graduate Studies Committee for visits to the Australian National Library in Canberra and the National Library of New Zealand in Wellington. In 1999 Sue Thomas presented earlier and different versions of the chapter on Jean Rhys at the Colonial Eye conference, held at the University of Tasmania, and the Third Biennial Conference of the Australian Association for Caribbean Studies (AACS), held at La Trobe University. She thanks her audiences, the organizers of the Colonial Eye conference, her co-organizers of the AACS Conference, and the La Trobe Faculty of Humanities and Social Sciences Research and Graduate Studies Committee for the travel grant that enabled her to attend the Tasmanian conference.

The authors and publisher gratefully acknowledge permission for use of the following material by Jean Rhys: 'Triple Sec' (Jean Rhys Papers), 'Essay on England' (Jean Rhys Papers), 'Cowslips' (Jean Rhys Papers), Orange Notebook (Jean Rhys Papers), 'New story' (Jean Rhys Papers), and 'The Ant Civilisation. The Kingdom of the Human Ants' (British Library, Add. Ms. 57856, f. 151–2). All material is used by permission of the Jean Rhys Estate. Selections from the Jean Rhys Papers are used by permission of the Department of Special Collections, McFarlin Library, University of Tulsa, Oklahoma. The Estate of Christina Stead and Professor Margaret Harris, literary trustee, have given permission to quote from the papers of Christina Stead.

Ron Geering has encouraged the research on Stead. Francis Wyndham, Rhys's literary executor, and Lori Curtis, Curator of Special Collections at the University of Tulsa, have facilitated the research on Rhys.

As Head of the School of English at La Trobe University Richard Freadman has been warmly supportive of the project. Clive Bloom offered useful advice on the initial publishing proposal. For a generous sharing of ideas and help in locating materials we thank Karen Hewitt, Peter Hulme and Martin Prochazka.

We are especially grateful to our families, friends, colleagues, and Palgrave editors (Julian Honer, Charmian Hearne, Elinor Birne and Ann Marangos) for their patience and support.

Introduction: 'Mother Country'

Contemplating in 1840 the imperial reach of the Catholic Church, Thomas Babington Macaulay imagined in a distant future 'some traveller from New Zealand [who] shall, in the midst of a vast solitude, take his stand on a broken arch of London Bridge to sketch the ruins of St Paul's' ('Von Ranke' 39). A British colonial taking as an object of aesthetic creativity a recognisably English scene is a speculative curiosity. Australasia had been celebrated in his Minute on Indian Education (1835) as one of the 'great European communities which are rising' in the southern hemisphere through the spread of the English language and of education in a British and European epistemological tradition. The other was in the 'south of Africa' (428). In India he envisioned the reach of that language and tradition to be the 'form[ation of] a class who may be interpreters between us and the millions whom we govern; a class of persons Indian in blood and colour, but English in taste, in opinions, in morals, and in intellect' (430). Twentieth-century writers from the British empire and its decolonizing nations regularly attest to the ways in which being English-speaking and having been educated in the knowledges English makes available has produced England as the centre of an imperial cartography, as a country of the imagination, and as a conflicted site of affiliation (and disaffiliation) encapsulated in the phrase 'mother country'. Sam Selvon, who emigrated to England from Trinidad in 1950, remembers, for example, in 'Finding West Indian Identity in London':

> There was also a feeling for the English countryside and landscape which had possessed me from schoolday reading of the English poets. In the hot tropical atmosphere I dreamed of green fields and rolling downs, of purling streams and daffodils and tulips, thatched cottages

1

and quiet pubs nestling in the valleys. And I wanted to see for myself the leafless trees covered with snow as depicted on Christmas post-cards.

(58)

In this book we are interested in England and representations of England, English life and English people as a 'contact zone'. Mary Louise Pratt uses the term 'contact zone' to describe 'the space of colonial encounters, the space in which peoples geographically and historically separated come into contact with each other and establish ongoing relations' (6). The concept 'foreground[s] the interactive, improvisational dimensions of colonial encounters', shifting attention to 'how subjects are constituted in and by their relations to each other' by concentrating on 'copresence, interaction, interlocking understandings and practices, often within radically asymmetrical relations of power' (7). Pratt's contact zones are outside Europe, located in its imperial territories. Our extension of Pratt's ' "contact" perspective' facilitates 'a dialectic and historicized approach' (6–7) to the fiction, topics, genres and authors we analyse. We suggest explicitly and implicitly that 'England' is a site of multivalent 'contact' for writers whose perspectives have been shaped by historically localized varieties of British colonialism and continuing processes of anti-colonialism and decolonization. In his anthology *Extravagant Strangers: A Literature of Belonging* (1997) Caryl Phillips demonstrates that 'English literature has, for at least 200 years, been shaped and influenced by outsiders'. He includes selections of 'British writers who are outsiders in the most clear-cut way – those not born in Britain' (x). The writers in our study rather were born in the British empire or in states which were part of it, or were born outside Britain and grew up in its empire. We highlight variously the relations between writers and their English material as they exert 'narrative rights' to it (Philip Cohen, 'Who' 20) and work to make it intelligible through genre and generic conventions, between writers and England as mythical and sociopolitical place, and between their fictive colonial subjects and England. Further, we are concerned with the processes of decolonization which take place through contact with and life in England as visitors, expatriates, or immigrants, and the manner in which these processes are mediated through questions of race, gender, class, ethnicity, desire, and national and political belonging. By addressing authors as 'actor[s] and agent[s]', rather than as merely 'screen[s]' or 'ground[s] or 'resource[s]' in the production of representations and knowledges (Haraway 198), we draw attention to the transculturative dimensions of the fiction we analyse, the ways in which the writers have 'select[ed] and invent[ed]' from (Pratt 6), transformed the literary traditions, conventions, and intertexts made available to them through British imperialism and its post-independence cultural residues. We indicate that this transculturative process does not necessarily underscore an inherently progressive politics. Its politics may be ambivalent, or at times, for instance, grounded in heterosexism or reactionary gender or class values.

Our interest in writing this book was prompted by our sense that recent critical scholarship on the 'historical and discursive constructedness of *Englishness*, as itself a form of ethnicity' (Bhabha, 'Re-inventing Britain' n.p.). was marginalizing, sometimes wilfully, the voices we discuss here. Robert Colls and Philip Dodd, the editors of *Englishness: Politics and Culture 1880–1920* (1986), note of their collection of essays that '[t]here are omissions. Because we could not find a suitable and willing contributor, there is no account of what "the Empire" or part of it, thought of the English' (Preface n.p.). Judy Giles and Tim Middleton in their editorial Introduction to *Writing Englishness 1900–1950: An Introductory Sourcebook on National Identity* (1995) argue: 'To include those attempts to rework the English's versions of what it means to be English, or to offer those perspectives on England generated in the Commonwealth and other foreign contexts, would be to give weight to perspectives which, in the period, lacked any real impact on the dominant sense of what it meant to be English' (3). The claim is dismissive, ignoring, for example, the cultural impact of Rudyard Kipling's writing and elaboration of imperial mission. Their chronology does not include royal commissions on immigration, key immigration debates, racist riots in Liverpool in 1948, or the arrival of the *Empire Windrush* in 1948 with 492 Jamaican passengers, an event usually read as initiating post-Second World War 'coloured' immigration to Britain. Our study covers 'contact' and generic transculturation in more sustained ways than Simon Gikandi's *Maps of Englishness: Writing Identity in the Culture of Colonialism* (1996) and Ian Baucom's *Out of Place: Englishness, Empire and the Locations of Identity* (1999). Our focus, too, is more literary than Gikandi's and Baucom's.

The historical scope of our book is pointed. We include analyses of the work of colonial and ex-colonial writers published before 1950, situating it in crucial historical and intertextual moments. Our addressing of such questions as race and modernity, for example, is also, then, informed by a sense of some of the shifting historical understandings of 'race' and the racialization of English bodies politic. This gives a longer view of the 'political narrative of "race"' in England, which, as Barnor Hesse observes more generally, is now popularly thought to have begun after 1945. This period is 'referred to as the period of settlement, as if Black settlement began in the second half of the twentieth century' (163). It is also one in which 'race' has become synonymous with Blackness, an effect of racism focused on and moral panics over immigration from the so-called 'New Commonwealth'. Writers from both the 'Old Commonwealth' (Canada, Australia, New Zealand, and, from 1902 until 1961, South Africa) and the 'New Commonwealth' are the focus of our study. The first pair of texts considered in our book, Sara Jeannette Duncan's *Cousin Cinderella* and Rudyard Kipling's 'The Mother Hive', are shaped by and in response to a moral panic over and royal commission into 'alien' immigration to Britain in the first decade of the twentieth century. The 'aliens' then were principally Jewish and European.

There is sustained critical interest in the authors that we analyse. Some of the fiction has been brought together in productive ways before under the signs of multicultural or diaspora studies. We think here, in particular, of *Other Britain, Other British: Contemporary Multicultural Fiction* (edited by A. Robert Lee, 1995), and, using the West Indian diaspora in Britain as an example, of recent collections like *The Routledge Reader in Caribbean Literature* (edited by Alison Donnell and Sarah Lawson Welsh (1996), which usefully highlights expatriation and immigration, 'The Windrush Commemorative Issue: West Indians in Britain, 1948–1998', *Kunapipi*, 20.1 (1998) (edited by David Dabydeen), and *Empire Windrush: Fifty Years of Writing about Black Britain* (edited by Onyekachi Wambu, 1998). Our focus is on representations of England and Englishness, and we are alert to the distinctions the authors in our study make between England and Britain, the English and the British. The British Council and Arts Council of England are currently sponsoring events as part of a 'Re-inventing Britain' programme. The programme, inaugurated in 1997, operates under the sign of 'the *hybrid* cosmopolitanism of contemporary metropolitan life'. In his manifesto, Homi Bhabha criticizes multiculturalist understandings of culture as 'primarily concerned with the attribution of identity (individual or collective) and the conferral of authenticity (custom, tradition, ritual)'. Instead he proposes that culture is 'more about the activity of negotiating, regulating and authorising competing, often conflicting demands for collective self-representation' and that 'the definition of cultural process' shift to a concern with 'articulation rather than authentication' ('Re-inventing Britain'). The Economic and Social Research Council UK is funding a Transnational Communities Research Programme, the chief investigators of which are Tom Cheesman, Marie Gillespie, Deniz Göktürk, John Goodby, John McLeod and Sujala Singh. They coin the term 'axial writing': '"Axes" are lines of communication, trade and travel which connect pairs of significant sites within the multicentred networks of transnational communities: e.g. London-Delhi, or Berlin-Istanbul. "Axial writing" thematizes past and present traffic along axes; it also forms part of that traffic itself' ('Transnational Communities'). The 'new cosmopolitanism' and 'axial writing' have a particular contemporary resonance; we do, however, excavate difficult histories of cosmopolitanism and of traffic along axes with one site in England.

Our book is organized in two parts, Part I, 'Mapping Some Territory', a set of survey chapters, and Part II a set of studies of individual authors. In Chapter 1 'Colouring the English' Sue Thomas analyses representations of English people and the normative whiteness of English culture in fiction by Duncan, Kipling, Olive Schreiner, Jean Rhys, Pauline Melville, Samuel Selvon, and Randolph Stow. Focusing on a small range of texts, she works to elucidate the historical, geographical and narrative contingencies of the representations. Chapters 2 and 3, Ann Blake's '"A Literature of Belonging": Re-writing the Domestic Novel' and Leela Gandhi's '"Learning Me Your Language": England in the Postcolonial *Bildungsroman*' analyse the transculturation of specific fictional genres. The studies each place this process in large historical frames. Chapter 2 addresses the ways in which colonial and ex-colonial writers reshape the patterns of domestic narrative to accommodate the unresolved everyday struggles of outsiders with displacement and resettlement. The senses of displacement are sociopolitical, cultural and even imaginative as the daily realities of English life place pressure on colonial myths of England as mother or home or land of opportunity. While the chapter ranges widely and suggestively across primarily post-1945 fiction, novels by Dan Jacobson, George Lamming, Marilyn Duckworth, V.S. Naipaul, Samuel Selvon, Caryl Phillips, and Abdulrazak Gurnah are given more extended treatment. Chapter 3 turns to the encounter between India and English imperialism elaborated as England-as-education in the history of English pedagogy in India. That encounter, she argues, has exercised a transculturating influence on the Anglophone Indian *Bildungsroman*, a genre conventionally celebrated as realizing the principles of civil society through its commitment to the ideals of self-formation and self-development. She examines, in particular, the traditions of *bhakti*, or devotional culture, as a site of anti-colonial critique and affect. The temporal reach of her chapter situates the histories of *Bildung* in fictional texts like Amit Chaudhuri's *Afternoon Raag* and

Amitav Ghosh's *The Shadow Lines* in relation to those in earlier autobiographical texts by Mohandas Gandhi and Nirad Chaudhuri. Physical journeys to England are juxtaposed with England experienced as colonial culture in India.

For our Author Studies (Chapters 4–11) we have chosen writers from different cultural and historical backgrounds and generations: Katherine Mansfield (b. 1888, New Zealand, d. 1923); Jean Rhys (b. 1890, Dominica, d. 1979), Christina Stead (b. 1902, Australia, d. 1983), Doris Lessing (b. 1919, Persia, now Iran; grew up in Rhodesia, now Zimbabwe), V.S. Naipaul (b. 1932, Trinidad), Buchi Emecheta (b. 1944, Nigeria), Salman Rushdie (b. 1947, India), and David Dabydeen (b. 1955, British Guiana, now Guyana). Of these writers only Stead was born in an independent state, a federated Australia having gained independence in 1901. Rushdie was born two months before Indian independence. The choice of authors for close study does, in part, reflect our earlier individual scholarly competences. We have individually published on Stead, Rushdie, and Rhys. The chapters are arranged by date of birth of the chosen authors. This organization contributes manifoldly to the historical resonance of the book. Our choice of writers was not always easy. We settled on writers whose *oeuvre* engaged in a sustained way with English material or whose fiction has become central to contemporary critical debates over meanings of Englishness. In having to limit our range in both parts of the book we are also aware that writers from some colonial and decolonizing contexts – perhaps most notably Ireland – are not represented, and that the coverage of other contexts, like Canada or east Africa, is thin. Our necessary omissions point, though, to the richness and vitality of our topic.

Part I
Mapping Some Territory

1
Colouring the English

Sue Thomas

> This is England Hester said and I watched it through the train-window divided into squares like pocket-handkerchiefs; a small tidy look it had everywhere fenced off from everywhere else – what are those things – those are haystacks – oh are those haystacks – I had read about England ever since I could read – smaller meaner everything is never mind – this is London – hundreds thousands of white people white people rushing along and the dark houses all alike frowning down one after the other all alike all stuck together – the streets like smooth shut-in ravines and the dark houses frowning down.
>
> Jean Rhys, *Voyage in the Dark* (1934) 15–16

Rhys's white Creole narrator Anna Morgan is from Dominica, a West Indian island with a very small white population. Her first impressions of England and the English highlight the predominant whiteness of the urban mass, which is immediately visible to her. This is an inversion of the characteristic 'invisibility of whiteness as a racial position in white (which is to say dominant) discourse' (Dyer 3). Lyn Pykett argues that in Europe at the end of the nineteenth century 'the urban mass became *the* distinguishing characteristic of the modern condition, and also a motive for modernism' (33). The West Indian modernist voices of narrator and author in *Voyage in the Dark*, exemplified in the surreal register of the final part of the cited passage, are grounded in critique of the assimilative imperative of this mass, its disciplining disapproval of Anna's cultural difference. This disapproval is represented as an enclosing and exclusive sameness. The xenophobia to which English people subject Anna is articulated in the novel through business involving flowers, horticultural tropes and a discourse of breeding which Philip Cohen

9

suggests is one of the 'essential idioms [of Anglo-Saxon] racism' integral to 'a model of racial degeneration focused on certain peoples and places as "breeding grounds" of vice and disease' ('Perversions' 63–4). Anna's disidentification with Englishness is also characterized by her corporeal memory of the Caribbean, structured by modernist primitivist dichotomies, in which whiteness, synonymous with English cultural and middle-class gender identity, is associated with the coldness and stillness of death. In Rhys's childhood black Dominican women would wear white head gears and kerchiefs across their shoulders to bury Carnival. Anna's corporeal memory of the Caribbean becomes her transcendental anchor in modernity. The ethnographizing of the English and the transculturation of metropolitan aesthetic practice, motive, genre and thematics are enabling conditions for assumption of voice-agency by Anna as first-person narrator and by Rhys. Their voice-agencies have a history that extends beyond the novel's temporal and cultural setting.

Alistair Bonnett observes that 'Whiteness is a centred identity. In other words, Whiteness has, at least within the modern era and within Western societies, tended to be constructed as a norm, an unchanging and unproblematic location, a position from which all other identities come to be marked by their difference'. He urges examination of the 'social construction of Whiteness' (146).[1] Alien, colonial, and black are identities marked in British imperial history by their difference from a white English norm. In this chapter I proceed to analyse representations of the 'historical and geographical contingency' (Bonnett, 'White Studies' 146) of Englishness, normatively white, in a range of texts, principally *Cousin Cinderella* by Sara Jeannette Duncan (b. 1861, Canada), 'The Mother Hive' by Rudyard Kipling (b. 1865, India), *From Man to Man, or Perhaps Only...* by Olive Schreiner (b. 1855, South Africa), 'Triple Sec' by Jean Rhys (b. 1890, Dominica), 'A Disguised Land' by Pauline Melville (b. 1948, Guyana), *The Lonely Londoners* by Samuel Selvon (b. 1923, Trinidad), and *The Girl Green as Elderflower* by Randolph Stow (b. 1935, Australia). The representations, as my opening discussion of *Voyage in the Dark* suggests, have their own narrative contingencies. I use the term colouring in the title of the chapter to emphasize that the authors are making visible the distinctiveness whiteness of English bodies politic and generalizing the character of the English as they see them.

The first section of the chapter 'Democracy and English Tradition' is organized around a discussion of *Cousin Cinderella* (1908) and 'The Mother Hive' (1909), both of which thematize an English/alien dichotomy. Politically both Duncan and Kipling were conservatives. Misao

Dean characterizes Duncan as a 'pink tory: "pro-British in culture, pro-Canadian in aspirations for the future, socially committed to community and responsibility and, therefore, fearful of individualist, republican "democracy"' (*Difference* 16).[2] In *Cousin Cinderella* her democratic support of meritocracy and 'belief that the preservation of Empire was the preservation of a concept of ideal value in the face of materialism' (111) are played out through the relations between Canadians and the English aristocracy in romance plots. In the second section 'Negotiating the Modern Babylon' I analyse an English/white colonial dichotomy in *From Man to Man, or Perhaps Only...* (1926) and 'Triple Sec' (1924) as it is shaped through representations of London as the modern Babylon: 'So London is sometimes called, on account of its wealth, luxury, and dissipation' (Brewer). I turn then to a discussion of a white English/black colonial dichotomy in 'A Disguised Land' (1990) and a historically newer Rastafarian representation of England as a modern Babylon:

> **Babylon**. 1. In Jamaica, a common name for the police. 2. In Rastafari, a name which refers to any evil force, any institution or system of thought which is anti-progressive, investing in the oppression and division of people throughout the world. 3. A Rasta concept derived from both the Old and New Testaments. It is especially associated with the Book of Revelation and to the decadence of ancient Babylonia. In contemporary times Rasta sees Western powers (especially England, the United States, and Western influenced Jamaican society as current manifestations of ancient Rome and Babylon.
>
> (Mulvaney)

Both of the texts I deal with in the final section 'Living in White Men's Houses' thematize accommodations to English life on the parts of colonial men, black West Indians in *The Lonely Londoners* (1956) and a white colonial in *The Girl Green as Elderflower* (1980). Throughout I attend to the ways in which questions of gender and sexuality and the historical moments of the narratives inflect the colouring of the English.

I make use of Walter Benjamin's concept of the transcendental anchor in modernity as elaborated by Angelika Rauch. In doing so I acknowledge Stuart Hall's point that, contrary to stock Marxist accounts, modernity was a product of European imperialism, of 'the process of conquest, exploration first, then conquest, then the decimation of indigenous people, then the transportation around the world, of blood and violence that went into the making of the world market' ('Caribbean

Culture' 29). Benjamin suggests that 'transcendental anchoring is essential to the constitution of the subject and self-understanding', that there is a 'myth of wholeness and the transcendental that is embedded in the experience of subjectivity in the aesthetic realm', and that:

> [t]he individual's psychological adaptation to a fragmented world... proceeds by libidinally investing the various broken pieces of the past and treating them as souvenirs of a blissful experience of wholeness. Meaning in this modern world of fragments is now formed by the subject's conception of these fragmentary pieces as fetishes, as means for a substitute experience of bliss.
>
> (Rauch 80–81)

Democracy and English tradition

In Sara Jeannette Duncan's *Cousin Cinderella* (1908) the Hon. John Trent, an emigrant Yorkshireman of unspecified class background, decides to send his children Graham and Mary on a visit to England as living 'samples' (10) of Canada's 'future greatness' (7) at a time of English New Imperialist fervour. This desire conforms to a practice of colonial exhibition in the imperial centre, but he also anticipates that the quality of his children will be testament to his own masculine enterprise in Greater Britain. Mary, who finds the distinctive first-person narrative voice of a Canadian girl through telling a cross-cultural comedy of manners and romance enjoined by travel, implies that this spirit of her father's was imprisoned in his early English years (8–9). This accords with Dyer's observation that enterprise is seen to be a special property of the white man, and that imperialism is '[t]he most important vehicle' for its 'exercise' and 'display', giving it 'an unprecedented horizon of expansion, of dangers to face, of material – goods, terrain, people – to organise' (31). In Canada John Trent's enterprise is realized in 'business, wealth creation, the building of nations, the organisation of labour' (Dyer 31). His anxiety, however, about his marriage to a (white) Canadian woman is apparent in his sentiment that his children might be ' "nothing but a pair of colonial editions" ' (9). Lord Peter Doleford, the representative of young England to whom Mary will eventually be engaged, finds England 'a kind of penal servitude': the Colonies of the British empire, 'the open', offer the English scope to 'always be in the management'. He does, though, have sufficient democratic scruple to declare that political office derived from hereditary title is 'a rotten borough' (142).

Duncan's most pointed commentary on English racial thinking and politics is provided by her ironic, indeed often satirical representation of the Duchess of Dulwich and her conversations with Mary. For English aristocratic women empire is, in the abstract, the sphere of patriotic duty. In 1903 there had been in Britain a Royal Commission on Alien Immigration. The term alien referred principally to Jewish, Italian, German, and East European people. The Commission refuted 'the contention that immigrants were unclean and unhealthy' and suggested that immigration 'made only a minor contribution to pre-existing problems' in the areas of 'housing and employment' (Dummett and Nicol 100–1). Mary observes the poor bathing habits of the English, and ironically the Duchess's contemptuous demands on her English secretaries are such that they routinely become unhealthy. The Duchess has been appointed to a Royal Commission on the Assimilation of Aliens charged with investigating ' "the quickest and most effective methods" ' of transforming aliens into ' "loyal British subjects[.] ... How most permanently to bind them to us, to win their affections, to educate them in British standards and traditions" ' in light of ' "their national, political or religious prejudices" ' (98). Her own prejudices are clearly apparent in her preferred sweeping solution to the presence of aliens: repatriation. She has a high public profile on the question of repatriation of Jewish people. She upholds the codes of aristocratic breeding – which linked 'notions of social pedigree and ancestral blood to a hierarchy of human sensibilities' (Cohen, 'Perversions' 64) – and for all her sense of herself as a repository of reason and disinterest (Lloyd 'Race under Representation' 64) is repeatedly demonstrated to judge with reference to stereotypes of class, gender, religion, nation, and race. Mary is delighted at her own 'perhaps, not good literary manners' in sharing her mockery of 'feudal' deference to the Duchess with her audience (347); the delight undercuts the Duchess's stereotype of the loyal Canadian. The deference to aristocratic title is irreconcilable with the liberal middle-class meritocratic sentiment on which the Trents as representatives of young Canada and its nationalism pride themselves. Ironically the Duchess exercises political influence while women are kept behind a grille in the houses of parliament, 'in a cage' remarks an American character (157).

The Duchess has decided views on miscegenation, which racialize white colonials. While acknowledging the visibly white Trents as part of the Anglo-Saxon family, at one point she asks Mary, on the evidence of Graham being 'so very dark and distinguished', about 'Indian blood' in the family, and brushes aside Mary's disavowal (283). The probability that the physical distinction signals 'rather a noble strain' reconciles the

Duchess to the prospect (284). This is arguably an identification 'with the Noble Savage as one of Nature's Gentlemen' (Cohen, 'Perversions' 66). Her anxieties about the 'corrupting influence of bourgeois "materialism"' (66) are deflected on to self-made colonial men identified, too, as import by source of wealth, as in '"Australian mutton"' (Duncan 348). She separates them out as a different species from the English, the infertility of their marriages against '"Nature"' to aristocratic English women (348) being an implicit sign of this. Robert Young notes that in nineteenth-century racial hybridity theory 'the argument that the different races of men were different species hinged on the question of whether the product of a union between different races were fertile or not' (8).

The country house, and the class structures and 'spatial moral order' (Said, *Culture and Imperialism* 94) it classically instantiates, are represented by Duncan as institutions which cannot be sustained economically by their English aristocratic inheritors: they need 'overseas sustenance' (Said, *Culture and Imperialism* 107). They are financially embarrassed by 'complications' unspecifiable in polite company (Duncan 252), or like Lord Peter constrained by virtue of lesser intelligence or financial backing in an increasingly bourgeois capitalist economy (140–1). In material terms intermarriage with wealthy (white) colonials or Americans may replenish depleted family coffers and genealogical symbols of English heritage and 'national virtues' (238) like the country house. The Duchess's niece Barbara will contemplate engagement with Graham as 'a necessary part of a scheme by which she might be perpetuated, or at least continued, as she was' (178). The Lippingtons derive a living from colonial governorships.

For both Mary and Graham the country house is a *lieu de mémoire*, an 'embodiment' of a 'sense of historical continuity' (Nora 7). Mary, though, clearly recognizes that its racial 'identity-enchanting' capacity (Baucom 19) is an artefact of their internalization 'ever since we could read' of representational conventions of English novels (Duncan 222). This recognition facilitates an awareness of the performative dimension of English ruling-class order on this site. Graham fetishizes dilapidated Tudor Pavis Court as the ultimate symbol of 'his moral birthright', 'the common wealth of aesthetics that is so much richer and more rewarding where the Empire began' (148), and as such is metonymic of a 'vaster imperial cartography of culture and discipline' (Baucom 170). The project of improving Pavis Court through the injection of his capital becomes Graham's transcendental anchor in modernity; his sincerity in personal relationships, however, will ensure that his engagement to

Barbara is short-lived. The 'seditious' aspect of her writing and Lord Doleford's 'features' provide the transcendental anchor for Mary. His 'features at once suggested a race and then a type and then an order, and a kind of direct correspondence of character...I don't know why he made me think of a Crusader...unless it was that sign of purpose and intention, which would be, one felt, as simple and high as modern circumstances permitted' (Duncan 108). Misao Dean observes that in allegorical terms Mary's engagement signals 'the advantages represented by the ideals of British history, and shows how Canada, too, can use her dowry, and her ability to make alliances to further the idealist challenge to materialism' (Introduction xix). Mary's likening of Lord Doleford to a Crusader is telling: the Crusader is a 'hero of pre-capitalist adventure' who draws on 'the chivalric code of honour to guide his actions' (Dawson 59), and arguably an early exemplar of the conflation of ' "White", "Europe" and "Christian"...that imparted moral, cultural and territorial content to Whiteness' 'from the late medieval period onwards' (Bonnett, 'Constructions' 175).

Rudyard Kipling's political allegory 'The Mother Hive' (1909) shares a historical moment with *Cousin Cinderella*: the turn-of-the-century moral panic about the alien presence in England, his own 'favourite foreign country' (qtd. in Birkenhead 243). The allegory addresses contemporary concerns about national efficiency and the quality of the national 'stock' or 'blood' (Kipling 85, 95). Janet Oppenheim explains that:

> [d]uring the Edwardian decade, the ambiguous phrase 'national efficiency' expressed diverse, but profound, concerns about British ability to compete in the modern world. Around the slogan of national efficiency gathered proponents of child welfare, housing reform, state support of motherhood, imperial expansion, and military preparedness alike. Strange alliances proliferated.... The anxiety and hatred that created the bugbear of 'racial decline' focused on no single target, but created an enormous conceptual muddle in which all prejudices could flourish.
>
> (267)

Kipling had by the early 1900s 'established himself as a public spokesman on behalf of a Tory populism characterized by the ideals of patriotism, the glory of the Empire, and the value of hard work and dedication to one's duty in all classes' (Montefiore 274). In Kipling's story the bee hive with its monarch and clearly demarcated division of labour on class and gender lines is his symbol of *English* national efficiency and tradition and his anxiety about racial decline is focalized through species difference. The hive is an instance of the conceptualization of a society as an organism, a model 'appealing to . . . post-Darwinian social evolutionists', in which 'diversity was turned into *specialization*' (Langer 109–10) and social inequalities were naturalized.

A wax-moth, which uses the deceptively 'chaste folds' of her grey wings to conceal 'her ceaseless egg-dropping', is Kipling's alien, a ghostly spreader of deathly newness identified with decadent modernity (86). She is a 'monster of reproduction' (Dyer 215) in several senses: she reproduces her species; beneath a cover of familial rhetoric she spreads insurrection in the form of liberal democratic, socialist, women's emancipist and racially tolerant 'principles' and talk about 'feelings' among the inexperienced young who are tolerant of 'any sort of stranger' (Kipling 85–6, 94); and her presence leads to the birth of 'oddities' – 'drones with workers' stomachs; workers with drones' stomachs; and albinos and mixed-leggers who can't pack pollen' who become Kipling's type of the intellectual (94). With reference to the discourse of breeding integral to Anglo-Saxon racism, the wax-moth as a figure of '*ideological contagion*' coalesces several strands of the association of 'heretical currents of European "free" thinking' with particular racial groups – the Wandering Jew and the Irish – and racializes as other 'a domestic tradition of radical dissent' (Cohen, 'Perversions' 74). The susceptibility of the hive to infiltration is grounded in the stock being 'old and overcrowded . . . where bees are too thick on the comb there must be sickness or parasites', the 'worn wings and nerves' of some 'old workers', and a guard's momentary loss of concentration, metonymic of a failure of military and anti-immigration preparedness (Kipling 85). These weaknesses are standard themes in the Edwardian moral panic about national efficiency. Bernard Mandeville in *The Fable of the Bees* had proposed 'that the economic prosperity of great nations is dependent on the vices of their inhabitants' (Harth 19) – 'Luxury', 'Ease', 'Lust', 'Vanity', 'Cheat', 'Pride' (Mandeville, 'The Grumbling Hive' 63–4, 75). Kipling associates such vices with degeneration. His hive's future is secured by the 'sound bees' (98), who remain loyal to their duties and the traditional wisdom of the queen, and exercise a 'hereditary hatred' of the alien and alien values (87). A god-like beekeeper scourges and 'disinfect[s]' the rotten hive (107).

Negotiating the modern Babylon

In 1885 W.T. Stead published in the *Pall Mall Gazette* a sensational series of articles on the 'traffic in girls in London's vice emporiums'

(Walkowitz 81) entitled 'Maiden Tribute of Modern Babylon', a spearhead of the campaign to raise the age of consent for girls from 13 to 16. His title is still the most familiar description of London as 'modern Babylon'. Judith Walkowitz has compellingly analysed the narrative layers of the articles. She cites the manner in which through melodrama 'class exploitation...was imaginatively represented and personalized as sexual exploitation of the daughter, which was a threat to family hierarchy and an infringement of male working-class prerogatives' (86). In *From Man to Man* and 'Triple Sec' the colonial female protagonists in London are displaced from their families and economically vulnerable. Schreiner and Rhys rework older melodramatic stories of London as a place of sexual danger, unpacking a nexus among imperial, class and sexual exploitation that belies sentimental family romances of empire.[3]

An early version of Olive Schreiner's posthumously published *From Man to Man, or Perhaps Only...* (1926) was submitted to Chapman and Hall in 1881; she revised it sporadically over the remainder of her life. Cherry Clayton suggests that she was never 'to find a satisfactory form' (60) for her narrative of the lives of two white middle-class South African sisters, the intellectual Rebekah and the simpler Bertie, the 'first exiled woman in South African literature' (66). In the novel the middle-class masculine body politic of England is split between the white cousins of the two, Frank and John-Ferdinand, who look to South Africa for wives and as a field for enterprise, and an Ashkenazi Jewish man, identified only as the Jew, and his second cousin, identified only as the Jew's cousin. Rebekah marries Frank and stays in South Africa. Bertie, often called Baby-Bertie by the narrative voice, is seduced when 16 by Percy Lawrie, her 'delicate' tutor from England (Schreiner, *From* 81), spurned by an idolizing John-Ferdinand when she confesses to having been seduced, and escapes the social consequences of gossip about it by departing South Africa for London with the wealthy Jew. Schreiner carefully notes the Jew's 'slightly bent shoulders', 'dull oriental pallor', 'piercing dark eyes' and 'stiffly curling' hair (328). This suggests that she may be alluding to the 'white Negro' model of Jewishness in which the 'black and the Jew were associated not merely because they were both "outsiders" but because qualities ascribed to one became the means of identifying the difference of the other' (Gilman 35). That the Jew's sexual desire for Bertie is grounded in her physical resemblance to his sister in childhood draws on a stereotype of the incestuous Eastern Jew (Gilman 110). The Jew keeps Bertie in opulence as his mistress, until, misunderstanding her conduct with his cousin, he unceremoniously casts her out into the street. Destitute and unskilled, she joins this second man. Bertie's family last hears of her having 'landed in a brothel in Soho', although near the novel's end Rebekah thinks that she may have heard her 'long, reckless, gurgling' laughter emanating from a dissolute 'motley crowd' of 'coloured men and boys, white loafers, coloured and white women in gaudy finery or squalor' (Schreiner, *From* 448–9). Anne McClintock observes: 'The radical thrust of the book... is that Bertie's luxurious confinement and Rebekah's martyred solitude [in marriage] are merely different kinds of prostitution. Indeed, Bertie's strange, rich laugh at the end hints at a fate more free and vital than the suffocating tedium of her velvet jail' (288). In her reading the laugh is definitely Bertie's. Rebekah can imagine Bertie in this 'motley' context, which suggests that she unconsciously links her sense of Bertie's style of prostitution with racial mixing.

Bertie is Schreiner's colonial version of the innocent country girl or child (her childlike face and childish desires are often noted) coerced by social and economic pressures to trade her sexual favours in the metropolis. In the evolutionary discourse of the novel Bertie's 'low forehead' underlines her capacity for degeneration (*From* 333). By drawing on Jewish stereotypes Schreiner emblematizes the more phobic aspects of Englishness within her feminist and anti-imperial polemical frame: 'foreign capitalist hands' (Clayton 73) and imperial exploitation of black colonial labour in the diamond mines; and England as a site of mobile entrepreneurialism, consumption, idolatry of money, sensuality and perverse sexual pleasure. The Jew fetishizes Bertie's beauty and her skin, which becomes progressively whiter in her indolent captivity within his home. Her movement outside the house is severely constrained and strictly supervised, because he territorializes the street and the urban mass as a place of thieves. He derives sensual pleasure from gazing at Bertie and contemplating his seemingly exclusive property right in her. This is a reworking of the stereotypical representation of the Jew as a 'merchant in flesh' (Cohen, 'Perversions' 22) and as an enslaver to luxury. Bertie's condition in England accords with the late nineteenth-century typology of the autoerotic woman (Dijkstra 64–82); business involving her stroking kittens lying on her lap is Schreiner's most explicit representation of autoerotic lassitude. Marianna Torgovnick suggests that in late nineteenth-century representations of the prostitute, when her genitals are covered, a cat is used to figure them (102). Both Bertie's and the Jew's sexualities are nonreproductive.

Bertie is represented largely through Schreiner's typology of the modern 'effete wife, concubine, or prostitute' elaborated in her feminist tract *Woman and Labour* (1911):

> The need for her physical labour having gone, and mental industry not having taken its place, she bedecked and scented her person, or had it bedecked and scented for her, she lay upon her sofa, or drove or was carried out in her vehicle, and, loaded with jewels, she sought by dissipations and amusements to fill up the inordinate blank left by the lack of productive activity.... [T]he hand whitened and frame softened[.] . . . Finely clad, tenderly housed, life became for her merely the gratification of her own physical and sexual appetites, and the appetites of the male, through the stimulation of which she could maintain herself. And whether as kept wife, kept mistress, or prostitute, she contributed nothing to the active and sustaining labours of her society.... She was the 'fine lady,' the human female parasite – the most deadly microbe which can make its appearance on the surface of any social organism.
>
> (81–2)

For Schreiner this sex parasitism is a sign of racial degeneration (104) that threatens European nation, civilization and empire. In her view it is a product of modernity, of evolutionary specialization, mechanization, and the accumulation of surplus wealth under capitalism, and of 'the gradual disappearance of women's work and the decreasing value and status alloted to reproductive labour' (Felski 157). Rita Felski notes of Schreiner's revolutionary 'plea for female liberation' that it 'reproduces a powerfully gendered cluster of metaphors which counterposes the laboring, healthy, and virile body to the insidious threat of passivity, femininity, and disease' (157). This binary is represented respectively by Rebekah and by Bertie enclosed by a morbid Englishness.

In *From Man to Man* grey is the pervasive colour of England. On one page alone there are references to 'dull grey light', 'grey damp' that 'was everywhere', 'dead yellow-grey brick' and a 'great grey cat'. The 'grey damp' 'seem[s] to ooze' from the all-alike buildings (Schreiner, *From* 353). Grey becomes metonymic of assimilative imperative and enclosure in England. Combined with her want of work and homesickness, it causes Bertie to become severely depressed, a process Schreiner documents naturalistically. This is the 'condition of morbid inactivity' to which 'modern civilisation' has 'reduced' her (Schreiner, *Woman* 49).

The colour is also indicative of Bertie's liminal moral condition (neither white nor black in Schreiner's view) while she is in the Jew's protection. While as kept woman Bertie has a social subjectivity for the narrative voice, as a reported common prostitute she has none. For Schreiner prostitution is a problem to be 'dealt with, either from the moral or the scientific standpoint' (*Woman* 83n).

In Jean Rhys's oeuvre there are quite a few abject figures who inhabit the upper storeys of English houses. Antoinette ('Bertha') Cosway Mason, imprisoned in Rochester's country house and a 'grey wrapper' of Englishness in *Wide Sargasso Sea* (1966), is the best known;[4] the first of them, and the only male, is in 'Triple Sec' (1924), Rhys's first and still unpublished novel. In 'Triple Sec' Rhys's white Creole protagonist is named Suzy Gray. Her patronym, like the colour grey more generally in Rhys's fiction, is metonymic of the cultural and moral disciplining of her as a colonial, working-class female subject in England. 'Triple Sec' is based on diaries Rhys kept during the 1910s; H. Pearl Adam edited them. Ethel, the masseuse who employs Suzy Gray as a manicurist, rents a flat that will also serve as a business, but the landlord's 'weird-looking' illegitimate son has a bedroom on the third floor of the flat, as does Suzy. Suzy's bedroom has been 'all done up in white and looks so fresh and dainty' ('Triple Sec' 51). Rhys doubles the characters under the signs of illegitimate sexuality and marginality in the family of white Englishness. The boy, whose work is indeterminate, is 'miserable and white-faced with a sort of hunted expression' (50). Suzy, too, feels as if 'somebody were hunting' her (27). That 'somebody' is identified as a 'horrid' 'night' aspect of London – 'like a great black animal – that pounces – and claws you up' (24).

The image, which reworks the usual imperial association of the centre of empire with light, compresses the beastliness of the men among whom she circulates, sickeningly for her, as part of a 'common pool' (Sedgwick 251) of working-class women, the sexual use, exchange, and conspicuous consumption of whom in front of other men secure upper middle-class homosociality. A popular place to pick up women is called the Empire ('Triple Sec' 94). The heterosexuality of the white men, English and American, who consume Suzy sexually is represented as largely vampiric and predatory, their money as corrupting of the social and sexual morals of women. The men operate outside the codes of 'moral' or 'domestic manliness' which developed through the nineteenth century (Dawson 65). The darkness of the sexuality has princi-pally Christian, but also racial referents, and accords with established melodramatic conventions in which London is represented as a place of sexual danger. Judith Walkowitz cogently draws the connection between melodrama and pornography, arguing that they:

> contained the same sexual script, which focussed on the transgression of class boundaries in the male pursuit of the female object of desire, the association of sex and violence, and the presumption of aggressive male sexuality bearing down on a passive asexual female. Both foregrounded power relations by emphasizing situation and underplaying character. Whereas melodrama permitted some power reversals and sympathy for the plight of the heroine/victim, late-Victorian pornography usually prohibited the female victim from mounting any resistance or telling her version of the story.
>
> (97)

The effect on Suzy of the 'clawing' and of her assimilation as innocent colonial into a disciplining set of class and gender relations in England is depression, which begins in a 'horrible, hurting, black, desolate, *rotten feeling*' (24), works its way through her sense of being 'quite dead inside' (33), and develops after an abortion into a major depressive episode which reduces her to a 'melancholy skeleton' (120). Suzy sums it up as 'I've been in blackness' (126).

The Christian imaginary of Suzy's narrative is also apparent in a dream which encapsulates her relation to the English as a mass: 'In my dream I always have fallen by the way and crowds and crowds of people pass and pass and trample me' (124). The allusion to Jesus's parable of the Good Samaritan implicitly represents the English as unneighbourly, wanting in Christian 'compassion' (Luke 10: 33), and Suzy's experience among them as a falling 'among thieves, which stripped' her of her 'raiment, and wounded' her, 'and departed, leaving' her 'half dead' (Luke 10: 30). Her raiment at the opening of the novel is two outfits made for her in which she does not 'look quite grown up': a white dress, which emblematizes the youth and innocence Tony, her first seducer, fetishizes in her appearance, and a 'grey coat and skirt' ('Triple Sec' 7). There are several scenes of stripping, for example, her nudity for Tony and the artists for whom she will model, the spectacle of herself as skeleton and a doctor's reduction of her to the craving for sex he mirrors back to her in medical diagrams of female reproductive organs. Her dispossession is summed up as 'Money lost, little lost – honour lost, much lost', but her determination not to lose the 'pluck' which would signal 'all lost' effects a turning point in her life: the 'blackness lifted up' (126). Adam Potkay and Sandra Burr outline the centrality of the notion of a 'universal

Christian community that transcends caste distinctions of race' in the abolitionist theology which characterizes the assumption of voice-agency by black British writers of the eighteenth century, Olaudah Equiano and Quobna Ottabah Cuguano, and provides their 'measure' of white society (13–14). Suzy's Biblical reference to an ideal of Christian community that transcends caste distinctions (English/colonial, male/ female, virtuous woman/'fallen' woman) also offers her a higher moral ground from which to speak in judgement of the English. The quality, 'pluck', which will redeem Suzy from blackness is one associated with British imperial masculinity in juvenile literature for boys.[5] She projects herself as a potential 'dare-devil Dorothy' ('Triple Sec' 126), a fantasy of racializing empowerment which meshes with her sacred imaginary[6] in moments when her sense of the cruelty of divine providence produces a conviction that 'the devil is ever so much so powerful than God and that he arranges most things' ('Triple Sec' 33).

Suzy's most benign relations to the English develop during a convalescence in the country and during her residence in a boarding house peopled by other ethnic outsiders in wartime England. Her convalescence gives her 'tantalising glimpses of peace and calm' (195), of a possible set of alternative social relations in England with 'nice people, kind people, nice men too I daresay who'd neither make love nor be rudely indifferent *or* brutal' (198). Her country visit is staged between a farm and a country house, both *lieux de mémoire* associated with English domestic idyll. Suzy revels in the English garden, and the patronage of Lady Marjorie who presents her with 'quantities of roses from a big tree just outside the room where she gave me tea generally' (197). Roses are a stock signifier of England. The appreciation of nature and the idealized social relations which structure Suzy's stay proffer her an imagining of redemption – 'Now buck up, pull yourself together' (198) – to 'set against the fragmenting and undermining effects of anxiety' (Dawson 282). In 1919 she is living in a boarding-house community of Greek, Italian, and South American immigrants and Belgian refugees. It is learning to laugh inside along with 'a mixture of dislike and contempt' for the English they express which more surely restores her spirits, even though she still identifies herself as English in relation to them (Rhys, 'Triple Sec' 216). The Irish landlady has a 'benevolent' attitude to the casual sex of couples she caters for in some of her rooms (218), unlike the 'smug-faced people who sleep in their little beds each night and snore and say "How shocking!"' whom Suzy despises (127).

Edward Said has observed that 'aborted childbirths' in literature of the modernist period suggest the 'difficulties of filiation ... the pressure to produce new and different ways of conceiving human relationships . . . social bonds' (*World* 17). Placed on the margins of the imperial family romance and Christian community, Suzy's affiliations are with her diary (writing) and friends Jennie Kent, Pamela and Raoul Poupèye (who is a displaced highbrow member of that boarding-house community). These become her transcendental anchors in modernity.

As befits the protagonist of female Gothic narrative, Suzy is economically dispossessed and her family origins are largely obscured. When Rhys returned to the diaries on which 'Triple Sec' is based, and reworked the early material as *Voyage in the Dark* the grounds for Anna Morgan's dispossession are made explicit: the failure of the economic modernization project in Dominica integral to the New Imperialism of Joseph Chamberlain and her English stepmother's appropriation of the inheritance intended for her by her dead father. In the first version of Part IV of the novel Anna's Uncle Bo, referring to the economic plight of the planter class in Dominica, complains that the 'English' monies intended to compensate slave-owners for the abolition of slavery 'stayed in the good old home coop' (386). This is Rhys's reworking of the motif of falling among English thieves from 'Triple Sec'. Uncle Bo's complaint is more topical than it might first appear, as *Voyage in the Dark* was published in the year that marked the centenary of the introduction of the apprenticeship labour system, the first stage in the abolition of slavery. In her delirium Anna remembers fragments of her sexual 'fall'; the history of West Indian plantocracies was being conceptualized in the period as the 'fall' of the planter class.[7]

Recently Gary Boire has argued that male imperialism defines 'the (sexed) child-body as a colonial space' (qtd. in Clayton 123). Percy Lawrie, John-Ferdinand and the Jew fetishize Bertie's child-like features in *From Man to Man* and Tony fetishizes Suzy's innocence in 'Triple Sec', desiring her to dress in ways that give her a child-like quality. Sexual abuse emerged publicly in the West as a category of child abuse in 1975; child abuse as a medicalized category of cruelty to children in the early 1960s (Hacking 275, 269). In the wake of this, some recent narratives by ex-colonial writers explore imperial relations or the effects of empire and its aftermath on relations within black families in England through the abusive treatment of the sexed child-body. Examples include Barbara Hanrahan's *The Albatross Muff* (1977), Joan Riley's *The Unbelonging* (1985), Buchi Emecheta's *Gwendolen* (1989), and David Dabydeen's *A Harlot's Progress* (1999). *Gwendolen* is discussed in Chapter 9 and *A Harlot's Progress* in Chapter 11.

In Pauline Melville's 'A Disguised Land' (1990) the protagonist Winsome has from the age of fourteen a recurring dream about England in which she has been 'sentenced to death' and the 'informal friendliness' of white people makes her fearful and silences her (41–2). England is a place of camouflage (46) and death-in-life captivity, in which she merely 'appear[s] to be free' (41). A first child of Hyacinth's, Winsome had been raised in Jamaica by her grandmother; Hyacinth had married in Britain, had three legitimate children and pursued material dreams. She 'cussed' at the thought of eleven-year-old Winsome being sent to join her. Winsome's Jamaican accent occasions 'teasing' from her half-siblings and her blackness 'taunting' and contempt from schoolchildren and her mother (42). To support her children she practises petty fraud. In this she is an anancy figure, anancy being in African Caribbean folklore the trickster who uses his or her wits to survive slavery and a dominant white culture. Appearing in court the day before her third child is due, Winsome is sentenced to twelve months imprisonment, and gives birth in the prison hospital. She escapes with her newly born child to rejoin her other children, and consents to her friend Sonia's suggestion that the wickedness of the sentence be exposed through a television interview before she surrenders herself and the child. ' "God, I feel awful," giggled the production assistant behind her clip-board to the director. "I feel as if I'd captured a runaway slave or something" ' (52). Back in jail Winsome dreams of her funeral, her death proffering 'freedom from the land of enslavement and pilgrimage through the wilderness' (Potkay and Burr 10) with 'bright flowers' on her chest, pointedly contrasted with the 'arid courtroom, the drained grey jail and the pristine hospital' (Melville 53, 50). 'The whiteness hurt her eyes' in hospital (47), the television lights 'drained the room of colour and made everything harsh and pale' (51): white Englishness has become an oppressive cultural atmosphere of psychological and epistemic violence. Her relationship with her boyfriend Junior Watson has entailed physical violence. A Rasta character, Levi, speaks of the 'Babylon writings' in court, 'writings on the walls to do harm to black people. Ancient spells fi mek us confuse when we stand in de dock deh' (44–5). Winsome reads only the word 'HONI' (evil) from the crest on the wall behind the judge. Melville's narrative endorses Levi's view, one which accords with an 'anti-capitalist' theme of urban black settlement in England which Paul Gilroy suggests has a 'historical resonance in diaspora culture and can be traced directly and indirectly back to the formative experience of slavery': attention to 'the role of the law' as an instrument of the state, 'challenging capitalist legality to live up to the expansive promises of its democratic rhetoric' (*Small Acts* 36). Melville juxtaposes the rule of English law with an 'alternative secular moral standard', common decency in treatment of pregnant women, articulated through Sonia, which has the capacity to appeal to 'popular sovereignty', and a 'divine version' of justice articulated through Levi (*Small Acts* 36).

Living in white men's houses

Samuel Selvon's *The Lonely Londoners* (1956) is set in the mid-1950s when 'English people start to make rab about how too much West Indians coming to the country' (8) and 'big discussion going on in Parliament about the situation' (8). The context is a bill presented to Cabinet and the efforts of Sir Cyril Osborne to 'introduce a Private Member's Bill in 1955 to control coloured immigration' and the moral panics over the changing racial composition of Britain in which they intervened. The themes of Osborne's anti-'coloured' rhetoric were criminality, disease, parasitism on the welfare system, and excessive reproduction (Dummett and Nicol 180). In a reworking of the famous racial recognition scene in Frantz Fanon's *Black Skin, White Masks*, published as *Peau Noire, Masques Blancs* in 1952,[8] Selvon particularly highlights the everyday racism experienced by a group of West Indian male immigrants, and the ways in which they cope with this. (David Dabydeen's reworking of the same scene in *The Intended* is discussed in chapter 11.) In *Black Skin, White Masks* Fanon describes the effects of the racist gaze on a black man when a white French boy fearfully declares to his mother ' "Look, a Negro!" ' and Fanon recognizes that the child understands his blackness through fixed racial stereotype (Fanon 111). The scene is crucial to Homi Bhabha's elaboration of 'the problematic of seeing/ being seen' where skin as a sign of racial difference is 'the most visible of fetishes' (*Location* 76, 78).

Selvon's improvization on Fanon's scene occurs in an extended passage on his character Galahad's sharpness, with sharpness being used in a range of its meanings. ' "Mummy, look at that black man!" ' a child says, 'look[ing] up' at Sir Galahad. The mother, educating the child in public politeness, tells the child, ' "You mustn't say that, dear!" ' Inured to such affronts, Galahad 'pat the child cheek, and the child cower and shrink and begin to cry', and compliments the mother on how 'sweet' the child is and asks the child its name 'putting on the old English accent'. The mother's respectability is threatened by her being seen by 'so many white people around' to be talking with a black man. Like Fanon, Galahad subjects his blackness to an examination – in response to such incidents, and to a scene of adult hypocrisy in which he over-hears two white men in a lavatory complain about 'how these black bastards have the lavatory dirty' and when he emerges from the cubicle 'they say hello mate have a cigarette'. Galahad 'watch the colour of his hand' and 'talking to the colour Black, as if is a person, telling it that it is not *he* who causing botheration in the place, but Black'. In this self-division Galahad equates Blackness with suffering, with difficulties in finding '[a] little work, a little food, a little place to sleep', in 'get[ting] by'. White people he theorizes 'don't like... the colour Black' (*LL* 71–3). As Stefano Harney notes, Selvon and Galahad are confident of black 'Caribbean innocence' (107). The innocence is articulated within two discursive fields, secular and divine (Christian) law. While a pigmentoc-racy materially tied to 'class position and privilege' operated in the Caribbean, in Britain 'no regard was paid to the complex hierarchy of shades by the "host" society'. Post-Second World War Caribbean immi-grants were 'regarded monolithically as "coloureds", "West Indians", "blacks", "immigrants", and even "wogs" with no reference to differ-ential shades' (Winston James 234, 239). Galahad's fellow Trinidadian friend Moses Aloetta compliments Galahad on his 'sharp theory', advis-ing him to write about it. Another friend of Moses' has responded more aggressively to a sign 'saying Keep the Water White' by 'want[ing] to get in big argument with the white people standing around' (*LL* 71–3). Galahad's 'aesthetic of redemption from racial subordination' at work and in public places (Gilroy, *Small Acts* 37) is focused on his own highly controlled sartorial sharpness, cultivation and performance of a 'cool' style of masculinity, gazing at 'sharp craft' (white women), and contem-plating sexual consumption of 'white pussy' (*LL* 71, 74). White women are also objectified as 'skin' (71). His public touch of a white woman, Daisy, in breach of a miscegenation taboo produces 'loud tones' in the eyes of white onlookers; he thinks they 'must be bawl to see black man so familiar with white girl' (74).

Galahad's aesthetic is an early version of one that Gilroy finds char-acteristic of contemporary forms of black urban culture in England. Galahad's cool black body is 'celebrated' by himself and by the narrator 'as an instrument of pleasure rather than an instrument of labour.... [T]he space allocated for recovery and recuperation' outside desultory work 'is assertively and provocatively occupied by the pursuit of leisure and pleasure' (*Small Acts* 36). Selvon implies that cool is an empowering performative taking back of his body and being from the negating scopic drive of white English people,[9] a reintegrating transcendental anchor in 1950s English modernity. Certainly the empowerment is not through 'control over political and economic institutions' (Kelley 248). Cool becomes a highly gendered means of restoring the injured male subject.[10] It is a 1950s 'styling' of the racialized body which entails 'a settlement in and with' it (Hall, 'Aspiration and Attitude' 40). Curdella Forbes, positing an authentic Caribbean model of masculinity grounded in an 'ordered society' located within patterns of traditional family life, argues that Selvon's characters exhibit a 'psychic absence of gender'(50). The black family is for her 'the approved, natural site where ethnicity and racial culture are reproduced' (Gilroy, *Small Acts* 197). Forbes identifies the black matriarch Tanty as the 'iconoclastic' agent (55) and 'means of this process of cultural reproduction' (Gilroy, *Small Acts* 197). Only she attains the status of Subject (Forbes 55). The homosocial bonding of Selvon's 'fellars', effected in part through conspicuously sharing 'ballads' about serially consuming 'white pussy', lies outside Forbes's family model.

Selvon emblematizes the negativity of life and the English in London in the 'kind of grey nasty colour' of the English winter, a colour linked with 'tightness and strain' in the 'faces' of white English people. The sun 'giv[es] no heat at all and the atmosphere like a sullen twilight' (*LL* 86). This negativity informs Moses' vision of:

> a great aimlessness, a great restless, swaying movement that leaving you standing in the same spot. As if a forlorn shadow of doom fall on all the spades in the country. As if he could see the black faces bobbing up and down in the millions of white, strained faces, everybody hustling along the Strand, the spades jostling in the crowd, bewildered, hopeless. As if, on the surface, things don't look so bad, but when you go down a little, you bounce up a kind of misery and pathos and a frightening – what? He don't know the right word, but he have the right feeling in his heart.
>
> (126)

Harney observes that Moses' 'principal source of . . . despair . . . is not blackness or minority status as such, but the existence of that river of millions of "white strained faces". The source of misery and fear is that white flow, and it is for this flow that Moses can find no meaning' (106). Selvon counterpoints Moses' sense of the white mass here with its faces in summer in a celebrated passage delivered in the narrative voice about sexual cruising. In summer in parks 'smile everywhere you turn the English people smiling isn't it a lovely day as if the sun burn away all the tightness and strain' (*LL* 86). It is a 'night . . . world turn upside down and everybody hustling that is life that is London' in which 'sex life gone wild' (93). It is this carnivalesque aspect of the urban mass that becomes the motive for Selvon's playful modernist improvization on the Molly Bloom section of James Joyce's *Ulysses*. Stasis – 'standing in the same spot', 'thoughts so heavy like he [Moses] unable to move his own body' (126) – contrasts with a serial mobility to which Galahad and Moses have different responses based on their personalities. The narrative voice insists 'that it ain't have no discrimination [among men] when it come to that [cruising] in the park in the summer' (88). Cruising – a world of sexual barter cross-cut with desire and exploitation – is an activity of men, working-class prostitutes and higher-class white women or couples desirous of sexual exoticism. The men sexually objectify women, the prostitutes sexually and economically objectify the men as paying customers, black men and women are sexually desired as the racially exotic ('primitive', 'cruder' sexually), the men in particular in sexual scenarios variously involving voyeurism (92). For the black men white women are racially exotic; the black prostitutes make white men 'pay big money' for the 'big thrill' of their racial difference (91). Alluding to Homer's *The Odyssey*, Selvon's narrative voice repeatedly refers to the sexually frustrated or prudes who would 'cork their ears' rather than listen to siren voices or its own siren ballad (91, 92, 93). For Selvon this siren England has the most fluid racial boundaries.

Randolph Stow's *The Girl Green as Elderflower* (1980) has two contemporary historical moments: 1961 and 1978. The protagonist Crispin Clare explains: 'I was born in South Africa, of a New Zealand mother and a father born in India. My mother and I sat out the war in New Zealand. After that, my father was in Malaya. Then he was in Kenya, and I went to school in Devon. The end of the Empire was pretty confusing to families like mine' (31). His father has as a minister of religion represented the soul-making mission of empire; Cris has tried to serve its scientific dimension. Cris's confusion in the wake of decolonization is exacerbated by his experience as 'a very raw anthropologist, working for one of the colonial governments' (30), during which he had 'grown unused to white men's houses' (4) and spoken Biga-Kiriwina (a Trobriand Islands language), trying to keep hold of his whiteness through writing in English. He had felt 'cut adrift', having 'lost the feeling of being a white man'. After developing malaria, malnutrition, and a 'delayed mourning reaction', he had begun to imagine conspiracies among his anthropological subjects against him (75–6) and attempted suicide by hanging. The novel is the narrative of his recovery and regeneration from January to May 1961 in his family's English heartland in Suffolk. Selvon's characters try to familiarize and accommodate themselves in London through turning their experiences into ballads, stories for sharing among male friends; Cris's regeneration is effected through the lonelier occupation of rewriting medieval stories he has read. Through the reworkings he 'is able to project the burden of his own illness on to the victims of the legends, and so to begin to reify that illness as something past and separate, like the legends' (Hassall 153). Stow himself has described his interest in the work of medieval writers like Ralph of Coggeshall as a quest 'perhaps for racial roots', ancestral connection through 'archetypes' (Kavanagh and Kuch 239–40). The colours white and green, which dominate the landscape, and Cris's writing become his transcendental anchors in modernity.

Cris's reconciliation with his Anglo-Saxon heritage entails a disavowal of medieval and late twentieth-century English racism. His story '*Concerning a boy and a girl emerging from the earth*' includes an eye witness account of the near extermination of the Jewish community in Lynn (now King's Lynn) in Norfolk in the twelfth century. In the story '*Concerning a wild man caught in the sea*' Stow alludes to the rise of the neo-Nazi National Front and Conservative Party Prime Minister Margaret Thatcher's remarks in January 1978:

> If we went on as we were, then by the end of the century there would be 4 million people of the New Commonwealth or Pakistan here. Now that is an awful lot and I think it means that people are really rather afraid that this country might be swamped by people with a different culture. And, you know, the British character has done so much for democracy, for law, and done so much throughout the world, that if there is a fear that it might be swamped, people are going to react and be rather hostile to those coming in.
>
> (qtd. in Miles and Phizacklea 5)

This sentiment expressed the 'shift to a racialized conception of collective identity' which would be 'codified in the 1981 British Nationality Act' (Baucom 12). In Stow's novel Corporal Snart uses the language of swamping, rationalizing his physical and sexual violence towards Silvester, an exotic merman. The violence includes homosexual anal rape of Silvester with a bottle. Stow wrote *The Girl Green as Elderflower* in early 1979, at a time when the National Front in Britain, working in the name of protecting ' "our British Native Stock" by terminating "coloured immigration" ' (Paul 178), was gearing up for a general election campaign. (The Conservative Party's reactionary position on immigration would undermine the Front's electoral support.) Private John Westoft, one of Cris's alter egos in the story, defends Silvester, telling Snart to 'stick your National Front up your national backside', and predicts that 'England's going to do to you lot . . . what Silvester do to raw fish', something that will make him 'laugh like a drain' (Stow 95). The liberal idealism of Britain is identified here as English and mobilized through homophobia. The political violence of the 'racialized conception of collective identity' is identified with repressed homosexuality, and with masculinity practised as terror and torture.

In *Political Inversions: Homosexuality, Fascism, and the Modernist Imaginary* Andrew Hewitt asks why homosexuality 'provides the vehicle for the representation of fascism' (262). Stow's use of homosexuality in this way accords with 'a heterosexist model that figures the homosexual as an abomination to historical generation – or to the generation of history' (Hewitt 19). In the novel, too, the threat of effeminization is developed in relation to a thematic of historical generation. Cris describes himself towards the novel's close as a '[f]ailed man of action' (Stow 141); in a decolonizing historical moment empire has not secured for him a white masculine gender identity exercised through enterprise, a process implicitly marked as effeminizing. The novel and Cris's story '*Concerning a wild man caught in the sea*' exhibit an unresolved homosexual panic. Cris's mourning for empire and the white man it might have made him is, as Hewitt suggests more generally of post-Second World War mourning, 'intrinsically sexualized; . . . the desire for a restorative process of mourning will be figured repeatedly as a desired return to heterosexuality' (252). Stow's allusions to T.S. Eliot's *The Waste Land* position this return as a grail.

Stow's fantasy figures of otherness through whom Cris plays out his fraught desire for heterosexual normality are wild men or wild children. They are a Green Man with 'a face made of summer leaves, not sinister but pitilessly amused' at Cris at the novel's opening (4), Silvester the merman, and two green-skinned children. Such wild figures were in the middle ages 'pagan' symbols 'most openly linked to sexual pleasure, erotic passion, and carnal love' (Bartra 100). Greenness was associated with death and the devil. Cohen argues that the 'profane and highly sexed character' of the Wild Man and Woman 'was the antithesis of the moral order represented by the Catholic Church: it expressed everything which was repressed by the chivalric code of the nobility and which could not be brought under seigneurial cultivation and control' ('Perversions' 49). Significantly Cris's crisis of masculinity is worked through in relation to that chivalric code rather than the 'mercantile imaginary' of modern adventure romance which is '"the energizing myth of English imperialism"' and 'imbued with the imaginative resonance of colonial power relations underpinned by science and technology' (Dawson 59).[11]

The representations of English people and of the contours of English racism and xenophobia in the work of visiting, expatriate or immigrant writers during or after empire are contingent on the historical moments of each text and the historical discourses engaged by the writers. The colourings of the English are produced also by narrative contingency, and cultural and historical interpretations grounded as much in intertextual literary and generic references as in a putative reality.

Notes

1. Bonnett capitalizes 'the initial letter of "racial" terms . . . in order to signify that such expressions are being employed as sociopolitical rather than biological categories. Lower-case initial letters are used . . . to signal the term's employment as a natural, as opposed to a social, construct' ('Constructions' 189 n.1). The contexts in which I use the word white indicate whether a social or natural construct is being referred to.
2. She is citing Robin Mathews, *Canadian Literature, Surrender or Revolution*, who is discussing the pink toryism of Susanna Moodie.
3. See McClintock 44–5.
4. Other examples include an old woman who lives upstairs from Julia Martin in *After Leaving Mr Mackenzie* and the mulatto woman in Serge's story and a diseased kitten in *Good Morning, Midnight*. On the significance of these figures see Thomas, *Worlding* 90, 125–8. The quotation from *Wide Sargasso Sea* is on 152.
5. Richards cites examples of popular imperialism in literature for boys that include the concept of 'pluck'. See his quotations from the work of G.A. Henty on 93 and 94. Alfred Harmsworth published a half-penny weekly titled *Pluck*, one of its '[h]ealthy papers for manly boys'. This phrase is used in the title of an essay cited by Richards (108, n. 60), John Springhall's '"Healthy papers for manly boys": imperialism and race in the Harmsworths' halfpenny boys' papers of the 1890s and 1900s' in *Imperialism and Juvenile Literature*, ed. Richards.
6. Baucom 201.
7. See, as a prime and influential instance, Lowell Joseph Ragatz, *The Fall of the Planter Class* (1928).
8. Fanon argues earlier in his book that '[t]o speak a language is to take on a world, a culture' (38), and that contempt for Antillean Creoles (languages) is a sign of colonial alienation. *The Lonely Londoners* is written in a stylized West Indian Creole.
9. Robin D.G. Kelley writes about the way in which communal leisure, focussed in his example on dance halls, allowed many working-class African Americans of the 1940s 'who daily endured backbreaking wage work, low income, long

hours, and pervasive racism' to 'recuperate, to take back their bodies' (238). Bhabha theorizes the ways in which 'colonial power' is enacted through 'the regime of the *scopic drive*', arguing that 'surveillance' through the look 'must depend for its effectivity on "the *active consent* which is its real or mythical correlate (but always real as myth) and establishes in the scopic space the illusion of the object relation' (my emphasis). The ambivalence of this form of "consent" in objectification – real as mythical – is the *ambivalence* on which the stereotype turns' (*Location* 76).

10. I am indebted here to Herman Beavers's suggestion about the function of cool in the comedy of Richard Pryor (257).

11. Dawson is quoting from Martin Green's *Dreams of Adventure, Deeds of Empire.*

2
'A Literature of Belonging': Re-writing the Domestic Novel

Ann Blake

> Not all migrants are powerless. They impose their needs on their new earth, bringing their own coherence to the new-found land, imagining it afresh.
>
> Salman Rushdie, *The Satanic Verses*

When Sir Thomas Bertram returns to Mansfield Park from Antigua he enjoys, if only for a short while, 'the delight of his sensations in being again in his own dear house, in the centre of his family after such a separation' (149). Houses and household economies always hold an important place in Austen's novels, but *Mansfield Park* seems set on exploring the complex of desires and experiences evoked in 'being at home'. As soon as Sir Thomas goes to his 'own dear room' (152) he finds furniture moved and other signs of change made in his absence which make his house no longer homely. Fanny Price's homecoming is more distressing, beginning with her father barely acknowledging her presence. Soon she realises, with pain and guilt, that the family home is 'the very reverse of what she would have wished' (322). These are moments which concentrate the essential concerns of the domestic novel, whether realist or modernist, which relate familiar, everyday experience – at Mansfield Park or in Mrs Dalloway's Westminster – with belonging and identity.

The daily life of the family, centred on the home, seems at first an unlikely subject for colonial or ex-colonial writers newly arrived in England. For them, arrival was not literally a return home, satisfactory or not, though in the once common colonial locution the journey to unfamiliar England was 'going home'. Nevertheless, many writers produced recognizably domestic novels, based on the migrant experience of looking for a new home. And the problems encountered by Sir Thomas and Fanny, temporary or more permanent, suggest why this kind of fiction was attractive. Looking *in* rather than *back*, the novels' concern is with immigration rather than the diaspora, their focus closer to the expatriate's than the exile's (Ramraj 228). 'Everyday England' for these writers is, after all, both everyday and as in the 'Proper London' of Rushdie's Chamcha, the end of a voyage.

Though it is the experience of exile, literal or metaphoric, that is more usually associated with modernist writing, 'expatriate' fictions too, rarely remain within the bounds of traditional realism. Experimental in form and language, they make over the patterns of domestic narrative to accommodate the unresolved day to day struggles of the outsider. They constitute a recognizable body of writing with its own recurrent 'ritual moments' (Nixon 73) – the evocation of the hugeness of the city, or the scene where the newcomer is met by an earlier arrival, and senses the changes that have happened to him or her. In the spirit of Ishiguro's remarks about *The Remains of the Day*, these novels reshape fantasies about 'a certain kind of mythical England' (qtd. in O'Brien 789), the ideas of the country with which they arrived.

In a discussion of exiled and expatriate writers, Kanaganayakam cites one who views the expatriate as privileged, enjoying 'a mobility of mind . . . to which we as writers should lay claim: a doubling instead of a split' (203). But this perspective can be doubly disconcerting. Dan Jacobson, the white South African writer who came to London first in 1950 and settled there in 1954, describes a two-sided impact of arrival in his novel *The Evidence of Love* (1960) when the narrator considers 'What it means for a South African to come to England'. He suggests it can perhaps 'best be compared with what it means for a provincial in England to come to London', only to reject the comparison as 'no more than a dim metaphor' for this complex, unsettling experience: 'England makes unreal all they have done, all they have been, outside her; but grants no reality to what they may become within her. They would not have her any less than she is; yet they can never forgive her for being all that she is' (140).

An encounter with a female personification of England more personally hostile and repelling appears in a piece by William Plomer, a forerunner of Jacobson's from South Africa. Plomer's essay appeared in *Coming to London* (1957), a collection intended by its British editor (John Lehmann) to present 'literary London as it appeared to newcomers approaching it through various ports and sallies' (4). For Plomer (as for Jacobson) there was more to coming to London than joining a literary scene: it meant encountering the 'complacent, insular and hypocritical' English (15) who are figured in his essay by 'an upper-middle-class ungentlewoman' on the channel crossing. He interprets the arrogance in her voice as 'trying to convey that her position in life was so assured – racially, socially, and economically – that she has no need to worry about her want of feminine grace' (13). Her words are designed to be overheard, he thinks, and to put him down: '"Everybody has an expression as if they were just going to take the first fence.". . . . It seemed as if she wanted us all to know that the language of the hunting field was natural to her, and that if it was not natural to us, so much the worse for us, whatever we were' (14).

Plomer obliges his *London Magazine* readers to see through his eyes those English 'types' whose 'ignorance of the non-British peoples of the world was tinged with contempt'. In a penetrating consideration of the imaginative persistence of such encounters, George Lamming observed: 'just because the so-called colonial situation and its institutions may have been transferred into something else', this does not mean there is an equivalent transfer of their 'human-lived contents': they persist, as a 'continuing *psychic* experience' (Lamming, 'Caribbean Novelist' 120), and may, in time, feed into imaginative recreations of domestic life in the metropolis.

When writers arrived they did so with their own impressions of England, and especially of the middle class. To quote Jacobson again: 'I felt myself to be involved very deeply, and very early, with an idea of England,' and 'most of that idea' came from 'books, comics, and magazines' ('No Return' 14). Familiarity with enveloping myths of Englishness was no adequate preparation for actual experience, and, as Plomer's 'ungentlewoman' suggests, what was amusing in a book might be unpleasant in real life. While Lehmann thought of writers coming to London in terms of discovering a place in an 'intellectual scene', what awaited many immigrants, students and travellers, was displacement and isolation from families, exacerbated by the post-war housing situation, and, for many, by racial hostility. Yet the England they found, if not the 'new land and a new future' they hoped for (Phillips, 'A Dream' 106), was material for the writer – though, notably, not for V. S. Naipaul. In a much-quoted passage in *The Enigma of Arrival* he acknowledges that when he arrived from Trinidad he had in front of him 'a subject . . . that could have been [his] own':

> Because in 1950 in London I was at the beginning of that great movement of peoples that was to take place in the second half of the twentieth century – a movement and a cultural mixing greater

than the peopling of the United States, which was essentially a movement of Europeans to the New World. This was a movement between
all the continents.... Cities like London were to change.

(130)

Though he did not then grasp this 'great subject', others did, and set
about transforming the domestic novel to accommodate it, as they
explored what it might mean to write of making a home in England,
'however cold and hostile it may be' (Innes 22). Not all newcomers
settle, of course, or even wish to do so: the possibility of *going back
home* is there, offering an alternative resolution. However, in immigrant
fiction of this generation, the desire for a dwelling place is a dominant
theme, and, as James Procter remarks, one quite at odds with the tendency of more recent fiction to embrace, and even celebrate, 'homelessness' (22).

Just coming to England meant acting out an episode in a domestic
narrative. In the colonial story, travelling to the metropolis – the colony's mother city – represents the return of offspring to the parent. The
mutual ties and tensions of the colonial relationship have conventionally been figured in familial metaphors, usually of parent and child but
sometimes of a marriage. Orwell likened imperial England to 'a rather
stuffy Victorian family' whose poor relations are 'horribly sat upon', a
family in which there is 'a deep conspiracy of silence about the source of
the family income' (68). Such metaphors of colonialism are embedded
in the deeper levels of these domestic novels, and when they come to the
surface, colonial ties take on the intensity of intimate familial relations.
When Buchi Emecheta's Adah discovers that white people lie, and a life-
long myth is dispelled, she is the adolescent disillusioned about her
parents. In Abdulrazak Gurnah's *Admiring Silence*, betrayal by an English
spouse is an analogue for a disappointed love of England. And when the
expectation, or hope, that England will appreciate or welcome the newcomer is met with indifference, the disappointment is literal, not metaphoric. In a London room in Lamming's *The Emigrants* (1954) a
Jamaican remarks how 'for generations an' generations we'd been
offerin' them a love they never even try to return'; and in language
that has an explicitly familial intensity he speaks of the pain and hatred
the colonial tie may generate: '' Tis almost like w'at children might feel
for parents who never treat them right,' ... 'W'at you say 'bout the hate
disappearin' if only there wus a sign of friendship' (186).

Lamming's later novel *Water with Berries* (1971) incorporates, in a
contemporary English version of Prospero's family, a domestic allegory

of colonialism. Cruelty and perversion dominate the Prospero figure's colonial rule on a Caribbean estate. He has snatched Miranda, here not his child but the daughter of his wife and brother, and imprisoned her on the island. In his dual role of impotent Englishman and sugar plantation owner he presides over abuse and acts of bestiality against the girl and the islanders. All who come into contact with him and survive live out lives distorted by the violent past. Taking up Lamming's term quoted earlier, Peter Hulme identifies this allegory as a predominantly 'psychic', rather than political, reading of colonialism ('Lamming' 124–5). This horrific re-imagining of the family/colonialism analogy has a coherence and intensity which makes the novel a revelation of the inner desires and pleasures of colonial power, as well as its crimes.

Of those who were to write of the English domestic scene in the twentieth century the earliest to arrive were, like Katherine Mansfield, Christina Stead, and Patrick White, descendants of English colonial settlers. But the great flowering of writing from colonies and former colonies is post-war, beginning in 1954 with Lamming's *The Emigrants*, the simplicity of its title now underlining its originality, and the work of Selvon, Naipaul, Harris, Colin MacInnes, Lessing, Jacobson, Duckworth, Emecheta, and numerous others. Their novels appeared in a literary environment in which, according to Walter Allen's 1954 study of the English novel, among the most significant writers were Greene, Cary, Golding, Powell, Bowen, and Hartley (343). What he nominates is an English fiction much taken up with the niceties of social mobility within a narrow range, and rarely acknowledging either non-whites or a working class. As novels and plays of the so-called Angry Young Men began to appear, and make different voices heard, so too did signs of a rapidly changing Britain: racial tension increased, and legislation to control it grew more severe. It is now possible to review this body of post-war writing through the work of a second generation. With hindsight, they revise earlier fictions of post-imperial England, while in their novels with a contemporary setting they interpret domestic life in a Britain transformed by the immigrants' return 'home'.

Making contact

London is an open-armed but still unwelcoming imperial mother in much post-war fiction of arrival, but not inevitably: 'Headquarters' (Lamming, *Pleasures* 24) may also appear 'foreign'. In the passage quoted earlier, and in 'No Return', Jacobson writes of settling and belonging in

England; but in his fiction the phenomenon of displacement has no consistent colonial slant. For his white South African figures London is essentially the modernist anonymous city. This is its attraction to the couple who eventually marry at the end of his South African Jewish family saga, *The Beginners*. Standing together on Primrose Hill they look down on the 'simple geography of London, a wide flat valley, between two ranges of low hills.' The city is immense: 'It simply filled the valley as a dream fills the mind' (424). Both have decided to stay in London, and, standing exposed on the skyline, they feel obliged to justify their decision: 'How could it be done, in the face of the vast indifference, the city sprawled immeasurably beneath them? Yet that indifference was surely one of the reasons for their choice' (425). In *The Evidence of Love* a more troubled sense of the city's immensity reflects the mental state of the lovers. A young 'Coloured' man, Kenneth Makeer, light enough to 'pass' for white, has been sent to London from South Africa to study law, paid for by his patron, Miss Bentwisch. There he falls in love with Isabel, his patron's niece. Unable to see a way out of his situation, he comes close to breakdown, and then the city exacerbates, and mirrors, his feelings. Walking about the streets after Miss Bentwisch's death Kenneth is grieving, and fearful about his life ahead. London itself becomes the object of his fears: 'vast in its details and vast over all, echoing, incomprehensible' (176). With Isabel this nightmare disappears: 'with her the streets of the city did not run endlessly and meaninglessly, one into the other and beyond; but wheeled around a certain centre of life, and the centre sustained them, though they were so massive and immoveable and indifferent...' (198).

In the short story 'Trial and Error', once again alienation interacts with other emotional states. A South African couple are living in a village, and though happy at first – 'They were in a foreign country; and yet they were at home' (104) – displacement eventually worsens the strains in their relationship. Quarrels break out and eventually Jennifer goes off to stay in London, and then writes saying she has fallen in love, and will not return. This crisis fills Arnold with a sense of their isolation. When he contemplates going to search for her, the thought of that 'huge, dark, crowded city' (111) frightens him. He has no one there to whom he can turn for 'succour'. Overwhelmed by the thought of life without her, he goes out into the night and walks in the village, ending up at the churchyard. To him this is now a place of alien spiritual traditions and family ties: in spite of all his learning, he feels lost and, in a resonant 'imperial' phrase, more 'ignorant than the most ignorant savage' (112). The wife returns and the marriage is patched up, but not before the story has communicated its sense of expatriate isolation as an episode of existential panic. But there is no emphasis on the location of his displacement as either English or metropolitan.

A Gap in the Spectrum (1959), the first novel of the New Zealand writer, Marilyn Duckworth, is, in contrast, dominated by the perception of London by the newcomer, Diana. At first she is in a women's hostel but cannot remember how she got there. She too endures a dislocation between her old and new self, which here manifests itself as loss of memory. In the London winter Diana feels 'in a different world' (81). She notices everywhere a mysterious new red colour, which is at first disconcerting, even painful. Associated traditionally, of course, with passion and sexuality, it connotes for her Europe (against a grey New Zealand), and London as a dangerous city of sexual crimes. Gradually she comes to find it more pleasant and, at the end, dyes her hair red – literally taking on the local colouration, a strand of symbolism recalling Mansfield's earlier evocation of London as the sexualized city.

The narrative centres on the virgin Diana's taking a lover. That he is English – even if for him to fulfil this role they have to go to Paris – goes against the stereotype of the English male as sexually inhibited. But in finding Stephen, and at the same time a connection with England, the novel's outcome completes a romantic scenario frequent in novels of arrival. This resolution, though uneasy in this particular instance, has, of course, a counterpart in colonial narratives of arrival and conquest. There the colonizing invader/settler performs – in Mary Louise Pratt's terms – an 'anti-conquest': he assumes possession of the country, and of a local woman, and may even take her, like Pocahontas, or Rhys's Annette Cosway, away with him.

In a narrative where it is a traveller, male or female, *from* the colony who is arriving and finding a mate, this pattern of events tends to be shrouded in qualifications and undertones. Rarely does the ex-colonist's romantic achievement of a foreign partner amount to anything as straightforward as a narrative of possession, or even acceptance and assimilation. Indeed, in the hands of a confidently critical observer of England and Empire such as Christina Stead, the romantic plot is turned right around and carries a negative judgment of life in the metropolis. In *Miss Herbert (the Suburban Wife)*, the Swiss Heinrich Charles sees marrying the English woman Eleanor as a fast route into the middle class. But in a novel that characterises that class as complacent and narrow, his desire condemns him. The romantic fate of the sympathetic figure of Teresa in Stead's *For Love Alone* also has a critical edge. Teresa comes to London and finds a job with James Quick, and they fall in love. But theirs is an anti-English alliance: Quick is not an Englishman but an American, and, moreover, one amused by the English upper classes' inclination to scorn colonials, including Americans. This couple cheerfully dispenses with England and the English and goes off to Paris.

In the romantic plots of ex-colonial writers, tensions provoked by perceived inequalities, or their 'psychic residue' (Hulme, 'Lamming' 125), in colonial-metropolitan relationships contribute to the romance's failure. In Naipaul's *The Mimic Men*, Ralph Singh and those around him anticipate these difficulties. That Singh would return to his Caribbean island of Isabella after his time as a student in London married to an English woman is spitefully predicted: he will be unable to resist the allure of what a French woman friend on Isabella calls, in the local slang, 'whitey pokey'. He marries Sandra, the first English-speaking woman with whom he has a relationship. She is a satisfactory sexual partner, but provides no access to belonging to England – implying that his expectation that she would do so was part of her appeal. Sandra, with her 'gift of the phrase' (78) and 'North London tongue' (79), is *of* the city but has no feeling of community *with* it, or with her family. Filled with a hatred of the 'common', and hungry, after the war years, for luxury, it is obvious what she hopes to gain from the marriage. Once back on the island they join 'a haphazard disordered and mixed society in which there could be nothing like damaging exclusion', a circle linked by 'expatriate and fantastically cosmopolitan wives or girl friends', without loyalties or depths; 'for everyone the past had been cut away' (66). Sandra's complex reaction to the island society, which includes taking on some of her husband's own fears and loathing of it, drives her into open hostility. As a result, *she* is then seen as a 'common' East End girl, rescued by a man 'besotted by the glamour of her race' (79). She leaves him and the island, but not for England. Later, on his return to London, Singh encounters Lady Stockwell's daughter, Stella. During the week he spends with her he enjoys the illusion of being close to 'a way of looking at the city and being in it, a way of appearing to manage it and organize it for a series of separate, perfect pleasures. . . . It was a creation, of the city I had once sought: an unexpected fulfilment' (275–6).

The English novels of Lamming and Sam Selvon, published in the 1950s and 1960s, evoke a male culture where high among the attractions of London for 'the boys' are English and Continental girls who believe 'the black boys so nice and could give them plenty thrills people wouldn't believe' (*LL* 92). Selvon celebrates summer as an idyllic time of sexual pleasure: 'it ain't have no discrimination when it come to that in the park in the summer' (88). The womenfolk put the men's preference for white women down to their being 'too fast', 'The things they will do, no decent girl from home would ever dream of' (*Emigrants* 147); some men want to marry them, but not vice versa, they note. These marriages won't work, or so says Selvon's Moses, the old London hand, speaking of students such as Naipaul's Singh: 'They go back with English wife and what happen? . . . the places where their white wife could go, they can't go. Next thing you hear, the wife horning them and the marriage gone puff' (*LL* 117).

When the woman is the newcomer, if there is any contact between her and an Englishman, the uneasy mood of Duckworth's Diana with her lover is the norm. In Doris Lessing's *The Golden Notebook* (1962) Anna, the white writer from Africa, does not form a relationship with an Englishman; her lovers are a European refugee and an American.[1] In *The Four-Gated City* (1969) Martha first meets up with Jack, whom she had known in Africa, and her relationship with the central figure, Mark Coldridge, lacks commitment from both sides. In both novels and particularly the first, Lessing is, of course, asserting that conventional marriage is dead and the conventional domestic novel now unwritable, but her women's choice of men remains striking. In novels of the post-war period relations between those arriving from colonies or former colonies and English people are typically transient or unsuccessful. An established couple, such as the Nigerian Mr Noble, and his wife Sue, the gipsy-like 'big blond woman' from Birmingham, in whose house Adah lives in *Second-Class Citizen*, appear occasionally but not at the narrative's centre.

Living on the edge

London, V.S. Pritchett's study of the city points out, has always been a city of transients and aliens: 'A large population floats. Millions have not been here for more than a generation' (28). But this was not the case in the predominantly middle-and upper-class society depicted in many home-produced English novels of the 1950s and 1960s, with their established networks resting securely on an ancestral experience of England. Newly arrived writers were likely to find themselves part of a transient metropolitan life, and wrote of it from a position that no English novelist could experience. Naipaul twice briefly recreates this to him unexpectedly bizarre milieu – in *The Enigma of Arrival*, in the narrator's Earls Court boarding house, and in the first part of *The Mimic Men*. The young Singh experiences a growing dissociation between himself and the city, 'so three-dimensional, so rooted in its soil' (*MM* 32), which saps the individual's 'solidity'. In contrast to the sensation defined with such confidence by an islander friend: 'Where you born, man, you born' (205), in London 'Each person concealed his own darkness' (33). With so many nations together, there was no community of experience and language, and though these circumstances lend themselves to comic episodes of misunderstanding and cultural bewilderment among lodgers, in Lamming's *The Emigrants* the confused life in student hostels assumes the shades of nightmare.

As for the lives of the English, everyday domestic events, observable in smaller cities and towns, were in London disconcertingly hidden. Singh learns of his landlord's death only after the cremation: 'It was disquieting . . . this secrecy and swiftness of a London death' (*MM* 8). Tornado in *The Emigrants*, who knows London from his time in the RAF, explains why this is so: 'Nobody ask questions and nobody give answers. You see this the minute you put foot in London. The way the houses build was that people doan' have nothing to do with one another. You can live an' die in yuh room an' the people next door never say boo to you no matter how long you inhabit that place' (76).

This observation on the lack of community is often repeated. The city is in every sense 'divide up in little worlds' (*LL* 58). Without shared domestic spaces such as the Nigerian 'compound' which Emecheta looks back to, a sustaining community is hard to create. The English think of all blacks in London as 'West Indians' and assume they know each other, but they are, as Selvon's title has it, *Lonely Londoners*, scattered throughout the city. Lamming and Selvon document the struggle of 'emigrants' and 'Londoners' with poverty, racism, police harassment, all contributing to a spatially segregated, demoralising existence: 'Alone, circumscribed by the night and the neutral staring walls, . . . All life became an immediate situation from which action was the only escape. And their action was limited to the labour of a casual hand in a London factory' (*Emigrants* 187).

They are shut away in basements and crowded rooms, caged up, or, like Harris in *The Housing Lark*, actually imprisoned. The need for a 'yard' transforms basement rooms into a substitute shared space, a haven (Procter 23–4). Long endurance of these conditions leaves Selvon's Moses overcome by 'a great aimlessness . . . that leaving you standing in the same spot' (*LL* 125), and he turns to writing about this fragmentary existence. Except for this metaliterary closing these narratives frequently find no conclusion beyond hesitation between returning home, after saving for the fare, and staying. The discontinuous, episodic form of *The Emigrants* and *The Lonely Londoners* mirrors a story which has 'no beginning or end' (Nasta 58). These lives fall outside the usual patterns of the domestic novel.

Setting up home

Displacement inspires the impulse to set up home. Even the drifter Gallows who comes to England 'by accident' is convinced that 'if a man have a house he establish his right to live' (*HL* 49). Naipaul remains sceptical about this possibility in any but the literal sense: 'his writing is about unhousing and remaining unhoused' (Muhkerjee qtd. in Gorra 64, Theroux 242). For all immigrants finding accommodation was an ordeal. As Stead remarked in 1958: 'The landlords are rampant, raging and this is a Landlords' Government and nothing else (*Letters 1*, 169). Africans, West Indians, Indians, Pakistanis and Bangladeshis who trailed the streets looking for housing faced 'No Coloureds' signs in the windows. Fictional retellings of the search for accommodation appear in repeated scenes of applicants being turned away, or forced to live in disgusting conditions. This struggle to set up home is paralleled by the writers' efforts to establish a literary base, to take over novelistic premises and do them out in a new style of language. Sushiela Nasta's essay on Selvon's London novels pursues this line, and points to the invention of a 'consciously chosen Caribbean literary English' (53), a Creolization of language and form. But while this comment is well made, housing in these novels is not primarily symbolic; as Selvon insisted: 'these material things become very important when one gets out of one's own land' (Interview with Nazareth 432).

Indeed his short novel *The Housing Lark* (1965) centres on this matter, with the success of a cooperative housing scheme bringing the narrative to an unusually joyful resolution. The scheme to buy a house is initiated by women and carried through by their determination, and typically it is women who in these narratives of immigration set up the home, and with it a claim on the country (Innes 22). The men, even if employed as 'casual hands', are less likely to take this route to settlement, unless, like 'Big City', they become landlords. Emecheta's Adah, a woman of unparalleled determination, is another success. *In the Ditch* reaches a conclusion when Adah and her family of five children move out of the welfare housing ironically called 'the Mansions', and into 'the matchboxes', an insubstantial but new maisonette flat, 'just in front of the famous Regent's Park' (128). Living in 'a middle-class neighbourhood' had been Adah's dream and she achieves it.

The modernist, linguistically innovative novels of Selvon, and the more conventional ones of Emecheta, though based in different immigrant communities, share a sense of the social and psychological obstacles to setting up home. The effort is initially sustained by the elation of being at last in London, 'the dream city' of so many novels including *The Satanic Verses* (37), but that is soon lowered by practical difficulties, and 'the wounded low esteem of racial contempt' (Gurnah 'Displacement' 11): even the resourceful Adah, when perpetually treated as an inferior, finds herself beginning to act like one. When the English are not actively, or covertly hostile, using 'the old diplomacy' (*LL* 47), living among them is still depressing. England to Adah is a silent country, English reticence and bottled up feelings epitomized for her by an English Christmas: it is indeed 'silent night holy night', without fireworks or rejoicing. Five Past Twelve in *The Lonely Londoners* agrees. Disappointed by the Lord Mayor's Show, he complains: 'They too slack in this city the people too quiet' (95). However, for women one compensation is the perception that in England they have rights. When Lewis beats his wife he is warned that he is not in Jamaica now (*LL* 53). For Adah too, who endures a long trial of hardship, London offers freedom from exploitation by her stepfamily in Nigeria, and her violent husband, and freedom to write. At the end of *Second-Class Citizen* her husband burns her first manuscript, but this is not going to stop her.

Representations of self-establishment on a still wider scale appear in these early novels. In his study of housing in novels of Selvon and Lamming, Procter characterizes the dwellings as 'West Indian strongholds, "colonized" sections of London' (30). Nasta too, as just mentioned, describes Selvon attempting a 'literary decolonisation' which colonises 'Englan' in reverse' (57). Metaphors of colonisation for occurrences of literal and linguistic or literary settlement are irresistible for describing the processes set in motion when British subjects from beyond England return in the last days of Empire. The everyday events of post-war immigrant settlement did indeed begin a material transformation of domestic culture. This process is epitomized when Tanty, in *The Housing Lark*, insists that her London grocer adopt the Caribbean system of credit: he takes down his 'No Credit' sign and replaces it with a picture of the royal wedding. London is becoming the *City of Spades* of MacInnes's 1957 title, 'spades all over the place' (*LL* 23). If forced to live in a 'black enclave' (Nasta 55) they can rename its boundaries: Bayswater becomes 'Water', Marble Arch 'the Arch', 'the Gate'. Harris, the Trinidadian would-be-Englishman, with his gentleman's clothes and copy of

The Times, is not just a ridiculous mimic man. It is he who organizes a dance in the St Pancras Town Hall and puts Caribbean social life on display, much to the envy of the white Londoners who fight to get in. In *The Housing Lark* an organized outing, a coach trip to Hampton Court, has even more significance. 'Hamdon Court', thus renamed, is redefined. By being there, with 'all them Englishers looking on' (118), and talking of 'the old Henry...watching his chicks,...studying which one to behead and which one to make a stroke with' (117), the community asserts its distinctive participation in a shared historic tradition. As the people in the party enjoy their banquet and lie drinking and chatting on 'the green banks of old father Thames' (120), the narrative gives a particular legitimacy and even power to their presence, especially when they return the gaze to those who stare at them:

> now and then...sedate Englishers wonder what the arse them black people talking about, and the boats on the river, every time a boat-load pass Syl waving to them, and you could see them white people getting high kicks as they wave back. You could imagine the talk that going on on the boat: 'Look dear, come and see, there's a party of Jamaicans on the bank.' And big excitement on the boat, everybody rushing to the gunnels (is a pity some of them don't break their arse and fall in the Thames) to see.
>
> (126–7)

This novel of 1965 celebrates a transformation of domestic life in Britain, which Enoch Powell was to attack in 1968 as a dilution of Englishness, and an infringement of English domestic space (Baucom 15). While Moses still dreams of going home, others are settling in.

Two nations

English readers did not need ex-colonial writers to remind them that 'England is the most class-ridden country under the sun' (Orwell 67). Home-produced novels are etched with what Lessing summed up wearily as 'this business of Britain's class system' (*Walking in the Shade* 59). But ex-colonial writers saw the system afresh. What she and others are most compelled to comment on is the working class – the ruling classes were relatively familiar from colonial experience, and from English fiction. Stead, Lessing, and other sympathisers from the left, saw little that gave hope of change: 'The working classes, the lower classes, have "internalised" their station in life' (60). The rich 'would never believe what it like in a grim place like Harrow Road or Notting Hill' (*LL* 58). But the division between rich and poor was accepted: 'People don't talk about things like that again, they come to kind of accept that is so the world is, that it bound to have rich and poor, that it bound to have some who live by the Grace and others who have plenty' (*LL* 58).

The 'emigrants' saw the conditions of working-class Londoners at close range, because they worked and lived alongside them. As a result, to quote Selvon further: 'It have a kind of communal feeling with the Working Class and the spades, because when you poor things does level out, it don't have much up and down' (*LL* 59). Emecheta's Adah held a well-paid job as a librarian in Nigeria but in London, her husband explains, as an African she is a 'second-class citizen'. Domestic fiction seen from the perspective of Adah was something rare. For many of Emecheta's critics *In the Ditch* (1972) was the first book they had read 'about the English working class written by a foreigner living among them' (Emecheta, *Head above Water* 76). Until the advent of Sillitoe and Braine English novelists still saw England predominantly as middle-class and white, and though workers, the poor and servants did appear, the point of view remained the same.

The publication of *Lucky Jim* (1954) roused Somerset Maugham to deplore a 'new class on the British scene'; 'l'école de Butler', was Evelyn Waugh's derisory phrase for these writers (Green 134–5). Waugh's reaction, if eccentric, suggests the gulf between the extremes of English society. If novels by grammar-school scholarship students, such as Amis and Wain, of the exploits of Lucky Jims raised such wrath, Selvon and Emecheta wrote of people who were still further down the ladder. Theirs were novels of an urban underclass of the basement ghetto, 'the ditch'. In 'the mansions' Adah learns the codes of the welfare-dependent poor, where it is not done to take a job, or to aspire, as she does, to move out. The reactions elicited by close-up images of the demoralisation and hardship of working-class life by ex-colonial novelists corroborate Selvon's impression of the ignorance of a predominantly middle-class readership. According to one reviewer, Emecheta's novel *In the Ditch* 'tells simply and readably what it is like to fall by the wayside in these days of affluence',[2] where 'the wayside' labels the life of poor families as abnormal. Lessing's being a single parent with a young son and little money saw her living in a working-class area, an experience which lies behind arguably her most successful 'English' book: *In Pursuit of the English*. Her autobiography tells how her fellow novelist Penelope Gilliatt made the assumption that she had done so 'to get material' (*Walking* 319). It simply did not occur to Gilliatt that a poor woman with a child had little choice. More recently, one reviewer of Gurnah's *Dottie* (1990), where Dottie is an Adah-like figure, condemned the novel as too relentlessly a tale of misery, implying it was incredible and exaggerated.[3]

Except for occasional sorties into the world of publishing, ex-colonial novelists rarely invade the English upper classes. The genteel literary world that Stead presents so scathingly in *Miss Herbert* appears in both Lessing and Jacobson. *The Beginners* has a satirical vignette of the establishment, a Teviot Square party given by an upper-class publishing couple. The devoted Lord and Lady Warrenton are, with their children, a much (and often self-) publicized ideal family of their class. Snippets of conversation, along with the lady in a 'hideous hat' (367), establish that this 'grand company' is not really grand, and neither is a publishing house ruled by the necessity to invest in 'the very latest thing, in any line' (373). Lessing's *The Four-Gated City* puts Martha in contact with wealthy members of the London establishment. When she and Mark visit the Georgian country house of Mark's mother and stepfather, the novel registers the apartness of such places from the England most people experience; these houses 'feed on a different air to that breathed by ordinary houses'. The visitors' contrasting reactions enact a class division: 'Mark approached it as the kind of place one lived in; Martha as a sort of inhabitable museum' (368). Martha is impressed by the conformity of the upper middle-class, in spite of the occasional communists and other radicals in their ranks, and intrigued by a form of sexual behaviour which she thinks of as 'playing nurseries' (70). It reappears for instance when Stella in *The Mimic Men*, in bed with Singh, insists on reading *Winnie the Pooh*. Lamming's images of the upper classes in *The Emigrants* follow his overarching conception of colonial relations as a perverse domesticity. When the Caribbean writer Collis visits the factory owner Pearson and his wife, the cold propriety of their middle-class household envelops him with the density of 'an entire climate'. His whole visit, recounted at an excruciatingly slow pace, is an arid ordeal. In the figure of Frederick, 'Tall, bony, emasculated' (217) and formerly in the colonial service, the novel has a dazzling instance of the stereotype sexually inadequate English male found in this environment. In an attempt to overcome his 'deficiency' (220) Frederick engages in threesome efforts at sex with Peggy, who passes as his wife, and with Collis, but once he learns of her bisexual 'irregularity' (244) he abandons her and, in the tortuous plot, returns to the Jamaican woman he previously jilted (thereby exposing her to ridiculing calypsos) because she was too dark skinned. He will marry her as a penance, and return to Africa.

Inside Britain now

Few writers took up the challenge of writing a novel of English domestic life without an outsider figure. In 1941 Patrick White published *The Living and the Dead*, his only novel set entirely in England, while Lessing, after many years of residence in London, has written of the English from the inside in her novels of the 1980s and 1990s, *The Fifth Child*, *The Good Terrorist*, and *Love, Again*. But in the post-war period Stead's *Cotters' England* and *Miss Herbert (the Suburban Wife)*, and Naipaul's *Mr Stone and the Knights Companion* stand out as rare instances. All three have at their centre a distinctively English, if eccentric, figure, presented without explicit judgment or reflection, but the attitudes of the writers to their material show nothing of an insider's inhibitions or self-censoring. Readers will recognise in these novels the concerns and features of style which characterize the writers' distinctive literary worlds, but each does more than put on an English persona here. Since these three novels will reappear in later chapters it is sufficient to note that in all of them English domestic life is grim, ugly, even horrific. Both of the Stead novels mount an attack on what for her are the determining structures of English domestic life; Naipaul, less radical, satirises a London Nobody, Mr Stone and his household, but finally moves beyond satire to find him pitiable. Being exposed to a critical outsider's recreation of England presented from the inside was, for some English readers, a disconcerting experience. Theroux reports that a woman attacked Naipaul over *Mr Stone* at London dinner party in his honour: ' "You wrote a dishonest book about London – *Mr Stone*. Nothing in that book is true. You totally misrepresent the way we live." ' (290).

A distinctively late twentieth-century refashioning of the 'insider' novel has now emerged in the work of David Dabydeen, Abulrazak Gurnah, Hanif Kureishi, Caryl Phillips and Salman Rushdie – and others, the second generation of ex-colonial writers, all either immigrants or the children of post-war immigrants born in England. Selvon revealed in an interview that when he was writing *The Lonely Londoners* in a modified Trinidadian English he was always thinking, 'perhaps unconsciously, of an English audience' and asking himself would these people understand it? (Nazareth 424–5). This later fiction speaks to a readership enlivened by 40 years of post-imperial 'cultural diversity'. In addition, it is in close contact with theoretical and critical debates on issues of nationalism and cosmopolitanism, national identity and cultural mutation, and both contributes to the intellectual ferment and, in some cases, bears the print of dominant theoretical concerns.

The issue of redefining a volatile post-imperial national identity finds a home in second-wave novels of the 1980s and 1990s in stories of discovering or inventing a personal identity. Discontinuous time-scales and double locations shape their narrative patterns, as the migrants journey back and forth, actually or in recollection, seeking to understand a hybrid existence. In this generation of writers, migrancy is a flexible term, and embraces moving between different regions of Britain, as in this recollection of Kureishi's: 'I remember coming from the suburbs and not belonging and getting to London and thinking, Where am I? Who am I?' ('London' 9) An answer to the question may be self-invention; in London, it seemed to Kureishi, 'you can make yourself up' (13). In its more traditional forms, this fiction seeks to explore the question Gurnah put to himself: 'what happens to people who are in every respect part of a place, but who neither feel part of a place, nor are regarded as being part of a place'.[4]

One reply, aligned to scholarly historical investigations, substitutes another question: how did these people get here? Novels revisit the recent British history of immigration, and oblige contemporary readers to remember the Peter Griffiths' slogan, 'If you want a nigger neighbour, vote Labour', Enoch Powell, and discriminatory legislation, as if to keep the ugly record in view. Reaching further back still, Phillips and Dabydeen, drawing on published studies of the black presence in Britain (in Dabydeen's case, his own), ground their migrant figures in a long past, looking back – with Lamming – to the writing of *The Tempest* and the first slave-taking voyages (Hulme, '*Tempest*'). This is to set domestic life in an overtly political context. An alternative psychological focus brings the novel of belonging and exclusion nearer to the domestic novel. These two kinds can be identified in the critically acclaimed 'English' fiction of Phillips and Gurnah.

Phillips's *The Final Passage* (1985) retells a story of Caribbean emigration in the Teddy Boy era of the late 1950s.[5] This story, however, is of emigration as a near fatal mistake: at the end the woman who is at its centre will, if she survives, return home. Earlier novels by male novelists centred on a group of men who travelled to England to work. Here, as is more frequent in second generation novels, a woman's experience is the focus. Leila, child of a Caribbean mother and an English father, follows her ailing mother to England with her small son and his father, the flamboyant, feckless Michael. All these figures remain largely enigmatic, their individual motivations left unspoken (Innes 25), with emphasis falling instead on the conditions of life in London for the Caribbean immigrant. The matters of day to day living, especially the domestic violence and the search for accommodation, recall Emecheta's London novels, but with the figure of Mary, the neighbour who befriends Leila, Phillips develops a characteristic historical point about attitudes to women. Mary quotes her Mother saying that 'as soon as Hitler hangs his clogs up', women will 'be back skivvying and scurrying like there's nothing in our heads' (174). But above all, this is a novel that announces the concern with the history of slavery and the African diaspora that is developed in Phillips' later fiction. With a title immediately suggesting the 'middle passage' of slaves across the Atlantic, it takes a long view of Caribbean emigration. Leila's journey links the presence in post-war Britain of these Caribbean descendants of African slaves to English involvement in slavery, that unfinished story 'that has stained British society' (Phillips, 'Interview' 27).

Crossing the River traces the fantastically extended life stories of three children sold by their desperate father into slavery on the West African coast in the eighteenth century. The boy Travis reappears in the novel's last section as a GI stationed on a Yorkshire airfield in the Second World War. He falls in with love with Joyce, a young woman from a steel town. When they meet, Joyce's husband is in prison for black marketeering but, when free to marry, they do so. Their story is told through entries in Joyce's diary, from 1938 with one last one in 1963, but jumbled out of order, forcing the reader to piece together a sequence of events, and reflect on what permitted it to take the shape it does.

Along with other recent British fiction the novel takes up a subject from the Second World War, but here in order to discover a 'black presence' in England, and a story of racial persecution – the victimization of Travis by the Military Police, well before post-war immigration. Throughout this story of the low-class marginalized woman and her lover, constructions of class and gender interact with racial feeling. Unconventional and non-racist, Joyce forges a brave alliance of those disadvantaged by gender, class and race, only to lose Travis to the war, and their son to an orphanage. She is a figure more familiar perhaps from feminist fiction of the 1970s, here convincingly located by Phillips in the previous generation.

With Joyce's 'migration' to the village the small incidents of daily life recorded in the diary build up an image of a wartime community threaded through with class and regional differences, and hostile to an 'uninvited outsider' like Joyce (129). To her the village is a 'bleak and silly little' place, 'filled with its own self-importance' (150). The community differentiates itself as 'up here' (174), in the North, and against the town where the shameless girls come from who frequent the camp (212). Joyce has a quick sense of class ideology in the village. She is not impressed when a 'couple of toffs' join the home guard (136); the rich in 1939 are 'already hiding from the war' (141). Dissenting from the pervasive patriotism, she becomes good at 'learning the difference between the official stories and the evidence before [her] eyes' (165). She counts the costs of the war in her own terms, and scorns the notion that, with everyone pulling together, England is now classless: 'Classless my arse. A toffe-nosed bugger's still a toffe-nosed bugger to me' (188).

Abdulrazak Gurnah's novels set or partly set in England, *Pilgrims Way, Dottie* and *Admiring Silence*, also take up the damaging day to day experiences of migration and black Britishness. Their central figures endure demands to produce exotic tales, or to confirm myths of Empire, while being frustrated by their fellow Britons' ignorance and consequent failure to acknowledge their British status: '*Where are you from?...*"England"', Dottie replies (213). Gurnah characteristically heightens the complexity of the context in which the reader contemplates these situations by setting them against a representation of Africa which does not idealize the pre-colonial past (Bardolph 81), or, for that matter, the present. These narratives recognise the slave-owning Muslims in East Coast Africa, the brutality and destructiveness of some anti-colonial movements, and the repression practiced by post-independence governments. In *Admiring Silence* the narrator returns home to discover his now 'independent' East African city has become a mire of inefficiency and corruption in the hands of 'armed thugs' and 'flabby devils' (192), Conrad's phrase for Belgian colonists here used to denounce corrupt African administrators. London, whatever its drawbacks, has unblocked toilets, running water and a health service. But, in this context of the postcolonial domestic novel, what most distinguishes Gurnah's novels is that themes of racial violence, the legacy of slavery, and cultural definitions of the British subject, together with the migrant's search for family and identity – for 'home', are here incorporated in many-layered narratives of family relationships and marriage, the domestic novel's traditional matter.

In *Pilgrims Way* (1988), as in the later *Admiring Silence* (1996), a student from East Africa comes to England and finds a 'wife'. Daud, soon too poor to study, becomes a hospital orderly, and meets a nurse, Catherine. She choses Daud over her conventional doctor partner, and there, with a nod to convention, the novel ends. In *Admiring Silence* the relationship between the central couple has become brittle. Emma Willoughby, a university teacher – who as a post-structuralist critic deplores closure – and the unnamed schoolteacher narrator have been together for twenty years and have a 17-year-old daughter, Amelia. The Austen and Thackeray associations of these names, with an irony intermittently deployed by both narrator and narrative, point to the failure of this story and its English female figures, and by implication of England itself, to find resolution in accord with the traditional romantic novel. Both these novels, and *Dottie* too, are, in classic realist style, peopled by a variety of figures: landlords, friends, rivals and parents, black and white, seen at home or at work in hospital, factories, in pubs or at parties. This enables them to present the clash of racial attitudes between the older and younger generations in the 1960s, the period of the original encounters in these novels. Emma's parents' lies and euphemisms do not conceal their horror that their daughter has a black boyfriend. Daud's contemporary, the good looking, confident Karta brags of his sexual relationship with his white teacher. If for him it has overtones of revenge – a racial replay of fuck the rich – for her, Karta is a chic accessory. Catherine and Daud manage to avoid such old and new racialist stereotypes, with Catherine delighted not to become the bride of the young doctor, and the displaced and often fearful Daud finding in Catherine a home. *Pilgrims Way* is an affecting narrative, which both draws on and revitalises the hackneyed patterns of desire of the hospital romance. It does so by delicately tracing the younger generation's effort to develop relationships that, while not pretending to transcend or deny black–white difference, put aside categorical positions and make space for other significant human differences.

Admiring Silence begins with the narrator raging to his wife about colonialism, the 'decadent English', and then, with 'overloaded ironies', condemning whining ex-colonials for not enduring their lot in England with the dignity of a Pocahontas. His joyous finding of Emma has happened years earlier. A middle-class rebel against conventionality, and her mother's 'obsessions with class and neighbours and foreigners' (24), she refused to marry. Her parents exemplify the split in ideologies of post-imperial British nationality re-examined by Baucom in the context of the 1981 British Nationality Act (6–14), the father glorying in the achievements of the Empire, the mother disavowing its returning subjects. To relieve his rage, the narrator feeds the father outrageous stories to confirm his belief in imperial paternalism and the benefits of colonial rule.

He has also made up stories for Emma about his African family, and for himself, especially about his schoolteacher father. And, as the reader listens to the voice devising a new version of the story of his childhood, it becomes clear that this is a series of consoling narratives, invented in response to his displacement, his guilt about his relationship with Emma, and, as is revealed once he goes back to Africa to see his own family, his distress at his father's disappearance and his mother's remarriage. Thus his return brings memories of what was, and was resented, as well as an awareness that this is 'no longer home' (170). There are also painful new discoveries. He learns from his mother that his father did not die, he 'just left' (124) before his son was born, stowing away perhaps, and never wrote to anyone. The father's abandonment of his pregnant wife, and his subsequent silence, thus precisely foreshadow the narrator's own uneasiness at abandoning Africa and his family, and his ensuing reluctance to tell them about his relationship with an English woman. He was unable to tell Emma that his mother remarried and that he was brought up by a well to do, respected stepfather, and still hides from his stepson role. That he refers to his stepfather as Uncle suggests an idealization of the lost father, conflicting with disappointment, betrayal, and anger.

Thus *Admiring Silence*, like *Mansfield Park*, examines 'being at home'. In the course of his visit his family takes pains to find him a bride. Finally compelled to tell them about Emma, he leaves, only to find on his return that she has 'found someone else'. She, the first and only woman he has loved, as he comes to understand while in Africa, was his 'home'; now he has no reason for being in England any more. The double journey of leaving and then returning to the home country's post-independence political turmoil, and then leaving again, with a homelessness made acute by betrayals, recalls Naipaul's narrative of displacement and broken marriage in *The Mimic Men*.

The narrator initially raged at contemporary England and ends complaining of his daughter – a 'hard, metropolitan creature who could take everything in her stride' (217). For Rushdie's Chamcha, 'the debasing of Englishness by the English was a thing too painful to contemplate' (*Satanic Verses* 75). Here the attitude to this rage is less ridiculing. The underlying parallel with the narrator's unhappy familial situation suggests that his feeling about England and his colonial past is a disappointment amounting to betrayal. His quick understanding of the Indian woman whom he meets on the plane returning to London reinforces the parallel. She too feels that England is like a lost lover, and (as he guesses) it emerges that her husband has left her, after many years of marriage, as Emma has left him. On the flight he also realizes he has lost his passport. In the episode in which he explains to the disconcerted official that what he has lost is a *British* passport, post-imperial England replicates on an official level the fact that Emma no longer accords him recognition. His experience of loss is multiplying.

Gurnah's earlier work, *Dottie* (1990), rewrites the novel of immigrant struggle for a 'better break' (*Emigrants* 52). What is different here is that the figures are emphatically 'British'. Dottie appears first as a young girl in a Carlisle flat. The mother who has struggled to support her children by prostitution is now dying, leaving Dottie with a younger half-sister and -brother to care for. All are, like Kureishi's Karim, English men and women, 'born and bred, almost' (*The Buddha of Suburbia* 3). Dottie's full name – Dottie Badour Fatwa Balfour – hints at a complicated family history. It goes back to soon after the First World War and her grandfather's arrival and settlement in Cardiff's Tiger Bay.[6] In colonists' terms, she is a third generation settler. *Dottie* is domestic fiction with a vengeance: it is about housing, furniture, and loans. Dottie's battle to find the courage to keep alive in spite of poverty and exploitation recalls that of Adah. Gurnah's female central figure marks the book as a 'second generation' text, but in its representation of Dottie's working-class milieu it has no obvious rival except perhaps *Cotters' England*. Dottie is intelligent and diffidently begins to read and educate herself. But before this process takes hold, her dealings with landlords, welfare workers, the prison system and the mental hospital where her family end up, are all shaped by her social position as a poor black woman. Adah, an educated professional woman, found herself consciously and unconsciously imitating poor English people, but Dottie, who works in a food-processing factory, is one of them. Gurnah's novel succeeds in presenting this experience from the 'insider' view of the black fellow-worker.

In this narrative of hardship and exploitation, the reader is caught up in Dottie's struggle, wishing her success, and fearing that she may lose what she has gained. Around her, again recalling the density of a classic realist novel, Gurnah interweaves stories that bring together African, Caribbean and white English figures. These intraracial and cross-racial relationships offer a dual insider–outsider perspective, unlike earlier ex-colonial fiction where white people remain distant. But though herself an 'outsider', the connections which Dottie feels are not with Africa, the middle east or the Caribbean, but with the black faces she sees in her London, that is, in Brixton and Balham, such as the old black man she remembers from visits to the library and who turns out to contribute to the novel's satisfying conclusion. This does not solve the questions of who Dottie is or where she comes from, but origins are now irrelevant:

her education has begun and she has, in the journalist Michael, an 'African-English likely lover' (Lee, 'Long Day's Journey' 120).

In 'Notes towards a Redefinition of Englishness', Michael Gorra recalls Orwell's conviction that however England changed after the war, it would go on being 'recognizably England'. But instead, Gorra points out, citing Larkin and Pym, recent British writing evokes a sense that 'England is out of touch with its own contemporary reality' (162). For writing that *is* in touch readers can look to Gurnah, and his contemporary ex-colonials. While the press and television contemplate yet again the death of Britain, these fictions offer an imaginative approach to the on-going cultural transformation of England brought about by her diverse British subjects.

Notes

1. In Anna's Yellow Notebook, her fictionalized version of her life, this lover becomes Paul Tanner, a working-class Englishman who, like the refugee, is a doctor. At the end of the novel, in the Golden Notebook, Anna tries to imagine the two figures ideally combined (528–9).
2. The *Sunday Telegraph*, quoted from the back cover of *In the Ditch*.
3. *Literary Review*, June 1988, qtd. in Lee, 'Long Day's Journey' 119.
4. Transcript of 'Book Shelf' BBC Radio 4, November 1992, also quoted in Lee, 'Long Day's Journey' 111.
5. For Phillips' acknowledgment of Selvon's importance to him, see 'Interview: "Crossing the River"' 34–5.
6. For the history of this community, see Dennis, *Frontlines*, 143–59.

3
'Learning Me Your Language': England in the Postcolonial *Bildungsroman*

Leela Gandhi

> ... Remember
> First to possess his books; for without them
> He's but a sot, as I am; nor hath not
> One spirit to command ...
>
>

The Tempest, III. ii. 91–4

> But in the end, even though it meant shutting himself away, the books won. They ruled over him: for him that bookcase had all the order the world lacked. I used to think it was love, but I know better now. He was afraid; afraid of the power of science and those books of his; afraid that if he disowned them they would destroy him.
>
>

Amitav Ghosh, *The Circle of Reason* (395)

The *Bildungsroman* has long been regarded as pre-eminent in the history of the realist novel. Yet, specialists of the genre insist that contrary to claims about its successful transmission, out of its late-eighteenth and early nineteenth-century German homeland, the *Bildungsroman* is a bad traveller. Closer examination reveals that the catalogue of European novels said to belong to the family of the genre are, in fact, prodigal creatures with scant regard for their structural and generic obligations. In most cases, as M. Bakhtin notes, the *Bildungsroman* functions as an arbitrary and promiscuous category 'requiring only the presence of the hero's development and emergence in the novel' (Bakhtin 20).

Given the case for the *Bildungsroman*'s poor transmission within Europe itself, there is reason to be doubly sceptical about its postcolonial appropriation. Can a genre which loses its integrity on what are, in effect, domestic flights, sustain the cultural effort of a journey 'out' to the distant colonial world, especially after a prolonged stop-over in England? Is it possible, in other words, to see the clear shape of Goethe's 'Englished' presence in, say, Singapore, Lagos, Gurgaon?[1] Seeking an affirmative answer to these questions, this chapter aims to foreground the conditions in which the *Bildungsroman* can, and does, successfully travel to the non-West. For the sake of argumentative coherence, my focus is specifically on the genre's emigration, or 'voyage out', rather than on those narratives of 'alternative development' which characterize diasporic or immigrant accounts of the 'voyage into' England/Europe. In so doing, I do not aim to disqualify these latter narratives from the status of *Bildungsroman*, so much as to make a case for the particular politics which underscore the transmission of the genre or, its 'arrival' in the colonial world.[2] So too, rather than generalizing the encounter between European culture and the non-European world, I have restricted this discussion to post/colonial India and its encounter with English imperialism. The Indian example is by no means paradigmatic. It is offered as but one historically synchronous case study among others. A more precise understanding of *Bildungsroman* through which such a 'case study' might proceed, however, requires that we revisit, at greater leisure, the alleged problem of the genre's poor communicability. The following chapter will, briefly, address itself to this task. In the main, it will specify the conditions under which the *Bildungsroman* can be said to have arrived, and been 'received', in post/colonial India. The question of its 'reception', as I will argue, with reference to some paradigmatic textual examples, offers a unique perspective on the place of England in the Indian imagination.

Bildung or *roman*

In an essay which concerns itself with problems of generic transmission, Jeffrey Sammons argues that the *Bildungsroman*'s unsuccessful itineration is not so much the fault of its imprecise European imitators, as it is a symptom of the genre's own intrinsically 'unfulfilled' nature, even in its German elaborations (Sammons 32).[3] Although the *Bildungsroman* is credited with a dominance over the nineteenth-century German novel, actual examples seem disproportionately few and far between: 'hardly more than a dozen titles have been commonly adduced for the century and a quarter from the advent of Romanticism until the First World War, and a large part of the discussion has been focused upon the

single archetypal example, Goethe's *Wilhelm Meisters Lehrjahre'* (31).[4]
However, and as Sammons admits, this reading is hard to reconcile
with the enduring intellectual interest generated by the *Bildungsroman*,
both within and outside Germany, and among illustrious commentators
who include the likes of Hegel, Carlyle, Shaftesbury.

The apparent discrepancy between the profuse philosophical reflections provoked by the genre, on the one hand, and the paucity of actual
Bildungsromane, on the other, can, however, be resolved, if we recognize
that the *Bildungsroman* is not so much a fully articulated aesthetic
development, as the purveyor-in-novel-form of the characteristically
bourgeois concept of *Bildung* or 'self-education'. So, for instance, in the
first available discussion of the genre, by Professor Karl (von) Morgenstern of Dorpat, in a series of lectures delivered between 1819 and 1820,[5]
the *Bildungsroman* is celebrated as a form which realizes the principles of
civil society through its commitment to the ideals of self-formation and
self-development. 'One's own powers', Morgenstern writes in explana-
tion of *Bildung*, 'they should be awakened, strengthened, purified in the
individual from the ground up' (173; qtd. in Martini 6). And elsewhere,
as a corollary to this view of self-regulation, he laments at large about
the perils of over-government: 'Let state constitutions perish – of mon-
archies and republics alike' (351; qtd. in Martini). Over a century later,
in 1932, we find Thomas Mann praising Goethe in startlingly similar
terms, not so much for his contribution to the novel form, but rather,
for giving utterance to 'the idea of training, "upbringing," in such a way
that this idea forms a bridge and transition from the world of the inner
self to society and the social concept' (67). Goethe's exemplary execu-
tion of this idea, Mann adds, confirms his status 'as a representative of
the classic-humanistic period' (67). Scholars of the *Bildungsroman* agree
that the ideological content of *Bildung*, celebrated by Morgenstern and
Mann, among others, is a symptomatic product of the *Aufklarung*, or,
Enlightenment:[6] a body of thought associated, in turn, with the cultural
politics of European imperialism.[7]

As is well known, the Enlightenment philosophes predicated their
project of political reform upon the contiguous reform of education
and pedagogy.[8] Thus, their overarching manifesto for the realization of
a self-regulating civil society, free from the interventions of a despotic
and zealous State, found expression even in their most narrowly conceived curricular reforms. In the main, their pedagogic efforts consisted
in replacing bookish and formal learning, and the 'over-education'
endorsed within scholastic methods of teaching, with a renewed human-
ist program of self-development or auto-didacticism. Accordingly,

Locke bemoans the distorting effects of rote-learning and routine, and recommends a greater emphasis on vocational training. In the same tradition, Rousseau, Hamlet-like, laments the tyranny of 'words, more words, still more words' (qtd. in Gay 544), seeking instead, the benefits of a 'natural' education acquired in the classroom of human experience. In each of these cases, learning is clearly privileged as a schooling in citizenship,[9] which is conceived, in turn, within Rousseau's etymology, as the capacity for self-government. So, if Rousseau's citizen is, as Gay writes, 'at once ruler and ruled, lawgiver and subject' (550), he acquires this capacity through the habits of self-formation instilled by his education.

The reformist underpinnings of this vision are self-evident. But, re-examining the philosophes' version of *paiedeia* or civil education (or, indeed, *Bildung*), more critically, it is also possible to detect at least two dangerous faultlines. First, a program that enforces a rigid symmetry between the capacity for culture/education, on the one hand, and political rights/citizenship, on the other, can easily become selective in its application. For, in the grand rhetoric of *Aufklarung*, can we not already presage the shape of a prejudice which might refuse political rights or self-government to those who are considered to lack – for reasons of gender, race, class, culture, sexuality – the capacity for self-formation?[10] Second, the discourse of citizenship/training promoted by the philosophes, and embodied within *Bildung*, can also be read as an intensely conservative discourse of socialization, viz; one which aims to achieve the symbolic legitimation of authority.[11] Indeed, it could be argued that far from encouraging individual autonomy, *Bildung* gestures toward a pedagogic ideal that promotes a subtle internalization of the law within its bourgeois pupils. Franco Moretti's comments on the political culture of *Bildung* are apposite here:

> It is not sufficient for modern bourgeois society simply to subdue the drives that oppose the standards of 'normality'. It is also necessary that as a 'free individual', not as a fearful subject but as a convinced citizen, one perceives the social norms as *one's own*. One must *internalise* them and fuse external compulsion with internal impulses into a new unity, until the former is no longer distinguishable from the latter. This fusion is what we call 'consent' or 'legitimation'.
>
> (16)

The constraints of this discussion only allow us to hint at the continuities between the conservative content of *Aufklarung/Bildung*, and the culture of late-eighteenth/nineteenth-century European imperialism. But already, following on from the points elaborated above, we can see how the talismanic association of pedagogic and political privileges, within Enlightenment thought, paves the way for 'the civilizing mission.' For now, not only can Europe deny self-government to seemingly 'unformed' or 'undeveloped' cultures, it can also justify its imperial intervention into these cultures as an ethically motivated and historically expedient pedagogic initiative.[12] So too, if 'education' enables the European State to train the 'consent' of its own bourgeois citizenry, it is instrumental, within a colonial context, in securing the hegemony of empire.[13] The only difference is this: in its European transmission, the narrative and ideology of *Bildung* aims to produce citizens; on its colonial travels, however, it aims, somewhat differently, to produce subjects. Thus, when English education arrives in India, shot through with all the residual rhetoric of its Enlightenment ideologues, but equally, fraught with terrible ethical contradictions, how do the Indians receive it? How do they write the story of their subjection to imperial *Bildung*? The next section will examine this response, and its variety, with specific reference to the British educational policy in colonial India. It is in this response, furthermore, that we can begin seek the historical materials for a postcolonial *Bildungsroman*.

Goethe in Gurgaon

English or 'Anglicist' education formally arrives in India with the 1835 English Education Act of Governor-General William Bentick, and the rhetoric surrounding this piece of legislation certainly reflects the hegemonic aspirations of imperial policy makers.[14] Writing to Bentick earlier that year, on 2 January 1835, William Adam, newly commissioned to compile a report on the state of education in Bengal, sounds very much like an *Aufklarer* (philosophe) in colonial clothing. The State, he proposes, must develop an educational model whereby the rule of force is replaced, in degrees, by the training of native consent to colonial rule: 'to labour successfully for them, we must labour with them; and to labour successfully with them, we must get them to labour willingly with us. We must make them, in short, the instruments of their own improvement'.[15] That English education is an improvement on its 'Oriental' counterpart, Macaulay announces in no uncertain terms with his 1835 Minute on English education; notoriously privileging a single shelf of European books over all the libraries of the East.[16] But this, of course, is only one side of the story. For, the narrative of English education in India owes its plot as much to the manipulations of Indian reformers as it does to the prose of imperialism. As early as 1817, clamorous demands for liberal Western training from Calcutta's chattering classes, result in the founding of the *avant garde* Hindu College, where, as Nirad Chaudhuri observes, beef, drink and Shakespeare soon prove to be equally *de rigueur* (181). So too, in 1823, it is the liberal reformer Rammohun Roy who urges the State actively to promote Western education, at a time when imperial administrators appear to believe that the interests of British hegemony would be better served through a culturally sensitive promotion of 'native' culture and 'oriental' learning.[17]

Already the site of collaboration between the native elite and colonial rulers, then, the English pedagogic intervention into India takes shape as a hybrid creature, where the political interests of the colonizer/tutor are cross-bred with the cultural aspirations of the colonized/pupil. Early Indian rationalism, especially, needs little imperial encouragement to concede the superior tutorship of England. Catching nationalism at an incipient moment when colonialism is still perceived as a cure, however unpleasant, for the moral ill-health of Indian civilization, rationalists like Henry Louis Vivian Derozio (1809–31) reinforce their fierce advocacy of English education with an equally fierce denunciation of Hindu scripture.[18] Writing, in this vein, in 1854, the poet Michael Madhusudan Dutt combines a paen to colonialism – 'it is the glorious mission of the Anglo-Saxon to regenerate, to renovate the Hindu race' – with a passionate hymn to the English language: ' . . . give me the literature, the language of the Anglo-Saxon: Banish Peto, banish Bardolf, banish Poins: but for sweet Falstaff, kind Jack Falstaff, banish him not the Harry's company; banish plump Jack and banish all the world! I say, give me the language – the beautiful language of the Anglo-Saxon' (532–3).[19]

But rationalism is not the only response to the advent of English education in colonial India. Caught at the busy intersection of old and new learning, in a milieu where education has become an intensely self conscious project, the over-stimulated Indian middle-class reader/student also proves resistant to the civilizing pretensions of colonial pedagogy. And in the ensuing debate, or recasting of England as a problem of knowledge, we can begin to make out the shape of at least two, albeit overlapping, perspectives, which can be claimed as proto-narratives for a postcolonial *Bildungsroman*. The first narrative, symptomatic of the cultural nationalism making its presence felt later in the nineteenth-century, undermines the tutorship of England by proposing a defensive case for the discipleship of the West to Indian spirituality. And, even as

England and India face each other in a pedagogic deadlock, a second narrative, often collapsed into the appropriative fabric of cultural nationalism/religious revivalism, announces, as we will see, its radical rejection of all formal and received knowledges.

It is now almost a truism that nineteenth-century cultural nationalism or 'religious revivalism' redresses the psychological/cultural damage inflicted by Western learning through opposing claims about the spiritual precedence of Indian civilization.[20] And among the numerous spokesmen for this project, Narendranath Datta, or, Swami Vivekananda (1863–1902), offers a paradigmatic example. A Hindu philosopher, sanayasi, and favoured devotee of the mystic Sri Ramakrishna Paramahmsa (to whom we will turn later in this discussion), Vivekananda follows his contemporaries in conceding only the material and practical benefits of Western knowledge. But, more radically, he extends this discourse further, to insist upon the Western need for spiritual instruction from India. Thus, drastically reversing the protocols of colonial pedagogy, Vivekananda undertakes a long and varied sojourn in the USA and in England, very much in the spirit of a teacher.[21] Despite his triumphant Western debut in the USA, at the 1883 Parliament of Religions in Chicago, however, he is especially overcome by pedagogic energy on his two trips to England, where he offers regular classes of Vedantic instruction, in addition to giving several courses of lectures at galleries, clubs, to Theosophists, and to educational societies.[22] In his accounts of this mission to England, and speaking in an idiom which anticipates Gandhian *ahimsa* or non-violence, Vivekananda claims 'spirituality' as the prerogative of a defeated or subject culture: 'Spiritual ideas have always come from the downtrodden (Jews and Greece).'[23] Asserting the ethical priority of victims over victors, and so, turning imperialism itself into Indian advantage, Vivekananda refashions India as the custodian of England's lost conscience.[24] Notably, however, and in keeping with the many paradoxes of nationalist thought, Vivekananda's English sojourn leaves him very impressed with the (secular) educational apparatuses of the British state.[25] These, he recommends, without any apparent sense of self-contradiction, as a model for Indian nationalism: 'Education, education, education alone! Travelling through many cities of Europe and observing in them the comforts and education of even the poor people, there was brought to my mind the state of our own poor people and I used to shed tears. What made the difference? Education was the answer I got...'.[26] And indeed, by the end of the nineteenth century, when Vivekananda writes these words, education has increasingly been brought under the jurisdiction of nationalism. As

Partha Chatterjee tells us, in addition to those schools and colleges instituted under the patronage of the colonial state, 'In Bengal, from the second half of the nineteenth century, it was the new elite that took the lead in mobilising a "national" effort to start schools in every part of the province and then to produce suitable educational literature' (9).

Through the nineteenth-century, as England and India sometimes collaborate, and sometimes compete, on the subject of pedagogy, a dissident minority demands attention for its radical rejection of all formal education. We find this story taking shape in the – for lack of a better terminology – guru 'cults' of the late-nineteenth and early twentieth century, notable for their appeal not only to the education-weary Indian middle-classes but also, and powerfully, to dissenting late Victorian English radicals.[27] This buried and collaborative Indo-Anglian critique of knowledge, imperial and nationalist, is ushered into the margins of colonial history under the aegis of what can only be called a 'modern' *bhakti* revival. First appearing in fifth/sixth-century India, the diverse and recurring traditions of *bhakti*, or devotional culture, are best explained in A. K. Ramanujan's words, 'as a countersystem, opposed to classical and orthodox systems, say, in their views about caste, gender, or the idea of god' (10). So too, in its very syncretism and populism, *bhakti* has consistently gained its energy from a peculiar anti-intellectualism, which struggles, first, to liberate knowledge from its formalized or bookish associations and, second, to resituate it, with the help of a *guru*, within the affective irregularities of devotional experience. Typically, then, the fifteenth-century *bhakta*, Kabir, celebrates his illiteracy and, in that spirit, pours scorn on orthodox learning: 'Teaching and preaching, their mouths/ filled up with sand. / While they watched the fields of others, / their own crops were eaten'; or, even more irreverently: 'What can the poor guru do / if the student's a lout? / Teach till you're blue, / you're blowing through bamboo' (126, 127). Divesting received knowledge, none too gently, of its claim to the truth, Kabir redirects his audience to the ontological priority of the heart: 'I've shouted for four ages: the true form's in your heart' (124).

These sentiments are given new expression by the numerous gurus who appear on the Indian scene, through the late-nineteenth and early-twentieth centuries. Of these, Sri Ramakrishna Paramahamsa (b. 1836–4) has attracted the most critical attention for his strong appeal to the English educated Calcutta intelligentsia, eager to escape from the prison-house of reason.[28] Tellingly, the various accounts of his life are replete with episodes concerning the liberation of students and scholars from the dogma of 'book-learning'. So, for instance, Ramakrishna's anglicized disciple, 'M.', is disabused of the false notion 'that a person who is educated and who studies books acquires knowledge';[29] and another realizes that, 'what I could not acquire by reading cart-loads of books, he has got without turning over a single page' (Sri Ramakrishna 159). The South Indian guru, Sri Ramana Maharishi (b. 1880–), advocates *bhakti* along similar lines, by directing his disciples away from the mind to the heart.[30] Ramana's own 'enlightenment' begins with his momentous decision to drop out of school: 'What is the use of books and school for me now?'[31]

A more focused critique of European 'intellectualism' comes from Sri Aurobindo (b. 1872–), the one guru with a first hand experience of English learning, acquired through a schooling at St Paul's, London, and then, at King's College, Cambridge.[32] Sri Aurobindo's considerable corpus is informed by the effort to liberate philosophy from dry 'speculations of the intellectual kind, a kind of metaphysical analysis which labours to define notions, to select ideas and discriminate those that are true, to logicize truth . . .' (*The Upanishads* 3). In his letters, he writes, in a similar vein, about the perils of producing philosophy like 'a labourer in a thought factory' (*On Himself* 84).

How far, then, does the Indian resistance to colonial *Bildung*, sketched in this section, inform the writing of post/colonial *Bildungsromane*? And what is the place of England in these narratives? The concluding section will seek the residual influence of the nineteenth-century Indian response to England-as-education in two sets of texts which exemplify, respectively, the colonial and postcolonial 'renaissance' in Indo-Anglian writing. The first group, comprising Gandhi's *The Story of My Experiments with Truth* (1927–29), G. V. Desani's *All About H. Hatterr* (1948), and Nirad Chaudhuri's *Autobiography of an Unknown Indian* (1951), reflects the politics and aesthetics of 'the Gandhian whirlwind' phase of Indian letters.[33] The second, postcolonial group, consisting of Upamanyu Chatterjee, Amit Chaudhuri, Arundhati Roy, Amitav Ghosh and Pankaj Mishra, includes some of the principal novelists of the 'Rushdie generation'.[34]

Bildungsroman, Indian-style

First published between 1927 and 1929, Mohandas Karamchand Gandhi's autobiography records the eccentric self-education, or 'experiments with truth', of its famous author. An account of the formative years preceding his involvement in the Indian national movement, *The Story of My Experiments With Truth* includes an irreverent account of Gandhi's

adventures and legal training in England between 1888 and 1891. Valu-
able as a testimony from one among the earliest generation of Indian
students in England, the book is doubly significant as a record of Gandhi's unorthodox views about education, which he approaches in the
spirit of passive resistance: under sufferance, albeit non-violently. Stub-
bornly refusing to acknowledge the utility or benefits of book-lore, this
autobiography adopts a *bhakta*'s perspective on all formal learning.

Of the new English schools in Rajkot, where he receives his early
education, Gandhi only recalls his disregard for academic achievement,
and regret that his teachers failed to give him an adequate 'knowledge of
self' (45). The only type of education to which Gandhi gives credence, in
this phase, comes informally or accidentally. A *mantra* he receives from
an old servant of the family to cure his childish 'fear of ghosts and
spirits', is privileged as religious initiation (45). Equally favoured are
the lessons he learns, by negative example, from a 'bad friend' who
lures him into the perilous paths of smoking, meat-eating and sexual
depravity (33–41). Gandhi's childhood bias toward 'the school of experience' (190) becomes doctrinaire in adult life. As a parent, he refuses
his sons a formal, 'artificial education . . . in England or South Africa';
and, much later, in 1920, he draws Indian students into the Non-
co-operation movement by calling them 'out . . . from those citadels of
slavery – their schools and colleges' (191).

Gandhi represents his own decision to study in England as pragmatic
and opportunistic, based on the prevailing (and lamentable) taste
among Indian employers for England-returned barristers, and also, on
the reputed ease of the Bar examination. *Contra* Macaulay, Gandhi's
England offers a respite from, rather than improvement upon, the onerous challenge of his Indian studies: 'Nothing could have been more
welcome for me. I was fighting shy of my difficult studies' (49). Also
important to these preparations, is Gandhi's decision to travel to England despite prevailing caste prohibitions and familial anxieties about
the contaminations of Western culture. By foregrounding his personal
vows of abstinence, Gandhi assures his family, and so, his readers, that
he approaches England as a seriously self-regulating individual, already
immune to its false influences and temptations. Morally armed and
pedagogically recalcitrant: this is the mood that Gandhi brings to bear
on every moment of his English training.

Upon arrival, a friend confirms that the young Indian must advance
on England more as an anthropologist than as a student: 'We come to
England not so much for the purposes of studies as for gaining experience of English life and customs' (57). While immersing himself in the

frivolous protocols of English 'manners', then, Gandhi noisily bemoans the simplicity of his prescribed syllabus. And the 'uselessness' of his textual English education is a theme to which he frequently returns later in the book: 'I had read the laws, but not learnt how to practice the law' (88). The instruction whose worth he does concede, however, is acquired through his association with marginalized groups; in the company of Vegetarians and Theosophists, especially, he re-discovers as 'knowledge' the unexamined tenets of his own Hindu upbringing.[35]

The Story of My Experiments with Truth is not really an 'authentic' account of Gandhi's English sojourn. Its implicit nationalist apologetics and cultural contestations reveal the voice of a man already at the vanguard of the anti-colonial movement; and one, who has announced in *Hind Swaraj*, his categorical rejection of English or modern civilization. A more 'truthful' account of Gandhi's first impressions of England is offered in his *Guide to London*, composed between 1893 and 1899, where he records the simple enthusiasm of a twenty-four year old man: 'I thought to myself if I go to England not only shall I become a barrister... but I shall be able to see England, the land of philosophers and poets, the very centre of civilisation' (68). Yet, as an account of self-development, *My Experiments* is noteworthy in that it refuses both the anti-English invective of *Hind Swaraj*, and the colonial adulation of the *Guide*, in favour of an affectionate, if somewhat trivializing, representation of the place of England in his education. If anything, the England of Gandhi's autobiography is fashioned as a recreational rather than pedagogic space: 'time out' for the man slated to become a 'mahatma'.

As distinct from Gandhi, Nirad Chauduri's *The Autobiography of an Unknown Indian* (1951) is a paen to bookish learning, yet, one with a peculiarly colonial twist in its tale. An account of the first 25 years of the author's life in colonial India, Chaudhuri's *Autobiography* describes his affective and intellectual formation, attributing the former to India, and the latter to England. The influence of India and Hinduism, Chaudhuri dismisses as pathological (207): a mix of 'synaesthesia' (205), 'moods' (207) and seasonal associations. By contrast, England is praised, in the book's infamous dedication, as teacher and preceptor, *par excellence*: 'To the memory of the British Empire in India, which conferred subjecthood on us but withheld citizenship; to which yet every one of us threw out the challenge: "*Civis Brittanicus Sum*" because all that was good and living within us was made, shaped, and quickened by that same British rule'. As the text unfolds, however, these rigid boundaries between affect and knowledge, India and England, collapse, revealing a troubling symbiosis between the author's cultural influences.

Throughout the book, Chaudhuri postulates England as a culture of books; an 'idea' which carries within itself the scholarly magic of philology, taxonomy and historiography.[36] But, with a curious evasiveness which contradicts the mood of his dedication, Chaudhuri constantly appropriates his textual love for England as a self-generated passion: produced by his own volition, than by the inducements of imperial civilizers. So, in 1911, he tells us, when the British empire was busily representing itself in India through the material and bureaucratic splendour of the Delhi Darbar, 'for me the most memorable experience was my first acquaintance with the *Encyclopaedia Brittanica* in its newly published eleventh edition' (292). Elsewhere, Chaudhuri insistently indigenizes his bookishness, even – and paradoxically – representing it as a version of *bhakti*. The Hindu, he instructs us, is free to worship God in three ways: 'first, through knowledge; secondly, through action; and lastly, through love' (190). The love of Shakespeare, he argues, could well be claimed as the first type of worship, were it not for the fact that the devotional excess of Indian Bardolatory is much more suggestive of *bhakti*, than the *yoga* of knowledge: 'the idea we cherished that our Shakespeare worship was *jnanayoga*, or intellectual contemplation, was certainly an illusion. Scholarship was perhaps the least element in it. What we were really doing with him was to worship him in the third mode of Hindu religious culture – adoration' (190).[37]

The appeal to *bhakti*, in this instance, could well be rhetorical; borne of a desire to assert the compatibility of English book and Hindu idiom. But, even in its effort to seek the consonance of these competing traditions, Chaudhuri's *Bildungsroman*-after-a-fashion, bespeaks the influence of Indian rationalism: that curious blend of balanced eclecticism and – *pace* Derozio and Dutt – excess. And if eclecticism accounts for his receptivity to the knowledge of England, its dark shadow, 'excess', or, the 'emotion of scholarship' (325), is responsible, as Chaudhuri tells us (not without some pride), for his immunity to the formal rules of English education: 'I had been attempting or rather prospecting too much ... I came to acquire a deep knowledge of certain aspects of certain subjects very unusual in a student of my age ... I disliked and even despised exams' (352). Failing at university, Chaudhuri dissociates his avid pursuit of European book-lore from the strictures of colonial tutelage. Albeit through a different route, then, his discourse on learning, no less than Gandhi's, amplifies the prickly narrative of colonial autodidacticism.

G. V. Desani's *Bildungsroman, All About H. Hatterr* (1948), recalls a more recognizably Gandhian incredulity about the value of received education. Set in British India, the novel is more or less a growing up story about the education of the eponymous and mad-hatterish hero H. Hatterr, son of a European merchant seaman and a lady from Penang. Described by Burgess as 'a grotesque autodidact who has built up a remarkable vocabulary with the aid of an English dictionary and a French and Latin primer', Hatterr demonstrates – *vide* Joyce – a profound colonial resistance to the tutelage of English grammar. Equally refractory toward formal pedagogy, Hatterr's picaresque efforts to acquire the meaning of life from Seven Sages (deadlier than their corresponding sins), leave him disenchanted with the religious affectations of Indian culture, on the one hand, and the social hypocrisies of British culture, on the other. If Oriental learning is the preserve of charlatans and fake sages, Occidental learning consists in the fraudulence of titles and accreditations; the pellicle of 'men who are *D. Litt.* – which title means Light of the World – and who, in the past, had access to the most *expensive* of the British private schools, Eaten, Westmoreland, Shrewsbury, 'Arrow, Charter's House, Rugby-Football, the Gun Co. Winchester, and, oh! attend, the *most* mystic of them all, the *'Ell See See!'* (103). Knowledge, the disenchanted hero realizes at the end of his journey, consists in its absence, and the meaning of life in its meaninglessness: a truth, both more reliable and less expensive.

Unique among writers of the 'Gandhian whirlwind' for his confident Indianizing of the English language, Desani is commonly regarded as the most significant precursor for the 'Rushdie generation'. Yet, where Desani's prose is appreciably defiant *vis-à-vis* prevailing linguistic and narrative conventions, the hybrid idom which marks the novelists of the 1980s is already derivative, gathering interest with the passage of colonial time. For, the aesthetics of the post-Rushdie generation, as Rukun Advani argues, is shaped by writers with 'no direct or lived experience of colonialism and the national movement... and... little to do with the English as a people, or a presence, or as an oppressive race...' (16). *Masala* English notwithstanding, however, the *Bildungsromane* which dominate the literary output of this generation continue to rehearse recognizably colonial responses toward English/Western education.

Upamanyu Chatterjee's *English, August: An Indian Story* (1988) is a case in point. Agastya Sen, the hero of this novel, has never been to England. Yet, and this is the burden of his youthful angst, he experiences Englishness everywhere as the stubborn residuum of empire, adhering, on the one hand, to his anglicized education and, on the other, to the archaic structures of the Indian civil service, to which he has recently been appointed. As the novel opens, he is posted, for the purpose of his training, to a small provincial town in the South. And it is here, through the dope-haze of his inert afternoons in Madna, that he contemplates, *ad nauseam*, the burden of his deracination. If some fault accrues to his Cambridge-style college in Delhi University – 'a parody, a complete farce' (24) – the cultural plot of Agastya's life goes drastically off-course, much earlier, at a boarding-school with a reputation for England-returned English teachers. Here, he develops a deforming infatuation with Anglo-Indian boys: 'Agastya's envy... had blurted out, he wished he had been Anglo-Indian, that he had Keith or Alan for a name, that he spoke English with their accent' (2). As a price for this show of school-boy vulnerability, Agastya is baptized, anew, under the sign of his desire; his many nicknames conveying the content of his embarrassing Eng-land-love: 'From that day his friends had more new names for him, he became the school's "last Englishman," or just "hey English"... and like most names, they had paled with the passage of time and place, all but August...' (2). The hero's re-education, then, shows him growing out of his received nicknames into the greater dignity of 'Agastya': a name he shares with an ancient Indian sage. It is only through the labour of owning his own tradition – and, so, disowning the false effects of his English education – that 'English, August', as the title of the novel tells us, can become the proper protagonist of 'an Indian story'. The accidental pun of an amateur astrologer, reinforces this conceit: 'You will leave this place after August for a place you want to... Whatever it be, you shall be happy after August' (33).

To become properly post-August or post-colonial, then, Agastya begins by cataloguing his distaste for every manifestation of western education; a burgeoning list which includes, a Rhodes scholar who has 'already picked up an accent from somewhere' (172); an insalubrious uncle with a questionable degree from 'some obscure American univer-sity' (147); a Cambridge-educated civil servant with a bad case of Raj nostalgia (39), and, Nirad Chaudhuri, through whose offices it is, alleg-edly, possible to gain an introduction 'to that lovely bugger, who loves us all, what's his name, Enoch Powell...' (93). Rejecting also, the colo-nial contaminants of his civil service training (English literature, we are reminded, is a compulsory subject for the civil service exam), Agastya submits – *pace* his anti-colonial ancestors – to the divergent tutelage of the *Bhagavad Gita*. 'The mind', he learns, in the words attributed to Krishna, 'is indeed restless, Arjuna: it is indeed hard to train. But by constant practice and by freedom from passions the mind in truth can be trained' (84). Chatterjee's recommended transition from the books of

England, to the authority of the *Gita*, is founded, of course, on the history of the cultural contestations which long accompanied the colonial encounter. But, written in a milieu where all formal training/education appears to be incurably infected by the history of that encounter, *English, August* also submits, in the end, to a fantasy of self-development; equally recalcitrant to colonial and postcolonial education.

A similar recalcitrance to English education characterizes the hero of Amit Chaudhuri's *Afternoon Raag*. A student at Oxford, Chaudhuri's narrator-hero approaches his life in the imperial metropole with muted postcolonial confusion, vacillating, 'between clinging to my Indianness, or letting it go, between being nostalgic or looking toward the future' (129). This excess of options, he recognizes, bespeaks a privileged relation to England that offers, in context, merely one choice among many. Impervious, then, to the authority of Englishness, the narrator approaches his education with similar detachment: underwhelmed by his teachers, and desultory in his own academic efforts. His alter-ego, in this Oxford sojourn, is a man called Sharma, portrayed affectionately, if patronizingly, as a guileless colonial aspirant, upon whom England exerts a 'more direct, more immediately generous' influence, and whose instruction, in turn, he craves rather more devoutly: 'he became friendly: computer-friendly, party-friendly, library-friendly, super-market-friendly' (127).

Unlike Sharma, the hero sees the University as a setting for his erotic, rather than pedagogic, development. And in narrating the uneven course of his mildly conflicting love affairs with two women students, Shehnaz and Mandira, he wilfully transforms the academic rituals of the city, its semesters, dons, libraries, tutorials, students, into an elaborate backdrop for his unfolding romantic drama. While evading the academic claims of Oxford, thus, the only kind of 'learning' to which the narrator accords any serious attention, consists in the tradition of Indian classical music, and much of the novel describes his initiation into this tradition under the watchful supervision of his guru in Bombay.

In Arundhati Roy's *The God of Small Things* (1997), an anti-diasporic, homeward-facing novel, which looks askance at all adult and 'foreign' knowledge, Oxford is transformed, rather more negatively, into a scene of emotional and academic failure. It is here, at Balliol, that the protagonist's beloved uncle, Chacko, betrays the promise of his early youth through a bad and premature marriage to a baker's daughter. Insolvent, divorced, and burdened with the ignominy of a poor degree, he returns home to the enduring scorn of his alienated sister: 'She said: (a) Going to

Oxford didn't make you clever. (b) Cleverness didn't necessarily make a good prime minister. (c) If a person couldn't even run a pickle factory profitably, how was that person going to run a whole country' (56). Throughout the narrative Chacko himself bemoans the psychological damage of the colonial encounter: 'A war that has made us adore our conquerors and despise ourselves' (53).

Amitav Ghosh is another writer who participates in a colonial critique of European knowledge, but, in an idiom that conveys the healing passage of time. In his *The Shadow Lines* (1988), while England is crucial to the story of the narrator's development, it is recuperated as the scene of affective ties, rather than the locus of his formal education. Trained, rather pointedly, in India, in a Calcutta school and, then, at the University of Delhi, the narrator leaves for England on a brief archive trip; the main interest of this journey consisting in his renewal of the two-generation long friendship between his own family, the Datta-Chaudhuri's, and the English family, Price. By taking friendship as his preferred metaphor for the Indo-British encounter, Ghosh's novel departs radically from the affective pessimism which famously concludes Forster's *A Passage To India*: ' "Why can't we be friends now?" said the other, holding him affectionately. "It's what I want. It's what you want." But the horses didn't want it – they swerved apart; the earth didn't want it . . . . "No, not yet," said the sky, "No, not there" ' (289). But, far from being a simple reflection of the historical changes, viz., the end of colonialism, upon which the deferred friendship of Aziz and Fielding must wait, *The Shadow Lines* is intensely self-conscious and motivated in its projection of the enduring compact between the Prices and the Datta-Chaudhuris. For Ghosh's undertaking in this novel, and elsewhere, consists in exhuming the small, interlocking lives and intimacies which are subjugated, or deterritorialized, by the grand narrative of the colonial encounter. And, in so doing, he upholds the former as the only available exit from the prisonhouse of History. Yet, of course, despite the ethical and narrative complexity of the affective annotations at the margins of History, it is only, as we have learnt from Lyotard, the grand-narratives that count as knowledge, which make it, in other words, to the archive.

The 'growing up' of Ghosh's narrator is, in context, really the story of his developing capacity to view the archive, and with it, all received precepts, with incredulity. His task is to loosen the grip of his 'own small puritanical world, in which children were sent to school to learn how to cling to their gentility by proving themselves in the examination hall' (23). And it is in travelling to England – imaginatively, as a child, and physically, as a young scholar – that he learns, progressively, to see past the formal truth, or, Knowledge-proper, which jealously polices the shadow lines between nations, peoples, temporalities. His guide in this mission, is a cousin, Tridib, from whom he inherits a *bhakta*'s interest in the 'unknowable'. ' "He said to me once", the narrator recalls, "that one could never know anything except through desire, real desire . . . a longing for everything that was not in oneself . . . that carried one beyond the limits of the mind" ' (29). And if this wisdom re-animates a familiar theme in the literature and thought of the post/colonial Indian subcontinent, *The Shadow Lines* charts new territory in its attempt to imagine an extra-curricular relationship with England itself: free from the agonism of thought and founded, instead, on the even ground of empathy and affection.

The mood of Anglo-Indian collaboration which informs Ghosh's critique of colonial knowledge reappears, albeit in a more detached idiom, in Pankaj Mishra's *The Romantics* (2000), which tells the story of a young Indian student, Samar, and his life among European and American expatriates in the ancient city of Benares. For both the Western and Indian characters in this novel, India is privileged as the repository of real knowledge; a knowledge which consists, furthermore, in recognizing the limits of formal/orthodox instruction. The truth of books, we are told, is always preceded by the imperatives of life. And this, of course, is also the wisdom of the *Bildungsroman*: a narrative that, as we have seen, privileges 'natural' development over 'artificial' or pedagogic influences.

What, then, is the burden of the present discussion? That, in the course of developing a uniquely Indian, anti-enlightenment critique of colonial pedagogy, post/colonial Indian thinkers and writers find themselves, paradoxically, repeating the *Aufklarere'* (philosophes') opposition to bookish and formal knowledge, in favour of autonomous self-formation? And that, in so doing, they become, *mutatis mutandis* a copy of that by which they felt themselves to be oppressed?[38] On the other hand, we might read the post/colonial *Bildungsroman* as an appropriative narrative, differing from its European counterparts in the following way: where the Enlightenment philosophes, and their imperial inheritors, use *Bildung* to elicit consent (to the British State), the anti-colonial *Bildungroman* deploys the discourse of self mastery to produce a counter-system, genuinely sceptical in the face of received colonial authority. In other words, we could argue that the writing of a post/colonial *Bildungsroman* produces a narrative self-development that ultimately denies legitimation, with varying degrees of success, to the colonial authority of English education. And so, as Rushdie might say, newness enters the world.

Notes

1. Goethe's *Wilhelm Meisters Lehrjahre* is commonly regarded as the archetypal *Bildungsroman*. It was translated into English by Thomas Carlyle in 1824.
2. The migrant narrative is intrinsically coded like the picaresque novel to which the *Bildungsroman* sometimes owes its inheritance. Equally, *Bildungsroman*-type narratives produced within multicultural/racial Britain are enormously useful as an index of changing social and economic realities, demonstrating also, the insistent commerce between the cultural and socio-political domain, between genres and societies.
3. Here Sammons simply corroborates the controversial reading first proposed by Jurgen Jacobs (271–8).
4. Hinton Thomas is illuminating on the apparent dearth of German *Bildungsromane* (177–8).
5. While Wilhelm Dilthey is normally credited with defining and historicizing the term *Bildungsroman* in 1906, Fritz Martini's landmark article establishes Morgenstern's prior usage (1–25).
6. See Martini 9–11.
7. See Leela Gandhi 23–41.
8. See Peter Gay 501.
9. Montesquieu is representative in his claim that 'the laws of education . . . prepare us to be citizens' (qtd. in Gay 512).
10. Hinton Thomas, in particular, argues that early ideologues of National Socialism invoked *Bildung* to authenticate a system of cultural and political exclusions.
11. Hardin offers an instructive definition of *Bildung* as, 'a collective name for the cultural and spiritual values of a specific people or social stratum in a given historical epoch and by extension the achievement of learning about that same body of knowledge and acceptance of the value system it implies' (xii).
12. See, in this context, David Lloyd's excellent discussion of *Bildung* (which he reads through Schiller, and somewhat contentiously, as 'aesthetic education') and Arnold's *On the Study of Celtic Literature* (1867): 'Their incapacity for sustained formative work having been made manifest in the aesthetic sphere, which already provides the criteria by which formal development is seen as the measure of political maturity, the Celtic peoples must perforce subordinate themselves to peoples whose "genius" is more politically, formatively directed' ('Arnold' 147).
13. Gauri Viswanathan offers the most detailed case for the links between education, culture and the hegemony of the imperial British Government in India.
14. See Vishwanathan 23–44.
15. Qtd. in Arabinda Poddar 104 and Manju Dalmia 46.
16. This Minute is commonly regarded as the catalyst for Bentick's 1835 Act.
17. A member of the 1823 Committee of Public Instruction in Bengal, Rammohun Roy requests Governor-General Lord Amherst to abandon plans for the proposed Sanskrit College in Calcutta in favour of a college which might promote the study of 'natural philosophy' and the sciences (see Lola Chatterjee 300; and Percival Spear 161–2).

18. For a useful nineteenth-century biography of Derozio, see Thomas Edwards. Manju Dalmia provides an interesting contemporary analysis of Derozio as English teacher.

19. Also qtd. in Sisir Kumar Das (88).

20. Partha Chatterjee famously argues this case: 'The greater one's success in imitating Western skills in the material domain, therefore, the greater the need to preserve the distinctness of one's spiritual culture. This formula is, I think, a fundamental feature of anticolonial nationalisms is Asia and Africa' (6).

21. See Raychaudhuri for an account of Vivekananda's itinerary (254–5).

22. Romain Rolland gives a full description of this activity (90–91).

23. Letter to Francis Leggett, July 6, 1896, qtd. in Rolland 89–90.

24. For Vivekananda's arguments regarding India's spiritual gift to the West see Raychaudhuri 242, 248, 256.

25. 'The British Empire with all its drawbacks is the greatest machine that ever existed for the dissemination of ideas...'. Letter to Leggett.

26. Quoted in Atmaprana 22.

27. The vast and complex subject of the late-Victorian disciple would require another full length study. In the main, however, the theosophists provided a significant catalyst for much of the spiritual traffic between West and East through the nineteenth century. But theirs was, by no means, an exclusive monopoly; Western disciples were drawn to Indian gurus through a range of other routes and methods. Of the very few sympathetic treatments of this subject, Kumari Jayawardena's study of Western women and South Asia stands out for its acute readings of theosophists, mystics and devotees (175–207). For informative but antagonistic readings of Indian spirituality and the West see Peter Washington's book on Theosophy and Anthony Storr's study of the guru phenomenon. Storr's essay on Paul Brunton is especially relevant (151–71).

28. See Partha Chatterjee 35–75, Raychaudhuri 232–41 and Parama Roy 92–127.

29. Qtd. in Isherwood 263.

30. See the testimony of Arthur Osborne, one of Sri Ramana's numerous English disciples 36, 70–1.

31. For an account for this event, see, 'Who' (7).

32. See Peter Heehs for an excellent short biography of Sri Aurobindo.

33. The 'Gandhian whirlwind' is M. K. Naik's evocative and influential formulation.

34. For the emergence of the 'Rushdie generation' see Advani and Mee.

35. For Gandhi's and late-Victorian radicalism, see James Hunt 18–36, and Arnold Hills 76–98.

36. See Nirad Chaudhuri (184–8).

37. In *A Passage to England*, Chaudhuri claims bookishness as a defiantly Indian trait, resented, or held in envy, by imperial England: 'It did not become an Indian...to air...contempt for literature which came naturally to an English Barbarian, and to pretend that he was brought up on the *Pink 'Un* from

childhood was even more unbecoming. But there were in the olden days in India a class of Indians trained to behave in that way by a class of Englishmen. An Englishman of this type resented our devotion to English literature as a sort of illicit attention to his wife, whom he himself was neglecting for his mistress, sport' (21).

38. The phrase is an echo of Seamus Deane, on anti-colonial nationalism: 'it is *mutatis mutandis* a copy of that by which it felt itself to be oppressed' (8).

Part II
Author Studies

4
Katherine Mansfield and the Rejection of England

Ann Blake

'Then you are an English woman?' 'Well, hardly –'
'The Luftbad'

The opening of Katherine Mansfield's birthplace to the public in 1988, the hundredth anniversary of her birth, accorded her a unique status – 'a position, in relation to the literature of New Zealand, not unlike Shakespeare's for 'English' in general: a position of priority and pre-eminence' (Hardy 76). Although Mansfield spent half her life in England and Europe, and roughly half her 90-odd stories are set there, according to many accounts she is always the New Zealander. A longstanding judgment is that her best work derives from her Wellington childhood.[1] In her stories, the beach in early morning, the city, its houses and gardens take on the quality of myth. In an alternative view, Mansfield is the international modernist, and, with Joyce or Lawrence, a traveller and exile (O'Sullivan 5–15). Attention has now turned to Mansfield's colonial context.[2] In the paradigms of postcolonialism, her white-settler society, defining itself by its difference from the Maori, can never be authentically 'English'. It is rather a hybrid, produced by the colonial setting, that mimics Englishness. Mansfield defined a similarly interstitial position for the colonial, and personally repudiated it, in the diary of her trek in the Urewera region of New Zealand in 1907. She was then nineteen, and back after three years at school in London. On meeting some English tourists, she wrote: 'it is splendid to see once again real English people. I am so tired & sick of the third rate article. Give me the Maori and the tourist but nothing between' (*Notebooks* 1, 140). Any consideration of Mansfield's writing representing the English has to take notice of her shifting understanding of her colonial identity, and place in colonial history.

79

New Zealand critics point out that, for readers today, the Wellington household of Mansfield's childhood stories is not typical of the New Zealand of the period, but rather 'a sheltered enclave of Anglophile gentility' (Alcock 63). The Grandmother, Mrs Fairchild, the most sympathetically presented adult, is no longer taken as embodying the best of early New Zealand, but rather 'the ancestral virtues of England and upper middle-class England at that' (Alcock 60). If, in London, Mansfield was the colonial exile in the metropolis, she was nevertheless, in Bridget Orr's phrase, 'a member of the colonising elite ('Reading' 49). After her initial enthusiasm Mansfield felt increasingly that she and England 'simply [didn't] get on': 'We have nothing to say to each other; we are always meeting as strangers' (*Letters* 4, 178). A bed of geraniums could make her feel she was 'the little colonial', 'a stranger – an alien', who had the impudence to pretend she lived there (*Notebooks* 2, 166). But though, in a late letter, Mansfield aligned herself with the South African Sarah Gertrude Millin, as a 'transplanted' writer, this was not always where the emphasis fell (Clayton, 'Olive Schreiner and Katherine Mansfield' 37). She saw herself and her English husband, John Middleton Murry, as writing to win places in an English literary tradition and in 1921, two years before her death, she wrote in her notebook of 'we English' (2, 283).

Mansfield's first story, 'Enna Blake', is set in England. Published in her school magazine when she was nine, it tells how a girl of 'about ten' is invited to stay with her friend Lucy in Torquay. When she wrote it, Mansfield had never seen England, but her parents were there at the time, 'a fact reflected in the story', the editor suggests (*Stories* 544). Though the choice of location may well derive from thoughts of them, it has a wider implication. The adoption of an English setting suggests she shared her family's perception of its close relation to England, their sense of a virtual contiguity of the two countries. The milieu of well to do settlers such as the Beauchamps extended back to London and the countryside where their relatives still lived. This did not mean they were always at their ease when visiting England. In Woolf's *The Waves* (1931) Louis is embarrassed that his father is a banker in Australia, a literary instance apposite to Mansfield, another colonial banker's child (Tomalin 7). Mansfield herself records being belittled for her colonial background. When the principal of her English school asked if anyone had been chased by a wild bull Mansfield, eager to play a part, put up her hand, only to be told that she did not count because she was a 'little savage from New Zealand' (*Notebooks* 2, 31). But while she was later to write more seriously of feeling alienated in England, in 1908 she saw herself, optimistically, moving between London and New Zealand, and repeatedly sketched an autobiographical narrative of 'a dual existence' (*Notebooks* 1, 111–12, 122, 220).

Mansfield's father, Harold Beauchamp, was born in Australia in 1858, his own father having left England in 1848, and, after some time on the Victorian goldfields, settling in New Zealand. Harold established himself in Wellington and became prosperous. While emigrant families throughout the Empire spoke of England as 'home', Beauchamp and his family actually went home often. He made the seven-week voyage twelve times, first in 1889 just after Mansfield was born. He was there in 1911 for the Coronation, and in 1923, the year he received a knighthood, attended a garden party at Buckingham Palace. In 1903 he sent his three oldest daughters to finish their education at a London school. For him, the role of a colonial leader entailed maintaining such connections.

With an aunt as chaperone, Mansfield spent three years at Queen's College, Harley Street, an unusually progressive establishment. Term-time excursions had no supervisors, and the city was at their feet, an intoxicating sensation for Mansfield, captured in an early 'Vignette – Westminster Cathedral'. She writes of climbing the tower with her friend Vere: 'We leaned far over the parapet, and the four winds of Heaven seemed to beat upon us both. A long strand of your hair blew across my face, and the voice of London thundered out some stupendous, colossal, overwhelming fugue to the whole world' (*Notebooks* 1, 131). This evocation of adolescent passion in and for the city itself also permeates the novel, 'Juliet', which Mansfield began when still at school: 'She was alone in London – glorious thought. Three years of study before her. And then all of Life to plunge into' (*Notebooks* 1, 66). Similar pieces date from the months after Mansfield's parents had taken her back to Wellington, her father refusing to consider her wish to return: 'My Father spoke of my returning as damned rot' (*Notebooks* 1, 79). She longed for London, as from exile: 'Isn't it terrible to love anything so much. I do not care at all for men – but London – it is Life' (*Notebooks* 1, 108). In one sketch, written before her return, the city calls seductively to her: 'Convention has long since sought her bed – . . . Permeate your senses with the heady perfume of Night. Let nothing remain hidden.' (*Notebooks* 1, 74) Mansfield transformed these longings into stories of a romantic encounter in a café, in 'The Education of Audrey', or the fantasies of a milliner's assistant, in 'The Tiredness of Rosabel'. London is the modern city, a place of female freedom, sexual adventure and possible exploitation – a 'sexualized' city (Sydney Janet Kaplan 170).

Alongside this imaginary city life, Mansfield pursued another fantasy that amounted to an imaginative cross-racial assimilation with the Maori. She gave the women at the centre of her stories Maori names: 'Rewa', and 'Maata'. Maata was actually a wealthy Wellington school friend, Maata Mahupuku, whose ancestors were Maori chiefs. Mansfield writes of being 'powerfully enamoured' of her, and an experience with her, which she referred to at the time as 'unclean', made her aware of her bisexuality (*Notebooks* 1, 104). She had also encountered the Maori in other circumstances. There was the 'endless family of halfcastes' (*Notebooks* 2, 24) who lived across the road, as well as those she met on her trip in the Urewera. Her diary, recording language and customs, testifies to her interest, but, as Orr has persuasively argued, her descriptive styles do not suggest she rebelled against the 'the racial bias' of the time (Orr, 'Free people' 165). She felt quite at ease in acquiring what she described as 'a Maori Kit' (*Notebooks* 1, 141). Later, in Europe, she wore her Maori costume to dinner parties (Tomalin 59), even hinting that she had Maori ancestry. For Orr this self-dramatization, especially in the figure 'Maata', is an attempt to counteract the insecurity she experienced as the expatriate colonial hybrid, by adopting an idealized form of the 'exotic aristocrat' ('Free people' 166–7).

Once she returned to London in 1908 to begin her artist's life, she set off almost at once to Belgium. This initiated a pattern of travel, which was to be repeated, and echoed in her stories, whether to meet a lover or to be alone to write, but always to put herself at risk. Her goal was not London, but adventure, she explained to Dorothy Brett in 1921: 'And by Adventure I mean – yes – the wonderful feeling that one can lean out of heaven knows what window tonight – one can wander under heaven knows what flowery trees. Strange songs sound at the windows, the wine bottle is a new shape, a perfectly new moon shines outside . . .' (*Letters* 4, 269–70). Keeping her distance from her family's English connections, she launched herself into a world of musicians and writers, and into 'a series of disastrous misjudgments' (*Notebooks* 1, xx) which saw her within 15 months fall in love, become pregnant, marry a man (not the child's father) whom she left immediately, travel to Bavaria with her mother, and suffer a miscarriage. Only when back in London again at the beginning of 1910 was she able to pursue her aim: 'I must be an authoress' (*Notebooks* 1, 123). To establish herself she wrote for a specific market, the socialist Orage's *avant-garde* journal, *New Age*. (Orage had accepted her 'The Child-Who-Was-Tired', now generally reckoned to be indebted to Chekhov.) Her *New Age* stories flatter English readers, and play on anti-German prejudice recently fanned by a successful West-End play (*Stories* 547). They take a satirical view of a group of the German middle-class gathered in a pension to take the *Wasserkur*. Some, 'At "Lehmann's"' and 'Frau Brechenmacher Attends a Wedding' for instance, were more testing of the progressive sympathies of *New Age* readers, with their images of 'gross, insensitive German males [who] dominate and enslave their fraus and turn them into domestic animals' (C. K. Stead 31). At their most serious, the stories' exposure of cruelty and grossness in middle-class attitudes to women, marriage and the body is directed at an international bourgeoisie.

The successful publication of the pension stories in 1911,[3] led to experimental sketches in dialogue, where the English become the target, and then to her English stories. Mansfield turns her back on bourgeois society, and her inspiration is in marginal people, working-class women, servants, or Bohemians and the hangers-on in the art world, and later the English abroad. Never are the English put comfortably plumb centre. To some male critics it seemed that Mansfield wrote as an exile, belonging 'neither to England nor New Zealand' (Pritchett), out of touch with her subjects. She was a 'malicious woman' who lacked 'heart' (O'Connor 130–1), and wrote about disagreeable people. Today these might appear to be the judgments of readers unused to seeing contemporary society through the eyes of a woman writer who, in de Beauvoir's phrase, 'questioned the world' (qtd. in Fullbrook 7–8). That satirical tone, censured as 'brittle' or 'malicious', was at times Mansfield's explicit aim. What she feared was producing something less: mere mockery (*Notebooks* 1, 283).

But as Pritchett sensed, Mansfield felt that she did not belong. Life *was* a joyous experience, but less so in England. Her relationship with Murry, often itself distressing, contributed to her uneasy social position: 'I don't like Jack's family. I could never <u>bear</u> to have them live <u>with</u> us' (*Notebooks* 2, 143). A working-class scholarship boy, Murry was, like their friend D. H. Lawrence, an outsider in the upper-class literary world.[4] Moreover, Murry and Mansfield were poor, finding it difficult to make ends meet, in London especially. For all its hostility to conventions, Bloomsbury had its reservations about Mansfield. In a letter to Virginia Woolf, Roger Fry wrote of 'the under-world that Murry and K.M. come from and really belong to because however much they read they never could get the cultured attitude'.[5] However, to women in this circle, Lady Ottoline Morrell, Brett and Woolf, Mansfield seemed, Tomalin suggests, 'blessedly fortunate and free, appearing from the far side of the world unfettered by the restrictions they had had to break through' (54). Ottoline Morrell took up both her and Murry and invited them to her house-parties. The fictional version Mansfield made of these gatherings is, again, critical. 'In Confidence' is a sharp sketch of a weekend of intellectual and emotional pretentiousness. If Bloomsbury looked askance at Mansfield, she returned their disapproval.

In the London stories, Mansfield ridicules affected alternatives to conventional middle-class manners, such as the self-conscious *avant-garde*. In 'Bliss' and the later 'Marriage à la Mode', as in 'In Confidence', this milieu, described by Murry as 'the bare fringe of cultivated society' (*Katherine Mansfield* 9), is rife with personal dishonesty and betrayal. Bertha, the wife in 'Bliss', appears to have at last awakened to a passionate response to life and to her husband: 'Why be given a body if you have to keep it shut up in a case like a rare, rare fiddle?' But on that very day, at the end of her dinner party, she discovers that Harry is having an affair with Pearl, the woman who has in part inspired this liberation. Among Bertha's guests are the ludicrously named Norman Knights and the poet Eddie Warren. Mrs Knight explains how her 'most amusing orange coat' has 'upset' the stodgy middle-class passengers on their train, and the poet tells in heavily stressed phrases of his *'dreadful* experience with a taxi-man' (*Stories* 309). While Bertha marvels with Pearl at a blossoming pear tree in the moonlight, the conversation rattles on, as Warren recommends a new poem which 'begins with an *incredibly* beautiful line: "Why Must it Always be Tomato Soup?"' (314). Against this grotesquely modernist chatter Bertha sees her husband and the elegantly cool Pearl in each other's arms. The story then breaks off, with Bertha's exclamation "'O what is going to happen now?"', the pear tree, 'as lovely as ever', and a sense of human isolation. 'Marriage à la Mode', written expressly for the conventional readers of the *Sphere*, is less detached and abrupt. Here the breaking of a marriage is a romantic narrative, rather than an edgy modern story of the impossibility of communication.

The warmest feeling for those living on the fringe of bourgeois society in Mansfield's stories goes to working women and servants, such as the milliner's assistant in 'The Tiredness of Rosabel', 'The Lady's Maid' and the char lady, 'Ma Parker'. Inspired possibly by Chekhov's stories of servants, and drawing on women Mansfield had met, the stories reflect her concern with the emotional and sexual vulnerability of women on their own. But though Mansfield's sympathy is not in doubt, that is not enough to ensure success in bridging the differences of class. Her prose, always close to the cadences of speech or inner thought, is here mimicking uneducated speakers, and this puts Mansfield at risk of indulging that talent which sustained her as performer of monologues at ladies' afternoon parties, and left Leonard Woolf remembering her as someone who made him laugh more than anyone else ever did (L. Woolf, *Beginning Again* 204). What Mansfield herself called a 'black hole'[6] can appear when the writer's tricks of thought sit implausibly with the imagined speaker, or when mimicry slips into mockery. At times, it was as if for Mansfield 'the lower classes' were 'merely people who say "perishall" when they mean "parasol"' (O'Connor 133). But 'Pictures', the story of an aging contralto, the *demi-mondaine* Ada Moss, avoids these flaws. It begins on a cold morning in a 'Bloomsbury top-floor back', smelling of 'soot and face powder and the paper of fried potatoes she brought in for supper the night before' (*Stories* 323–4). Firmly located in streets, shabby offices and ABC cafes, the story follows Ada's going the rounds of the agents looking for work, recording one knock back after another. Her long day, pathetically sustained by daydreams of success, ends with her being picked up by 'a very stout gentleman wearing a very small hat that floated on the top of his head like a little yacht'. He buys her a drink and she sails 'after the little yacht out of the café' (330). The effect is neither sentimental, nor reassuring: going off with 'the very stout gentleman' is hardly a conventionally consoling image. But because the episode is free of moralizing the desperate Ada is able to achieve a moment of triumph.

The pathos and humour of these stories is not confined to women who are servants or *demi-mondaines*. In the finest of them, 'The Daughters of the Late Colonel', Constantia and Josephine are the relics of an English imperial household, emotionally stunted by their father's tyranny. This story depicts an essentially English life, beginning with the daughters' social isolation that derives from their connection with the colonial service. They were in India with their father, where their mother died of snakebite. Now their father is dead, their brother Benny is in Ceylon, and they have ended up in their London home, running in terror of their servant who treats them – 'the old tabbies' – with contempt, and bullied by their father's nurse. The house keeps their mementoes of the colonial years, a Buddha, a Hindu screen, an Indian carpet, the sunlight revealing its rich red colour. But the life of both England and India has dried within the daughters and been replaced by trivialities and absent-mindedness. Their last memories of anything amounting to action are from long ago, of pushing Benny into the Round Pond when they were children. If they had an amorous adventure they can barely recall it. Now though they are liberated from the father's bullying, they cannot believe they are. London impinges on their home, with cabs clip-clopping past, their nephew

Cyril rushing in between appointments at Paddington and Victoria, the organ grinder under the window, the sparrows. But nothing is available to them except an intermittent sense of disappointment and loss. The broken phrases which end the story mark their inability to hang onto even the remnants of a desiring self. Alpers writes that this 'outstanding story' of Londoners is 'a study of Londoners who seem to know almost no one in the city where they live' (*Stories* xxi). And this is only to be expected of these returned colonists, displaced figures of a type that will reappear in post-imperial fiction.

Mansfield's stories of the English abroad have their origin in her own preference for France. 'Katherine always seemed happy and more free in France, and hoped for peace to do her work in this land of her adoption', explained her devoted friend, LM (*Memoirs* 94). Her notebooks and letters register surges of feeling against England and the English, including her husband, which grew more intense as the years passed. One outburst, in London in 1919, was set off by Murry's saying that the place he would most like to be was in a Sussex farmhouse. The notebook races on:

No, I don't want England. England is of no use to me. What do I mean by that? I mean there never has been, there never will be any rapprochement between us – never. There is the inexplicable fact that I love my typical english husband for all the strangeness between us. I do lament that he is not warm, ardent, eager, full of quick response, careless, spendthrift of himself, vividly alive, high spirited. But it makes no difference to my love. But the lack of these qualities in his country I HATE – these & others – the lack of its appeal – that is what I chiefly hate. I would not care if I never saw the english country again. Even in its flowering I feel deeply antagonistic to it, & I will never change.

(2, 167)

But the 'crawly froggies' too were hateful at times: 'With them it is always rutting time. See them come dancing and sniffing round a woman's skirts' (*Notebooks* 2, 145); 'the french bourgeoisie' who avoided her, and stared disapprovingly at her, were abominable (*Letters* 2, 52), and in these moods Mansfield could long to be in England. In 'The Lost Battle', 'Miss Brill' and 'The Little Governess' Mansfield dramatized the sexual fears, whether of attack or ridicule, of solitary women travelling. What is missing in them (except perhaps for the autobiographical 'An Indiscreet Journey') is the aggressive disgust of Mansfield's outbursts,

and the adventurousness of her notebook descriptions of her own jour-
neyings. These conflicting feelings, associated with travel and risk, with
their erotic undercurrents, do surface however in her remarkable experimental story '*Je ne parle pas français*'. The first person narrator is the
Parisian Duquette, a pimp and gigolo, and a pretentious modernist
writer. In his discontinuous, fragmentary narrative, he confides his
intimate thoughts and desires, including his first sexual experiences
with his family's African laundress. He has an acquaintance, Dick Harmon, an English man of letters, and cherishes him as a curiosity. Dick
comes to Paris with an English woman, Mouse, and then finds he
cannot bring himself to 'hurt' his mother by continuing the affair. He
abandons Mouse, and returns alone. She, unable to speak any French
except '*je ne parle pas français*', can only weep. Though intrigued by her,
Duquette does nothing to help. When he later comes across a memento
of her, his reaction is to be impressed by his capacity to experience a
'grand moment', 'an intensity of feeling' (*Stories* 280). To Woolf this was
a story that breathed 'nothing but hate' (V. Woolf, *Diary* I, 216), but its
surface is unruffled by personal attachments: it is no mere vendetta
against an English husband or a French lover, their inadequacies or
treacheries.[7]

Later stories of the English abroad derive from months spent in rented
rooms and hotels in France, Italy and Switzerland, where Mansfield was
advised to live after her tuberculosis was diagnosed. In these stories the
English are seen against an alien background, exposed to the gaze of the
locals. In 'The Dove's Nest' the complacency and chauvinism beneath
the English mother's timorous opinions is at first left to the reader's
sense of irony, but later the limited responses of both mother and
daughter to their American male guest are shown up by their French
maid and cook. In these stories a physical and emotional inhibitedness,
like Dick Harmon's, is characterised as English in contrast to a European,
and especially French, sensuality and spontaneity, precisely the qualities
mentioned in the notebook entry as lacking in Murry.

In 'Poison' and 'The Escape', both stories of unhappy couples abroad,
their conflicts are exacerbated by unfamiliar, hot, if beautiful, settings.
Differences between them emerge in the shorthand of national stereotypes. 'Honeymoon' begins with a happy newly married couple, but as
they listen to an old man singing with a café band their situation
darkens. His song of passion and grief touches the local audience and
also the English wife. Like Laura in 'The Garden Party', she becomes
aware of the coexistence of happiness with mortality. But 'George had
been feeling differently' (*Stories* 538), and his resistance to the song and

its singer, expressed in distinctively 'English' slang – 'old codger' – amounts to an inability to share her understanding which threatens their marriage at its very beginning.

'Englishness' is a key feature in the story 'The Man Without a Temperament'. Its original title, 'The Exile', refers to an Englishman in Italy. He is caring for his sick wife in a hotel in late November. The narrative is detached from the consciousness of both principal figures who are observed through the responses of the Italian staff and the cosmopolitan group of guests, an American honeymoon couple, an American dowager, an Italian countess and a General, her companion. The man is seen standing still, waiting. He stares, 'blinking vacant', he yawns, fetches a shawl, and repeatedly turns his signet ring. His one sign of frustration greater than this is when he calls noisily for the lift. Thereafter the manager, as if to register that he fully understands the Englishman's situation, makes a point of his not being kept waiting again. Mansfield juxtaposes to this half-alive figure the lively honeymoon couple, a servant girl who mocks him with her question: '*Vous desirez, Monsieur?*', and three girls in the garden who take off their 'drawers' and hold up their skirts to play in tubs of water. When one sees 'The Englishman' she shrieks and they all run away. The wife wonders why they were so frightened, 'Surely they were much too young to...' (*Stories* 335–6), her unfinished phrase alluding to sexual feeling, an unspeakable issue in their lives. The garden of the hotel, and the hillside beside the road, all abundantly alive and warm, offer a silent contrast. The guests are explicit in their criticism. The American woman catches Robert yawning:

> '*Vous avez voo ça!*', said the American Woman.
> 'He is not a man,' said the Two Topknots, 'he is an ox. I say to my sister in the morning and at night when we are in bed, I tell her – *No* man is he, but an ox!'
>
> (*Stories* 335)

In their carriage the General and the Countess come upon Robert walking:

> 'There he goes,' she said spitefully.
> But the General gave a loud caw and refused to look.
> 'It is the Englishman,' said the driver, turning round and smiling. And the Countess threw up her hands and nodded so amiably that he spat with satisfaction and gave the stumbling horse a cut.
>
> (*Stories* 337)

Two flashbacks to the life Robert and his wife in England delicately suggest another point of view. In one Robert remembers a snowfall in London and showing their cat its first snow, and in the other, a November walk across fields, 'swinging along in the drifting rain and dusk', before a cheerful evening with his wife and friends. The varying degrees of sympathy for the husband which this story evokes in readers testify to its fine balancing of restraint and spontaneity, understatement and ebullience. Here the contrasting of national stereotypes has become a subtler questioning of English and non-English styles of behaviour, which then enriches the working out of one of Mansfield's most characteristic themes – solitude and frustration in human communication – in the tragic story of the incompatible needs of Robert and his sick wife.

Mansfield's work, moving between English and New Zealand subjects, mirrors the shape of her life. As she transports material from one setting to another, or treats the same themes in different settings, there is a crossover, a hybridity even, in her writing.[8] Unlike many writers to be considered in this book, Mansfield had no interest in England, apart from its writers. London was at first an escape from her family and what to her were their essentially bourgeois, commercial values. It was a joy, and a 'kick off' (as she called an inspiration, a starting point) for her stories and her career. Later, shaded by memories of the War, England became in her imagination associated with inhibition and male inadequacy, even a metaphor for human unhappiness. England was where Murry (but not Lawrence) felt most at ease; for her, it was nothing less than 'a kind of *negation*' (*Letters* 4, 255). But the hostility that she felt does not determine the value of these stories, any more than her illness, her unhappy marriage, or 'the anxieties attendant on colonial subjectivity' (Orr, 'Free People' 167).

Notes

1. Murry promoted this view, and associated a shift to New Zealand subjects with Mansfield's grief at her brother's death in 1915 (*Katherine Mansfield* 11–14), an idea laid to rest by C. K. Stead, who pointed out that Mansfield began her first story based on her Wellington childhood in 1914 (35–7).
2. See the essays of Linda Hardy and Bridget Orr.
3. Mansfield later disparaged this book (*Notebooks* 2, 191) and refused republication. Suggested explanations include an unwillingness to be associated with a chauvinistic attitude to Germany, as implying their greater blame for the horrors of the war (Fullbrook 53), or embarrassment about the borrowing

from Chekhov in 'The-Child-Who-Was-Tired' (Tomalin 208–9). Nevertheless, she offered a copy to Ottoline Morrell in 1917 (*Letters* 1, 292).

4. Murry wrote: 'Yet London disappointed us. Katherine used to sing a darkie song:

> London's no place for me – and I don't like London town.
> London societee – has turned me down.

And it expressed our feelings.'
They were happier out of town with the Lawrences who 'had no more liking for London than we had ourselves'. 'John Middleton Murry', *Coming to London*, ed. John Lehmann (London: Phoenix House, 1957) 105–6.

5. 4–5 September, 1921, qtd. in S. P. Rosenbaum, ed., *The Bloomsbury Group: A Collection of Memoirs and Commentary* (Toronto: University Press, 1995) 37.

6. Referring to Alice in 'At The Bay' (VIII); see *Stories* 457–60, and 571.

7. Resemblances have been detected between the fictional characters and Mansfield, her lover, the French writer, Francis Carco and Murry. Mansfield met Carco with Murry in Paris, and later travelled behind the lines to visit him in 1915, as in 'An Indiscreet Journey'. '*Je ne parle pas français*' possibly draws on an episode in Murry's early life in Paris, recounted in his autobiography, *Between Two Worlds*.

8. For further discussion of this phenomenon, and instances, see Pritchett on the 'web that is ingeniously spun between these places' (England and New Zealand), R. King (99–103) and Fullbrook (102).

5
Looking from 'This Curious Limbo': Jean Rhys

Sue Thomas

Jean Rhys's unpublished and undated autobiographical 'Essay on England'[1] opens with the declaration that it is her 'LAST WILL AND TESTAMENT of thought' ([1]). A will is a disposition of property and sentiment prepared for reading after one's death. Rhys implies, however, that she is writing already from a place of death: 'this curious limbo, which is England' (3–4). To Rhys growing up Ella Gwendolen Rees Williams[2] in turn-of-the-century Roseau, Dominica, 'England was a wonderful place' given imaginative form through her reading of English books, and the 'English thoughts' imparted by her education ([1]). In *Smile Please: An Unfinished Autobiography* (1979), Rhys narrates her childhood as a series of failures to realize an oceanic desire, in turn for her mother, black servants as surrogate maternal figures, the Dominican landscape, and finally the alternate world of the English book, in which she might 'blot out the real world which was so puzzling' to her, with its complexities of sex, religion, racial politics and tension, class, and gender (62). On arrival in England Rhys's colonial cultural difference cannot be assimilated to a middle-class English feminine norm and this consigns her to a limbo, a place of the socially cast aside or outside, a place of abandonment ('Essay' 3–4). Limbo is, too, in Dante's *Inferno*, a place 'where the Unbaptized and the Virtuous Pagans dwell "suspended"', excluded 'from the positive bliss of God's presence' (Sayers 91). There there is:

> No sound of grief except the sound of sighing...
> Grief, not for torment, but for loss undying...
>
> (Dante 92)

Intertextually Rhys's limbo as a metaphorical and worldly state is characterized by her exclusion from or loss of the possibility of the 'Grace,

Justice, and Charity' of people in Christian community or empire (Sayers 69). In Rhys's writing about her own emotional, cultural and geographical journeys to England and Englishness and those of her white Creole fictional protagonists – Suzy Gray in 'Triple Sec' (1924), Anna Morgan in *Voyage in the Dark* (1934), Antoinette Cosway Mason in *Wide Sargasso Sea* (1966), the unnamed narrator of 'Temps Perdi' (1967), and 'West Indies' in 'Overture and Beginners Please' (1968) – the end of *Bildung* is not an assimilated identity but the discovery of the culturally *constitutive* function of English xenophobia and misogyny.[3] They are exposed to a 'coldness and brutality' that 'proves the storybook England to have been a lie' (Raiskin 149).

A crucial shift in Rhys's attitudes towards England and the English between 1940 and 1959 is registered in the stories on which Rhys was working during this period. In 1940 Rhys was arrested on a charge of being drunk and disorderly. She had reportedly uttered a 'stream of abuse of the English race,' in the memory of one witness, 'I am a West Indian, and I hate the English. They are a b——— mean and dirty lot' (Angier 413). 'As far as I know I am white – but I have no country really now,' Rhys wrote in 1959 (*Letters* 172). Rhys's disidentification with England and the English is territorialized differently in these quotations: as being 'West Indian' in 1940; as 'no country really now' in 1959, signifying both a double failure of assimilation to nationalist sentiment and a strong sense of being dispossessed. These feelings could also be cross-cut with a resignation to the fact of being in England: 'This is an English room in an English pub. That is an English tree, and all the books you read are English books' (*Smile* 165). In later life Rhys would claim only a West Indian childhood, speaking of 'my childhood there', '*being* born in the West Indies', being 'brought up in Dominica' (qtd. in Gregg 2). Of the West Indies of her childhood she writes in 1956: 'never was anything more vanished and forgotten. Or lovely' (*Letters* 133). The stories about the return of white Creole protagonists to Dominica during the 1930s – 'Temps Perdi' and 'The Imperial Road' – emphasise their alienation, their difficulties in making meaning of their experience, and feeling themselves to be objects of reverse racism for black Dominicans.[4] I analyse Rhys's representations of England and Englishness as marks of the 'culturally racialized' colonial subject split 'between what assimilation absorbs and what it necessarily produces as its residue' (Lloyd, 'Race under Representation' 85). The processes of identification and disidentification I describe are compressed in particular tropologies and thematics in her late fiction, and I work to situate them in relation to her responses to Caribbean nationalism, large-scale post-war immigration from the Caribbean and decolonization of the British empire.[5]

Biographer Carole Angier argues that Rhys's disidentification with Englishness is a symptom of Rhys's individual pathology, a 'borderline personality disorder', which occasionally manifested itself as madness (657–8). 'Borderlines,' explains Theodore Millon, 'typically experience extended periods of dejection and disillusionment, interspersed on occasion with brief excursions of euphoria and significantly more frequent episodes of irritability, self-destructive acts, and impulsive anger' (177). Angier's pathologization of Rhys is preceded by speculation that she was of mixed race ancestry. She cites Ford Madox Ford's, Rosamund Lehmann's and Mollie Stoner's sense that 'there was black blood in her', a sense, I note, based on uncritical adoption of a stereotype of white Creoles: that they may merely be passing for white. Angier then offers a physiognomical reading of Rhys's ancestry: her 'black blood...showed especially in her eyes...[which are] like a black person's eyes in a white face' (656). Drafts of stories first written during the 1940s in the Orange Notebook, Angier insists, are 'fill[ed]' with Rhys's 'swelling obsessions': 'her hatred of England, England's hatred of women (England's hatred of her)' (415). Her attitudes to Englishness are being implicitly and uncritically framed by a 'tragic mulatto' stereotype. A couple of the published stories, according to Angier, also exhibit Rhys's 'insect obsession' and 'machine obsession' (416). Rhys's Second World War stories – 'A Solid House' (1963), 'Temps Perdi,' 'I Spy a Stranger' (1969), and 'The Insect World' (1973) – 'are', she writes, 'all too close for comfort to Jean's madness of that time, and their drafts are even closer' (426). These stories were originally part of *The Sound of the River*, a collection Rhys offered to Constable in 1946. In this chapter I analyse two of them – 'I Spy a Stranger' and 'The Insect World' – the unpublished 'Cowslips,' Grace Poole's narrative in *Wide Sargasso Sea*, and 'Let Them Call It Jazz' in an effort to comprehend some of the meanings of her 'reversed gaze at the culture of Englishness' (Gikandi 19) and of its phantasmatic dimensions.[6]

In 'I Spy a Stranger' Rhys juxtaposes the unreflective middle-class Englishness of sisters Mrs Hudson and Mrs Trant with the values of Laura, a repatriated Englishwoman, who, because of long residence in continental Europe, exposure to foreign views of the English and critical intelligence, has become the object of xenophobic suspicion and has been institutionalized as insane. The wartime blackouts metonymically represent war and the insularity of the English. In *Forever England* Alison Light describes the kind of 'intimate and everyday' conservative

Englishness typified in Rhys's Mrs Hudson and Mrs Trant. Light suggests that its emphasis on 'the English as a nice, decent, essentially private people' 'could...recast the imperial, as well as the national idea of Englishness' (11). '[S]haped by the experience of dislocation after the First World War and fuelled by essentially pacific rather than aggressive urges', the 'conservative embracing of modernity', she argues, focused 'upon the quiet life, on a celebration of the known and the familiar' (12). Rhys highlights the everyday viciousness with which social and patriotic conformity is upheld by Mrs Hudson and Mrs Trant and by gossip. Particularly in her denunciation of English misogyny in her diary, Laura flagrantly violates the standards of 'reticence and verbal self-control' integral to this model of Englishness (Light 12), which is cast by Laura as a social 'mechanism' which reduces 'human beings' to 'cog[s]' (119). As William Leiss observes, from the mid-nineteenth century, fears about the routinization of society and culture and the powerlessness of the individual, were 'to be fleshed out as a favorite device in fiction', often projected through images of machines and with 'the root metaphor of autonomy/automaton' (119). Rhys associates Mrs Hudson's and Mrs Trant's Englishness with cliches about femininity – 'a girl ought to play safe, ought to go with the tide, it was a bad sign when a girl liked unpopular people' ('I Spy' 122). In Light's terms, Laura exhibits emotions – concern for friends still in Europe, anger, defiance of local opinion, unsociability – 'which threaten to return and trouble the calm of conservatism's sexual and social economies and suggest at what cost the ideals of femininity and of private life were maintained' (13).

Light suggests that '[m]ost frequently the value attached to the literary' in this ideology of Englishness 'was the clearest way of distancing oneself from the experience offered by forms of "mass" entertainment and leisure' (12). In Rhys's story it is Laura who uses this classing strategy. Laura's prose in her diary implies that she has a 'writer's mentality and sensitivity' (Light 12); she uses her reading and her collection of cuttings of misogynist propaganda from newspapers to distance herself from the mass values she despises and the 'horrible games' based on suspicion the locals play 'to take their minds off the real horror' (116): war, the situation of people in mainland Europe, themselves, the misogyny which 'has settled down and become an atmosphere, or, if you like, a climate' (120).

Laura's intelligence and moral position are linked in the story with extreme whiteness, with ' "Too much light" ' (122), which is, more objectively, the *merest glimmer* (125). The ideal imagined reader of

Laura's exercise book with its cuttings and diary reflections, and indeed interlocutor of Laura's reception of her reading, is an anti-English European friend, Blanca. Laura collects the misogynist propaganda ' "For Blanca" ' (121); she writes in her book that 'Blanca's voice, her face, the things she used to say haunted me' (120). Blanca's name carries multiple resonances from French, German and English. It suggests that she is white(r) or shinier at core, free of blemishes. She is a disembodied presence in Laura's life. In *Imagination at War* Adam Piette notes the commonness of the idea of ghostliness and haunting in writing about the home front (56–7). Laura remembers her part in 'endless, futile arguments' with Blanca in which the war was read as an imperial, racialized contest between Germany and England (Nordics and Anglo-Saxons), and Blanca's 'acrimonious' denunciations of the ' "extraordinary attitude" ' of the English ' "to women" ' ('I Spy' 120). The memory of Blanca and the sentiments and ideas which could be voiced in their conversations become Laura's transcendental anchor in the xenophobic modernity of wartime provincial England. Laura's project in her exercise book 'compensates for the loss of experience and the debilitation of agency in an industrialized [mechanized] world' (Rauch 85); it also focusses her attention on more immediate horrors than those to which her friends in Europe may be subject.

Richard Dyer argues in general terms that 'extreme whiteness' is functional 'in relation to ordinary whiteness and white hegemony', 'is perhaps even a condition of establishing whiteness as ordinary.... Extreme whiteness ... leaves a residue, a way of being that is not marked as white [by its viewers], in which white people can see themselves' (222–3). In 'I Spy a Stranger', structured as a discussion between Mrs Hudson and Mrs Trant about Laura and the exercise book she has left behind, their ordinary whiteness – marked as Anglo-Saxon, English, dehumanizing and giving women no room to 'breathe' (123) – is secured by their distancing of themselves from the extreme whiteness Laura represents in her ghostly absence.

The story's ambivalence about the Englishness it criticizes is registered through the responses of characters to two rose beds which function as stock emblems of England, the English spirit in wartime, and the aestheticized nationalism invested in them. On the mace which represented British imperial authority in Dominica England is symbolized by a rose, and the rose trope in white Dominican writing, including Rhys's, is highly charged.[7] Initially in 'I Spy a Stranger' Mrs Trant, the sister more threatened by Laura, is comforted by the continuity symbolized in the flowering of the 'flame-coloured' roses ([114]), metonymic of

English people, as they were constructed in the 'gallant and cozy myths' of the Blitz in 'propaganda and newspaper rhetoric' (Piette 71): 'strong; hardened by the east coast wind' from Europe, 'fierce, defiant... dazzling' ('I Spy' 114).[8] After reading Laura's exercise book, Mrs Trant complains of the 'stifling' weather, 'Too much light', and her sense of the roses shifts, and they become metonymic of Laura herself: 'their colour was trying. The brilliant, cloudless sky did that. It made them unfamiliar, therefore menacing, therefore, of course, unreal' (122). Rhys implicitly links Laura's dissident spirit with the heroic English qualities Mrs Trant had earlier aestheticized in the roses, suggesting ironically that Laura is their true bearer. Mrs Hudson remembers Laura's final (to her unintelligible) conversation as she departs for the cheap sanatorium in which she is to be institutionalized. It is about the 'exquisite' roses. Laura insists, '"let them live... One forgets the roses – always a mistake." She stood there staring at them as if she had never seen roses before and talking away – something about how they couldn't do it, that it wouldn't happen. "Not while there are roses," she said two or three times' (126). The roses become emblematic of a transcendent, implicitly English spirit, more aesthetically satisfying and inspirational than the physical resistance to imprisonment she has attempted. The life in the roses is what cannot be absorbed by the processes which would assimilate her into the mechanism of mid-twentieth-century little Englandism. Rhys characteristically associates England with greys and whites, rather than intense and vibrant colours like red, a colour dichotomy subtended by racialized modernist primitivist binaries: England/ tropics; death/life; coldness/vitality; drabness/gaiety; self-control/emotion; white/black.

'Cowslips', structured as reminiscence, set during the Second World War and written after 1964, thematizes a reconciliation with a more archaic (indeed anti-modern, anti-democratic), rural Englishness. Welshness and Englishness are elided. In the story the social order on the Gower Peninsula in Wales is residually feudal, ruled over by the 'redoubtable' Lady B. The narrator finds that 'all the women had some quality, a sort of self confidence that English women seldom had' ([1]). She is ravished by the spectacle of nature – a field of cowslips and a view from a 'hill of bracken' ([2]), a 'broad panorama anchored in the seer', whose eye is '[u]nheroic, unparticularized, egoless', which Mary Louise Pratt argues is integral to the imperial travel trope (Pratt 209, 60). But she is also ravished by the belief-system she thinks is dissolved into it: keeping people out. She argues with her partner: 'if you let everybody in they'd destroy it. It wouldn't be there any more. They wouldn't mean to.

But they would. [...] "They will grab. Before you know where you are, there's nothing left"' ('Cowslips' [2]). Female and national integrity and historical tradition are anchored symbolically in the aestheticized landscape. The narrator resists the temptation to look out from the hill again after she is told that the area contains snakes 'in that weather, and though not poisonous, that they did bite sometimes when disturbed' ([2]). Rhys associates the imperial travel gaze through Eden symbolism with potential exposure to moral fall. But the usual connotations of the colour yellow in Rhys's fiction – 'fresh sunshine and clear hope and promise when tropical, or dangerously threatening or depressing when associated with white people or grey weather' (Savory Fido 8) – shift here. Ironically the narrator will 'grab' by picking a waterlily, but the rankling admonition by Lady B's gamekeeper is smoothed over by the arrival of Lady B 'a few days after [...] with some flowers' and an invitation to tea ([3]). Undaunted by Lady B's 'large case of stuffed birds, all labelled and all British' ([3]), the narrator decides that she likes her. In the story the banal and indulgent ironizing distance between the narrative and authorial voices identifies the narrator as misanthropic, and the appeal of the ideology of exclusion as being grounded in this generalized misanthropy and in the flattery afforded by Lady B's gestures of atonement. The more critical voice, the narrator's partner's, who suggests that her view is premised on 'awfully selfish' and unutilitarian principles ([3]), is marginalized and ineffective. The narrator's grasp of the political dimension of her view, especially in relation to democratic social principles and refugee and immigration policies, is never tested.

Denise Riley has argued that British social policy concerning women during the 1940s was characterized by 'overemphasis on the role of mother' and 'their desexualization as workers' (261). In the unpublished essay 'The Ant Civilisation', and in 'The Insect World' Rhys engages intertextually with these representations of women. Her insect metaphors resonate with the mordant humour and cultural and racialized political contestation expressed in insect metaphors for the English, 'English' Creoles and the English state which circulated in late nineteenth- and early twentieth-century Dominica. Local white people, for example, were called cockroaches by the non-white population, and in a poem published in the *Dominica Dial* on the occasion of Queen Victoria's golden jubilee the royal family – metonymic of the English state – are characterized as 'German drones' and 'bloated parasites', and their circle as 'locusts', all of them living off the labour of workers (F). In 'The Ant Civilisation', part of a lecture on 'Woman' in England, 'The

Kingdom of the Human Ants', ostensibly 'delivered when' she 'was drunk from sadness', Rhys rails against the 'process' which changes women from individuals 'into the neuter – the ant female', a creature whose 'unused force & tenderness' turns her 'sour'. The process comprises a 'repressive education' which values (heterosexual) love as 'anti-social,' ridiculing it and rendering women 'a thing to have children by & enrich the antheap'. '[N]early all English books & authors slavishly serve the ant civilisation', she writes. 'Do not blame them too much for the Niagara of repression is beating on them & breaking their hearts – To live or not to live'.

Rhys's image of England as an antheap is not original, and points to the possibility that she is countering journalist Philip Gibbs' view in *England Speaks* (1935), a commemoration of George V's Silver Jubilee and the myth of the transcendent individuality of the English people.[9] He describes London as 'a monstrous ant-heap with millions of little ants, all with little individual instincts, desires, characters, dreams, busy with their particular adventure' (64). Here the 'terrible danger' of a mechanistic modernization, a 'standardisation' of thought and character brought about by mass culture is most apparent, but he takes comfort in a 'long tradition' of 'intense' individualism in the 'English character' (66), which is 'still' at its 'innermost core ... firmly defensive of individual rights' (67). He observes that the English 'imagine' themselves to share a 'dislike of "ballyhoo",... shyness and secret reserves,... sense of humour, and ... distrust of emotionalism and self-exhibition' (2). In draft material for stories for *The Sound of the River* in the Orange Notebook Rhys represents the English not as defenders of *women's* rights; rather she describes the English wife as being positioned as a 'music hall joke', 'a stunted servant' of the husband's 'protective instinct', prevented 'from trying to earn a decent living otherwise than as unpaid char & cook' ([136]-[7]).

In *Maps of Englishness* Simon Gikandi notes that 'the great categories that came to define the modern age – race and citizenship, civility and authority, for example – were haunted, from the start, by the colonial question' (3). Rhys demonstrates how these categories and gender, as lived mundanely by Audrey in 'The Insect World,' are haunted by unstable colonial binaries: self/other, white/black, temperate/tropical, civilization/savagery. 'The Insect World' is set during the fly bombing of London and Audrey passes nightmarish, she thinks 'haunted' 'piles of rubble' (133). Another historical context, compressed in the primitivist figure of the 'easily worked up' 'surly' native (128), is the decay of Britain's imperial political and cultural authority during the 1930s and

1940s in the context of rising colonial nationalism and political unrest. English Audrey's horror at her own aging, the failure of her expectations of romance and motherhood, her sexual frustration and desexualization as worker are projected through a surreal transformation of older women and workers into termite-like tropical insects and of crowds of people in the Tube into jiggers. Parasitic female jiggers burrow under the human skin and lay eggs. Their hosts are unwittingly 'infected' ('Insect' 132). Audrey has read about the insects in a second-hand book, annotated with misogynist comments by a previous owner. Not just by writing about colonial otherness, as Gikandi suggests, but also by reading about it, the metropolitan imperial subject 'could be drawn into the sites of what it assumed to be colonial difference and turn them into indispensible spaces of self-reflection' (xviii). Audrey feels herself to be twins: one the lower-middle-class epitome of the conservative Englishness Light elaborates, even down to desiring a girlish grey dress; the other 'lost, betrayed, forsaken, a wanderer in a very dark wood' ('Insect' 126). Judith Kegan Gardiner generalizes from her own response to the story, suggesting that readers 'can identify with both. We can understand the pain in Audrey's persecuted mind and also stand outside her, sharing her "twin" viewpoint' (42). Gardiner links Audrey's 'paranoid fear of invasion' with 'the anticommunism, racism, and anti-Semitism of the 1940s,' but also notes that it 'seems entirely sensible as the psychology of the air raid victim' (43). The metamorphoses of streetscape and of English people in Audrey's imagination augur also, however, the postwar industrial decay and changing racial composition of London. Her apocalyptic vision produced by what Rhys represents as an atavistic savagery within her echoes for the story's 1970s readers the figurative dimension of 1950s and 1960s British racism directed against black and Asian immigrants: infection, excessive reproduction, decay, parasitism brought from the tropics.

In late nineteenth- and early twentieth-century Dominica Englishness was represented in the public sphere by journalist members of the 'Mulatto Ascendency' as the other of nascent Dominican nationalism, and as synonymous with whiteness, 'negrophobia', social exclusivity on racial lines, and maintenance of a racialized social hierarchy through enjoyment of special material privileges (Thomas, '"Human Ants"'). Ceremonially Englishness was identified with 'the shade and protection of a civilizing administration' ('Arrival' [3]), the British national anthem, and shows of imperial loyalty. In 'New story', a reworking of a 1938 autobiographical fragment,[10] Rhys indicates that the white Creole child is for English settler children always already not English.

The child is identified in the story as 'an inferior being (breed) – a Colonial. My mother says Colonials are not Ladies and Gentlemen, my mother says – etc., etc.' (1); in the autobiographical fragment at best Rhys can be in the eyes of English children British, understood as an imperial category (Black Exercise Book [76]). Disidentifying with Englishness, preferring to be more exotically 'French or Spanish or something', the child in 'New story' commits in the eyes of the English children '[b]lasphemy', and is labelled 'a dirty little Colonial', 'also mad – stark, staring mad' (1).[11] Rhys's school atlas spatialized the globe, she says in 'Essay on England', not only through maps, but through lists of Exports and Imports and of Characters of the Inhabitants. She improbably remembers her atlas telling her of the English, among other things, 'religious instincts very strongly developed, but a religion that will not require them to make any sacrifice of material advantages whatsoever'. The abject spectre which causes her to disavow these 'instincts', a disavowal labelled 'Socialist Gwen' by her family and occasioning their emotional bullying of her, is the colonial racialized class hierarchy in which 'the white people should have everything and the black people have nothing, in money' ('Essay' 2). She feels this spectre again in England in the 'poverty and misery' of the working class, especially women: 'I couldn't get used to the idea that white women could look like that', that is, 'poor' and 'ugly' (4). Non-white West Indian immigrants also record this initial shock at the living conditions of white working-class English people.[12] Winston James argues that this shock has salutary functions in challenging the 'erroneous association of white people...with superordination: the mystique of whiteness dissolves in the air of a class-stratified English society' (243).

In giving a point of view to Grace Poole in her rewriting of Charlotte Brontë's *Jane Eyre* as *Wide Sargasso Sea*, Rhys has her justify her work as Antoinette/Bertha's keeper to Leah: ' *"After all the house is big and safe, a shelter from the world outside which, say what you like, can be a black and cruel world to a woman."* ' Her sympathy with Creole Antoinette is grounded in her sense that her charge *"lives in her own darkness"* (146). Her language of blackness and darkness accords with two sets of early nineteenth-century British discourses of emancipation, one which drew analogies between the positions of slaves and the white British working class, and one which drew analogies between the positions of slaves and white British women (Sharpe 40). The difference Grace notes between herself and Antoinette – that Antoinette *"hasn't lost her spirit. She's still fierce"* (Rhys, *Sargasso* 146) – identifies her with the rebel slave; Grace, like the xenophobic Rochester, who comes to read his wife through ethnographic stereotypes about white Creoles, may see Antoinette as a figure of miscegenation. The scruples Grace had about her prospective work and the secrecy to which it binds her (' "*I don't serve the devil for no money*" ') is allayed by the money, doubled by Mrs Eff (Brontë's Mrs Fairfax) on Rochester's instruction if she is ' "*satisfactory*" ' (145). Grace does not successfully hide from Antoinette the economic relations with the 'devil' which structure their relationship. Antoinette observes her at night 'counting money. She holds a gold piece in her hand and smiles. Then she puts it all into a canvas bag with a drawstring and hangs the bag around her neck so that it is hidden in her dress' (147). 'Gold is the idol they [the English] worship', insists Antoinette (154), Rhys drawing an implicit parallel between Rochester's and Grace's mercenariness. 'Her name oughtn't to be Grace. Names matter', thinks Antoinette (147). The difference between the Grace who feels protected by the '*thick walls*' of Thornfield Hall (146) and the incarcerated Antoinette is emblematized by what each thinks is secreted in the room: the gold held so close to Grace's person and Antoinette's red dress, sign for Rochester of Antoinette's intemperance and unchastity (152), for Rhys of her experiential otherness among the English, internalized as corporeal memory and a differently acculturated structure of desire and pleasure, and racialized as degeneracy.[13]

'Let Them Call It Jazz' is unique in Rhys's oeuvre, the only story with a black Creole narrative voice, that of Selina Davis, a young Dominican or Martinican immigrant to 1950s England.[14] Rhys frames the story historically in relation to the white English racism which would manifest itself in the Notting Hill race riots of 1958 and the indifference of British feminist traditions to the everyday reality of such immigrants as working women.[15] As with white Creole Anna Morgan in *Voyage in the Dark*, for Selina Davis memories of the Caribbean function as a sustaining space of otherness; they, and a determination to hold on to her experiential difference of view in the face of racialized cultural misreading, allow Selina to preserve her psychological and cultural integrity. Rhys's sympathetic and politicized identification with Selina's point of view and her sharp observations of the racism to which the destitute Selina is subjected by a landlady, a seeming protector figure (Mr Sims), neighbours, and the law may be traced back developmentally to the disaffiliation from Englishness called 'Socialist Gwen' in her childhood.

Rhys's representations of the English in her late short fiction are characterized by conflicted processes of identification and disidentification, related to a shifting sense of her own cultural identity. Her disaffiliation – her 'curious limbo' – opened for her a space from which to gaze critically, but also ambivalently, at historically contingent models of Englishness, their gendered manifestations in everyday lives, the cultural narratives through which they were constituted and consolidated, and the ways in which colonized peoples and racialized sexual economies integral to twentieth-century European imperialism were crucial elements of those narratives.

Notes

1. The handwriting indicates that the essay was written before 1964.
2. Rhys's middle name is spelt Gwendolen or Gwendoline in various documents, and by Rhys herself (Savory, *Jean Rhys* 228–9 n.7).
3. My formulation of this point is indebted to Lloyd, 'Race under Representation' 85.
4. Rhys herself had visited Dominica in 1936.
5. The first phase of decolonization for Dominica was membership of the West Indies Federation that, after protracted negotiations with Britain, had achieved self-government in 1958. Dominica became independent in 1978.
6. My emphasis on the contradictory and ambiguous in Rhys's representations of England and English characters contrasts with Nancy Hemond Brown's argument that Rhys's 'attitude to England and the values it represented' were consistent throughout her writing career: 'England meant to her everything she despised' (8).
7. See Chapter 1 of Thomas, *The Worlding of Jean Rhys*.
8. Gregg reads the roses as consistent 'metonyms for the absent Laura' (168). Savory discusses Rhys's use of the roses as 'stylistic motifs' (169), but does not interpret the roses as being symbolic of Englishness.
9. Mr Severn in Rhys's 'Tigers Are Better-Looking' is a journalist who writes for an Australian newspaper. In the story a questioning of his masculinity – being called a 'tame grey mare' – brings on a short-lived crisis in his ability to write a 'swell article' on the King's Jubilee (64). Rhys had begun work on the story by 1938.
10. There is more than one typescript titled 'New story' among the Jean Rhys Papers at the University of Tulsa. The one to which I refer begins 'My relations with little English boys and girls' (1).
11. When Rhys worked 'New story' into 'The Day They Burned the Books', the preference makes the English children think the white West Indian protagonist 'too killingly funny, quite ridiculous' (39).
12. For examples see Winston James 240–2.
13. My analysis of Grace differs from more romanticized readings like Caroline Rody's: 'Rhys's unfailing readerly/writerly intelligence locates in Grace the very emblem in *Jane Eyre* of erased, unnarrated female existence'. Her narrative function, she suggests, is to provide a '"knowing" . . . and sympathetic' view of Antoinette/Bertha and to ground 'clear parallels drawn between her life and Antoinette's – and Mrs. Eff's and Leah's' (224–5). Mona Fayad reads Grace as an exemplar of the figure of the '"male-woman"' theorized by Mary

Daly who '"pleases her masters by selling out her own kind"' (236). She overlooks the ethnic difference between Grace and Antoinette and its implications.

14. More typically in Rhys's fiction set in England non-white characters have minor roles: a nurse in 'Rapunzel, Rapunzel', a pub patron in 'Tigers Are Better-Looking', and a hawker in 'Who Knows What's Up in the Attic'.

15. I discuss the historical intertexts of the story more fully in 'Modernity, voice and window-breaking'. Angier minutely documents Rhys's disputes with Beckenham neighbours between 1948 and 1950, convictions on charges of wilful and malicious damage to property, assault, and being drunk and disorderly, and her remand in custody in Holloway Prison in 1948 (442–54), on which Rhys based Selina's experiences of English law. Angier writes of Selina 'clearly' speaking 'for Jean' (446), a critical move which accords with her view that Rhys 'knew so little, and wrote only about herself' (218).

6
A 'Very Backward Country': Christina Stead and the English Class System

Ann Blake

In 1935 the Australian expatriate novelist, Christina Stead, sailed from Cherbourg to New York. A third generation Australian, she had left Sydney in 1928 for London and found a job in a grain dealer's office as stenographer. Her employer was a New York Marxist economist and novelist, William Blake (Wilhelm Blech) who at once became her companion and eventually husband. With him she moved to Paris to work in a private bank until its sudden failure forced the move to New York. Apart from *For Love Alone* (1945), a coming to England novel, Stead's English fiction, two novels and some short stories, was written in the 1950s, late in her career. Both novels are obsessive studies of repellent and fascinating women, based on people Stead knew well. Through the lives of those around these central figures, the books construct a damning analysis of the country. They do more than offer a resistance to the colonial power: they attack it, and as if from within. Unlike most novels of England by outsiders, there is no figure remotely corresponding to Stead in them. Nevertheless the novels' critical attitude is unmistakable. Stead's understanding of the colonial parent, and her powers as a political novelist in the broadest sense were well refined by the time she wrote of 'grey-spidery'[1] England. Her idiosyncratic vision is already apparent in, for instance, a much earlier piece, an article she drafted on that first visit to the USA, comparing the English with Americans.

Though the United States was still recovering from the depression, Stead's first impressions were positive. She assured her American readers that she came from 'a commonwealth which loves America, regards it as the rising English-speaking nation'.[2] Theirs was a country, and a climate, very unlike England: 'a land of riches' ready to race into the future, 'a skyrocket waiting to be let off'. On her first day in Boston she thought herself 'in a sort of socialist commonwealth'. A policemen in shirt-sleeves called her taxi driver 'buddy' and officials of all sorts were 'amiable and not obsequious; what a change from the brass hats and brass buttons of Europe'. Then, still impressed but no longer approving, she comments on an 'obvious and outspoken' attitude to the workers, and to money. To the 'smooth and unrelenting' English, workers were 'necessary vermin or good imbeciles'. But in the United States the successful middle classes openly hated them because they produced 'trouble, disorder, and demands for better living'. Moreover, though there was inequality in the United States – and she saw in Boston 'the rottenest slum' – at least there was a 'democratic' expectation that everybody was in the 'scramble for boodle'. In England, in contrast, 'the upper classes try to prevent the workers from wanting food, clothing and warmth by praising fortitude, by teaching that money is the root of all evil . . .'.

From the first, England appeared to Stead a 'very backward country' (interview with Lidoff 207), both old fashioned and backward looking. In London in the late 1920s, she saw plenty of evidence of a clinging to the past. At the Tower she remarked on the 'sensational uniforms of red, black and gold' worn by various 'sentries', 'porters and janitors', while at the Bank of England:

> The functionaries in chief . . . wear also a long red gown after the style of doctors of medicine, with bits of dog's fur or rabbit-fur in rows, in the most regal style, and a cocked hat exactly like our hero Mr Bumble. It's really queer to keep running up against these old customs in the very centre of a modern city – or what passes for a modern city – I begin to have doubts about it all.
>
> (*Letters 1*, 4)

Though her doubts soon firmed, they did not trouble a young woman who was, in the 1930s, like many others, at her most radical, and who took a firmly internationalist position. Though never a party member, her attitudes were shaped by communist sympathies and in both small and larger matters she acted true to her internationalism. In spite of her dismissive view of England, she went as secretary with the English delegation to the Paris Congress of Writers for World Peace in 1935, rather to the surprise of the Australian writer, Nettie Palmer (Rowley 170–5), but it was characteristic of her outlook, and matched by her practice as a writer. In her pre-war novels, set in Sydney, Salzburg, Paris and London, the range of locations and topics never suggests a writer obliged to settle scores with the metropolitan parent. England is noticed, but not at the centre. Her cosmopolitan characters amuse each other making jokes about the English. In *The Beauties and Furies* the businessman Marpurgo heaps ironic praise on England, his adopted country: 'There's none so crooked and clever as the English: a remarkable race.' Their power is an historical enigma: how can one explain, he asks, 'the rise of a miserable, cold, infertile island in the German Ocean, half-barren hills, populated by a mixed race, often invaded, surrounded by enemies, . . . to its position as balancer of Europe's powers, the first of the Empires. What a people! What accounts for it? I am proud to be a Briton.'(370) Stead's second Paris novel, the massive *House of All Nations* (1938), 'about banking and full of crooks' (*Letters* I, 71), is set in 1931, the year England went off the gold standard and a significant moment in the decline of Britain as world power. Among its numerous international figures are two English businessmen, both convinced of England's probity, tolerance, and influence, and persuaded that the wealth which comes from the Empire is a sign of God's blessing on a job well done (324). While they insist that England will never go off the gold standard, the French Marxist Alphendéry declares her best days are over.

However Stead, who wrote in *Seven Poor Men of Sydney* of Anglo-Australian relations as ' "their Whitehall" . . . breakin' the sheep's back' (170), never underestimated England's ideological hold, or its manipulation of political and economic ties with the dominions, in spite of its declining influence. A letter to one of her brothers in Sydney suggests her insight into Australia's relations with the old Empire and with the strengthening imperialism of the United States. This was in 1937 when, after some months in Europe, she was back in New York, where she and Blake were to stay during the war.

> There is a lot of propaganda 'pro Australia' going about here at the moment, so I guess Britain is refusing you a loan, or is relinquishing her grip, or is getting weak in the Pacific, or has a treaty with Japan. I notice, under the cheesy jingoism of Mr Lyons, [Labour Prime Minister] a muscular trades-unionism once more making itself heard: I hope the two are combined to give the noble Englishman the noble order of the sack.[3]

Here ridicule of England, as 'the noble Englishman', along with imperial honours, 'the noble order of the sack', links together hostility to imperial exploitation and to the class system. Australia, Stead believed, was an unquestionably superior nation because of its egalitarianism. The country's formation, beginning in the industrial age and lacking a feudal past, made it 'naturally...a Labor commonwealth' (Whitehead 240). The letter goes on to identify the English enemy:

> I am not against the west Englishman, not the north Englishman from Hull or Liverpool, but I detest and despise the London Englishman who runs the Empire; they are the smuggest, bootlickingest, most class-saturated, most conceited and ignorant people I ever met. This only goes for the middle and Eton classes, too, the clerks and counter-jumpers and the white collar brigade of London. The underdog is smart, comical and lively, in London. But the 'intelligentzia' – woe is me....
>
> (*Letters 1*, 73–4)

It was the underdog who captured the attention of a novelist who was always on the far left, her socialist sympathies nourished by her father's 'natural socialism', and then by the international left wing circle she moved in with Blake. In line with this position, in London in 1937, with the banking novel complete, Stead began planning an English novel: 'If Bill didn't want to run from England so fast, I might tackle an English working class town (or Welsh), but I'm afraid I won't have the time to do it...'(*Letters 1*, 71). The move to the US put an end to this. Stead was a writer who needed to be, or to have been, immersed in the physical situation she wrote about.

By 1946 the radical left in New York was in disarray as the 'great fear' of communism took hold, and the hearings of the HUAC began. This was the last phase of that disillusionment with the United States as land of opportunity and haven of the huddled masses which is played out in all its agonies in *I'm Dying Laughing*, Stead's novel of the wealthy, and finally renegade, American socialists. For Stead and Blake the time had come to leave. With the return to Europe she took up plans for a novel which became *Cotters' England*. Through the war years there had been among the left in the US a hope that with peace would come radical change in Britain, but, as they saw it, this had not eventuated. *Cotters' England* reflects that further disappointment. As the reviewer in *Nation* wrote, it is a novel that asks 'why the English working-class movement has not made the revolution'.[4] To both Stead and Blake England was a country without hope: 'that strange lost island, in the twilight of history, yet immensely self-satisfied, self-congratulatory amidst ruins', as Blake wrote in 1947. The place they knew before the war was unrecognizable and this was not simply due to the blitz: 'the psychic differences are so profound.... the people are not robust, there is nothing to go for.... Five more years of "austerity" and then what? A parlous balancing of poverty, a perpetual lower level than pre-war, hanging on to a liquidating concern, the Empire'.[5] He ends with the observation that this 'new society' has yet to be revealed in literature, predicting precisely the subject of Stead's novel, a book which Angela Carter was to praise for its 'extremely important' analysis of 'postwar Britain' (*Expletives* 177). Slow to find a publisher, the novel finally appeared (under the title *Dark Places of the Heart*) in 1966 in New York and in London in 1967.

Cotters' England is above all a novel of the working class, an English counter-part to Stead's *Seven Poor Men of Sydney*. The Cotters are Nellie, a journalist, her brother Tom, an engineer, her sister Peggy who has lived at home with the parents, the parents themselves, and old uncle Sime. All come from an industrial city in the north east, 'Bridgehead grey' – an amalgamation of Newcastle and Gateshead. The regional setting alone makes this a remarkable novel. Few novelists had, at the time it was written, ventured into a far north provincial city (Pybus 41–2).[6] Equally remarkable is its focus on the working class, and the lack of self-consciousness with which Stead writes of them. The 'working class novel' is notoriously difficult to identify. *Cotters' England* admittedly has neither a worker author nor, apart from Uncle Sime, figures of workers; though born in the working class, Nellie, Tom, and the rest have become engineers, journalists, political activists, trades unionists. Nevertheless, though these activists argue fiercely amongst themselves, and the novel exposes the shortcomings of English socialism, its identification is always with the workers and their environment: no other voices are heard. In the autobiographical novel, *For Love Alone*, Teresa comes to England and discovers a rainy, class-ridden city of Lyons teashops, Bloomsbury boarding-houses, city offices and alleys, haunted by memories of Dickensian crime and misery, where the dusk falls 'like soot' (500): it is the setting for her experience. In *Cotters' England* London, indeed England, is more than that. This many-peopled novel has a more obvious political focus on the '*Lives of Obscure Men*' (Stead, 'Writer's Friends' 496)[7] and how England shapes them.

Though concerned for the suffering of the workers, the novel is deeply critical of all the English. In 1918 Lawrence (whose work is often recalled in comparison with Stead's) wrote: 'I feel that nothing but a quite bloody, merciless, almost anarchistic revolution will be any good for this country, a fearful chaos of smashing up' (*Letters* 3, 215). Stead and her circle agreed. More was needed than a reformist Labour government, supported by the workers. In the novel the radicals are in retreat. George, Nellie's trade unionist husband, abandons England and takes a job in an international Labour organization in Europe. England has, as he sees it, done its best to kill him and all his class; he is now determined not to die 'to save their England' (216). Nellie, the novel's central figure, based on Stead's communist journalist friend, Anne Dooley, is now, in George's eyes, deluded and ineffective politically. Once a strike leader, but now, he claims, 'a plain Fleet Street sobsister' (214), she pours out sentimental sympathy for the workers on their 'lonely road'. To her, workers are 'poor frail waifs', and her catch-cry is 'Life's an incurable disease'. Anyone who speaks of improvements is guilty of political grandstanding. Nellie embodies the limitations of the English left, which appeared to Stead determinedly unintellectual, and failing in its task of educating the people.

Cotters' England traces the ebbing of any hope of change to a 'hunger' which has weakened the will of the workers. It adopts a material, even physiological view of their sapped energies. Scenes in London recreate the post-war landscape of bombsites with 'weeds growing over the ruins' (219). Plaster falls, the ceiling comes down (310), families plead for accommodation, even 'an evil-smelling slum' (163). The war may be over but not the shortages of food and housing: as Nellie's brother Tom says: 'There are a lot of half-fed people about; that accounts for their troubles. They think it's misery, despair; it's not enough food and fun' (164). To Nellie this is 'crass materialism'.

Here, as in her earlier autobiographical novel, *The Man Who Loved Children*, the family is a destructive institution, fuelled by jealousy, and the need to dominate and possess. But this particular family, based on people whom Stead studied closely when she stayed with them in Newcastle, is also the product of its working-class history; it is stunted, and warped psychologically by the depression as much as by the war. Through Tom and Nellie the novel looks back to the period of unemployment and hunger which marked a whole generation. Tom sees himself as 'a thin fistful of skin and bone' (163). Size is a mark of class: 'Now in England the classes are divided by inches.'(110) Physical hunger and want have wasted all the family: '"it's a bloody tragedy.... The frustrated lives"' exclaims Nellie (45). Uncle Sime, the frail old bachelor, is a 'beached wreck', and Tom fears becoming like him in time (105). Tom himself is charming but non-sexual, 'heartless' according to Nellie. Fair-haired, 'wraith like', his slight body symbolizes an inability to act effectively which derives from the weakness of the under-nourished.

Also sapping political drive is the dead weight of tradition, an attach-ment to a past 'so old baronial, so out of date'.[8] As her responses to the Tower of London proclaim, Stead was not charmed by the heritage of English history or by its aesthetic legacy. Where Jacobson and Naipaul were moved by a sense of continuity and age in England,[9] *Cotters' England* deplores it. In her letters she was more outspoken than in her fiction in her attacks on tradition, and on the monarchy as the key to perpetuating this oppressive system: 'If the British working class knew in so many words, exactly how much they were paying for the British royal family, I mean the millions and millions, . . . but knew it as some know the 39 articles, don't tell me that would make NO DIFFERENCE to them . . . '.[10] But censorship ensured that they were not allowed to know, she maintained. *Cotters' England* presents dramatically, in con-versations and episodes, the consequences for social progress of ideo-logical pressures on an ill-informed electorate. Nothing fundamental has changed or is likely to. Tom attributes this to the persistence of 'feudal' England, an age-old class-bound conservatism and inertia which makes even Uncle Sime speak proudly of having a friend who worked on a Duke's estates. This England is 'shadowy', ancient, as the novel hints in its references to Stonehenge, the flint mines of Norfolk and the ballads of the border country: 'and all this is in the people, their unconscious thoughts and their language' ('Another View' 518).

As if in response to the stagnation of the country, there is no forward movement in the novel. The chapters circle around the groups of characters, in repetitive patterns of complaint, attack, and temporary reconciliation. There are political solutions to all this suffering and waste of human lives, but England has failed to find them. The novel's cumulative image of the country as almost overwhelmingly cold, dreary and locked in its past, is made all the more plausible by the grumbling acceptance of the people. The Cotters and their like muddle on, retreat-ing further into illusions, twisted, perverted even, for in Nellie's case the effects of 'hunger' take on more explicitly a dimension of sexual perversion. Living apparently on tea, cigarettes and alcohol, she is a psychological predator who uses sexual relationships to satisfy her need for power. Herself seduced into a mysterious Bohemianism in her youth, she then 'corrupted' her sister, and still holds her brother with a jealous, incestuous love. Her lesbianism is equally threatening. She lures women friends and protégés to her house, offering accommodation and the chance to 'introspect', wearing them down with her endless bullying, 'crooning' and lies. They too are 'food' for her.

Just after Stead finished *Cotters' England* she and Blake, tired of being harassed by European authorities, 'went to ground in austere, post-war Britain with seeming stoicism' (Sage, *House of Fiction* 45). There they stayed, Blake for the rest of his life (he died in 1968) and Stead until she returned to Australia in 1974. This was a bleak, exhausting time. England in 1953 was still in the grip of rationing and food shortages. The housing crisis saw them often on the move searching for better accommodation. Moreover, as 'Reds', their political affiliations caused constant anxiety. Unable to find publishers for their own fiction, they turned to 'drudging for publishers' (*Letters 1*, 180) and translation: 'very secondary (though not evil)' (*Letters 1*, 151). This experience of England in the 1950s she brought into her second English novel, *Miss Herbert (the Suburban Wife)*.

Stead is an uncompromising novelist. Her novels combine the large scale of nineteenth-century fiction with a modernist lack of plot, their structure marked by a repetition which grinds on, or builds up to a storm-like a climax. The novels offer no narrative commentary. Readers are left to discover the significance of figures such as Nellie or Eleanor Herbert – a 'nice woman', 'a Dumb Dora' (*Letters 1*, 180 and *2*, 69). Eleanor's life-story becomes an anatomy of English middle-class values, in all their ramifications, sexual, political and literary, and lays open all that Stead found most hypocritical, complacent and self-damaging. Eleanor is, like Nellie, recognizably a figure of 'England', and the novel, as Carter wrote, amounts to 'nothing more nor less than a representation of the home life of Britannia from the Twenties until almost the present day' (186). This was equally apparent to the American reviewer who saw the 'half-defeated spirit of contemporary England' mirrored in Eleanor's defeat: 'the life story of a British beauty is a metaphor for England in its present hour' (H. Yglesias 4). Stead brushed this aside: 'but I won't say I meant it that way'.[11]

Eleanor Herbert is a narcissistic woman of the 1930s who has illusions of becoming a writer. She hangs about the fringes of London literary society keeping up contacts, and reworking her stories with the help of writing manuals. Though she has many lovers, and later marries and has children, 'her sensuality is limited'. As in her writing, she is inhibited, bound by rules, as Stead explained; she knew nothing:

> except the timeworn project of being a good wife and mother, which
> she attacked blindly, just to put herself in the picture of the world as

she knew it – accepting the most banal ideas because safest.

(*Letters 2*, 135)

At times she appears 'modern' or 'open-minded', at others, the opposite. An admirer asks: 'How can George have such an old-fashioned sister? He told me you were very modern. You sound like Elinor Glyn' (150–1). When her behaviour is unconventional she is unable to admit it. Even her individual remarks are contradictory: 'It seems wicked wishing to want to be safe and married; and yet it's the fate of women, isn't it?' (71). Her underlying conservatism also shapes her political attitudes. Like the Englishmen in *House of all Nations*, she is unquestioningly loyal to the belief that England is the guardian of democracy, fair play and tolerance. She cannot accept the possibility that England might lose the war, or that her husband might not return to her.

However, after the war Eleanor is divorced. She moves to London with her children to find work in the commercial literary world referred to dismissively in the novel (though not by Eleanor) as 'Grub Street'. Stead here set out to write of 'the literary worker in England'.[12] This was how she described the novel's subject when she attempted to place it with a publisher in the German Democratic Republic, where Blake's books were selling. Eleanor exemplifies the willing exploitation of 'lower middle-class workers' with 'pretensions to gentility' who are anxious to be employed in a 'refined' occupation, though their rate of pay is less than that of floor cleaners. Miss Herbert and her like chose a 'pathetic existence', which amounts to the 'rejection of both creativity and a full life on the altar of false values'. In 1949 Stead already saw English publishers as the creatures of a ruling elite: 'Bill and I are facing the genteel tradition in British letters. The publishers are sweet little mistresses kept by the real governors of the country: some are pretty, some are sweet, some are money-grubbing, but all are cute little cuties and won't hear a nasty word about their masters.'[13] Once her 'sweatshop novel' was finished, Stead had little hope of seeing it in print: 'naturally no publisher will take it. Here. I hope in the USA someone may be found'(*Letters 1*, 180).

Though exploited by her 'genteel' employers, Eleanor is content, indeed, always eager to please. She readily agrees with the upper-class proprietor of the giant publishing house when he deplores political writing, where political means only left wing, and soon, without asking any questions, begins to gather and pass on information about her fellow writers. Sexually, Eleanor is equally attractive to the old-boy net work, and as biddable. She readily slips into the task of posing naked in classical positions to meet the tastes of the indolent Mr Quaidson. A gentleman-publisher uninterested in any book except one he has written, and the owner of a collection of instruments of torture and other mementoes of cruelty, Quaidson is himself a fine instance of English upper-class sexual decadence. Nellie and Eleanor, those female emblems of England, are also associated with what the novels characterise as perversion, but with them, in a complex way, this is felt as an effect of their 'environment': England made them.[14]

In 1952 Stead had applied for a grant from the Australian Commonwealth Literary Fund to write a novel of the 'New Australia', provisionally called 'Migrants'.[15] *Miss Herbert's* post-war chapters reflect the reverse process, the 'colonisation' of England. Eleanor's Swiss husband is a pre-war arrival. A would-be middle-class Englishman, he admires most a notion of respectability, which for him rests on assumptions of racial and class superiority, a view that reflects badly on both admirer and admired. Meanwhile it is clear that the England he imagines and aspires to join is changing fast. Drafts of the novel include long episodes, finally omitted, of Heinrich's ambitions to win favour in Tory circles through manipulating hostility to immigrants in a local housing association. In 'Days of the Roomers' and 'Accents', two short stories which make use of this *Miss Herbert* material, Stead writes of European Anglophile landlords hostile to students arriving from India and Pakistan to study in London. As is frequently represented in the fiction of ex-colonial writers, such newcomers experienced virulent hostility, especially from recent non-English settlers. Heinrich is one such. When he and Eleanor run a boarding house he refuses to take 'dark-skinned foreign students' (94). He also protests that the dustmen do not treat him with the respect due to a natural social superior. 'A Routine', another London housing story which Stead worked on at this time, takes up from the Englishman's point of view anxieties about what are perceived as threats to English identity from class and race. In this long story Noel is a tropical fish seller with a socialist wife. In their struggle to make ends meet they have taken to playing a trick, 'a routine', when they cannot pay the rent. Noel is humiliated by having to stoop to this, and by 'the conditions' in which they live. He whines in protest at post-war England, where his cherished place in the middle class is being eroded. He has to live in a 'slum', a 'place only foreigners would take' (430). 'This is my country' he complains, and now it is 'overrun by foreigners'. In the days of full employment he must endure the cheek of 'bloody porters shouting at you and bloody waiters talking back to you and wanting six pounds a week' (412). In *Miss Herbert* and in these stories of aspirants to the middle class, there is again no authorial or narrative commentary. However, in a dramatic mode, the narrative treats with scorn and pity their ambitions to join 'the white collar brigade of London'.

England was never a place Stead could feel at home. A true novelist of the left, she was uncompromising in her attack, and in her despair of improvement outside a communist system. Behind these novels stands a vehement critic of English inequality and political apathy, but her anger is that of a socialist more than of an ex-colonial. Her Marxist understanding of imperialism had in the 1930s led her to recognize the decline of the British Empire, and the shift of power and influence to the United States. Neither Britain nor its Empire was ever likely to make her feel despised and colonially inferior. She was not one of those Australian women abroad described in Pesman's study as sensing that metropolitan 'centres were to be approached with awe and deference' (5).

The deep pessimism of these English novels is made possible in part by Stead's position as unillusioned outsider: she can dare to see and speak because England was not *her place*. But the thoroughly dramatic mode of her fiction ensures that the despair is overlaid with ironic images of England carrying on as usual. Nellie and Eleanor, these warped products of England, live on. Indeed, they are moving blindly forward. Nellie becomes 'interested in the problems of the unknowable' (352), and the self-deluding Eleanor plans to write her autobiography.

Notes

1. To Neil Stewart, 21 October 1955, R. G. Geering, ed., *A Web of Friendship* 151, hereafter cited as *Letters 1*.
2. All quotations in this paragraph are from the draft, 'It is all a scramble for boodle', ed. Ron Geering 22–4.
3. Stead always insisted on the self-confidence of Australian culture and was impatient with the 'cultural cringe', the notion that Australia deferred to the old world. See for instance *Letters 1*, 126.
4. J. Yglesias 421. See also Terry Sturm 353.
5. Bill Blake to Florence James, 8 December 1948, Florence James Papers, Mitchell Library, State Library of New South Wales.
6. Stead may have known *The Islanders*, a novel set in Newcastle by the Soviet writer, Yevgeny Zamyatin, but her connections were personal, through Anne Dooley and her brother, Peter Kelly.
7. For this phrase, see Margaret Harris 142–3.
8. Letter to Gwen Walker-Smith, 16 July 1952, qtd. in Chris Williams 195.
9. For Jacobson on the 'real continuity in English life still' (in 1960), see 'No Return' 21; and in Naipaul, see, for instance, *The Enigma of Arrival* 51.
10. Draft letter to Anne Dooley, 21 January 1949, Stead Papers, MS 4967, National Library of Australia.

11. Letter to Jessie and Ettore Rella, 20 July 1976, R. G. Geering, ed., *Talking into the Typewriter* 135, hereafter cited as *Letters 2*.

12. This and later quotations in the paragraph are from a description of the novel intended for the 'intellectual in socialist countries', MS4967, National Library of Australia.

13. Unpublished letter to Florence James, 26 May 1949, Florence James papers.

14. Kate Lilley's 1993 essay offers a criticism of the novel's 'homophobic ethics'.

15. It was to include 'English workers, as say, an engineer or other worker from, say, Newcastle-upon-Tyne, or Hull', qtd. in Chris Williams 182–3. Stead's application was unsuccessful.

7
The London Observer: Doris Lessing

Ann Blake

To read Doris Lessing is to move into a world of change. Her realist fiction and space fiction alike take a long, broad view: 'All history is the history of empires rising and falling.'[1] At the end of the twentieth century men and women lead lives still driven, Lessing believes, by the upheavals of the First World War and then the Second; they are the 'children of violence'. This phrase, the title of her sequence of five novels about Martha Quest, refers to 'children' bred in an age of violence and inevitably damaged by that heritage.

Revolutionary processes have affected Lessing's own life. Persia, her birthplace, is now Iran, and Southern Rhodesia, where she lived until she came to London at the age of 30, is now Zimbabwe. The political institutions that dominated her early years have, likewise, been superseded. British colonial rule has gone from Africa. And the Communist Party (the small unofficial Rhodesian branch of which she joined in the struggle against colonial rule) has lost much of its power, and the empire of the Soviet Union too has broken up.

One may speculate that Lessing's colonial experience, growing up under a system which she saw as doomed to fall, and whose decline she worked to hasten, might well have instilled a heightened awareness of change, and a more positive feeling for it. In the fiction of this 'expert in unsettlement' (Sage, *Lessing* 11) at any rate, change, if often terrible in its consequences, is energising. Her writing relishes 'transitoriness' (*London Observed* 89) and feeds on social dynamism. When not being tossed in some political upheaval, her figures seek self-transformation, and her best known novel, *The Golden Notebook*, is a study of a woman who believes her identity and her world are fragmenting and flying apart. In her English novels, whether the emphasis is on the decaying war-damaged city, immigration, shifting attitudes, or political movements, new versions of the English and of England are always emerging. Her concern is not to identify the forces that drive these social transformations (apart from that dominating influence of the past) but their impact and the human responses they evoke.

Although the paradigm of the nostalgic exile is often employed in interpretations of particular facets of Lessing's work,[2] there is nothing of the stasis of nostalgia about her fiction – or her life. Both as a thinker and as a writer she has had the courage to recognize when she has reached an impasse, and to make a break and move on. Given this adventurousness, there is something to be learned from the fact that, since her arrival in 1949, she has made London her home. This choice suggests an underlying Anglocentrism, an orientation not entirely accounted for by family or her English literary inheritance, powerful though these influences were.[3] Anglocentric here carries no overtones of approval: she writes about England because it interests her. This prominence of England becomes more obvious when contrasted with the work of other twentieth-century novelists who turn to Europe, or the United States, or adopt the international perspective of her fellow-novelist of the left, Christina Stead.

Lessing's earliest fiction came out of Africa. *The Grass Is Singing* (1950) was followed by the short stories, *This Was the Old Chief's Country*; then came *Five*, a collection of 'short novels', all except one set in Africa, and the first of the autobiographical Martha Quest novels. *The Golden Notebook's* complex multi-narrative reworks Rhodesian material again, as do many of Lessing's most acclaimed short stories, and she has lately returned to her years in Africa once more in the volumes of autobiography, *Under My Skin* (1992) and *Walking in the Shade* (1994). *The Golden Notebook* (1962), in many ways a watershed in Lessing's career, was her first novel to be set largely in England. The final Martha Quest novel, *The Four-Gated City* (1968) is also set in England, and this is again the location of the more recent novels, *The Good Terrorist*, *The Fifth Child*, of the first third of its sequel, *Ben, in the World*, of *Love, Again* and of a collection of stories and sketches, *London Observed*.

When writing of Africa, Lessing soon sensed she faced difficulties in depicting Africans. The figure of Moses (in *The Grass Is Singing*) is unsuccessful, in her view, because she did not know enough of the African people to make him better (*Interviews* 100–01). Paralleling this remark is an admission that the young Englishman in that book, Tony Marston, was also 'very bad', and for the equivalent reason: her 'complete lack of experience of England' (*Interviews* 112). Together these comments suggest that Lessing was 'at home' in neither England nor Africa, and even more alienated than the white settler writer whom she defined, in a now often quoted phrase, as an exile not from England but from Africa.[4] But in fact Lessing does not present herself in the role of the postcolonial exile – like Naipaul, at home nowhere. Certainly she writes of longing for the landscape, as Martha does, when she moves from the bush into town: 'this frank embrace between the lifting breast of the land and the deep blue warmth of the sky is what exiles from Africa dream of; it is what they sicken for, no matter how hard they try to shut their minds against the memory of it' (*Martha Quest* 252). This is a passage that defines the 'home' of childhood. England in 1950 was, in contrast, disconcerting. By 1980 she remembered it being 'dull', 'so gray and lightless and grim and unpainted and bombed' (*Interviews* 88–9).[5] But for her counterpart, the Doris of *In Pursuit of the English*, it is bewildering: she is jolted by the sight of whites doing labouring work, at sea in interpreting English understatement, and the class divisions constantly trouble her. Lessing herself did not feel English, but she could, like Martha, '*pass*' (*F-G City* 42), because of her background, with its 'silver tea trays, English watercolours, Persian rugs, the classics in their red leather editions, the Liberty curtains', and the Army & Navy catalogue which 'regulated our lives' (*Under My Skin* 64, 71). But to fit in was not what she wanted. Instead she confronted England with the confidence of a self-taught, independent-minded woman of the left, deeply critical of English provinciality and xenophobia. For all her familiarity with an 'English' middle-class household, she was an outsider and this was an advantage, as she was often to explain. Whether in England or in Africa, as colonial or as communist, she was an outsider because she was a writer.

Southern Rhodesian settlers introduced Lessing to a version of English-ness, and her writing about England is shaped by this experience, baffling and diverse as it was. As Doris remarks in *In Pursuit of the English*, 'while the word *English* is tricky and elusive enough in England, this is nothing to the variety of meanings it might bear in a Colony, self-governing or otherwise' (2). This is no exaggeration. Martha Quest grows up in a house where her own parents' attitudes to England are in direct conflict. The father, maimed by his war injury and enraged by government denial of the horror of war, looks back with loathing to the small grey 'narrow and conventional' country. His wife, on the other hand, having arrived in the colony with the material and psychological trappings of English middle-class refinement, contemplates 'the hard and disappointing life she had led' (*Martha Quest* 70) and lives for the day when they will be able to afford to go home. Martha grows up between these two attitudes, determined not to become a 'petty-bour-geois colonial' (*A Proper Marriage* 149). Lessing makes the Quests, and other 'English' settlers, interstitial figures, situated between the 'Dutch' and those newly arrived from England. The Quests' acquaintance, Mrs Van Rensburg, with her eleven children, is easy-going and direct, in contrast to 'that English kind of cold, upper-class thing' (*Interviews* 100): 'English' is often in the colony just as much a description of a reserved manner as a national classification. Piet, a much-travelled painter, elaborates this stereotype: the English in Southern Africa 'can't cook. They can't eat'; colonial life makes them suspicious and conventional; and as for men in England, 'They are no good for women' (*In Pursuit* 20, 24). While the Afrikaners are close-knit, all Dutch Reformed churchgoers, the English, mutually suspicious in their 'innumerable subgroupings', come together only in their 'knowledge of ownership', 'this is a British country' (*Martha Quest* 56). Women newly arrived from England are seen to behave in a snobbish manner, which is felt to be quite inappropriate in a colony where class difference, the colonists like to say, 'does not exist' (*In Pursuit* 67). Newly arrived male settlers appear 'graceful' or 'effeminate', but the airmen, representatives of the working class, coming to train in Africa during the war, seem strangely undergrown and dwarfish. In colonial eyes England is a dangerous source of liberal ideas, a place where blacks are treated as equals, even by women (*Proper Marriage* 66). But to Martha and her circle, who see themselves living in a colony whose collapse cannot come too soon, it is politically progressive. In her view, responsibility for the oppression of the Africans lodges with people like the magistrate, Maynard, and the white settler government. She longs to escape.

Far from the changing metropolis, a form of English life is preserved fossil-like in the colonies, and especially in the imagination of the aging colonists. Their disappointment when they go back makes this obvious. When Mrs Quest returns to England after her husband's death, she cannot understand how Martha's acquaintances behave. She joins her old friends in complaining that England is 'being ruined by all these foreigners', and that the 'lower orders' are spoiled and show no respect (*F-G City* 312). Unable to discover the place she had left, she returns to her son in Africa. Later in the novel the Maynards, now retired and disapproving of their new 'soft' colonial government, also visit London. Both were once 'rebels' in their own eyes who had repudiated 'home' decades ago as conservative and tyrannical, only to recreate that tyranny themselves in the colony (*Proper Marriage* 330). Now, ill at ease in a smart new restaurant, they find nothing in London to like or admire. They try a cousin's farm in Devon, hoping to find 'sympathetic soil', only to be shocked by a grand-daughter arriving home for the weekend from one of the new universities with a West Indian boy friend. They too go back to Africa.

A sense of change and loss in postwar England also haunts *In Pursuit of the English*. Doris, fresh from Africa, jokes that English people are hard to find. Like Bushmen who disappear as you approach, they protest that they are not English at all, but Scots, Irish or Welsh. The Londoners she eventually meets are struggling to hang on to a sense of themselves and their country. Rose will not count Tynesiders as English, or her landlady, who has an Italian grandmother. She herself is English, of course, having lived all her life within a few streets, but even she subscribes to the myth that real English people live in the country. For the retired ex-colonial Colonel Bartowers, England is unrecognisable: it 'isn't the old country any longer' (74). In these days of a socialist government he is not proud to call himself English. Also disappointed by the present state of England is Wally James, foreman of the gang who comes to repair the landlady's war-damaged house. He believed a Labour Government meant things would be 'better for the working people' (210) but now the government gives with one hand and takes back with the other; and the arrival of 'all these blacks' means 'we'll have unemployment again' (212). Rose shares his disillusionment: 'All through the war, they kept saying, everything's going to be different', but things are no different for her (154). A young woman who cannot quite commit herself to marriage, the emotionally damaged Rose is a symbolic figure in this post-war country. Though as the German wife in *The Four-Gated City* maintains, the English were spared the worst terrors of invasion and occupation,[6] Lessing's fiction insists on the psychological as well as the physical damage caused by the blitz. But a more persistent concern is the damage done by class divisions.

Rose takes up this topic with the newcomer, Doris. She looks back with wistful affection to the blitz, when everyone sheltered together in the underground. She knows how working-class people are looked down on, and made fun of, and resents it. For her the war was a happier time – of national unity, of a Utopian classlessness. It was not just that then people were fed with the hope of better times ahead, but that 'The blitz made comrades of us all'.[7] Lessing explored class and the struggle to escape its boundaries in several of her early stories. In 'Notes for a Case History' (1954) an attractive, ambitious young working-class woman tries, like Becky Sharp, to marry up the social ladder: not for her the early marriage of her plainer girl friend. But the plot pattern twists and she fails to snare the young architect, and has to settle for a man from her own background. 'England *versus* England' (1963) tells the class story familiar from fiction of the 1950s and 1960s: the guilt and pain of the grammar school boy who goes to university and is torn between his family and the educated and therefore middle-class milieu he is now in. In 1994 Lessing wrote: 'Britain is two nations, all right... though it is a bit better now – not much' (*Walking in the Shade* 59), and her English fiction has remained concerned with the consequences of class feeling.

By the early 1960s, it seemed to Lessing that the very structures of English life were disintegrating. This intuition was the starting point for *The Golden Notebook*, and the figure of the progressive woman writer, Anna Wulf. When she exclaims 'Everything's cracking up' (9), Wulf means traditional sex roles, faith in soviet communism, and even the integrity of the writer, now the literary world has become an industry like everything else. In the later stages of the novel mental 'breakdown' emerges as another aspect of that turmoil and transformation in every sphere which Lessing's large novels of the 1960s set out to embody and analyse. In a 'Preface' (published in 1971) Lessing explained that *The Golden Notebook* was 'to give the ideological "feel" of our mid-century', and that her novel took on a new, fragmented form to do so (*Personal Voice* 32, 36). In her next, *The Four-Gated City*, the final Martha Quest novel, she again 'wanted to convey what London was like' (*Interviews* 139).

Lessing's term for the whole sequence, 'a *Bildungsroman*' (*F-G City* 711), while appropriate for the earlier volumes, does not suit this last one. It begins with a focus on Martha in the unfamiliar city, but soon moves off on a different trajectory, when she becomes involved with the well-to-do Coldridge family and their political and cultural activities. As Martha's life lacks direction and she drifts in response to the family's needs, the narrative widens to take in a panoramic view of the decades from the Labour victory in 1950 to the 1960s and, prophetically, to the 90s, culminating in the madness of a global nuclear, or possibly 'chemical', catastrophe. The currents of change which sweep the country into this future also transform beliefs, and behaviour. Class barriers begin to weaken but that is only one shift in a social and political environment where new attitudes to mental illness, sex and to much else, compete for attention, and television coverage, with new fashions in 'Make-up and clothes and food and the decoration of houses' (516). Lorna Sage suggested that Lessing here succeeded only in a grand registering of manners and mores, 'the small change of change' (*Lessing* 45). But how important it was to Lessing to chart this time of transformation, when war-grey London took on colour again, and then fell under the threat of destruction, can be judged by her attempt in the autobiography once again to record 'HOW WE WERE THINKING' during those postwar years (*Walking* 271). Late in the novel, Mark Coldridge and Martha, despairing of reason, or science, to offer solutions to world conflict, move the novel out into new spaces: and for Martha, to a dangerous exploration of 'inner space', through self-induced breakdown. Mark, whose first novel was *The City in the Desert*, leaves England for North Africa in his search for a better civilisation and a good city, only to perish in the catastrophe. In the novel's last pages 'little Englands' are growing up around the world in post-catastrophe settlements, the product of 'a sentimental nostalgia for an England that never was' (671), a phrase which hits off Lessing's constant scepticism about the cherishing of national myths. The settlements anticipate the England 'tourist experience' situated on the Isle of Wight in Julian Barnes's satirical novel, *England, England* (1998).

This was to be Lessing's last Anglocentric novel for some time. Then after twenty years of writing 'space fiction', she turned back to England in *The Good Terrorist* (1985), a novel about a group of unappealing, self-deluded urban militants living in a London squat who, after being scorned by the IRA, bomb a London hotel. In a review published in New York Denis Donaghue suggested that this book's ending offered comfort to middle-class readers, 'if only because their enemies, Alice and her friends, are so ludicrously inept' (qtd. in Maslen 45). But, as Elizabeth Maslen points out, if at the end the terrorist group drifts apart, they have killed five people and wounded many (45). Lessing is a tough, disconcerting writer, less likely to reassure readers than to remind them of their capacities for violence, or their primal relish of destruction, as in *The Fifth Child* (1988), her fable of the ferocious boy born in a upper middle-class family who also ends up joining an urban underclass. *The Good Terrorist* in fact struck Gayle Greene as dark even by Lessing's standards, in its despair of political action, and female nurturing (208); but earlier novels had already questioned both as sources of light or comfort. The alternative paths Lessing herself has explored, especially Sufism, or even feminism, may have given her readers hope, but her disillusion with progressive politics set in long ago. And in the relationship in *The Good Terrorist* between Alice, who plays the mother figure in the terrorist group, and Alice's mother, Lessing returns to the 'personal' version of her theme of the damaging inheritance from the past. As with Martha and her mother, the child–parent bond damages both. But it is, as Greene says, the blending in Alice of ugly, stupid and admirable qualities which is especially disconcerting, and typical of Lessing at her most 'unsettling' (210–14). On one level this novel invites comparison with Conrad, or Stead, in its depiction of political action as futile and self-indulgent. But the American novelist Alison Lurie also detects 'a personification of England itself' in Alice's 'English' qualities: 'fairness, acute sense of class differences, humor, courage, capacity for hard work, love of domestic coziness, and unease about sex' (qtd. in Greene 260), and, one might add, her xenophobia.

London Observed (1992) collects stories and sketches published between 1988 and 1992 and here an affection for London mitigates Lessing's toughness. This new tack, she explained, was a reaction to a fashion among the well-to-do 'to knock London' (*Interviews* 234). Many of the stories present Londoners who are more justifiably discontented, made angry by poverty, or by their impotence before the violence around them, or resentful of change or even of the city traffic. Two recalcitrant motorists cause a traffic jam rather than give way to each other; an Indian shop keeper and his white customer angrily plan a counter-raid on whoever 'did [his] car in', since the police 'don't want to know' (79); a desperate mother begs for money 'to feed [her] kids' and when helped cannot bring herself to 'even just look at' her helper (64, 71); a taxi-driver complains 'London was not what it was, it was full of people he didn't think were Londoners at all' (128). Nevertheless, the narrator wants to congratulate Londoners: 'for people so threatened they are doing, I think, rather well' (89). Some have 'come to terms with the impossible' (90), and their stories find resolution in moments when this happens. Others, 'Sparrows', 'Pleasures of the Park' and 'The New Café', are warm with appreciation of London life outdoors. If on occasion the observer–narrator adopts the alien's view, 'that other-worldly visitor so useful for enlivening our organs of comparison' (94), she enjoys what she sees: the city is 'like a great theatre' (129), as she demonstrates in 'In Defence of the Underground'. The recollections of the past recounted by the oldest inhabitants, 'It was all fields and little streams' (80), are an occasion for wonder, not regret, as are the residual traces of ancient times. But there is no sentimental looking back: Lessing coolly points out the lies of the nostalgia merchants, and their selective memories of the past.

With equal detachment two stories in this collection once again appraise 'Englishness'. In 'The Real Thing' an American, Jody, is incongruously enmeshed in an English double divorce and remarriage. All the ex-husbands and wives – except Jody – are the best of friends with their former spouses, and play out a satirical comedy, their politeness and conscientious, even fussy, fulfilment of domestic obligations seeming to Jody ever more like an English way of escaping the claims of passion, sexuality, and even self-respect. Both American directness and the polite, or self-deprecating, upper middle-class English willingness to settle for considerably less appear comic, but exaggerated: these are types, not individuals.[8] 'The Pit' offers a more penetrating study. Sarah and her ex-husband James see themselves as having positive 'English' qualities: polite, reticent, forbearing, and wholly unlike Rose, the second wife, who is loud, Jewish, unscrupulous and excessive: 'I have too much vitality, too much energy for the English!' (166). Sarah has heard of Rose's being in the concentration camps, and afterwards in occupied Europe, and 'closed the door' against the thought, telling herself the English, meaning people safe all their lives, could not understand such 'a horror outside ordinary living' (164). Forced to be in contact with Rose again, and fearing her unscrupulousness, she recognises that 'the camps' and 'all that' have made Rose what she is; indeed, her greedy clasping at what she wants 'brought her out of the black pit' (165). Inevitably 'Rose would never, ever, understand ordinary decency, commonsense, honesty. One did not learn these qualities when part of "all that"' (166). Though the story is sympathetic to Sarah, it firmly links the 'English' virtues of Sarah and James to their more favourable circumstances.

'Decency' is a key concept in Lessing's representation of self-congratulatory myths of Englishness, and the varying mood of her allusions to it measures her residual connection to the English. In the comic mode of *In Pursuit of the English* decency is at first a joke. At the age of six Doris decided that her father's violent attacks on people, provoked, for instance, by a man's referring to a young woman by her first name, must be a sign of madness. Once in England, she half-seriously recognizes that there his 'splendidly pathological character' would pass almost unnoticed. This comic account still allows 'decency' some respect. In contrast Martha's amazement at Mark Coldridge's assumption that the public school fosters a moral 'strength' which makes a 'gentleman' is serious and critical. It is clear Mark does not expect to find 'gentlemen', men he can 'trust', outside his own class (*F-G City* 147). In his last words on leaving England: 'there was no point in staying in Britain: it no longer stood for anything a civilized man could care for' (*F-G City* 670), his assumption that Britain had been the bastion of 'civilization' echoes this self-congratulation. Writing in her autobiography of the political events of 1956, Lessing refers to her own disillusionment with 'some old idea of Britain, or perhaps I should say England, embodying decency and fair play' (*Walking* 208). And interestingly, in this same volume, she records with some sympathy how a comment made on radio by Richard Hoggart about lost standards of English decency provoked a public welling up of regret. This, she implies, is something more than nostalgia, or an illusory belief in English values. There *are* reserves of integrity and honesty in Britain. The Lessing of the *London Observed* stories, detached as ever, allows her figures to demonstrate these qualities.

Ben, in the World (2000), a sequel to *The Fifth Child*, takes up again the persistence of decency, of respect and compassion for others, in a complex, fast-moving London. Ellen Biggs, an 80-year old widow, feeds, clothes, and cares for Ben, the now 18-year old strong shouldered, strangely hairy 'human animal' she finds starving in the supermarket. At times fiercely violent, perhaps a 'throwback', the guileless Ben, ever anxious to please, is as much at a loss before state welfare bureaucracy as before individual greed. Beginning in London, his story moves to Nice and then to Rio, as he falls victim to the global activities of drug-traffickers, filmmakers and geneticists. The London section evokes a milieu similar but not the same as that of the squatter-militants of *The Good Terrorist*. It is peopled by those like Ellen and her neighbour in their tower block who struggle to live decently on welfare payments, and, in the alleyways alongside, by prostitutes, pimps and drug-dealers, products of 'a hard childhood', 'bad parents' (41), and borstal (53), who also struggle to get by, some with, some completely without, compassion for others. The reader contemplates the dealings of these various Londoners with Ben through the lonely, scarce-comprehending eyes of the outsider. Ben too is an 'other-worldly visitor' (*London Observed* 94).

The didactic potential of the trope of the space traveller appeals to Lessing: 'It's the easiest way of trying to make the readers look at a human situation more sharply' (*Interviews* 44). She is always ready to uphold the authority of the outsider. In an exchange of letters with E. P. Thompson in the 1960s about his criticisms of *The Golden Notebook*, she dismissed his suggestion that she was 'something that wandered out of the bush dazzled by bright lights' as 'an easy way out of thinking about the kind of outsider's view someone with my kind of upbringing was bound to have about Europe' (*Walking* 344). Her definition of the writer, which appears several times in the autobiography, is someone who sees at a distance, and, it is understood, therefore sees how things are (*Under My Skin* 397). As an outsider, Lessing could claim to be exempt from a mood of rejection of England, and of home, which beset inter- and post-war English writers, and which has been variously associated with modernism, loss of Empire, and the Great War. She detected it persisting in the 60s among the 'package' of ideas fashionable in progressive circles: 'A contempt for our own country, Britain, so deeply felt it had not, then, been examined at all, showed itself in a steady nagging denigration of everything British' (*Walking* 347).

Her fiction maintains a more remote relationship than is implied by the phrase 'our own country'.[9] English writers, she notes in a *London Observed* sketch, tend to get out of London and live in the country; but she has not felt the need to do so. She has stayed there, and consequently her fictional England is predominantly a London milieu of intellectuals and politicians, of people on committees and the institutions they preside over. Her English novels offer images of the restless evolution of that world, observed at times with compassion, but from a distance. Similarly, she is always detached from her figures, even the most autobiographical. Her fiction puts her readers in touch with *her* understanding of her character's plight, rather than giving them the illusion of sharing the character's own perspective. Detachment is not so much a product of her response to the English: it is the hallmark of her work, a mark of its value as well as a description of its method.

Notes

1. Earl G. Ingersoll, ed., *Putting the Questions Differently* 114; hereafter cited as *Interviews*.
2. For example, Carey Kaplan argues that the Canopean dramatis personae exhibit 'the colonist's rootlessness and sense of separation', 'a staple of Lessing's work'. See 'Britain's Imperialist Past in Doris Lessing's Futurist Fiction' 149–8, 150. See also Rebecca Rourke, 'Doris Lessing: exile and exception', and Nicole Ward Jouve, 'Of mud and other matter – *The Children of Violence*', as well as Lessing's own comments quoted below on the exile of the white settler writer, and note 4.
3. 'Colonials ... arrived in England with expectations created by literature. "We will find the England of Shelley and Keats and Hopkins, of Dickens and Hardy and the Brontës and Jane Austen, we will breathe the generous airs of literature. We have been sustained in exile by the magnificence of the Word, and soon we will walk into our promised land"' (*Walking in the Shade* 25). For her reading, see *Under My Skin* 82, 88, 202, etc.
4. 'The Lost Tribe of the Kalahari' 700.
5. For memories of England from her early childhood visit as 'cold, damp, dreariness, ugliness, a series of snapshots illustrating my loathing for the place', see Doris Lessing, *A Small Personal Voice* 116; this collection is cited hereafter as *Personal Voice*.

6. Lessing's story 'The Pit' returns to this difference of experience, and in *Walking in the Shade* she refers to how people reach for the phrase 'You see, Britain hasn't been invaded for hundreds of years', when commenting on a British 'reluctance to understand extreme experience' (96).
7. Quoted from the *New Statesman*, 16 September 1950 in Kenneth O. Morgan, *Labour in Power 1945–1951* 296. For historical discussion of this particular aspect of the myth of the Blitz, and on class tension in the war years, see Angus Calder, *The Myth of the Blitz* esp. 34 and 59–64; and Ian McLaine, *Ministry of Morale* 93–8 (on class feeling and unity) and 177–85 (on the Beveridge report and post-war aspirations).
8. Similarly, Judith Kegan Gardiner, *Rhys, Stead, Lessing and the Politics of Empathy*, reads the English couples in 'Not a very Nice Story' as 'types' (105–6).
9. For a reading of Lessing's fiction as, in contrast, the work of a self-fashioned 'English writer', see Louise Yelin 57–107.

8
Made in England: V.S. Naipaul and English Fiction(s)

Leela Gandhi

In recent years the question of V.S. Naipaul's relationship to England has begun to complicate his hitherto negative reception within the postcolonial academy. While, in the 1980s, a generation of colonial discourse analysis-inspired critics were able to condemn him unequivocally as an apologist for empire, a new recuperation reveals Sir Vidia as a casualty of imperialism; a man more victim than collaborator. Something of this, albeit still incipient, shift in attitude belongs to the changing nature of postcolonial critique itself. If, following the example of Edward Said's *Orientalism*, the 1980s were preoccupied with imperial constructions or representations of the non-West, a new tendency – reflected in the concerns of this volume – seeks a reversal of the imperial gaze, asking what colonized cultures, and their travelling/writing figures, made of England and empire when they arrived as emigrants, expatriates, travellers, in the 'mother country'. Each of these perspectives, as we will see, offers a variant, if not opposing, assessment of Naipaul and his oeuvre.

Read solely through the dark glass of colonial discourse analysis, Naipaul does emerge as a native informant, colluding opportunistically with imperialist/neo-orientalist constructions of the third world. In his Caribbean travelogue *The Middle Passage* (1962), for instance, Naipaul's gaze upon his former homeland appears mediated, without qualification, through the condemnatory imperial prose of former Victorian travellers to the region. There is nothing to offset the ethnographic virulence of his Victorian authorities, Trollope, Froude, Kingsley; no 'alternative' bias gleaned from local sources divulges a subaltern speaking-back to empire. It is precisely this anachronistic 'allegiance to the imperial vantage point' which critics like Rob Nixon single out as proof positive of Naipaul's desperation to retain a, presumably conservative,

English constituency (47). Indeed, as Nixon would argue, Naipaul's literary success in England, especially through the 1970s, accrues, in part, from his racially secured license to condemn the third-world. Where an over-vigilant liberal/postcolonial thought police has scrupulously checked the racism and imperial nostalgia of English writers, Naipaul, allegedly, remains free to animate the outdated diction of empire. In the words of Joseph Epstein, 'It may be that among living writers only Naipaul is able to speak of "barbarian peoples"; only he can say things that . . . in the mouths of others would straight away be declared racism' (qtd. in Nixon, 118). There is, thus, a guilty and forbidden pleasure in reading this Naipaul, a convenient 'White Man's Brown Man' (Gorra 72), who has made his career, according to Said, as 'a witness for the Western prosecution' (53). For Said, who would debar the author entirely from the postcolonial counter-canon, Naipaul betrays the most shameful variety of eurocentricism, viz., that of 'a third-worlder denouncing his own people, not because they are victims of imperialism, but because they have an innate flaw, which is that they are not whites' ('Intellectuals' 79).

Over the last few years this strident and over-conscientious verdict on Naipaul has met with substantial resistance from at least two mutually sympathetic groups of critics. The first comprises West Indian scholars like Stephano Harney and Gordon Rohlehr and Caribbeanist John Thieme, who read Naipaul's pessimism about the postcolonial nation-state differently, as an indictment of imperialism. 'Imperialism and the wicked consequences of colonialism', Harney writes, 'are the central themes of Naipaul's work. The dismissive comments on the Third World are made in this context – a Third World disfigured by the greed and violence of the colonial powers' (145).[1] This appraisal is strongly corroborated by a second group of like minded metropolitan postcolonial critics, who include Sara Suleri, Michael Gorra and Ian Baucom. Refusing the rigid binary of empire and its colonial other, these scholars foreground the profound cultural/political ambivalence produced by the colonial encounter, and embodied in renegade writers like Naipaul. Naipaul's critique of England-as-empire, they suggest, is implicit in his irascible account of colonial complicity.

Accordingly, Gorra interprets Naipaul's impatience with the colonized world, and with the imitative postcolonial nation-state, positively, as an appeal for ideological change. It is impatience, he argues, which 'allies Naipaul with Fanon. . . . He has that kind of rage, the rage that in other men and women brought independence into being, that made the postcolonial world' (Gorra 110). In this reading, far from being a writer intent, as Nixon puts it, on 'ventriloquizing an English identity' (49), Naipaul's gaze upon Englishness is shown to reveal a greater self-reflexivity, and a bitter apprehension of his own implication in the workings of empire. Always writing himself into his critique of the postcolonial condition, his oeuvre concedes the existential cost of desiring metropolitan England from the colonial margin. 'The need for angry critiques of his work', then, as Suleri tells us, 'is now obsolete, or such critiques must be prepared to admit what each successive text from *An Area of Darkness* to *The Enigma of Arrival* makes increasingly clear: Naipaul has already been there before them and has been exquisitely angry with himself' (158).

We can, however, only begin to comprehend Naipaul's 'exquisite' self-loathing if we admit to our analysis something of his double vision of England itself: simultaneously the scene of desire and lack, faith and agnosticism, creativity and self-denudation. Keeping company with his critical allies, this chapter argues that Naipaul's 'England' is written up as a duplicitous entity – which he believes in, even though he knows it lies. In his writing, then, we find three distinct 'discoveries' of England's deceit, and so, three accounts of colonial deception. First, Naipaul's autobiographical work concerns itself with the bitter knowledge that, for all its pretensions to the contrary, the English canon is an incarnation of English imperialism. Secondly, in his ethnographic and travel literature, Naipaul addresses the lie of the 'civilizing mission'. In other words, closer examination reveals that, for all its apparent concern for the cultural and civilizational 'betterment' of its colonial subjects, the English empire was a profoundly narcissistic enterprise. And finally, in his rewriting of a familiar postcolonial trope, Naipaul battles with the discovery that the 'real' England bears little or no relation to the one imagined and constructed in the colonial periphery. The subsequent section looks at Naipaul's disclosure of his fraught relationship with the imperial metropolis, with a specific focus on his negotiations with the English canon.

The politics of literature

The paradox which informs Naipaul's writing is this: that if England is troped, consistently, as the land of opportunity, the place in which to 'arrive' decisively as a writer, it is also the scene of a terrible incarceration. The longing for England, thus, folds seamlessly into its antithesis, the desire for departure; a landscape once loved from afar proves, on closer acquaintance, to be tragically dystopian. This is the burden of

Naipaul's autobiographical, *The Enigma of Arrival* (1987). 'For years', he writes, 'in that far off island whose human history I had been discovering and writing about, I had dreamed of coming to England. But my life in England had been savourless, and much of it mean.... And just as once at home I had dreamed of being in England, so for years in England I had dreamed of leaving home' (95).

A related sense of the claustrophobia and inhospitality of English life marks *Mr Stone and the Knight's Companion* (1963), Naipaul's first and only novel with an entirely English setting, and exclusively English characters. Here, at the end of his professional career as a petty bureaucrat, Naipaul's hero attempts to extend and animate his barren future through marriage and a 'scheme' to rehabilitate the retired members of his Department. The inevitable, if heroic, failure of these efforts is amplified through the novel's insistence on the oppressive enclosure of the English scenes, habits and rituals which supply its narrative context. The routines of Mr Stone's single life lapse into the slightly more tedious routines of his marriage and domesticity. The confinement of everyday spaces – the 'unbearably hot and crowded' lunchtime pub, 'the damp and steaming queue into the underground' (24, 25) – find a correlative in the incurable insularity of the lives stunted by these spaces. Ironically, Naipaul writes himself and his world into this exhaustively 'English' novel only as the absent object of xenophobia, as a potential trespasser defying the interdiction imposed by his own blinkered characters. There is little accommodation for him in the Earl's Court residence, once occupied by Mr. Stone's wife, whose 'refuge of calm and respectability' is secured by a discrete ' "Europeans Only" card below the bell' (32). A similar sign appears to regulate the unthinking racism of Whimper (by name and by nature), office colleague and friend of the Stones, who is inexplicably and regularly 'driven to fury' by the 'sight of black men on the London streets' (112). And finally, as though mocking his exilic and deracinated author, there is Mr. Stone, who wisely prefers 'to spend his holidays in England', never leaving the shores of his island habitat.

Gazing steadfastly upon England in this early work, Naipaul finds it desolate and, implicitly, unwelcoming. In an essay, 'London' (*Overcrowded Baracoon*, 9–16), he explicates the negative impressions of England fictionalized in *Mr Stone*. Postulating England as a necessity, as the only place in which he can meaningfully exercise his vocation as a writer among writers, he simultaneously laments the insularity of English life, the absence of visible communal pleasures. Alienated by the baffling opacity of Englishness, his craft – much like Rushdie's –

concedes the gap between metropolitan location and non-metropolitan materials. England, as he tells us, 'it is the best place to write in. The problem for me is that it is not a place I can write about' (16). *The Enigma of Arrival* will revisit these early impressions about the frustrating inaccessibility of English 'materials'; the autobiographical pieces in *Finding the Centre* (1984) will, likewise, record Naipaul's belated recognition that he can only write about the home that he has so eagerly relinquished: 'To become a writer...I had thought it was necessary to leave... Actually to write, it was necessary to go back' (47). This prodigal return, of course, finds expression in, and as, his very first novel, *Miguel Street* (the third to be published), that already registers a formative ambivalence in Naipaul's relationship to the imperial metropolis.

In the Trinidadian 'vignettes' that comprise *Miguel Street*, England is exalted as the grammar of colonial aspiration, as the governing trope for opportunity and 'improvement'. At the same time, however, England and Englishness also emerge as shorthand for failure and deception. So, the hopeless Elias briefly wins the respect of his small community for the reason that his Cambridge School Certificate examination scripts will obtain a metropolitan audience: 'Errol said, "Everything Elias write not remaining here, you know. Every word that boy write going to England"' (*Miguel Street* 39). Destined to drive a scavenging cart, however, Elias's efforts are futile, and England is rapidly transformed into the scene of his repeated academic failure. Much the same, the unsuccessful calypso lyricist, B. Wordsworth, fails to fulfil the canonical expectations of his improbable name. And although the character 'Man-Man' sounds like an Englishman 'if you shut your eyes while he spoke', an open gaze reveals a madman, covering the local pavements of Miguel Street with cursive renditions of the English alphabet. Eventually, the narrator of this early *bildung* himself succumbs to the dream of arriving in England to become a literary man. 'Think', he is instructed by his benefactor Ganesh Pundit, 'It means going to London. It means seeing snow and seeing the Thames and the big Parliament' (218). But in order to secure this trip to London the narrator must bribe Ganesh Pundit (destined to become the protagonist of Naipaul's first published novel, *The Mystic Masseur*, 1957) and, thus, obtain an always, already illegitimate place in the imperial centre. As he prepares to board the aircraft to depart for his desired destination, a sudden trick of light projects a prophetic image: 'I left them all and walked briskly towards the aeroplane, not looking back, looking only at my shadow before me, a dancing dwarf on the tarmac' (222). So it is, that the act of leaving for England, which requires the 'corruption' of local culture, also produces the unsettling image of a shrunken and comically reduced self. What, then, is the basis for this desperately fraught perception of England? What, in the other words, accounts for Naipaul's particular crisis about Englishness?

In his autobiographical essay, 'Conrad's Darkness', Naipaul is illuminating on the subject of his own disappointed arrival in England: 'I suppose in my fantasy I had seen myself coming to England as to some purely literary region, where untrammelled by the accidents of history or background, I could make a romantic career for myself as a writer. But in the new world I felt that ground move below me' (216). Here, in summary, we have it: the wishful fabrication of England as the uncontaminated place of literature comes unstuck. Instead of delivering the political, cultural and historical amnesia that Naipaul devoutly seeks, England brings on the reverse: an acute consciousness of the damaged postcolonial world he has left behind; a world damaged, furthermore, by empire: 'The new politics, the curious reliance of men on institutions they were yet working to undermine . . . the corruption of causes, half-made societies that were doomed to remain half-made: these were the things that began to preoccupy me' (216). For Naipaul's detractors, a passage such as this is characteristic, confirming his arrival in England as an ideological departure from his own origins. But, is this harangue on the lamentable failure of the 'third'-world simply a sycophantic performance of his allegiance to the 'first', or, something rather more interesting? Could it be the unexpected knowledge, for instance, that England is (has always been) simultaneously the place of both empire and canon? To put this differently, it is, arguably, in England that, contrary to his deepest expectations, the colonial writer-aspirant finds himself pathetically trammelled by the accidents of both history and background.

Sara Suleri's insightful reading of Naipaul develops a similar viewpoint, casting his troubled relationship to England as a continuous struggle to sever canon from empire. Everywhere, Naipaul's writing is haunted by the desire (everywhere recognized as impossible) to apprehend the unproblematic autonomy of the canon, and to confirm, concomitantly, the immunity of English literature from the contagion of English imperialism. Naipaul, Suleri notes, 'records a perspective that . . . has no choice but to register its own bewilderment at the relation between education and empire, seduced as it was into the quaint belief that literature could somehow provide a respite from what it means to gain consciousness in a colonial world' (Suleri 150).

Even in his earliest excursions into writing, Naipaul is keenly aware that the principal deceit of European culture inheres in the racial exclusivity which undermines its apparent universality. The curiously Calvinist paradox of *la mission civilisatrice*, that Naipaul fully understands, is this: while England (with its European counterparts) represents the only possible cultural/civilizational truth, only some are chosen, by accident of birth, to have natural access to the privilege of this truth. And as his relentless pathologization of the 'mimic man' reveals, the colonial aspirant can only enter the compelling scene of Englishness, its exhaustive 'everything', as the subject of mutation and comedy. Such is the judgement he offers on, among others, the Anglophile Mr Mackay in, *The Middle Passage* (1962) who, 'like all good West Indians...was unwilling to hear anything against England' (18). The 'nigrescent' Pundit Ganesh Ramsumair, in *The Mystic Masseur*, is similarly mocked for inappropriately anglicizing his name, on arriving in England, to G. Ramsay Muir (215).

But what of the colonial reader/writer and his cultural and linguistic metamorphosis in the face of England? We might refer here, briefly, to Simon Gikandi's *Maps of Englishness*, which teases out, through the example of the *athomi* (Gikuyu converts to Christianity) something of the complex betrayal and self-loss which accompanies the practice of colonial education/reading. '*Athomi*', a tribal name literally meaning 'one who reads', signals a biblical literacy predicated upon a total, and ultimately unrewarded, rejection of the pre-colonial and pre-Christian past. As Gikandi observes, 'After all, what made the African readers *athomi* was not merely their newly acquired literacy but also their willingness – and capacity – to renounce their previous identities and narratives to enter an imperial future in which – many of them were to complain later – they were still marginal' (37). It is in 'Conrad's Darkness', again, that Naipaul touches upon his own experience of reading the English canon as a conversion, not dissimilar in its implications to that undergone by the *athomi*.

The essay seems to suggest, contra Bloom, that the postcolonial 'beginning poet' or *ephebe* comes to life and voice without sufficient anxiety about his influences. Exploring his own too ready acquiescence to the lessons of literary and other fathers, Naipaul's study bristles with the consequences of receiving a flawed and unexamined patrimony. Conrad, we are told at the end of this essay, 'died fifty years ago. In those fifty years his work has penetrated to many corners of the world which he saw as dark. It is a subject for Conradian meditation...' (227). The ironies of this conclusion – what Suleri calls the 'ambivalence of reading' – are complex. In the main, Naipaul points to the bizarre self-disregard involved in assiduously reading a writer whose oeuvre is, in some ways, a meditation upon the cultural impoverishment (the civil-izational darkness) of one's own world. And Conrad's verdict is compre-hensive, condemning both the geography and inhabitants of the colonized world: 'it extends to all men in these dark or remote places who, for whatever reason, are denied a clear vision of the world' (215). As a colonial reader, then, one cannot participate in the pleasures of Conrad, as it were, properly, from outside the logic of conversion. To concur with Conrad's verdict, as Naipaul does, is to authorize his estimation of the colonial world: '...in Conrad...I was...to find my feelings about the land exactly caught' (214).

There is another irony. Conrad's power as a storyteller, as Naipaul recognizes, is an effect of what Said has described as imperialism's 'structures of attitude and reference' (Said, *Culture and Imperialism*, 84). And, in this, Conrad's writing is typical of the fiction produced under the aegis of empire. As Said writes, 'imperialism and the novel fortified each other to such a degree that it is impossible...to read one without in some way dealing with the other' (84). Anticipating Said, 'Conrad's Darkness' concedes the symbiosis between imperialism and the canon. 'The great novelists', Naipaul insists, 'wrote about highly organised societies' (213); and later, attributing the death of the novel to the end of empire: 'the great societies that produced the great novels of the past have cracked' (227). Nowhere, then, is the question of literary influence more complicated: to admire the canon, and to emulate a precursor like Conrad, the latecoming postcolonial *ephebe* must consent to his own cultural and material dispossession. So too, in recognizing his cultural seduction by England, the colonial reader/writer is compelled to register the fact of his complicity in the work and lies of empire.

Keen to the ethical and existential compromises which mark colo-nized subjectivity, what does Naipaul have to say about the mentality of Empire? The following section will assess Naipaul's verdict on England's imperial narcissism.

Imperial narcissism

In his studies of India and the West Indies, Naipaul recognizes, and foregrounds, the colonial encounter as a pastoral relationship between the English metropolis and the far flung peripheries of empire. His insights, in this regard, are very close to those offered by Raymond Williams in *The Country and the City*. Williams, we might recall, reads the English pastoral as generic evidence for the fundamentally unequal relationship between metropolis and the rural periphery. In the course of its transmission, he argues, the form gradually becomes a pretext for the self-elaboration of metropolitan desire and identity. Concomitantly, the realities of country life all but disappear or, are actively repressed to achieve the projection of poetic/metropolitan conceits. 'The pastoral drama beginning with Tasso's *Aminta* (1572)', he writes, 'is...the creation of a princely court, in which the shepherd is an idealised mask, a courtly disguise: a traditionally innocent figure through whom, paradoxically, intrigue can be elaborated' (20).

Williams also acknowledges the pastoral underpinning of English colonialism. The paradigm of country and city, he tells us, has long exceeded the boundaries of the nation-state. Read especially as a set of overdetermined political and social relationships, the English pastoral has always sought a global provenance. In his words, 'Much of the real history of city and country within England itself is from an early date a history of the extension of a dominant model of capitalist development to include other regions of the world....Thus one of the last models of 'city and country' is the system we now know as imperialism' (279). Williams's reading here is, of course, authorized in Mill's earlier and explicit endorsement of colonial commerce as an extension of the city-country relation. 'These [outlying properties of ours]', he writes in his *Principles of Political Economy*, 'are hardly to be looked upon as countries carrying on an exchange of commodities with other countries, but more properly as outlying agricultural or manufacturing estates belonging to a larger community....The trade with the West Indies is hardly to be considered an external trade, but more resembles the traffic between town and country' (qtd. in Baucom 44).

While emphasizing the socio-economic content of the colonial pastoral, Williams points to the specifically cultural mutations of this form in, among others, Kipling, Maugham, Orwell, Joyce Cary and, of course, Conrad (see Williams 281). In the work of such writers he observes the distinct emergence of imperial territory as 'an idyllic retreat, an escape from debt or shame...an opportunity for making a fortune' (281). Naipaul's *An Area of Darkness* (1964) and *The Loss of El Dorado* (1969), it might be suggested, pursue a similar reading of the colonial pastoral in India and the West Indies. Both books foreground the 'colonies' as a new peripheral theatre for the performance of English identity.

In *An Area of Darkness*, the scene of the colonial pastoral is written out in the language of touristic disappointment. Naipaul approaches India in the hope of discovering the pre-colonial landscape of his childhood imagination, and finds England instead. Much of the book is a response to this unwelcome surprise. The opening pages, with their account of Naipaul's sea-borne approach to India, reveal, in advance, the traveller's determination to recover a Europe-free zone in his ancestral homeland. Anticipating the East, then, Naipaul registers the 'falling away' of Europe 'even in Greece' (10). And so, progressively, the journey sometimes yields up the satisfactions of 'withdrawn' imperialisms (11), and sometimes discloses a fearful racial alterity as 'the physique of Europe... melt[s] away' (13). Yet, if the approach to India satisfactorily delivers on the promise of Eastern difference, India itself appears tragically overcome by an irrevocably 'Englished' landscape. The demystification comes even before Naipaul sets foot on Indian soil: 'sitting in the launch about to tie up at the Bombay pier... the names on cranes and buildings were, so oddly, English' (16). For the rest of the journey, England proves ubiquitous, living 'in the shadow of imperial-grand houses' (188); 'in the division of country towns into "cantonments", "civil lines" and bazaars... in army officers messes... in the silver... in uniforms and moustaches... in mannerisms and jargon... in the clubs, the Sunday morning bingo... the *Daily Mirror*' (190).

Naipaul reacts to the ubiquity of England-in-India with a self-directed anger at his own belatedness. The journey described in *Area*, as he confesses elsewhere, is heavily invested with the desire to authenticate an 'original' fantasy about India: 'India was special to England; for 200 years there had been any number of English travellers accounts and, latterly, novels. I could not be that kind of traveller. *In travelling to India I was travelling to an un-English fantasy.* There was no model for me here. Foster nor Ackerly nor Kipling could help' (emphasis added, *Enigma* 141). In context, Naipaul's extreme aversion to the English possession of India is at least partly informed by the supersession of his autonomous fantasy by the very models he hopes to eschew: Kipling, Forster, Ackerly, and so on. And as Naipaul understands, a competition with these powerful predecessors for the creative rights of fantasy, is a bit like wishing colonialism away. And yet, the too excessive and insistent elaboration of Englishness in the subcontinent also betrays what we have described earlier as the logic of the colonial pastoral. For, in its self-referentiality, its very incongruity, the Englishness that Naipaul encounters in the land of his forbears, reveals a characteristically metropolitan self-regard. The Raj, as he bitterly concludes, 'was an expression of the English involvement with themselves rather than with the country they ruled' (201). Revealed as yet another rehearsal ground for the elaboration of English identity, postcolonial India bears witness to the symbiosis between imperialism and the emergence of the myth of

English nationalism. So, tracking the literary history of the word 'British' from Austen to Forster, Naipaul finds a telling shift from a geographical idea to a cultural ideal. 'Between the two uses of the word', as he writes, 'lie a hundred years of industrial and imperial power' (196). It is possibly in India that the English fully succumb to self-love. After empire, Naipaul tells us, the writers of the nineteenth-century begin to report, 'not on themselves but on their Englishness' (196).

If India is often cast, in Naipaul's oeuvre, as the preferred site for imperial self-elaboration, *The Loss of El Dorado* (1969) foregrounds the West Indies as another overlooked setting for England's self-consolidating performance. Framed by the European discovery of the new world, this monumental study substantiates what Naipaul himself describes as 'a colonial aspect of the taste for pastoral' (182). The book develops its thesis through a detailed account of the events surrounding the trial of a British governor, Picton, for the torture of one Luisa Calderon at the end of the eighteenth-century. Reading against the grain of Picton's trial, Naipaul transforms a congratulatory account about imperial legislative justice into a narrative more concerned with a struggle over the signification of Englishness. In the face of growing abolitionist concern about Britain's deteriorating image overseas, the Luisa Calderon 'cause' acquires an unexpected ideological urgency. Picton's style of rough imperialism is suddenly rendered obsolete by a newly conscientious jury of 'English radicals, English humanitarians, English patriots' (184). By the time prosecuting First Commissioner, William Fullarton, begins to elaborate 'Britishness as an ideal of justice and protection', Picton does not stand a chance. Altogether superseded by a new and improved imperial fashion, his indictment confirms Englishness as the real subject of the trial. His victims, meanwhile, remain faceless and nameless in the self-regarding din of 'London talk, from London people' (257). 'So much was written about the Negroes', Naipaul wryly observes, 'but the Negroes of 1800 remain as anonymous as the Indians of Las Casas three centuries ago. It is the silence of serfdom' (250).[2]

Troubled as he is by such examples of imperial narcissism, Naipaul refuses to forgive the colonial world for its own unrestrained capitulation to the myth of Englishness. This is the underlying theme, as it were, of *A Bend in the River* (1979). In a brief but significant episode in this novel, the character Indar describes, in such terms, a culturally alienating visit to India House in London. The visit leaves him with a sudden nightmarish apprehension of his own contrivance by England. A new perspective on the borrowed English costume he wears, the 'London building... which pretended to be of India' produces something like the estrangement that qualifies the conclusion of 'Conrad's Darkness'. As he puts it: 'I felt in that building I had lost an important idea of who I was. . . . For the first time in my life I was filled with colonial rage'. The rage is directed at England, at empire, but no less, also at 'the people who had allowed themselves to be corralled into a foreign fantasy' (152).[3]

To an extent, of course, Naipaul comes to believe too much in his own exposition of the cannibalism and ubiquity of empire. Indar's harsh indictment of colonial mimicry informs Naipaul's easy dismissal of Indian nationalism as an English invention.[4] The insistence that empire supplies the vocabulary for anti-colonial nationalism finds new expression in his judgement on other resistance movements in the colonized world. He readily and repeatedly dismisses négritude as a modernist invention, and in 'Michael X' (1980), Black Power is similarly condemned for its wholly derivative etymology. This study of the Black Power killings in Trinidad in 1972-73, accounts for the revolutionary 'negro' as an English projection, produced – much like the 'shepherd' of the conventional pastoral – for the entertainment of a listless metropolitan audience. Such then, is his verdict on Michael X: 'He was the total 1960's negro, in a London setting; and his very absence of originality, his plasticity, his ability to give people the kind of Negro they wanted, made him acceptable to journalists' (23). The damning notion of the anti-colonialist as an imperial mannequin is further developed in the character of Mr. Blackwhite, the colonial writer figure in *A Flag on the Island* (1967). Once marked by the apparent unauthenticity of his lurid English romances – 'all the time . . . only lords and ladies' (184) – Blackwhite is shown to be equally derivative when he starts to write nativist novels which are enthusiastically endorsed by his English audience. 'Discovered' by London, like Michael X and a host of Indian nationalists, he is rapidly dispatched to Cambridge to recuperate his colonized culture and 'to do some work on your language' (207).

In his studies of India and the West Indies, then, Naipaul bemoans the self-regard of empire. While pursuing the systematic 'manufacture' of Englishness in the colonial world he comes up against yet another aspect of imperial deceit, viz., the impassable gap between the imagined and the real England. And to this discovery we now turn, very briefly, in the final section.

The fiction of England

El Dorado, as we have seen, takes as its theme the shifting and 'constructed' nature of Englishness. Such too is the subject of *Area*, which confirms Englishness as a theatrical 'role' rather than a cultural reality. Indeed, Naipaul tells us here, colonial mimicry is facilitated by the invented rather than essential nature of Englishness: 'Almost the last true Englishmen...are Indians. It is a statement that has point only because it recognises the English "character" as a creation of fantasy' (*Area* 41). Elaborating these perceptions in his early travel-book, Naipaul pushes against the suspicious, 'full-bloodedness', or excessiveness, of England-in-India, to reveal an England which simply does not 'ring true' (190-91). So, for instance, in the overproduced architecture of the Raj, he finds an England which protests too much: 'Their grounds were a little too spacious; their ceilings a little too high, their columns and arches and pediments a little too rhetorical ... a little too grand for their purpose. ... They were appropriate to a conception of endeavour than to endeavour. It was embarrassing to be in these buildings' (33). Re-grafted into the alien top soil of Northern India, Eastern Africa, and South-East Asia, imperial Englishness, Naipaul suggests, transmutes into something all the stranger for its colonial riches.

Writing in a similar vein about life as a civil servant in the former Ceylon, Leonard Woolf points to the blurring of fiction and reality in the making of Anglo-Indic *burra sahibs* and *memsahibs*. He writes, 'The white people were...in many ways astonishingly like characters in a Kipling story. I could never make up my mind whether Kipling had moulded his characters accurately in the image of Anglo-Indian society or whether we were moulding our characters accurately in the image of Kipling story' (46). Naipaul's reiteration of this reading – 'at the height of their power, the British gave the impression of a people at play' – brings us in the presence of something that Baudrillard has called 'hyperreality'. In his work on the excessive consumerism that marks late-capitalism, Baudrillard, as is well known, describes a cultural condition given over to the indeterminate play of simulations and images. The predicament of advanced capitalism as he sees it, then, is this: that the lines dividing the real and the unreal gradually become indistinguishable. So much so that artificial or fictive simulations achieve a 'hyperreality'; in other words, they become more potently real than that which is real. So too, although in a world only just anticipating the culture of late-capitalism, colonial England becomes hyperreal in relation to its real/metropolitan counterpart. This is what Naipaul suggests when he tells us that 'to be English in India was to be larger than life' (*Area* 200).

Like many of his twentieth-century postcolonial counterparts, Naipaul discovers that the real England, encountered in the flesh, falls short of the hyperreal England, manufactured and imagined in the colonies. Such is the lament recorded in a range of his minor and major, fictional and autobiographical, 'arrival' narratives: 'I used to have a vision of a big city, it wasn't like this' (*In a Free State* 72); 'The Europe the aeroplane brought me to was not the Europe I had known all my life' (*Bend* 237); 'I no longer dream of ideal landscapes . . . all landscapes turn to land, the gold of the imagination to the lead of reality' (*Mimic Men* 13); 'England is not perhaps the country we thought it was' (*Overcrowded Baracoon* 21); 'I had come to England at the wrong time . . . I had come too late to find the England, the heart of Empire, which (like a provincial, from a far corner of empire) I had created in my fantasy' (*Enigma* 120).

On the face of it, there is nothing especially delphic about the text of Naipaul's disappointment. Measured against the English fictions of his colonial childhood, England itself simply fails to satisfy: a destination that falls short of tourist brochures. Indeed, the colonial migrant/traveller's disappointment with the real England is already a postcolonial trope; a commonplace which invariably attends the much-awaited journey into the imperial heartland. Yet, one feature of Naipaul's particular disappointment stands out, and deserves comment. It would appear that his complaint seems to accrue, in part, from the apparently contaminating presence in England of colonized people like himself. London, Naipaul's books reiterate, is soured by the ubiquity of the third world. The streets seem overcome by North Africans, East Africans, West Indians, Arabs, South Asians, and the flotsam of Europe, journeying in at the end of Empire. As Indar says to Salim in *A Bend in the River*: 'We've come here at the wrong time. . . . When we were in Africa, in the good old days . . . I don't suppose we thought it would be like this in Europe, or that the British passports we took out as protection against the Africans would actually bring us here, and that the Arabs would be in the streets outside' (247).

We could read a text like this as evidence, yet again, of Naipaul's adopted racism, or of his inherent conservatism. Naipaul, as Nixon insists, only criticizes England when he finds the over-liberal postimperial welfare state hastening 'national decline towards a third world degeneracy' (Nixon 36). On the other hand, his consciousness of the colonial presence in London could also be read as an attempt to divulge England's imperial legacy. For, as Said tells us, the residual history of empire is revealed precisely in such migrations from the 'developing' to the 'developed' world: 'a vast new population of Muslims, Africans, and West Indians from former colonial territories now resides in metropolitan Europe; even Italy, Germany and Scandinavia must today deal with these dislocations which are to a large extent the result of imperialism and decolonisation' (*Culture and Imperialism* 41).

The unwelcome surprise of finding East Africa in London is consistent with the material logic of the colonial pastoral, or, more specifically, with the reverse journeys provoked by its narratives. In *The Country and the City* Williams sees in successive rural emigrations to London, evidence of the dispossession produced, and long repressed, by the material practices underpinning pastoral poetry. The same reading, he writes, applies to the scene of colonial 'arrival' into the imperial metropolis: 'unemployment in the colonies prompted a reverse migration, and following an ancient pattern the displaced from the "country" areas came, following the wealth and the stories of wealth, to the "metropolitan" centre, where they were at once pushed in, overcrowded, among the indigenous poor, as had happened throughout in the development of cities' (283). Could it be that the reverse migrations foregrounded and lamented in Naipaul's books also register the savage inequities produced by empire? In other words, might we read his anger with the third-worlding of poor London as an anger about the repressed realities of the colonial encounter? There is enough in his prolific career that would suggest so.

Notes

1. See Farred for C. L. R. James' favourable assessment of Naipaul (42).
2. Gikandi's reading of the 1865 Morant Bay rebellion develops a similar perspective (69).
3. See also, 'Prologue to an Autobiography' (58).
4. See *Area of Darkness* (398).

9
Black Families in Buchi Emecheta's England(s)

Sue Thomas

The controversy over Buchi Emecheta's fiction is epitomized in Chikwe-nye Okonjo Ogunyemi characterization of Emecheta's 'been-to' writing career (220) as an optimization of the 'raw material' of 'her own story, her mothers's [sic] story, her father's story, her brother's story, her children's stories, and the stories of her friends and acquaintances in England' (229); and as a purveying of 'reprehensible aspects of Nigerian life retarding societal transformation' as 'exotic reading for her primary audience, the West' (233). Emecheta describes her first two published novels, *In the Ditch* (1972) and *Second-Class Citizen* (1974) as 'self-documentary' (*Head Above Water* 60), writing of the critical distance from her own experiences that she achieved by naming their protagonist Adah, 'meaning "daughter"' (58). Ogunyemi refers to the protagonist as Emecheta-Adah, and categorizes Emecheta's representation of Adah Obi's husband Francis in *Second-Class Citizen*, identified as Emecheta's ex-husband Sylvester Onwordi, as 'literature of insult' tantamount to murder of his spirit.[1] Afam Ebeogu refers to Emecheta's 'personal opinion about the male chauvinistic perversions in an African culture' (85). 'It is when you're out of your country that you can see the faults in your society,' Emecheta, who arrived in England aged seventeen in 1962, has commented. 'It has been my being in Europe that has made me see the disadvantages some Nigerian women are subjected to' (Interview 22). Emecheta is a qualified sociologist. In my reading of her fiction for adults set wholly or in large part in England – *In the Ditch*, *Second-Class Citizen*, *Gwendolen* (1989), and *Kehinde* (1994) and *The New Tribe* (2000) – I emphasize the critical frameworks from sociology which she brings to bear on her material. Paul Gilroy writes of the regularity of the ways in which 'contemporary political and economic crises of blacks' are seen to be 'most intensely lived in the area of gender relations where the symbolic reconstruction of community is projected onto an image of an ideal heterosexual couple. The patriarchal family is the preferred institution capable of reproducing the traditional roles, cultures, and sensibilities that can solve this state of affairs' (*Black Atlantic* 94). Emecheta projects different visions of community and communal reconstruction.

Looking back on her decision in her mid-twenties to return to study, Emecheta says that she 'wanted the type of discipline that would help me to be a good writer when I was forty' (*Head Above Water* 47). In a 1980 interview she comments: 'Literature has a lot to say about the social life of a people at a particular place and time. Because my first degree is in sociology, I always deal with my subject from a social angle. I form the social theory, then I expand the theory in the novel. I look for a problem strictly from a woman's point of view' (Interview 20). 'The more I went into sociological theories the more I could find their equivalent or what I termed their interpretation in real life', she writes (*Head Above Water* 57). Sylvester Onwordi had burnt the manuscript of her first novel *The Bride Price*. Inspired by books like Nell Dunn's *Poor Cow* and Monica Dickens's *One Pair of Hands* and *One Pair of Feet*, she determined while a student to write about her own 'social reality' (58), which she was mediating through social theory. She realized that her recent experiences as a Nigerian immigrant single mother with five young children in a North London block of council flats 'could be regarded as "anomie" or classlessness. I found I could relate my lack of any hope for the future and near personal despair to the same concept' (57–8). Anomie has been variously defined. Marco Orrù outlines a range of meanings: 'For some writers, anomie is the absence of cultural restraints on human aspirations, for others it denotes a conflict of belief-systems in a society; anomie also describes the imbalance between cultural goals and institutional means at either the social or the individual level, or a psychological condition of self-to-other alienation' (1–2). Understandings of anomie inform Emecheta's representations of her protagonists' negotiations of English and immigrant modernities in all five novels I will discuss, even when it is not the central 'subject' she mediates through sociological theory and the generic structures of her novels. In *Second-Class Citizen* the subject is 'the conflict of two cultures' (*Head Above Water* 105); *Gwendolen* focuses on incest and illiteracy; *Kehinde* on abortion and gendered cultural expectations; and *The New Tribe* on adoption and senses of belonging.

In the Ditch had several working titles – 'Observations', 'Social Realities', 'Life in London' (*Head Above Water* 64); to Emecheta's university colleagues it was '"Buchi's poverty book"', an aspect of her 'specializ[ation] in poverty and race' (96). The novel opens with Adah Obi being woken by the noise of her male 'room-mate, the Great Rat' (1). Its presence, encouraged by the food Adah is forced to store under her bed, signifies the threat to 'physical and moral hygiene' (Stallybrass and White 143) represented by the standard of accommodation of Adah and her young family in London. The novel is dedicated to Emecheta's father, a mordant gesture given that he revered England as the 'Kingdom of God' (*Head Above Water* 27). Adah thinks: 'Igbo people seldom separate from their husbands after the birth of five children. But in England, anything could be tried, and even done. It's a free country' (*Ditch* 5). Adah thinks that she will be 'free to keep her job, keep her kids, do her studies' and 'to ignore' with 'safe[ty]' the efforts of her Yoruba landlord to scare her into leaving (4). She will experience difficulties, however, finding the institutional means to realize simultaneously the first three of these goals. Moving from an illegally rented-out room of a council tenant to a block of council flats for 'problem families' (17), ironically named Pussy Cat Mansions, Adah finds herself 'in the ditch': in the 'hierarchy of the city', a slum dwelling (Stallybrass and White 145); moving down the social scale to welfare dependency; and a place of abandonment. There she is subjected to two kinds of social policing: she comes under the scrutiny and paternalistic interest of the Family Adviser, Carol; and she allows herself to be inculcated into the mores of the adult, mostly female neighbours in order to 'belong, socialise, participate' and to ameliorate any 'resentment' which might be directed at her or her children (*Ditch* 21–2), but the realization of this desire for peace entails a loss of individual purposiveness: she 'just had to drift along "making-do"' (76–7). The narrative voice characterizes the tenants of the Mansions as 'shiftless, rootless, with no rightful claim to anything. Just cut off ... none of them knew the beginning of their existence, the reason for their hand-to-mouth existence, or the result or future of that existence' (31). Adah eventually realizes that the welfare state had reduced them to a common condition 'of apathy, inadequacy and incompetence' (125), and determines not to 'lower herself any more for anything' (127). She has comforted herself that certain symbolic capital which accrues to her – a fine education in Nigeria, having had a Civil Service job in a 'white country' (71) – separates her out from the Mansions community.

Adah and her family's accommodations in room, council flat and finally maisonette flat instantiate different kinds of community available to her. Knowing the difficulty Adah will have finding accommodation, her Yoruba landlord profiteers on the rent he charges her, despite 'the rats, the cockroaches and the filth' (2). The washing of the 'dirty linen' of their relationship in public (5) – the illicitness of his renting the room; his efforts, with his wife's complicity, to scare her with a juju masquerade – sets in train her removal to Pussy Cat Mansions. The efficacy of juju in Nigeria is seemingly grounded for Adah in mystique: the closeness of her living with the Yoruba couple and her class contempt for the man's 'greasy second-hand lounge suit' renders his effort futile. A momentary sense of black 'racial loyalty' is induced in Adah by her sense of the probable racist referents of the juju spectacle for the white onlookers (Fishburn 56). At Pussy Cat Mansions Adah becomes enmeshed, by and large, in a female community: 'always a warm chat, a nice cup of tea and solidarity against any foe' (*Ditch* 71), even if her sense of her superior symbolic capital means that 'she can not identify with them' (Petersen 284). Mrs Cox is ' "Mum" for everybody', 'a working-class Wise Woman', who reminds 'Adah of most African matrons' in her 'sense of mutual help' (*Ditch* 65). The design of the flats suggests an African compound to Adah. 'To most of these women sex was like food. Love was dead, except the maternal love they had naturally for their kids,' observes the narrative voice (61). Adah may draw comfort from the breakdown of '[d]ifferences in culture, colour, backgrounds' (71), but not of differences in gender identity or signs of ethnic identity. She is mortified by the gender ambiguity of a person who takes the masculine lead in dancing with her at a pub to which she is taken by Whoopey and Carol, and goes 'cold' at the thought that 'she had been dancing with a woman'. The trendy clothes of the patrons which include gipsy, African and Moslem designs and a dance style, like the clothes, with 'no definite pattern as such – just anything . . . a sort of drift' (113–14) also disconcert her. Ogunyemi reads the Mansions community as one of the 'living dead', and Adah's situation there as an allegorical 'extension of Nigeria. Her dependence on Carol and others, colonial in essence, has to cease if she must come out of the ditch of dependence, immaturity, poverty, and inferiority' (235–6). This reading of the 'others' overlooks the ethnic mix of the tenants – Nigerian, West Indian, Irish, English – and the number of children identified as being of mixed race. The maisonette flat in Regent's Park to which Adah moves is by comparison with the Mansions ostentatiously and antiseptically white; and there she outfits herself and her children in 'new and clean' clothes. The flats are designed to reinforce the ideological model of the rational economic man: 'private', 'isolat[ed]' (129). And as with Robinson Crusoe, the pedagogical epitome of rational economic man in neoclassical capitalist economics, Adah, in spite of loneliness, grounds her

recovered sense of individual identity in feminine and racializing other-
ing, in her case of the women at the Mansions.[2] Ogunyemi's recuperation of the novel's closure for womanism because it 'incorporates white
people and black men' (237) is optimistic. Adah's shows of goodwill
towards anonymous black men and towards Whoopey, whose very
name sexualizes her and who earlier in the novel 'nod[s] her small
head vigorously like an African lizard resting in the shade' (52), are
underscored by condescension.

The title of *Second-Class Citizen* is a pointed allusion to a policy commitment in a 1966 manifesto of the Conservative Party, referred to by
Enoch Powell in his 'rivers of blood' speech. The commitment was to
'[e]nsure that all immigrants living in Britain are treated in all respects as
equal citizens and without discrimination' (Layton-Henry 218); Powell
offered a contentious reading of Edward Heath's insistence that 'we will
have no "first-class citizens" and "second-class citizens"' (285). Referring implicitly to the classic liberal idea of the private sphere being a
realm in which the state has limited 'legitimate authority to intervene'
(Jaggar 34), he asserts that the (here generically white) citizen had the
'right to discriminate in the management of his own affairs between one
fellow-citizen and another' (Powell 285). One of his prime examples
upholds the right to assert a colour bar in letting accommodation. 'I
kept writing about Powell in my essays and howling abuse at him during
seminars – I was almost as hysterical as he was. I felt as if I was doing
something against this man who thought he could ride on the backs of
black people in the race to Number 10 Downing Street,' Emecheta
acknowledges (*Head Above Water* 110). In searching for accommodation
Adah and Francis are confronted by notices saying '"Sorry, no coloureds"' (*Second-Class Citizen* 59). When Adah, shortly after her arrival in
England, complains about the standard of housing Francis has found for
her and her two children, Francis berates her, telling her that she might
live '"like an élite"' in Lagos, '"but the day you land in England, you
are a second-class citizen"', mocking her class consciousness about the
other Nigerian tenants and identifying it as 'white' by referring to her as
'"my dear young *lady*"' (30). Adah's cultural goals have been formed
within her Igbo community and by her schooling. They are shaped by
many of the forces which Ali Mazrui identifies as destroying African
community by developing individualism: 'Christianity, which weakened tribal custom; Western liberalism which emphasized "the right to
privacy and personal choice"; urbanization, which weakened "the constraints of collective village life"; Western capitalism, which taught the
"pursuit of personal profit"; "the rules of western [sic] education and

science," which stress individual accomplishments (summarized by Fishburn 60). Her father has revered the United Kingdom; the arrival of a Nigerian lawyer trained in the UK is triumphal. The Igbos are 'highly motivated by the middle-class values', and are 'realizing fast that one's saviour from poverty and disease was education' (3), although boys are its more favoured recipients. Literacy in non-African languages, mission schooling founded on Protestant individualism, and noticing that professions in Nigeria are dominated by 'English graduates' (8) fuel Adah's romance of upward social mobility in Nigeria through enhancing professional qualifications in England. Francis will study accountancy, Adah librarianship. These goals are frustrated by the institutionalized racism they encounter in England. The experience of racism, the unfamiliar institution of the nuclear family, and perceived crises of masculinity vitiate Francis's character. He turns his anger and his contempt on Adah, 'treating her as the object [on which] to work out his social failures and amibitions [sic]' (Oko 95). Emecheta documents the effects of pressures to succumb to second-class status on Francis and Adah as black citizens of England and on Adah as Igbo female on that institution so prized by Conservatives, the patriarchal nuclear family. Their marriage breaks down.

Ogunyemi argues that Emecheta 'silences Francis/Onwordi' (239), the 'untold story' being 'what happened to make Francis a changed creature in England', because she does not allow him to 'state his case' (243). Emecheta's narrative voice is more sympathetic to, though not uncritical of, Adah's point of view, and, as Petersen observes, the book becomes more 'centered on domestic issues that are vital to the survival and self-preservation of the woman: sex, motherhood, birth control, economic independence, and a sense of personal value' (285). Emecheta, however, works to incorporate Francis's story as a set of anomic responses to a diminished sense of masculinity and masculine authority.[3] The family becomes for Francis the final site on which he may redeem that masculinity, and on which his failures to do so become most intimately and destructively demeaning. For example, Adah's frigidity, largely a product of fear of pregnancy, is an affront to him. From Adah's point of view, he demands sex as a marital right; she finds it animalistic because of the self-to-other alienation that exists between them. His awareness of her growing hatred for him and desperate need to assert control over her lead him into acts of psychological, physical and epistemic violence, even his burning of the manuscript of her book. He is drawn to the rhetoric of the Jehovah's Witness Church, exhorting Adah to 'the diligence of the virtuous woman, whose price was above rubies ... Jehovah

God would bless such a woman. Her husband would be respected outside the gates' (84). For him the virtuous woman would affirm his worth
through unconditional love, obedience and service.

As Abioseh Michael Porter points out, *Second-Class Citizen* is a
Bildungsroman, in which Emecheta charts Adah's loss of 'naivete and
her juvenile interpretations of love, marriage, and "life outside school"
(as the narrator calls it)' (125). Emecheta emphasizes Adah's isolation
within the nuclear family in England, especially as Francis does not
encourage friendships. Looking back on her adolescence in Nigeria,
Adah remembers 'the love of her parents-in-law', her indulgence by
her servants, the respect of her sisters-in-law (18). She is isolated from
her early Nigerian neighbours in London by her snobbery, her pride in
claiming the goods of first-class citizenship, including a middle-class
job, and keeping her children with her, whereas most Nigerians practise
fostering their children out to a white foster mother, a 'social mother'
(36). 'England is a silent country; people are taught to bottle up their
feelings and screw them tight', thinks Adah (83). Many of her categorical comments – 'She had seen English men and women behave like
humans once or twice' (83) or 'Why was it that men took such a long
time to change, to adapt, to reconcile themselves to new situations'
(100), for example – are represented as being rather too sweeping,
grounded in the vicissitudes of their moments and part of a process of
bottling up her anger in private.

Her prospects of redemptive peace are not placed by Emecheta in the
heterosexual couple. She bonds in platonic friendship with Bill, an anti-
English white Canadian and library co-worker, through reading books
he recommends. James Baldwin gives her faith 'that black was beautiful'
(131). She identifies herself in England with a 'bird; grey, small, solitary,
but contented in its solitude . . . singing, hopping from one window
ledge to another, happy in its lonely freedom', thinking she will achieve
contentment through working to make her children 'enjoy being black,
be proud of being black' (120–1) and a Wordsworthian appreciation of
nature. Ogunyemi reads Adah's relationship with Bill as symbolic adultery, with Bill being the 'surrogate father' of the manuscript Francis
burns (238). She reads Francis's adultery with a white woman as a sign
of his 'degeneration' (243); her implication about Adah's 'adultery' is
clear. The breakdown of Adah and Francis's marriage is attributed ultimately to Adah's abandonment of 'the husband whose horizons were so
limited and limiting' (238). For Ogunyemi leaving a marriage is the act
of 'a Western woman' (230), unNigerian. As Gilroy remarks about the
trope of family in black political discourse based on an 'idea of original

African forms and codes', '[w]hat is racially and ethnically authentic is frequently defined by ideas about sexuality and distinctive patterns of interaction between men and women, which are taken to be expressive of essential difference' (*Small Acts* 197).

Gwendolen (1989), published as *The Family* in the US, was highly topical. 1990 was International Literacy Year; UNESCO had proposed the declaration of such a year in 1985. Marcela Ballara places the move in the context of '[e]ducation' being 'one of the inalienable rights of every person and ha[ving] been recognized as such in both the Universal Declaration of Human Rights and the Universal Covenant on Economic, Social and Cultural Rights' (17). As Christina Davis observes, 'education is really the key to Adah's empowerment' (17). In *Gwendolen* the illiteracy of Jamaican immigrants Sonia and Winston James, and their daughter Gwendolen, has a devastating impact on their lives. The Jameses become 'economic refugees' in England (52). In Jamaica illiteracy is accommodated socially through the practice of using letter-readers and letter-writers; in England the illiteracy of Winston and Sonia isolates them, exacerbates comprehension difficulties, and impairs their ability to provide the 'motivational climate' crucial in their children's acquisition of literacy (Paris and Wixson 38). From early childhood Gwendolen's labour has been crucial to her family; Emecheta makes the point that poverty and ingrained cultural practice dictate that the family has the right to her body. This is important, as researchers on sexual abuse have proposed 'the child's right to her own body' (Herman and Hirschman 204). Granny Naomi and Sonia control Gwendolen's work on the bee farm in Jamaica and within the home; Uncle Johnny, Granny Naomi's friend and lover, and Winston assume control over her body through sexual abuse of the child and incest with the adolescent respectively. The romance of England for Gwendolen, whose only formal education in Jamaica is a few months of cheap private lessons in which she practices writing '"Jesus Christ Our Lord"' (*Gwendolen* 17), is very different from Adah's. Winston's departure for England, the '"Moder Kontry"' (4) means that her parents marry: Gwendolen 'had no idea where or what England was' (2). Coerced by Uncle Johnny into keeping his sexual abuse secret, becoming a chronic bed-wetter as a result of the abuse, being publicly shamed as a bed-wetter, and then receiving little sympathetic support when the abuse becomes public knowledge, Gwendolen is introverted and isolated. News that she is to join her parents and siblings born in England excites her: she longs to recover the innocence of her 'happy, trusting' self, and to make friends who 'would not know about her bed-wetting past nor what Uncle Johnny had done' (28). Her experiences of school in London are catastrophically anomic, because of her literacy problems, being categorized as one of the 'ignorant poor' on the basis of race, 'her inability to understand London English', and her father's stammer (60–1), feeling 'degraded' by being placed in a remedial class, and her mother's failure to appreciate why girls needed to do homework 'when there was so much work that needed doing at home' (66–7). School, an instrument of the English state, becomes for her 'a place of humiliation, a place of shame' likened to her feelings about Uncle Johnny's invasion of 'the privacy of her body' (93); it makes her feel 'reduced as a person' (81). The narrative voice explicitly condemns the indifference of the school to her 'dignity as a person' which causes her disruptive behaviour (61), insisting that 'if anyone needs education it is the Gwendolens of this world' (83). After Gwendolen leaves home, Emmanuel, the young Greek friend thought to be the father of her child, patiently teaches her to read things relevant to her life, newspapers and a book by a black woman *A Black Person's Story*.

In her representation of father-daughter incest Emecheta adapts the findings of influential studies of the subject. For example, sociological research shows that '[f]or the daughter, the duty to fulfill her father's sexual demands may evolve almost as an extension of her role as "little mother" in the family' (Herman and Hirschman 45). This is close to Winston's view of his sexual right to his daughter. In these cases the mother is often 'ill, incapacitated, or for some reason emotionally unavailable to her husband and child' (Herman and Hirschman 45). At the time the incest takes place Sonia has returned to Jamaica, in the mistaken belief that her mother Naomi is ill (she cannot read the telegram which informs her that Naomi has died). Grieving, shocked, experiencing a stillbirth, she becomes in Jamaica 'not completely mad, but... not herself' (*Gwendolen* 111). Sonia cannot write to Winston, he cannot write to her, her Jamaican friends do not want to broach the sensitive topic of her having gone 'crazy' in a letter to her husband (112). A Nigerian friend of Winston's and parishioners of his charismatic church suspect his incest but do not reach out to support Gwendolen. When Winston hints at his incestuous desire, Ilochina the friend thinks that the man's West African cultural heritage has been killed by the legacy of slavery. He explains to Winston that incest is a 'sin against the Earth' and the ' "land is the soul and life-blood of a community. That the land never belonged to an individual. That from the land we are nourished. That when we die we go back to the land to manure it, in order to feed the next generation. That so our "Chi" or souls go in circles. That to offend the land or Earth was to offend something greater than one's soul"'. The perpetrator of incest would '"surely be killed by an earth force like thunder, ... natural electricity, drowning"' (121). Emecheta's retribution against Winston follows this precept. He is thrown '"into a drum of tar"' by a '"gas explosion"' at work (167). Ilochina says to Sonia: '"You buy everything here, even beautiful funerals. This is not like African people. In my town, our people will not bury your husband, I'm sorry to say. But here in England, money buys honour"' (168).

Gwendolen, who has given birth to a child by her father, is redeemed by the quality of her relationship with her daughter Iyamide, whose Yoruba name means '"my mother, my friend, my sister is here"' (177), greater literacy, and a trusting friendship with Emmanuel. The child's name marks a reconnection with her African heritage. Emecheta has evidently been criticized over the cross-racial aspect of the idealized male-female relationship between Gwendolen and Emmanuel. Ogunyemi reports that Emecheta 'retorted that it was not so much that redemption lay for troubled blacks through whites but that the modern family is beginning to take different forms among less racially conscious youths' (277).

In *Kehinde*, which is set in the late 1970s and early 1980s, Nigerian immigrants Kehinde and Albert Okolo are outwardly materially comfortable, but their marriage has inner tensions, which when played out lead to its breakdown. After 18 years in England they own 'a typical East London mid-terrace house', and sublet bedrooms (2), have two children, both work, Albert as a storekeeper and Kehinde as a bank clerk, and Albert can fantasize about returning to Nigeria, a place of 'sunshine, freedom, easy friendship, warmth' where he would be able to 'show off his new life style, his material success' (6). He feels that his masculine status is compromised by the more liberal gender norms of English life and the fact that his wife outearns him, and longs for the kind of life he imagines his father had: 'a life of comparative ease for men, where men were men and women were women, and one was respected as somebody'. Kehinde, Albert thinks, racializing her perceived disloyalty to his values, is 'full of herself, playing the role of a white, middle-class woman' (35). His nostalgia, like the 'idea of tradition' in contemporary black political discourse in the West analysed by Gilroy, 'provides a temporary home in which shelter and consolation from the vicious forces that threaten the racial community (imagined or otherwise) can be found' (*Black Atlantic* 188–9). Gilroy highlights the centrality of 'ideas about masculinity, femininity, and sexuality...in this redemptive journey back to Africa' (193). When Kehinde becomes pregnant, threatening the economic foundation of Albert's dream of return, he is prepared to compromise his Igbo moral understanding by coercing her into having an abortion. Kehinde's conservatism on Igbo womanliness becomes apparent in her vehement denunciation of Mary Elikwu. Mary's circumstances – separated from an abusive husband, six children, living in a council flat – parallel those of Adah in *In the Ditch* and of Emecheta at one stage of her life, and in her sense that women who have abortions are no better than street prostitutes. She derives a great deal of her womanly pride from playing the roles of mother and of the respectable wife of the 'Igbo family man in London' (*Kehinde* 35).

Personally Emecheta does not support abortion (*Head Above Water* 70); pointedly Kehinde comes to realize that her 'father's *chi* was coming back' in the embryo she had aborted (*Kehinde* 32). Kehinde's life after the shock of the decision to abort becomes a journey to 'self-awareness which finally enables her to act on her own behalf' (Gohrisch 134) and to a 'spiritual reunion' with her dead twin sister Taiwo (138). The young, unmarried white girl Julia in *The New Tribe*, adopted by the middle-class Arlingtons, becomes pregnant by working-class Ray, her sexual relationship with whom resulted from mutual loneliness, bore-dom and uncertainty. While Ray wants marriage and their child, and is confident of the support of his working-class family, Julia thinks this future is uninhabitable. Her adoptive mother Ginny Arlington arranges for her brother Robert to set up an abortion for Julia. Emecheta suggests that the decision to abort is based on an individualistic ethos and shame. The older Julia realizes that she could have been a tertiary student and a single mother, and now be enjoying the communal sense of having 'someone' (152). She also feels that she was not allowed enough time to think through the decision. Ray poses the question to Chester, the black protagonist of the novel, also adopted by the Arling-tons, 'Would you rather your mother had aborted you than had you adopted?' (59).

In *Kehinde* Emecheta contrasts the institutional means available to Albert and Kehinde after their staggered return to Nigeria for them to realize their cultural goals. Albert enters a polygamous marriage with a university lecturer, Rike, fathers more children, legally owns the pro-perty Kehinde has worked for and shipped back to Nigeria to enjoy been-to status, and enjoys the respectful formalities of the status accorded him as a man. Kehinde finds Albert healthy, 'more imposing' in his Nigerian-style clothes, 'exud[ing] a new confidence', 'thoroughly at home' (66), but is 'humiliated' by her sense of her lost marital status, her difficulties in finding work because of her age and lack of educational certificates, and the discipline meted out to her by Albert's sisters for want of deference to him (94). She comes to appreciate Mary Elikwu's decision to get tertiary qualifications to secure '[t]he saving grace' of independence (95). Albert's new marriage and health sour when he becomes unemployed, but by the novel's close he has taken yet another wife. Kehinde returns to Thatcherite London keen about the idea of greater economic independence, achieves a sociology degree, works as a cleaner before getting a civil service job, and takes a younger Caribbean lover, tenant Michael Gibson. The novel ends triumphally with Kehinde asserting her rights as a person to son Joshua, refusing to 'live' for her 'children' or be dispossessed of her house and looked after by him, justifying her new relationship, declaring ' "I just don't have the energy to be the carrier of everybody's burdens any more" ' (139), and affirming to the spirit of Taiwo, ' "Claiming my right does not make me less of a mother, not less of a woman. If anything it makes me more human" ' (141).

'Throughout the 1980s the field of adoption policy was one of the front lines of confrontation over the meaning of "race" in Britain', Phil Cohen explains. 'It was also the site of a great historical reckoning, where customary practices which had long characterised the British adoption scene were for the first time defined, and challenged as racist' (60). Emecheta implicitly places the story of Chester, the main narrative in *The New Tribe*, in the context of debates around transracial adoption and shifts in adoption practices and policy recommendations. His mother Catherine Mba, identified as Nigerian, has followed the publicity surrounding the Arlingtons's adoption of Julia, a child found abandoned in a Tesco bag. Pregnant again, this time with twins and a new partner, Catherine feels unable to continue raising her 18-month-old son, and requests that Social Services place Chester with the Christian Arlingtons. (Arthur Arlington is a vicar.) Emecheta dedicates the book '[t]o my students and friends at the Mental After Care Centre in Northampton, where we realize that many mental problems can be caused by people who mean well'. Catherine, the Arlingtons and Social Services 'mean well' by Chester in terms of the standards of the day. Catherine understands adoption as part of a 'civilising mission' (Cohen, 'Yesterday's words' 49). 'The Arlingtons', Emecheta writes, 'were like a good strong tree, under whose branches Chester and Julia sheltered' (*New Tribe* 10). In the Arlington marriage the needs of Arthur and Ginny often remain unarticulated, and this pattern is replicated in the adoptive children. Neither Social Services nor Arthur and Ginny understand Chester's cultural needs as a black child growing up in a small, insular, white community, in which his skin colour will always mark him out as different, not ordinary. This is particularly apparent in Ginny's main cultural concession to Chester's Nigerian heritage. She is largely ignorant about Nigeria, but does try to find out more in the local library. Finding no children's books about Africa there, she makes one for Chester, basing the story on 'an African folktale she had read' (8). The story becomes for Chester the unwitting starting point for an elaboration of a 'myth of origins' entailing 'exalted . . . parentage, associated with birth . . . family', coming into a 'rightful inheritance' in Nigeria which will 'magically' redress the 'wrongs suffered as a result of . . . abandonment' (Cohen 70). The myth compensates for the deracination of the 'black child adrift on the oceans of whiteness that Britain supposedly represents' (Gilroy, Foreword xii). In childhood he confides his myth, in which Catherine is not his birth mother, only to his adoptive sister Julia. Chester's scant sense of black British history is developed through chance attendance at a lecture about the eighteenth-century black Briton Olaudah Equiano. A copy of Equiano's slave narrative becomes as precious to Chester as his bible. Transracial adoption practices in the wake of the 'historical reckoning' to which Cohen refers are more aware of the potential problems for the child of deracination, displacement from ethnic communities, geographical dislocation from these communities, and the ignorance of prospective parents about her or his cultural background. Agencies handling adoptions are more likely to weigh these factors up in assessing possible placements.[4]

Emecheta emphasises Chester's feeling of unbelonging, produced often through small, casual acts of racism, but suggests through the black character Esther Willoughby that Chester's home is Britain. She tells him: 'We don't belong in Africa, we're British. Black British maybe, but this is our home now. . . . Look how black people have changed the face of British culture. Don't you want to be part of that?' (113). Chester's return to Nigeria is a saga of misadventure, cultural alienation and catastrophe. Like the Nigerian immigrant Enoch Ugwu, whom Chester chooses as a surrogate father figure, having originally met him by chance, Chester has to find ways, Emecheta suggests, to adapt to living as a responsible black man in a country in which to do so 'is a struggle' (83). The character strengths drawn out in Chester by life with the Arlingtons and the Ugwus are central to this process. The ending suggests that Chester and Esther are becoming a couple, and that Esther will help Chester realize a rightful place in black British culture.

Emecheta's novels *In the Ditch, Second-Class Citizen, Gwendolen, Kehinde* and *The New Tribe* focus on family life. The 'invocation of "race" as family is everywhere' in contemporary black political discourse, comments Gilroy (*Small Acts* 194). The visions of communal reconstruction Emecheta articulates through the empowering of her female protagonists are, often controversially, not centred on an idealized model of the black heterosexual couple, reproducing the cultural norms of an 'imagined, though not always imaginary, idea of original African forms and codes' (197). In *The New Tribe* Emecheta celebrates the potential of Chester and Esther as a couple, but their cultural being will be black British. Esther cites an apposite proverb: 'Africa is no longer our home. We have stayed away in the market too long, as Nigerians say' (145).

Notes

1. Ogunyemi writes: 'one can almost declare that she kills him with her one-sided disclosures, because insults and curses are injurious to the spirit' (242).
2. Adah likens herself to Crusoe (129). On Crusoe and rational economic man see Hewitson.
3. Eustace Palmer, overlooking this thematic, finds it 'incredible that a normal young man could be so consistently unreasonable' (28).
4. The debates around race and adoption policies are cogently set out in Gaber and Aldridge.

10

'Ellowen, Deeowen': Salman Rushdie and The Migrant's Desire

Leela Gandhi

The Satanic Verses, the only one of Salman Rushdie's novels to be set substantially in England, must be read within the paradigm established by his wider fictional project. Like his other novels, *The Satanic Verses* uses the discourse of migrancy as the launching pad for an attack on nationalism. And yet, this chapter will argue, for all his attempts to underscore the objective political validity of his anti-nationalist narratives, Rushdie's work is severely constrained by its libidinal sub-text. Departing from India, or arriving in England, his fiction is, as Fredric Jameson might put it, private rather than public, poetic rather than practical, therapeutic rather than political.[1] In his 'subcontinental' novels and themes, for instance, the author's private deliriums are more easily accessible to analysis. The émigré-hero's guilty pessimism about the home he is leaving, his patricidal fantasies, his obsessive fear of maternal engulfment, each cast a distinct shadow on the 'politics' of his revulsion for the nation. In contrast, in *The Satanic Verses*, and incidentally, in the few England scenes of *The Ground Beneath Her Feet*, it looks as though England has finally made a politics out of Rushdian migrancy. The former novel, especially, seems redolent of British new socialism and 'new social movements'. Drawing upon these sources quite explicitly, Rushdie identifies himself with the ideological forces that launched a powerful attack on conservative nationalism in the grim age of Thatcherism. But the allegorical commitments of his postmodern fiction backfire, revealing more than they intend in the text's misogyny, and disturbing thematization of postcolonial homosexual panic. Certainly, *The Satanic Verses* documents a revolutionary slice of contemporary British history, and, to be fair, it also explicates to good effect the migrant's subversive hybridization of the imperial metropolis. But what is the psychic cost of Rushdie's postcolonial hybridity? Which textual neuroses attend and complicate his negotiations with the English nation? Before turning to these questions in the main body of this chapter, let us begin with some context setting: first, through a consideration of Rushdie's politics of migrancy, and secondly, with a brief review of the Rushdian migrant's subjective struggle with the subcontinental nation.

Throughout his writing, Rushdie celebrates the migrant condition as the basis for an alternative epistemology. In *The Ground*, for instance, the redoubtable Sir Darius Cama develops a theory of 'outsideness' which proposes that 'the only people who see the whole picture are the ones who step out of the frame' (43). *Shame* extols the migrant as a magus who has achieved a 'conquest of gravity' (85) and, with it, unique gifts of humour and hopefulness. And an essay, 'The Location of Brazil', brings the distinct quality of zen to the art of migrant intelligence: 'The effect of mass migrations has been the creation of radically new types of human being.... The migrant suspects reality: having experienced several ways of being, he understands their illusory nature. To see things plainly you have to cross a frontier' (*Imaginary Homelands* 125).

If these hyperbolic apostrophes to migrancy verge on the nonsensical, they come with a deceptive critical sting. For migrancy is the ground from which Rushdie launches his bitter and often thoughtless critique of nationalism and other cognate solidarities or cults of belonging. In *Shame*, for instance, it is the migrant narrator – 'Outsider! Trespasser!' (28) – whose task it is to disclose the failure of the Pakistani nationalist project. Likewise, in *The Ground*, yet another emigrating narrator, Rai, ceaselessly laments the bankruptcy of the postcolonial Indian nation-state. In these and other novels, the onerous responsibility of dismantling nationalism devolves upon the migrant-figure for the reason that, as 'The Location of Brazil' tells us: 'To be a migrant is, perhaps, to be the only species of human being free of the shackles of nationalism (to say nothing of its ugly sister patriotism). It is a burdensome freedom' (124).

As is well acknowledged, it is in such assertions of its anti-national politics that Rushdie's 'migrant hypothesis' resonates with prevailing postcolonial orthodoxies.[2] Yet, reviewing his corpus more critically, we find that Rushdie's censure of the post*colonized* nation can be read as an apology for the emigration of his heroes. Seeking fictional exoneration for these émigré-heroes, he insists upon the uninhabitability of the subcontinent either by inventing a threat to their lives, or through the device of family quarrels and deaths which conclusively sever ties with 'home'. Moraes Zogoiby, hero of the densely Oedipal *The Moor's*

Last Sigh, for example, is compelled to go West to escape retribution for the murder of his mother's former lover, the Hindu communalist demagogue, Raman Fielding. As he is leaving, he comes to learn of the secret affair between his remote father and his own estranged beloved, Uma Saraswati. Embittered by the knowledge of Abraham Zogoiby's sexual treacheries, not to mention his implication in the corruptions of the Bombay underworld, the prodigal Moraes is offered one last libidinal satisfaction by the dream-work of the narrative. Abraham perishes in a bomb blast, allowing his son finally to disown his genetic and geographic origins. Looking down on his abandoned city from the transcendental vantage of an aeroplane, he rationalizes his exit, thus: 'There was nothing holding me to Bombay anymore. It was no longer my Bombay, no longer special.... Something had ended' (376). The oedipal investments of this novel, its patricidal fantasies, are re-worked in *The Ground*, where two heroes, Ormus and Rai, must lose fathers to facilitate their flight to England. Once again, in a narrative that replicates the tricky substitutions of the dream, Ormus Cama is free to approach the creative opportunities of England only after his brother, Cyrus, suffocates their father to death. Rai's father, by contrast, obligingly kills himself. Fortuitously orphaned, Rai is also able to flee the 'Caligulan barbarity of India' (248) following a direct threat to his life from corrupt politician Piloo Doodhwala. The refrain of his 'farewell, my country' is, accordingly, acutely defensive (248). 'As it happens I didn't go of my free will', he protests. 'As it happens I was driven out like a dog. I had to run for my life' (203). This iterative killing of fathers, and flight to creative freedom of sons, in Rushdie's emigrant narratives, is served with another disturbing fantasy about the physical destruction of the subcontinent. Pakistan goes up in flames at the end of *Shame*; Bombay blows apart under the impact of 3,000 kilograms of RDX explosive in *The Moor*; India is devastated by earthquakes in the 'Dies Irae' chapter of *The Ground*. Rushdie's vandalizing of the 'real' subcontinent, in such narrative conclusions, performs a perverse utopianization. It literally renders India/Pakistan into 'no place' so that they can be properly reclaimed as 'imaginary homelands', in other words, as fiction. 'Writers in my position', he writes, 'exiles or emigrants or expatriates ... will, in short, create fictions, not actual cities or villages, but invisible ones, imaginary homelands' (*Imaginary Homelands* 10). Constrained by such solipsism, Rushdie's assault on the subcontinent's nations is decisively poetic; the opportunistic work of therapy rather than the puritanical labour of the organic intellectual. More Freud than Marx (see Jameson 69).

Writing, as it were, under the 'sign of Freud' about the subcontinent, then, Rushdie makes his heroes secure their creativity by liberating themselves from their past. The past, he pontificates, 'is a country from which we have all emigrated', thus producing a *sententia* which immediately posits the departing migrant in an antagonistic and ironic relation to the category of subcontinental history. Lamenting the prior contamination of Pakistani history, the migrant-narrator of *Shame* treats the nation's archive as luggage which must be made to conform to airline restrictions and to the capacity of the traveller's suitcase: 'I, too, face the problem of history: what to retain, what to dump...' (87). On a similar note, an essay on deliberate errata and unreliable narration in *Midnight's Children* privileges (the migrant's) memory over (Indian) history, in the interests of story-telling. Saleem Sinai, it argues, achieves narrative 'meaning' in this novel through his semantic competition with, and denial of, historical authority: 'He wants so to shape his material that the reader will be forced to concede his central role. He is cutting up history to suit himself...' (24). Defiantly *sui generis*, the Rushdian emigre and his artefacts refuse to concede their prior fabrication by the forces of history.

In sharp contrast, writing about the migrant's condition in England – it would appear, under the 'sign of Marx' – Rushdie consecrates history as the cornucopia of revolutionary or political meaning. Now, liberation is to be secured in, rather than from, the past; history is a resource to be owned, rather than squandered with the careless profligacy of the emigre-hero: 'the past to which we belong is an English past, the history of immigrant Britain' (20). To this England-inspired historicism in Rushdie, and its implications for his (apparent) politicization of migrancy, we might now devote some attention.

Let us begin with the migrant clientele of the Hot Wax Club, scene of much of the political action in *The Satanic Verses*. Following the 'Brickhall' riots of this novel, racist police and prejudiced media-men will 'misread' the hip-hop, Hindi-pop subculture of the hot-waxers through the vector of ancient stereotypes: witchcraft, sexual perversion, cannibalism. But, we are instructed to read the clubbers differently, as historians disinterring the nation's past to reveal a secret history of immigration. Audio-visual in its preferred historiographical methods, the club is decorated with waxworks of England's notable but hitherto unacknowledged migrant ancestors: Mary Seacole, Abdul Karim, Grace Jones, Septimus Serverus, Ignatius Sancho. Far from cloistering this counter-pantheon within the language of hagiography, however, the deejay, Pinkwalla, uses the migrant past, strategically, to lay claim to the nation's present: '*Now-mi-feel-indignation-when-dem-talk-immigration-when-dem-make-insinuation-we-no-part-a-de-nation-anmi-make-proclamation-a-de-true-situation-how-we-make-contribution-since-de-Rome-Occupation*' (292). There is violence too in Pinkwalla's inspired scratch-and-mix history, which finds expression each night in the ritual burning of certain waxwork villains: 'Powell, Edward Long, all the local avatars of Legree . . . *Maggie-maggie-maggie*'(292, 293).

The politics of the Hot Wax Club are, in microcosm, the politics of *The Satanic Verses*; recognizing the line from Powell through to Thatcher as marking the emergence in England of a virulent conservative nationalism, scrupulously defined against the nation's coloured migrants. A brief background would be useful here. Responding to the collapse of empire, the malign genius of Powellism lay in revivifying the declining spirit of English patriotism by proposing an internal war against the coloured immigrants who had arrived in England during the 1950s and 1960s. What Powellism began, of course, Thatcher absorbed into the popular and administrative structures of the English nation-state.[3] Following the example of her predecessor, she was careful to transform the simple rhetoric of racism into a specifically nationalist invective against the immigrant, the foreigner, the outsider. Two specifically Thatcherite 'events' confirm the linking, within the 'new racism', of 'discourses of patriotism, nationalism, xenophobia, Englishness, Britishness' (Gilroy, *There Ain't* 43). First, by legalizing the concept of patriality – proof that one of your grandparents had been born in the UK as a qualification for citizenship – the Nationality Act of 1981 expressly excluded numerous coloured British migrants from the privilege of national membership.[4] Secondly, we must consider the fiasco that was Falklands. Using this episode as a tonic for Britain's post-imperial blues, Thatcher also drew upon a specifically anti-migrant discourse in her postulation of the Falklands intervention as a war to expel foreigners (here Argentinians) from British territory. In effect, telling the 'Argies' to go back where they came from, Thatcher's offensive cemented a costly opposition between the nation and its migrants.

Thatcher's England, then, supplies the context for *The Satanic Verses*. So too, Rushdie's developing ideas about the insurgent politics of migrancy owe much to the shifting ideology of the British Left during the late 1980's.[5] Faced by Thatcher's co-option of the old working class, the Left, as various commentators have observed, was compelled to patchwork an altogether new constituency out of Britain's female, unskilled, unemployed, black and migrant sub-class. Many of the essays gathered in Rushdie's *Imaginary Homelands* reflect the emergence and effects of some of these new alliances, especially the rise of a politicized migrant population, fiercely resistant to the exclusions of conservative nationalism, and quizzical about the claims of an alternative 'left' nationalism. But, as we have glimpsed already, it is in *The Satanic Verses* that Rushdie fully explores the politicization of migrant sensibility in late 1980s England. While he does this in part through the heteroglossia of the minor characters, the main exposition is through the dialectic between the competing migrant rationalities of Gibreel Farishta and Saladin Chamcha. The former is an ageing Bollywood Muslim movie star with an overtaxed talent for Hindu 'theologicals'; the latter an unemployed Anglophile radio artist with a gift for ventriloquizing the 'voices' of products in English advertizing jingles. Where Farishta has long mimicked the sacred gods of a rival religion, Chamcha has been parodist *par excellence* of the secular deities devoutly pursued by a rival race. Both are compelled, by magical realist circumstances, to exit from careers founded on the practice of inauthenticity. However, while Farishta, described as a migrant in the Ovidian mould, remains more or less 'continuous' through all the impurities and metamorphoses (desired and inflicted) which interpellate his existence, Chamcha, taking his cue from Lucretius, proves incapable of containing hybridity (see 427). He is inclined, instead, to shed the cloying skin of old selves in favour of the newer ones on offer. Consequently, where the Ovidian Farishta has the resources to maintain and to project his integrity – the truth of his own self – in the shifting English world around him, the Lucretian Chamcha is, by contrast, painfully impressionable. 'For are they not conjoined opposites, these two, each man the other's shadow?' Rushdie observes, 'One seeking to be transformed into the foreignness he admires, the other preferring, contemptuously, to transform . . .' (426).

If Gibreel – a secularized angel stolen from Islam – must redeem England, Chamcha's part is to be redeemed from England.[6] One politicizes, the other needs to be politicized. With a didacticism that seems generically inappropriate for the anti-realist novel, *The Satanic Verses* uses Chamcha as a text for the education of migrant desire, here the unsuitable love of Englishness. Plummeting to the ground, following the explosion of the aeroplane carrying him back to the Isles, Chamcha experiences this traumatic return as a Fall, with severe implications for his former habitation in the garden of England. Metamorphosed, upon descent, into a goat, he is allegorically brought into the shameful knowledge of his racial alterity. And, as Rushdie's text subtly displaces the authority of Genesis with that of Fanon, Chamcha discovers that his disgraceful knowledge of racial difference is an effect of the English gaze, tutored anew in Thatcher's England into racist ways of seeing. In *Black Skin, White Masks*, it will be remembered, Fanon attributes his painful knowledge of (monstrous) blackness to the estranging gaze of the white onlooker. The 'Look, a Negro!' which surgically excises his former wholeness, condemns Fanon to revise himself into a figure of negative alterity: 'My body was given back to me sprawled out, distorted, recoloured.... The Negro is an animal, the Negro is bad... The Negro is ugly' (112, 113). So too, in a detention centre for migrants who, like him, have been mutated into animals, Chamcha learns about the powers of racist description. A man altered into a 'manticore' instructs him, thus: 'They describe us.... That's all. They have the power of description, and we succumb to the pictures they construct' (168). To submit to the transformative powers of Englishness as a black man, Saladin Chamcha learns, is a dangerous thing.

Still seeking admission into the mother-country, however, Chamcha recites the magic of his citizenship to incredulous immigration officials, forgetting that after the Nationality Act, his colour and goatishness defy the requirements of patriality. Anyone, as Benedict Anderson once argued, 'can in theory learn the language of the nation they seek to join and through the process of naturalization become a citizen enjoying formal equality under the law' (Gilroy, *There Ain't* 45). So Chamcha naively believes, even though well before the constitutional injustices of 1981, Mr Powell had insisted that citizenship was a racial rather than legal privilege: 'the West Indian does not by being born in England, become an Englishman. In law he becomes a United Kingdom citizen by birth; in fact he is a West Indian or an Asian still' (qtd. in Gilroy, 46). The immigration officials harassing Chamcha remember all this. 'Look at yourself' – and again we are brought into the presence of that refrain from Fanon – 'You're a fucking Packy billy. Sally-who? – What kind of a name is that for an Englishman?' (163). It is at this moment that Chamcha experiences his first 'scrap of anger' (163); a righteous anger which will gradually prove an antidote to his goatish metamorphosis. But, in order to train his incipient oppositional rage, Chamcha must first enter the space of his people, seeking a new habitation among Bangladeshi resteraunters, Pakistani raconteurs, Rastas, migrants, others.

In forcing Chamcha into the 'space of the people', Rushdie appears to shed the agoraphobia and pessimism about grassroots politics which runs through his subcontinental novels. In *Midnight's Children*, for instance, it is the burgeoning crowd, the destructive people of India, who threaten the life of Saleem Sinai, and cast their long shadow upon the nation's posterity: 'they will trample me underfoot, the numbers marching one two three, four hundred million five hundred six, reducing me to specks of voiceless dust, just as in good time they will trample my son...and his son...until the thousand and first generation...' (463). Chamcha, by contrast, will be saved by his people. Excluded by England, he will discover a curative likeness among the hospitable population of the Shaandar Cafe's B&B. Here, the eminently desirable Mishal Sufyan will induct him into the dissident knowledge of 'the Street' (283): 'from her Chamcha learned the fables of the new Kurus and Pandavas, the white racists and black 'self-help' or vigilante posses starring in this modern *Mahabharata* or, more accurately, *Mahavilayet*' (283). Later in the novel, the reformed Chamcha will find himself part of a riot militating against the repressive forces of the State: 'Saladin Chamcha...found a *testudo* of helmet men with plastic shields at the ready moving towards him across the Fields at a steady, inexorable trot' (454).

And so, we might argue, the allegory of the Fall with which Rushdie inaugurates the process of Chamcha's consciousness-raising, finds a novel resolution. Like his scriptural predecessors, Chamcha experiences his rude expulsion from Eden as the loss of everything, which has, in his case, constituted the bounty of his Englishness: culture, city, wife, job. However, Rushdie insists – especially in this book – in a secular world it is still possible to protest against one's dispossession.[7] The victims of civil society (as opposed to those of a religious culture) can recover their dignity by taking positive action, and through an appeal to the law. So Chamcha proclaims in a speech which amply demonstrates his successful rehabilitation as a migrant opposed to the poisonous rhetoric of Thatcherite nationalism: 'When you've fallen from the sky, been abandoned by your friend, suffered police brutality, metamorphosed into a goat, lost your work as well as your wife, learned the power of hatred and regained human shape, what is there left to do but...demand your rights?' (402). In acknowledging this version of Chamcha's political renovation, however, we are still leaving out something crucial in the allegorical work of the Fall which afflicts him. Returning to the early 'immigration' scenes of *The Satanic Verses*, we discover in the novel's iterative evocation of Genesis, the suggestion that Chamcha's formative experience of racial alterity (or cultural dispossession) is accompanied by/as the disgrace of (homo)sexual knowledge. And, as we will see, in pursuing this other reading of Chamcha's Fall we come up against the complicating libidinal investments of Rushdie's novel.

What really happens to Saladin Chamcha in 'the windowless police van' that takes him to the detention centre? The question evokes – as it is possibly meant to – the query at the heart of *A Passage to India*: what really happens to Adela Quested in the Marabar caves? Like Forster, Rushdie refuses the inducements of an explicit rape narrative. And yet, in a perverse explication of the desire actually haunting the former text, he supplies his readers with a densely implicative catalogue of (homo)-sexual abuse. 'When they pulled his pyjamas down...', the scene begins, chronicling the precise moment and nature of Chamcha's goat-ish self-knowledge. His subsequent 'degradation' and humiliation is performed through the cheap innuendo of the officers, and in their relentless (homo)sexualization of racial violence:

> 'Opening up time, Packy; let's see what you're made of!' Red-and-white-stripes were dragged off the protesting Chamcha... 'What's this, the'?' joked Novak... giving it a playful tweak. 'Fancy one of us, maybe?'... 'no wonder he's so fucking *horny.*'
>
> (157–8)

If repressed in these scenes, homosexuality speaks its name and rises to the surface of the text in/as the language of allegation. The Liverpool supporters among the officers offend their Spurs colleagues 'by alleging that the great Danny Blanchflower was a "luxury" player, a cream puff, flower by name, pansy by nature; – whereupon the offended claque responded by shouting that in the case of Liverpool it was the supporters who were the bum-boys' (161). In this angry confrontation, each faction is determined to demonstrate the homosexual identifications of the other (as they have earlier done with Chamcha). When they agree, then, to vent their combined fury on Chamcha – 'to demonstrate exactly what they meant by "tearing apart", "bollocking", "bottling" and the like', what, we may ask again, really happens? Two things. First, the senior officers turn a blind eye to the frenzy of their juniors with that notorious phrase which has long haunted the history of the rape mis-trial, viz; 'boys would have their fun' (162). Second, and as we know, Chamcha starts to be cured of England: ' *"This isn't England", he thought, not for the first or the last time.* How could it be, after all; where in all that moderate and common-sensical land was there room for such a police van in whose interior such events as these might plausibly transpire?' (emphasis added, 158).[8]

The police van episode is a small scene in a massive book. Never-theless, Rushdie's dramatization of homosexual panic at the origins of

Chamcha's political education must give pause. Why does Chamcha have to undergo a specifically homosexual humiliation in order to achieve a distance from England? How can we explain the performative homophobia of the text, its postulation of homosexual activity only as violation or racism or *threat*? Two other novels illuminate the concerns of the present discussion. In *The Ground*, Ormus Cama's convalescence from the sickness of England-love is also intimately bound up with the strength of his emerging homophobia. Arriving in England, he discovers that he is the object of homosexual obsession for Mull Standish, his benefactor and employer on the sea-based Radio Freddie. Desperate to abandon ship – 'Let me out of here' – Ormus only agrees to stay under the terms of a firm 'no sex' proviso (273, 263).[9] Already alert to (homo)-sexual panic, Cama's prejudice is further sharpened after repeated raids on Radio Freddie from sodomitical drug squad cops. Hawthorne and Waldo Standish (the homosexual's sons) are amused about these repeated incursions: 'My fucking rectum's getting so habituated to being probed by these rozzers' rubber-gloved fingers...it's beginning to like it. Waldo gravely assents. Probably something in the genes' (278). Notably, Cama's reaction to these examinations is articulated specifically in opposition to Hawthorne's and Waldo's, as an unamused disidentification from homosexual desire and, with it, from England: 'Ormus, however, finds it hard to see the funny side. Naked and inno-cent before the officers of the law, suffering their jolly rogerings, he shakes with rage and shame. *This in an England his father never knew, at whose existence he could not have guessed*' (emphasis added, 278). Later in the novel, in another revealing and anxious assertion of heterosexual preference, Cama will begin a punitive sexual relationship with the lesbian lover of Standish's former wife (see 288–9, 296).

If Chamcha and Cama demonstrate the circuits, in Rushdie's fiction, between homophobia and revolutionary anglophobia, Aires da Gama, in *The Moor*, explicates the reverse, viz; the wires connecting homosexu-ality and reactionary anglophilia. The novel constantly asserts the seam-lessness between da Gama's apologies for empire (he has an English bulldog called Jawaharlal) and his incurable homosexuality. Tellingly, Rushdie insistently invokes cliches of effeminacy and impotence to describe da Gama's sexual deviance: 'He bowed to her...the bow of a Restoration dandy, his right hand spiralling foppishly outwards, the right foot extended, its toe deliciously cocked...' (49). The effeminizing of Aires da Gama is instructive, for it helps us to understand Chamcha's and Cama's homosexual panic as an updated or residual version of older fears about colonial emasculation. Sara Suleri is apposite here. In a reading which productively dissociates gender from the imperial 'feminisation of the colonised subcontinent',[10] Suleri draws attention, anew, to the homoerotic economy of the colonial encounter. The 'discourse of effeminacy', she argues, 'makes evident that the colonial gaze is not directed to the inscrutability of an Eastern bride but to the greater sexual ambivalence of the effeminate groom' (Suleri 16). Suleri carefully foregrounds the positive and mutual imperatives of desire within the colonial homoerotic economy. However, as she acknowledges, the rhetoric of colonized effeminacy also finds expression as imperial invective and so, as colonial phobia/anxiety. Indeed, it is precisely in response to the fear of effeminacy that subcontinental nationalism, all too often, devotes itself to a dubious re-masculation of the race. Read with reference to this background, Chamcha's (and Cama's) homosexual panic is revealed for what it is: the other side of the heterosexual aggression with which Gibreel Farishta approaches a feminized England (the two men, we might recall, are described as 'conjoined opposites'). Thus, clearly reversing the sexual politics of empire, *The Satanic Verses* submits to a derivative rendition of the 'postcolonial moment' as a project predominantly, if not exclusively, concerned with the recuperation and noisy reassertion of colonial masculinity. And if, as we have seen, this project aligns itself – as it must – with the forces of homophobia, it also borrows heavily, as we will see, from the forces of misogyny.

In the much celebrated 'A City Visible but Unseen' section of the book, Gibreel proposes to 'tropicalize' London (354). The introduction of a national siesta, improved street life, flamboyant flora and fauna, spicier food', will, he believes, positively transform 'British reserve' and the 'English commitment to a "high workrate"' (355). But, while this section demonstrates the culturally disruptive genius of Gibreel's migrant imagination, let us not forget that he also achieves the project of adulterating Englishness through the conduit of the female (English) body. His arrival in England begins as a sexual encounter with Rosa Diamond who, as Homi Bhabha observes, 'represents the English *Heim* or homeland' in – as he neglects to observe – pointedly feminized form (Bhabha, *Location* 167).[11] To transgress the borders of this body and arrive in England, Gibreel must insert himself into the place of Rosa's dead husband, Henry Diamond, thus activating Bhabha's favoured trope of colonial mimicry, but also a Rushdian one of postcolonial adultery.

The Rosa Diamond episode uses the female body, allegorically, to convey the migrant's voyage into the imperial metropolis. Elsewhere, the text asserts the female body's metonymic relation to Englishness.

Gibreel's sexual conquest of the icy Allie Cone has a clearly contiguous relation to his cultural conquest (tropicalizing) of England. So too, Saladin Chamcha's 'naturalization' as an Englishman is secured and signified through his marriage to the aristocratic Pamela Lovelace. Co-opted in this way for the allegorical and metonymic work of the text, the female body is postulated as the site of sexual unreliability, thus earning the powerful misogyny that runs through this novel.[12] Pamela, for instance, becomes the figure of adultery in the novel, her affair with Chamcha's friend Vijay Joshi simply a playing out, as Talal Asad writes, 'of her marriage as racial adultery' (Asad 297). Establishing its place in the tradition of anti-feminist satire, the novel progressively insists upon the physical and mortalizing effects, ala Eve, of Pamela's sexual impurities. The migrant's permeation of England, is signified here in/as the corruption of the female form. Confronting her after their long and treacherous separation, Chamcha is cured of love, once again through the onset of sexual nausea: 'Pamela, with her too-bright brightness, her face like a saintly mask behind which who knows what worms feasted on rotting meat . . . her shaven head under its absurd turban, her whiskey breath, and the hard thing that had entered the little lines around her mouth' (402). Colluding in Chamcha's second, misogynistic recuperation from the love of England, the narrative takes its final revenge on Pamela Lovelace by causing her to die in an accidental fire, along with her illicit lover, and their unborn half-caste child. The novel's second heroine, Allie Cone suffers a similar fate. She is pushed to her death from a multi-storey building (her Fall) by her jealous lover Gibreel Farishta, on the suspicion of adultery.

With some hermeneutical effort, perhaps we can find the novel's self-critique secreted within the bitterness of its own narrative conclusions. Of late, we have learnt to regard with suspicion the masculinism of most nationalist projects: conservative and oppositional. How tragic, Rushdie's novel seems to say that even the most diligent critique of nationness should resolve itself in such a terrible vendetta against effeminacy, both in women and in men. Let us pursue the possibility of such an 'opening' in the text. *The Satanic Verses*, I have been arguing, is not the political novel that it claims, and is taken to be. Indeed, *pace* Jameson, it has much more to do 'with the domain of sexuality and the unconscious than that of the public world of classes, of the economic, and of secular political power' (69). In making this claim, however, I am not suggesting that the 'domain of sexuality' is inadmissible within the 'domain of politics'. The theoretical battles within feminism, and the emergence of 'queer theory', have gone a long way toward proving otherwise. Nor do I seek to propose that 'the story of the private individual destiny' (69) can never achieve the status of the political. The postmodern condition, as we have learnt from Lyotard and Jameson, among others, is characterized by precisely those social struggles that are scattered, disorderly and intimately bound up with questions of subjectivity. My contention, then, is this: that through the self-contradictions of which it is hardly aware – its textual unconscious – *The Satanic Verses* demonstrates the impossibility of a 'pure politics'. The migrant's critique of Englishness, in this novel, cannot escape the complicating impurities of the migrant's desire. There is wisdom in this unpalatable knowledge, especially when we consider the extent of postcolonialism's unexamined investments in migrancy. Where the theorists tell us that migrancy is better politics than nationalism, more purely radical as a form of anti-imperialism, the novelist betrays the reverse. And, thus, if *The Satanic Verses* fails spectacularly in its attempt to offer us an 'organic' political perspective on England, it is instructive precisely because it fails.[13]

Notes

1. Jameson's distinction between libidinal and political narratives is useful, even though his 'worlding' of this distinction remains questionable.
2. For an enthusiastic celebration of migrancy in Rushdie's fiction see Homi Bhabha (*Location* 164–70; 223–9) and Ian Baucom (200–18).
3. Tom Nairn (256–91) is instructive about Powell's part in the making of conservative English nationalism.
4. See *Imaginary Homelands*, 136–8, for Rushdie's attack on the Nationality Act.
5. See Stuart Hall and Martin Jacquesi, ed., *The Politics of Thatcherism*, and Hall, *The Hard Road to Renewal*. For the rise of anti-racist/migrant politics within British 'new social movements', see Paul Gilroy, *There Ain't No Black in the Union Jack*.
6. See Baucom 208–9.
7. Compare Gibreel's thoughts on God's 'unwillingness to permit dissent among his lieutenants... and... denial of moral choice to his creations' (354).
8. It is telling that Saladin Chamcha is conclusively cured of Bombay/India following an abusive homosexual encounter: 'It seemed to him that everything loathsome, everything he had come to revile about his home town, had come together in the stranger's bony embrace, and now he had escaped that evil skeleton he must also escape Bombay, or die' (38).
9. Standish is represented as a 'good homosexual' precisely because of his ability to control his sexuality: 'Never in all the years of their partnership did he sexually importune the artist whom he helped build into a world superstar' (285).

10. The separation of gender and sexuality is more fully explored within queer theory. As Sedgwick observes 'there is always at least the potential for an analytic distance between gender and sexuality' (30).

11. Chamcha's Englishness is also elaborated in/as a more conventional fantasy about sex with the queen: 'he found himself dreaming of the Queen, of making tender love to the monarch. She was the body of Britain, the avatar of the State, and he had chosen her, joined with her. . .' (169).

12. For a persuasive reading of migrancy and misogyny elsewhere in Rushdie's fiction see Aijaz Ahmad (123–58).

13. As Gayatri Spivak observes about *The Satanic Verses*: '. . . I am more interested in failed texts. What is the use of a "successful text"?' (223).

11
Liberating 'contrasting spaces': David Dabydeen

Sue Thomas

David Dabydeen describes *Slave Song* (1984), his first volume of poems, as being 'largely concerned with the exploration of the erotic energies of the colonial experience' (*Slave Song* 10). 'The British Empire...was as much a pornographic as an economic project', he proposes ('On Not Being Milton' 61).[1] Dabydeen's later volumes of poetry *Coolie Odyssey* (1988) and *Turner: New & Selected Poems* (1994) and his novels *The Intended* (1991), *Disappearance* (1993), *The Counting House* (1996), and *A Harlot's Progress* (1999) offer further imaginative elaborations of this proposition. The central male protagonists of *The Intended* (1991) and *Disappearance* (1993) are, like Dabydeen, from Guyana, and their intellectual histories and sexualities are indicative of alienation from community and self. Their phantasmatic identifications and disidentifications with England and Englishness are projected in the novels through their relationships with white Englishwomen and their shifting responses to and psychological investments in specific *lieux de mémoire*, 'tradition-soaked places' – 'textual, monumental, topographic' – invested with the capacity to 'secure and bestow English identity' (Baucom 18). In *The Intended* Oxford University, an English village, and a white-'skinned' doll, in *Disappearance* an English garden and the English coast have these resonances for their unnamed expatriate protagonists; their voyages of return in memory to Guyana bring them greater 'self-recognition'. Dabydeen's scholarly work, most notably *Hogarth's Blacks* (1987) and his edited collection *The Black Presence in English Literature* (1985), has focussed to a large extent on countering the 'invisibility' of black people in English art and literary history, and demonstrating the implications of their presence. Dabydeen effects in *A Harlot's Progress* a searing 'reconfiguration' of the 'scenes' of William Hogarth's 'A Harlot's Progress' (Interview with Stein 29) and

'The Four Stages of Cruelty' by having the black servant boy in Plate 2 of the first of these series tell his life story.[2] He also reconfigures in the novel Thomas Pringle's editorial presence in *The History of Mary Prince, a West Indian Slave, related by herself* (1831), the first published slave narrative of a black British woman, and the sexual dealings, floggings, and medical attentions pertaining to his slaves recorded so minutely in the diaries of Thomas Thistlewood, an Englishman who lived in Jamaica from 1750 to 1786. The 'inner sickness' of eighteenth-century and early nineteenth-century English culture (265) becomes visible in *A Harlot's Progress* through the story of the variously named African slave Mungo/Perseus/Noah and on his flesh.

The identity of the first-person immigrant narrator of *The Intended* is grounded in abjection: a desire for the invisibility of the racial and cultural difference emblematized in his brown skin, for 'exempt[ion] from the normal rules of lineage and privilege' (195) which determine Englishness, for 'escape from this dirt and shame called Balham, this coon condition, this ignorance that prevents me from knowing anything, not even who we are, who they are' (230). The 'we' here are a 'regrouping of the Asian diaspora in a South London schoolyard' – Shaz, 'born in Britain' 'of Pakistani parents'; Nasim, 'more authentically Moslem'; Patel, 'of Hindu stock'; and the narrator, 'an Indian West-Indian Guyanese, the most mixed-up of the lot' (5) – and Joseph Countryman, a Rastafarian, a curiously gifted illiterate seer, who commits suicide by self-immolation. '[R]eminding' him of his 'dark shadow, drawing' him 'back to' his 'dark self' (196), Joseph and writing about Joseph guide the narrator to acknowledge what cannot be absorbed by his ambition for assimilation. Dabydeen's Jungian language implicitly represents the assimilative 'I' as the persona: 'a way of responding to a demand from some collective [in *The Intended* the English and the cathexis of masculinity to individualism] that is characteristic' (Singer 164). 'The shadow', June Singer explains, 'is a dominant of the personal unconscious and consists of all those uncivilized desires and emotions that are incompatible with social standards and with the persona; it is all that we are ashamed of' (165). The narrator's persona and shadow are structured by epidermalization of the psychological and epistemic violence of racism. For him the shadow comprises atavistic 'savagery', 'mess', 'soiling and vandalism and the gaze of the ignorant' (*Intended* 197–8). In writing his life, the narrator retrieves the shadow back into himself 'as native to psyche, native to a quest for unity through contrasting elements, through the ceaseless tasks of the creative imagination to digest and liberate contrasting spaces rather than succumb to implacable polarisations' (Harris, Author's Note 8).

His abjection is compressed in his fear of being 'a lump of aborted, anonymous flesh' (198), unsouled, 'drowned in a sense of orphaned neglect' (*Intended* 121); his desire for transcendence of late 1960s and early 1970s postmodernity is summed up in his anxiously repeated wish to 'be somebody, some recognisable shape' (198). Joseph explains to the narrator the effects of the racist gaze at the 'black man': 'You can't even see yourself, even if you stand in front of mirror, all you seeing is shape. But all the time they seeing you as animal, riot, nigger, but you know you is nothing, atoms, only image and legend in their minds. So to make yourself real you collect things, and you place them round your room like ritual, like black magic' (101). Joseph is thinking of carefully arranged possessions – a comb, cigarettes, matches, towel and shoes. '[G]ood examination results' (113) and books, 'decipher[ed]' to write essays (195), 'array[ed]' to impress Janet (121), a desired white girl whose village origins signify 'genteel Englishness' and its 'protections and confident virtues' (169), providing the 'nutrients of quiet scholarship', are the collections which promise to make him 'real.' Collections of books, like Oxford University Library, will become his 'cocoon', the womb from which he will 'emerge' as 'somebody' in his ambitious fantasy of self-regeneration, self-making (198). Shaz will collect women to pimp, and Patel wealth from the white customers he despises as '[w]alking banknotes' (199) or degenerate drug addicts.

The narrator's is an adult confession of an adolescent individualistic 'identification of an ego ideal that is white and whole' (Bhabha, *Location* 76), an identification which was his transcendental anchor in late 1960s and early 1970s postmodernity, but which he now understands as 'the pernicious effects of racial hierarchy in both Guyana and England' (Fee 113). In aesthetic terms the wholeness is premised on a fetishization of whiteness; 'to be calm, to write with grace and clarity, to make words which have status, to shape them into the craftsmanship of English china, coaches, period furniture, harpsichords, wigs, English anything' are the promises of whiteness (*Intended* 197). Dabydeen elsewhere identifies such a position as one of intellectual miscegenation, as taking the part of Ariel, becoming 'a mulatto and house-nigger... rather than stay a field-nigger (Caliban).... And to become mulattos, black people literally have to be fucked (and fucked up) first. Which brings us back to the pornography of Empire' ('On Not Being Milton' 73). If for his narrator 'black words' are the Creole of Albion Village in Guyana (*Intended* 148), it is a sign of his continuing alienation from his 'dark self' that the Creole in his narrative is confined to reconstructed dialogue in memories of Guyana and reports of the contents of his mother's letters.[3] Late 1960s and early 1970s postmodernity is emblematized by his fear of failure to self-birth, the World Cruise Ride at the Battersea Fun Fair replete with crass stereotypes of cultural and racial difference, the dominant cathexis of masculinity to commodified feminine sexuality especially through pornography and advertizing, the Asian shopkeeper in London, the 'messy' lives of immigrants (168) by contrast with the settled white English, and the 'blank faces' of white people 'suppressing their indignation and distress' at the 'vulgar rowdiness' of 'black West Indians' in public (177–8).

Dabydeen's account of his narrator's libidinal investment in Englishness is organized around several primal scenes: 'myths of the origin of the marking of the subject within the racist practices and discourses of a colonial culture' (Bhabha, *Location* 75–6). Two of these take place in British Guiana/Guyana. The first occurs during the State of Emergency declared in British Guiana in 1964 in response to interethnic violence precipitated by racialized political divisions over the Sandys Plan, a model of proportional electoral representation, proposed for an independent Guyana (Glasgow 126–30). The narrator refers to 'hunger everywhere, strikes, riots, bombs exploding late at night and people hiding in their houses as soon as darkness fell, with an arsenal of knives, cutlasses, sticks' (*Intended* 126); his mother, who barricades her children in her home on their returns from school, makes terrified allusion to events in Wismar, where people of East Indian descent were driven out by those of African descent: ' "Don't ever say that black people and we hate each other or your throat will cut and your sisters rape up like they do in Wismar. If anybody ask you anything . . . say we is all one people, all of we is neighbour and mattie" ' (129). His mother insists that the people of British Guiana are ' "colonial trash" ', and places her trust in British colonial paternalism over a Guyanese nationalism she sees as an imposition of an elite, 'some black and Indian educated people in Georgetown' (127–8). The threat of violence exacerbates the racialization of the body politic of British Guiana, and assertions of communal unity are defensive, belied by the scissors the mother keeps on hand to protect her family. White people appear on the scene in a role emblematic of benevolent state paternalism, supplying the schoolchildren with food.

The second primal scene, which significantly takes place in Albion Village, involves the narrator's sexual excitement as he undresses an exotic white doll, beholding its 'beautifully white and smooth' genitals, 'hairless, not like Ma's' (his maternal grandmother's), which are 'bushy and nasty-looking like a malabunta nest' (227). In *Slave Song* Dabydeen describes overdetermined 'native' 'lust' for the White Woman as 'inspiration, aspiration, assimilation into a superior scheme of things' (10); she symbolizes for the canecutter 'beauty, cleanliness and inner spiritual strength . . . she is removed from life whereas he is steeped in its flux and squalor' (53). The doll 'had creamy white skin, smooth and strangely different from anything I had ever seen before', the narrator of *The Intended* remembers, 'and a white cotton dress with tiny yellow flowers. It had short golden hair, curling prettily around the face, and pink lips. . . . I felt weak as it looked at me with blue eyes' (225–6). She is artifice: her smooth genitals give the lie to the labial lips of the young girl; her demeanour is fixed in a 'gentle smile' and the 'pink glow on her cheeks'. The spectacle produces in the narrator an acutely subjective consciousness of the 'unclean' materiality of his own body and village world, of his 'ragged' clothes, dark-skinned ugliness, sweat, scent, 'rough handling', and proximity to animal dung. The village, now objectified through racial stereotype as 'coolie and nigger people' and 'nastiness', would, he thinks, degrade her (226–7). His grandmother comes to stand as an emblem of the fate of impoverished East Indian Guyanese women: 'only bone white as the doll's skin . . . ugly and broken and scarred by the weather and time, its jaws set in silence, its eyes empty of feeling' (229). His aggression is fuelled by a sense of banal abandonment, as she fails to engage with the intellectual and emotional needs expressed in his questioning of her about the mystery of a cow's skull. The doll and the grandmother are normatively positioned by the narrator 'as the repository of the "race"' (Lola Young 96). In this memory he also recalls being 'aroused' by the 'power' of his grandfather's brother Richilo's obscene cursing of his grandmother (*Intended* 228).[4]

Dabydeen's theorization of the effects of the white gaze at blackness and brownness in England draws in large part from Frantz Fanon's moving account of the 'difficulties' which 'the man of color' experiences 'in the development of his bodily schema,' the 'slow composition of my *self* as a body in the middle of a spatial and temporal world' (*Black Skin, White Masks* 110–11). Joseph's 'all the time they seeing you as animal, riot, nigger, but you know you is nothing, atoms, only image and legend in their minds' recalls Fanon's description of the crumbling of his 'corporeal schema, its place taken by a racial epidermal schema' when a white French boy exclaims, '"Look, a Negro!"' and expresses a mortified and mortifying fear grounded in racial stereotype (111). 'I strive for anonymity, for invisibility,' Fanon writes (116). Making himself an object, a primal scene of racial formation, is 'an amputation, an excision, a hemorrhage that spattered [his] whole body with black blood' (112). Dabydeen figures such an 'amputation', 'excision', as 'a lump of aborted, anonymous flesh.' His metaphor resonates, too, with Enoch Powell's ' "We need to expel immigrants from the host body" ', which Dabydeen remembers as a key sign of the 'threat of violence' against immigrants in England, but also a sign of the 'continuity' of the 'sense of violence' carried by the Indian Guyanese child caught up in the reverberations of the 'Wismar episode' (Interview with Binder 69). It is worth recalling that Powell in his infamous 'rivers of blood' speech on immigration (1968) described as 'mad' Britain's 'annual inflow of some 50,000 dependents', people admitted under family reunion provisions of immigration law (Powell 283). Dabydeen's narrator is one such dependent.

The 'I' of *The Intended* is in some ways similar to the character of Jean Veneuse in René Maran's *Un homme pareil aux autres* (1947), on whom Fanon bases his discussion of 'The Man of Color and the White Woman'. Veneuse is an orphan sent to boarding school, 'forced into the habit of solitude, so that his best friends are his books.... Unable to be assimilated, unable to pass unnoticed, he consoles himself by associating with the dead, or at least the absent' (65) – the authors he reads. Drawing on the work of Germaine Guex, Fanon argues that Veneuse has an 'abandonment neurosis': ' "It is this tripod – the *anguish* created by every abandonment, the *aggression* to which it gives rise, and the *devaluation of self* that flows out of it – that supports the whole symptomatology of this neurosis" ' (73). Dabydeen's narrator's ambition works, sometimes precariously, to repress his mourning over his sense of abandonment, as 'Albion ghosts' follow him to England (*Intended* 70) through memory. The barely spoken of in his reconstructed life narrative is the story of reunion with his estranged, apparently alcoholic father, whom he initially joins in England where he has been sent to 'tek education' (38), and of his father placing him in the care of the state, which singularly fails to nurture him. For Islamic Nasim such conduct – on a par with 'marrying and breeding and divorcing and bequeathing the children to the welfare' – is a sign of the degeneracy of English family values (21).

As Dabydeen's narrator prepares to depart Albion Village Auntie Clarice, an elderly black woman, offers advice he finds riddling: ' "you is we, remember you is we" ' (40). His mother admonishes him, ' "Go and don't look back" ' (70), pleased to have 'one less mouth to feed' (238) the narrator thinks, planning that his education will allow him to support his Guyanese family financially and that he will reunite them all in

England. The riddle is recontextualized in the narrator's telling of Joseph's relation to his own Asian diasporic community. The narrator interprets Joseph's self-immolation as a potential sign of his Asian identification, a show that ' "you is we" ', and as a 'burning off' of his 'black skin', his epidermalized difference (197). He reminds Patel, who has become a shopkeeper, mercenary pornographer and drug-dealer, shortly before Joseph's death that Joseph is ' "one of us and and we're one of him" ' (240). The narrator's adolescent admission of Joseph to his community is premised largely on his admiration for his visionary abstract aesthetics, expressed conceptually, but not well realized technically, in film and comment on *Heart of Darkness*. While he identifies with Joseph as artist-in-the-making and as fellow former inmate of the Boy's Home, Joseph's meaning, as bearer of the sordidness of poverty, homelessness and self-destructive violence, and, aesthetically, 'blurred' shapes and 'confusions' (197) – of 'the misery of his kind of being' – is often repudiated. The narrator's adolescent persona relegates it as 'a constitutive outside to the subject, an abjected outside, which is, after all, "inside" the subject as its own founding repudiation' (Butler 3). His adult storytelling 'I' (eye) 're-sense[s] or rediscover[s] a scale of community', taking on in conscience the task 'of the creative imagination to digest and liberate contrasting spaces' (Harris, Author's Note 8). Joseph's spirituality, his Rastafarianism, however, is a virtually empty signifier for him. White girls are admitted temporarily to the narrator's diasporic community[5] under the sign of (hetero)sexuality as virgin (Janet) or whore (Monica). Each is represented as desiring surreptiously or having sexual agency, in tune with the period's sexual liberation, symbolized most aggressively in pornographic objectification and Shaz's pimping of Monica. Janet fantasizes female sexual agency through a contrast between 'sissy' daffodils, 'vulnerable images, things they [men] can control and dominate', metonymic of English femininity, and a preferred exotic Venus fly trap, a vagina dentata (*Intended* 205). In Dabydeen's reworking of the Othello-Desdemona myth, Janet is drawn 'to the body of alien experience [of the narrator] in preference to the familiarity of her own culture' ('On Not Being Milton' 73). In the narrator's transfigurative ambitious fantasy she is, however, her skin, an object of desired homosocial exchange between him and her father, an engineer from Wimbledon, withholder of 'stable community' (*Intended* 167). White men – racist gang, pub brawlers and patrons, borstal warden – are more generally the bearers of violence, and kept at a distance. Women and girls of the Asian diaspora in London become markers of the public shame of difference (15, 215) and of 'a sense of family' (26); when the narrator sees 'dark-skinned' Indian dolls 'with thick curly black hair' at Nasim's home he obliquely acknowledges sexual curiosity: 'I would have liked to examine them more closely... but I was swiftly overcome by a sense of shame' (23–4).

Both *The Intended* and *Disappearance* are shaped by the aesthetic of Wilson Harris.[6] The settings, too, are both material geographies and, at an allegorical level, geographies of the mind. Dabydeen's reconfiguring of Harris's poetic is indicated in the first epigraph of *Disappearance*, which is from the opening paragraph of Harris's *The Secret Ladder*. *The Secret Ladder* is a novel about a journey of psychic reintegration, in which the coast of British Guiana emblematizes 'the conscious outer self' which Fenwick must reconcile with 'the inner self', the unconscious (Gilkes 87–8). The African Guyanese narrator of *Disappearance* is an engineer, hired at the instigation of his professional mentor, a Professor Fenwick, to shore up crumbling cliffs on England's Hastings coast; Fenwick's corrupt management of the reclamation project disillusions him. Like Fenwick in *The Secret Ladder*, Dabydeen's narrator must reunite 'heart and head' (Gilkes 87). In his case the split has been generated by his libidinal investments in mastery of engineering technology represented by books and computations, a mastery which will make him 'somebody' (*Disappearance* 132), but which cuts him off from 'the sorrow of ancestral memory' (17), from the 'spirit living' in the Guyanese land (34) articulated by the illiterate Indian Guyanese seer Swami, the past he had let 'revert to bush' (64), and sexual pleasure. He comes to realize that his identity as an engineer is a 'dam', a marker of his desire for the historyless invisibility of his 'colour, culture or age' (132–3), a desire grounded in part on his internalization of his mother's colonial sense of the inferiority of black people to white.

His journey to greater psychological integration is catalysed by his growing inability to shield himself from the ancestral spiritual power in African masks in the home of his white English hostess Mrs Janet Rutherford, by her questioning of him about his past, and by the understanding he develops of her own contrastive psychic journey. Characteristically for a woman of her generation her 'life' was engineered to 'begin' when she met her husband Jack, and included her seduction by English patriotic rhetoric, mobilized in the 1950s to orchestrate a local campaign to save the cliffs, allegorically the conscious outer self of national identity. Dabydeen acidly links the hackneyed imperialist and xenophobic rhetoric of Mr Curtis, shored up against the contemporaneous demise of England's empire, to that of Margaret Thatcher, interviewed after the Royal Marines regained South Georgia during the

Falklands crisis, 'Rejoice! Rejoice!' Thatcher would triumphantly interpret the Falklands War as a 're-kindl[ing]' of the 'spirit' of a 'nation that
had built an Empire and ruled a quarter of the world' (qtd. in Barnett
150, 153). Mrs Rutherford's sojourn in Africa brought her to a new
understanding of her Englishness and of her 'own pitiable female condition' (*Disappearance* 78). There her desire to remain 'colourless and
invisible' (102) is unrealizable. She has to confront English exploitation
of its colonial subjects, emblematized in Jack's sexual exploitation of
local women and in imperial pilfering of colonial wealth and resources,
and the epistemic violence of empire, characterized by Jack's collection
of African masks for his own pornographic titillation, and by a colonial
education which romanticizes England and Englishness. Mrs Rutherford
tried in Africa to challenge this romanticization by teaching her pupils
of the violence and disease of English history recorded in the names of
English flowers. Back in England, her marriage over, she cultivates her
village garden, a 'gentle spectacle' of Englishness, 'engineered' as a
public mask for her anti-imperial eccentricity (67). She sublimates her
anger at English history and at Jack's humiliation of her in her 'engineering' of the garden. Dabydeen's epigraph from V.S. Naipaul's *The
Enigma of Arrival*, 'Was it Jack? I didn't take the person in; I was more
concerned with the strangeness of the walk, my own strangeness, and
the absurdity of my enquiry', highlights, among many other complex
intertextual resonances, the comparability of the West Indian narrators'
expanding comprehension of the constructedness of the 'English' garden, and the tradition it represents, as they come to read the figure of
the gardener in the landscape, but also the difference of their journeys.
Dabydeen's narrator acknowledges, 'It would take centuries for me to
grow into the English landscape, as it took centuries for a hybrid flower
to evolve' (131), and resolves to seek new beginnings in Guyana.

Paul Gilroy usefully observes that the 'return to slavery', 'so deeply
embedded in modernity', as a subject of 'imaginative writing' in the
black Atlantic 'arises from present conditions': 'it is formed by the need
to indict those forms of rationality which have been rendered implaus-
ible by their racially exclusive character and further to explore the
history of their complicity with terror systematically and rationally
practised as a form of political and economic administration' (*Black
Atlantic* 190, 220). Of his scholarship in *Hogarth's Blacks* Dabydeen
says, 'You had to take what was defined as English high culture and try
to find yourself in there.... [T]he academic work I have been doing on
eighteenth-century England has never been divorced from a personal
quest to belong to twentieth-century England' (Interview with Binder

72). For Dabydeen that belonging is grounded in a restorative social memory.

In *A Harlot's Progress* Dabydeen explicitly indicts the purportedly 'rational, scientific, and enlightened' outlook (Gilroy, *Black Atlantic* 220) of the producer/instigator of slave narrative, generically named here Thomas Pringle, after the Secretary of the Anti-Slavery Society from 1827 to 1834, who edited *The History of Mary Prince*. Mungo/Noah/Perseus is his recalcitrant informant: 'he would prefer to hoard the past and squirrel on it through miserable seasons' (*Harlot's Progress* 2). Dabydeen's Pringle is motivated by his sense of the utility ('dividends') of Mungo's narrative for the Committee for the Abolition of Slavery, and in this interest and condescendingly is prepared 'to colour and people a landscape out of his own imagination, thereby endowing Mungo with the gift of mind and eloquence' (3). Mungo thinks that Pringle's pen is a 'gravedigger's spade' (35). For him 'the book is no more than a splendidly adorned memorial and grave. To speak is to scoop out substance, to hollow out yourself, to make space within for your own burial'. He has 'kept in things as bulwarks against death' (34). Mungo resists Pringle's desire to fit his life narrative into preconceived schemas, to 'wash the Aethiop white, scrubbing off the colours of sin and greed that stained Mungo's skin as a result of slavery' (6).

Dabydeen also doubles back on his own critical ratiocinations on Hogarth's series 'A Harlot's Progress' (1732) in *Hogarth's Blacks*, his teasing out of the implication of 'black marginalized figures' in the 'complexity of the narrative' (Interview with Binder 72). Mungo/Noah/Perseus fears that Hogarth's 'A Harlot's Progress' will perpetuate an association of the Negro, generically male, 'with the indecencies of merchants and whores' such that subsequent generations will think of him as a 'pimp, pickpocket, purveyor of filth' (273). In Dabydeen's interpretations of 'A Harlot's Progress' and 'The Four Stages of Cruelty' (1750/51) in *Hogarth's Blacks* he emphasizes Hogarth's social critique, his 'bitter representation of the squalid and dehumanizing commercialism characteristic of the times' (*Hogarth's Blacks* 101). Dabydeen elucidates the black boy of Plate 2 in relation to the intricacies of Hogarth's thematics of corruption. He draws attention in his analysis of 'The Four Stages of Cruelty' to Hogarth's technique of 'juxtaposition of, or comparison between, the savage and the civilized . . . sometimes for satiric, sometimes for horrific effect' (62). Dabydeen, like Hogarth, inverts the manichean association of whiteness with civilization by representing England in *A Harlot's Progress* as a place of savagery, emblematized, for example, in Mungo's sense of the desire of 'poor white beasts with savage looks' on the streets of London to cannibalize him (158, 239, 266).

In his account of 'A Harlot's Progress' Dabydeen had passed over Hogarth's representation of the merchant in Plate 2 who draws his riches 'from colonial trade' and uses prostitutes (enslaved in his reading) as Jewish (*Hogarth's Blacks* 108). In *A Harlot's Progress* Mungo/Noah/Perseus acknowledges that Hogarth drew his Mr Gideon as 'the oldest Jew in the book, in terms of his cunning, his hoarding of coin, his purchase of Christian women' (273), and that Pringle, who 'believes' Hogarth's prints and pirates of them, 'sees danger to England's Christian fabric everywhere, in the shape of Jew and Papist, Jacobite and callous merchant' (275–6). It is as if Dabydeen is taking up the implications of Gilroy's critique of the way in which 'themes like the involvement of Jews in the slave trade are invoked as simple eloquent facts without the need of interpretation (214).

Caliban-like, Mungo/Noah/Perseus acknowledges that Captain Thistlewood (allusively a Prospero figure) 'taught' him 'language' (*Harlot's Progress* 57). With his acquisition of the English language he also acquires a Christian vocabulary and epistemology through which to understand and transcend his experiences of English people and their failures to recognize his individuality or his position as 'the ruined archive' of his own people, their 'resurrected expression, writing the discovery of the New World of Whitemen' (36). After being branded by the sadistic Thistlewood with a mark indicating he has 'been breached and made accustomed to men' (123), Mungo experiences Africa and his people as 'occasional glimpses and fragments of voices' in his head (152–3. In many ways those voices 'leech' his conscience (35); Mungo himself 'becomes exhausted by their [Thistlewood's, Betty's, Pringle's] need to repent, by the way they peck at themselves out of guilt and will use him to leech that guilt' (156). 'It is your love that I greed for, not the coinage of your guilt', he affirms (71). He comes to appreciate his functions for white people in relation to the 'epic pain' (276) that is the burden of their varieties of alienation from English modernity and their guilt over cruelties.

Dabydeen speaks of being 'doubled over in terms of an imaginative life', of having a 'double consciousness' of place as an 'arrivant' in England (Interview with Stein 28). 'Striving to be both European and black requires some specific forms of double consciousness', writes Gilroy, acknowledging the challenge of 'occupying the space between them [these unfinished identities] or trying to demonstrate their continuity' (*Black Atlantic* [1]). In his fiction Dabydeen takes up the challenge of this

consciousness, particularly through imaginative digestion and liberation of 'contrasting spaces', including critical revisiting of his own
scholarship.

Notes

1. Dabydeen attributes the phrase 'the pornography of empire' to Wilson Harris
   (Interview with Binder 75).
2. Dabydeen's narrative strategy here is similar to that in his long poem 'Turner'
   in which the 'submerged head of the African in the foreground' of J.M.W.
   Turner's 'Slavers Throwing Overboard the Dead and Dying' (1840) provides
   him with his point of critical and imaginative departure (*Turner* ix).
3. Benita Parry notes that '[t]he consequence of this separation is a fiction which,
   despite its deliberate juxtaposition of temporalities and its crossing of genre
   boundaries in mixing social and marvellous realism, personal testimony with
   detached commentary, does not rupture received fictional form' (89–90).
4. Mario Relich rightly points to Richilo as a 'kind of role-model' for the narrator
   as aspiring writer, but indulges his misogyny: 'he is squalid in a grand manner'
   (49–50).
5. My formulation of arguments about terms of admittance to community is
   indebted to Rey Chow.
6. Dabydeen's image of the cocoon in *The Intended* and his use of illiterate
   characters in *The Intended* and *Disappearance* are among his many reworkings
   of aspects of Harris's *The Secret Ladder*.

Works Cited

Advani, Rukun, 'Novelists in Residence', *Seminar* 384 (1991): 15–18.

Ahmad, Aijaz, *In Theory: Classes, Nations, Literatures.* Delhi and Oxford: Oxford University Press, 1992.

Alcock, Peter, 'An Aloe in the Garden: Something Essentially New Zealand in Miss Mansfield', *Journal of Commonwealth Literature* 11 (1977): 958–64.

Allen, Walter, *The English Novel: A Short Critical History.* 1954. Harmondsworth: Penguin, 1968.

Angier, Carole, *Jean Rhys: Life and Work.* Rev. edn. Harmondsworth: Penguin, 1992.

Arnold, Matthew, *On the Study of Celtic Literature, and Other Essays.* London: Dent, 1919.

'Arrival of the New Bishop of Roseau', *Dominica Guardian* 4 and 11 June 1902: [2]–[3].

Asad, Talal, *Genealogies of Religion: Discipline and Reasons of Power Christianity and Islam.* Baltimore and London: Johns Hopkins University Press, 1993.

Atmaprana, Pravrajika, *Sister Nivedita*, 1961. Calcutta: Sister Nivedita Girls School, 1992.

Austen, Jane, *Mansfield Park.* 1814. Ed. Kathleen Sutherland. Harmondsworth: Penguin, 1996.

Bakhtin, Mikhail M., 'The *Bildungsroman* and Its Significance in the History of the Novel: Toward a Historical Typology of the Novel', *Speech Genres and Other Late Essays.* Trans. Vern W. McGee. Eds Caryl Emerson and Michael Holquist. Austin: University of Texas Press, 1986. 10–59.

Ballara, Marcela, *Women and Literacy.* London and New Jersey: Zed, 1991.

Bardolph, Jacqueline, 'Abdulrazak Gurnah's *Paradise* and *Admiring Silence:* History, Stories and the Figure of the Uncle', *Contemporary African Fiction.* Ed. Derek Wright. Bayreuth African Studies 42. Bayreuth: Bayreuth University, 1997. 77–89.

——(ed.) *Short Fiction in the New Literatures in English, Proceedings of the Nice Conference of the European Association for Commonwealth Literatures and Language Studies.* Nice: Faculté des Lettres et Sciences Humaines de Nice, 1988.

Barnes, Julian, *England, England.* London: Cape, 1998.

Barnett, Anthony, *Iron Britannia.* London: Allison and Busby, 1982.

Bartra, Roger, *Wild Men in the Looking Glass: The Mythic Origins of European Otherness.* Trans. Carl T. Berrisford. Ann Arbor: University of Michigan Press, 1994.

Baucom, Ian, *Out of Place: Englishness, Empire, and the Locations of Identity.* Princeton, NJ: Princeton University Press, 1999.

Baudrillard, Jean, *Simulations.* New York: Semiotext(e), 1983.

Beavers, Herman, '"The Cool Pose": Intersectionality, Masculinity, and Quiescence in the Comedy and Films of Richard Pryor and Eddie Murphy'. Stecopoulos and Uebel 253–85.

Bhabha, Homi, *The Location of Culture.* London: Routledge, 1994.

——. 'Re-inventing Britain – a Manifesto', British Council homepage. n.pag. Online. Internet. 19 March 2000. Available http://old.britcoun.org/studies/stdmani.htm.

Birkenhead, Lord, *Rudyard Kipling*. 1978. London: Star, 1980.

Bonnett, Alastair, 'Constructions of Whiteness in European and American Anti-Racism', *Debating Cultural Hybridity: Multi-Cultural Identities and the Politics of Anti-Racism*. Eds Pnina Werbner and Tariq Modood. London: Zed, 1997. 173–92.

——, '"White Studies": The Problems and Projects of a New Research Agenda', *Theory, Culture and Society* 13.2 (1996): 145–55.

Brewer, E. Cobham, *The Dictionary of Phrase and Fable*. 1894 edn. New York: Avenel, 1978.

Brown, Nancy Hemond, 'England and the English in the Works of Jean Rhys', *Jean Rhys Review* 1.2 (Spring 1987): 8–20.

Butler, Judith, *Bodies that Matter: On the Discursive Limits of 'Sex'*. New York: Routledge, 1993.

Calder, Angus, *The Myth of the Blitz*. London: Cape, 1991.

Carter, Angela, 'Christina Stead', *Expletives Deleted: Selected Writings*. London: Chatto and Windus, 1992. 177–92.

——, 'In Love with the Tempest', *Sunday Times* 10 April 1983: 44.

Chatterjee, Lola, 'Landmarks in Official Educational Policy: Some Facts and Figures', Sunder Rajan 300–8.

Chatterjee, Partha, *The Nation and Its Fragments: Colonial and Postcolonial Histories*. Princeton: Princeton University Press, 1993.

Chatterjee, Upamanyu, *English August: An Indian Story*. Calcutta: Rupa, 1988.

Chaudhuri, Amit, *Afternoon Raag*. London: Minerva, 1994.

Chaudhuri, Nirad C., *The Autobiography of an Unknown Indian*. 1951. London: Hogarth, 1987.

——, *A Passage to England*. 1971. New Delhi: Orient, 1994.

Cheesman, Tom, Marie Gillespie, Deniz G, John Goodby, John McLeod, and Sujala Singh, 'Transnational Communities Research Programme', n. pag. Online. Internet. 19 March 2000. Available: http://www.swan.ac.uk/conferences/transcomm.

Chow, Rey, 'The Politics of Admittance: Female Sexual Agency, Miscegenation and the Formation of Community in Frantz Fanon', *The UTS Review* 1.1 (1995): 5–29.

Clayton, Cherry, *Olive Schreiner*. New York: Twayne, 1997.

——, 'Olive Schreiner and Katherine Mansfield; Artistic Transformations of the Outcast Figure by Two Colonial Women Writers', Bardolph, *Short Fiction* 31–9.

Cohen, Phil, 'Yesterday's Words, Tomorrows Worlds: from the Racialisation of Adoption to the Politics of Difference', Gaber and Aldridge, 43–76.

Cohen, Philip, 'The Perversions of Inheritance: Studies in the Making of Multi-Racist Britain', *Multi-Racist Britain*. Eds. Philip Cohen and Harwant S. Bains. Houndsmills: Macmillan Education, 1988. 9–118.

——, 'Who Needs an Island?', *New Formations* 33 (Spring 1998): 11–37.

Colls, Robert, and Philip Dodd (eds), *Englishness: Politics and Culture 1880–1920*. London: Croom Helm, 1986.

Dabydeen, David (ed.), *The Black Presence in English Literature*. Manchester: Manchester University Press, 1985.

——, *The Counting House.* 1996. London: Vintage, 1997.

——, *Disappearance.* London: Secker and Warburg, 1993.

——, *A Harlot's Progress.* London: Cape, 1999.

——, *Hogarth's Blacks: Images of Blacks in Eighteenth Century English Art.* 1985. Manchester: Manchester University Press, 1987.

——, *The Intended.* 1991. London: Minerva, 1992.

——, Interview with Wolfgang Binder. *Journal of West Indian Literature* 3.2 (Sept. 1989): 67–80.

——, Interview with Mark Stein. *Wasafiri* 29 (Spring 1999): 27–29.

——, 'On Not Being Milton: Nigger Talk in England Today', *Crisis and Creativity in the New Literatures in English.* Eds Geoffrey V. Davis and Hena Maes-Jelinek. Amsterdam: Rodopi, 1990. 61–74.

——, *Slave Song.* Sydney: Dangaroo, 1984.

——, *Turner: New and Selected Poems.* London: Cape, 1994.

——(ed.), *The Windrush Commemorative Issue: West Indians in Britain 1948–1998. Kunapipi* 20.1 (1998).

Dalmia, Manju, 'Derozio: English Teacher', Sunder Rajan 42–62.

Dante, *The Comedy of Dante Alighieri the Florentine. Cantica 1 Hell 'L'Inferno'.* Ed. and trans. Dorothy L. Sayers. 1949. Harmondsworth: Penguin, 1974.

Das, Sisir Kumar, *A History of Indian Literature: 1800–1910, Western Impact: Indian Response. Vol. 8.* Delhi: Sahitya Academy, 1991.

Davis, Christina, 'Mother and Writer: Means of Empowerment in the Work of Buchi Emecheta', *Commonwealth* 13.1 (1990): 13–21.

Dawson, Graham, *Soldier Heroes: British Adventure, Empire and the Imagining of Masculinities.* London and New York: Routledge, 1994.

Dean, Misao, Introduction. *Cousin Cinderella.* By Sara Jeannette Duncan. 1908. Ottawa: Tecumseh Press, 1994. vii–xxiii.

Dennis, Ferdinand, *Behind the Frontlines: Journey into Afro-Britain.* London: Gollancz, 1988.

Desani, G. V., *All About H. Hatterr.* 1950. New York: McPherson, 1990.

Dijkstra, Bram, *Idols of Perversity: Fantasies of Feminine Evil in Fin-de-Siècle Culture.* New York: Oxford University Press, 1986.

Donnell, Alison, and Sarah Lawson Welsh (eds), *The Routledge Reader in Caribbean Literature.* London and New York: Routledge, 1996.

Duckworth, Marilyn, *A Gap in the Spectrum.* 1959. Auckland: Oxford University Press, 1985.

Dummett, Ann, and Andrew Nicol, *Subjects, Citizens, Aliens and Others: Nationality and Immigration Law.* London: Weidenfeld and Nicolson, 1990.

Duncan, Sara Jeannette, *Cousin Cinderella.* 1908. Ottawa: Tecumseh Press, 1994.

Dutt, Michael Madhusudan, *Madhusudan Racanabali.* Calcutta: Sahitya Samsad, 1965.

Dyer, Richard, *White.* London: Routledge, 1997.

Ebeogu, Afam, 'Enter the Iconoclast: Buchi Emecheta and the Igbo Culture', *Commonwealth* 7.2 (1985): 83–94.

Edwards, Thomas, *Henry Derozio.* 1884. Calcutta: Riddhi India, 1980.

Emecheta, Buchi, *Gwendolen.* 1989. Oxford: Heinemann Educational, 1994.

——, *Head Above Water: An Autobiography.* 1986. Oxford: Heinemann Educational, 1994.

——, *In the Ditch.* Rev. edn. 1979. Oxford: Heinemann Educational, 1994.

——, 'An Interview with Buchi Emecheta'. By Davidson Umeh and Marie Umeh. *Ba Shiru* 12.2 (1981): 19–25.

——, *Kehinde*. Oxford: Heinemann Educational, 1994.

——, *The New Tribe*. Oxford: Heinemann, 2000.

——, *Second-Class Citizen*. 1974. London: Hodder and Stoughton, 1989.

F. [pseud.], 'A Jubilee Dirge', *Dominica Dial* 16 April 1887: [3].

Fanon, Frantz, *Black Skin, White Masks*. Trans. Charles Lam Markmann. 1967. London: Pluto, 1986.

Farred, Grant (ed.), *Rethinking C. L. R. James*. Oxford: Blackwell, 1996.

Fayad, Mona, 'Unquiet Ghosts: The Struggle for Representation in Jean Rhys's *Wide Sargasso Sea*', *Wide Sargasso Sea*. By Jean Rhys. Ed. Judith L. Raiskin. Norton Critical edn. New York: Norton, 1999. 225–40.

Fee, Margery, 'Resistance and Complicity in David Dabydeen's *The Intended*'. *Ariel: A Review of International English Literature* 24.1 (Jan. 1993): 107–26.

Felski, Rita, *The Gender of Modernity*. Cambridge, MA and London: Harvard University Press, 1995.

Fishburn, Katherine, *Reading Buchi Emecheta: Cross-Cultural Conversations*. Westport, CT and London: Greenwood, 1995.

Forbes, Curdella, 'Revisiting Samuel Selvon's Trilogy of Exile: Implications for Gender Consciousness and Gender Relations in Caribbean Culture', *Caribbean Quarterly* 43.4 (Dec. 1997): 47–63.

Fullbrook, Kate, *Katherine Mansfield*. Bloomington: Indiana University Press, 1986.

Gaber, Ivor, and Jane Aldridge (eds), *In the Best Interests of the Child: Culture, Identity and Transracial Adoption*. London: Free Association, 1994.

Gandhi, Leela, *Postcolonial Theory: A Critical Introduction*. Sydney: Allen & Unwin, 1998.

Gandhi, Mohandas K., *An Autobiography, or The Story of My Experiments with Truth*. 1927. 1929. Penguin: Harmondsworth, 1982.

——, 'Guide to London'. *Collected Works of Mahatma Gandhi: Vol. 1*. 1893–. Delhi, 1958.

——, *Hind Swaraj, or Indian Home Rule*. 1909. Ahmedabad: Navjivan, 1947.

Gardiner, Judith Kegan, *Rhys, Stead, Lessing, and the Politics of Empathy*. Bloomington: Indiana University Press, 1989.

Gay, Peter, *The Enlightenment: An Interpretation. Vol. 2: The Science of Freedom*. London: Weidenfeld and Nicholson, 1969.

Ghosh, Amitav, *The Circle of Reason*. Delhi: Roli, 1986.

——, *The Shadow Lines*. Delhi: Ravi Dayal, 1988.

Gibb, Phillip, *England Speaks: Being Talks with Road-Sweepers, Barbers, Statesmen, Lords and Ladies, Beggars, Farming Folk, Actors, Artists, Literary Gentlemen, Tramps, Down-and-Outs, Miners, Steel-Workers, Blacksmiths, The-Man-in-the-Street, High-Brows, Low-Brows, and All Manner of Folk of Humble and Exalted Rank with a Panorama of the English Scene in this Year of Grace 1935*. London: Heinemann, 1935.

Giles, Judy, and Tom Middleton (eds), *Writing Englishness 1900–1950: An Introductory Sourcebook on National Identity*. London and New York: Routledge, 1995.

Gilkes, Michael, *Wilson Harris and the Caribbean Novel*. London: Longman, 1975.

Gikandi, Simon, *Maps of Englishness: Writing Identity in the Culture of Colonialism*. NY: Columbia University Press, 1996.

Gilman, Sander L., *Difference and Pathology: Stereotypes of Sexuality, Race, and Madness*. Ithaca, NY: Cornell University Press, 1985.

Gilroy, Paul, *The Black Atlantic: Modernity and Double Consciousness*. London: Verso, 1993.

——, Foreword, Gaber and Aldridge, ix–xiii.

——, *Small Acts: Thoughts on the Politics of Black Cultures*. London: Serpent's Tail, 1993.

——, *There Aint No Black in the Union Jack: The Cultural Politics of Race and Nation*. London: Routledge, 1993.

Glasgow, Roy Arthur, *Guyana: Race and Politics among Africans and East Indians*. The Hague: Martinus Nijhoff, 1970.

Godman, David (ed.), *Be As You Are: The Teachings of Sri Ramana Maharishi*. Delhi: Penguin, 1985.

Gohrisch, Jana, 'Crossing the Boundaries of Cultures: Buchi Emecheta's Novels', *Anglistik and Englischunterricht* 60 (1996/97): 129–42.

Gorra, Michael, *After Empire: Scott, Naipaul, Rushdie*. Chicago: University of Chicago Press, 1997.

Green, Martin, *The English Novel in the Twentieth Century: The Doom of Empire*. London: Routledge and Kegan Paul, 1984.

Greene, Gayle, *Doris Lessing: The Poetics of Change*. Ann Arbor: University of Michigan Press, 1994.

Gregg, Veronica Marie, *Jean Rhys's Historical Imagination: Reading and Writing the Creole*. Chapel Hill: University of North Carolina Press, 1995.

Gurnah, Abdulrazak, *Admiring Silence*. 1996. Harmondsworth: Penguin, 1997.

——, 'Displacement and Transformation in *The Enigma of Arrival* and *The Satanic Verses*', Lee, *Other Britain* 5–20.

——, *Dottie*. London: Cape, 1990.

——, *Pilgrims Way*. London: Cape, 1988.

Hacking, Ian, 'The Making and Molding of Child Abuse', *Critical Inquiry* 17 (1991): 253–88.

Hall, Douglas, *In Miserable Slavery: Thomas Thistlewood in Jamaica, 1750–86*. London: Macmillan, 1989.

Hall, Stuart, 'Aspiration and Attitude . . . Reflections on Black Britain in the Nineties', *New Formations* 33 (Spring 1998): 38–46.

——, 'Caribbean Culture: Future Trends', *Caribbean Quarterly* 43.1–2 (Mar.–June 1997): 25–33.

——, *The Hard Road to Renewal: Thatcherism and the Crisis of the Left*. London & New York: Verso in association with *Marxism Today*, 1988.

—— and Jaques, Martin (eds), *The Politics of Thatcherism*. London: Lawrence & Wishart in association with *Marxism Today*, 1983.

Hanrahan, Barbara, *The Albatross Muff*. 1977. London: Chatto and Windus, 1986.

Haraway, Donna J., *Simians, Cyborgs and Women: The Reinvention of Nature*. New York: Routledge, 1991.

Hardin, James (ed.), *Reflection and Action: Essays on the* Bildungsroman. Columbia, SC: University of South Carolina Press, 1991.

Hardy, Linda, 'The Ghost of Katherine Mansfield', *Landfall: A New Zealand Quarterly* 43 (1989): 416–32.

Harney, Stefano, *Nationalism and Identity: Culture and the Imagination in a Caribbean Diaspora*. Kingston: University of the West Indies, and London: Zed, 1996.

Harris, Margaret, 'Names in Stead's *Seven Poor Men of Sydney*', *Reconnoitres: Essays in Australian Literature in Honour of G. A. Wilkes*. Eds Margaret Harris and Elizabeth Webby. South Melbourne: Sydney University Press, 1992. 142–53.

Harris, Wilson, Author's Note, *The Whole Armour* and *The Secret Ladder*. London: Faber, 1973. 7–10.

——, *The Whole Armour* and *The Secret Ladder*. London: Faber, 1973.

Harth, Phillip, 'Introduction', *The Fable of the Bees*. By Bernard Mandeville. Harmondsworth: Penguin, 1970. 7–46.

Hassall, Anthony J., *Strange Country: A Study of Randolph Stow*. Rev. edn. St Lucia: University of Queensland Press, 1990.

Heehs, Peter, *Sri Aurobindo: A Brief Biography*. Delhi: Oxford University Press, 1989.

Herman, Judith Lewis, and Lisa Hirschman, *Father–Daughter Incest*. Cambridge, MA and London: Harvard University Press, 1981.

Hesse, Barnor, 'Black to Front and Black Again: Racialization through contested times and spaces', *Place and the Politics of Identity*. Eds Michael Keith and Steve Pile. London: Routledge, 1993. 162–82.

Hewitson, Gillian, 'Deconstructing Robinson Crusoe: A Feminist Interrogation of "Rational Economic Man"', *Australian Feminist Studies* 20 (Summer 1994): 131–49.

Hewitt, Andrew, *Political Inversions: Homosexuality, Fascism, and the Modernist Imaginary*. Stanford: Stanford University Press, 1996.

Hills, Arnold, 'The Making of a Late-Victorian Hindu: M. K. Gandhi in London, 1888–1891', *Victorian Studies* (Autumn 1989): 76–98.

Hinton-Thomas, R., 'The Uses of *Bildung*', *German Life and Letters: A Quarterly Review* 30 (1976–77): 177–86.

Hope, Christopher, *Darkest England*. London: Macmillan. 1996.

Hulme, Peter, 'George Lamming and the Postcolonial Novel', *Recasting the World: Writing after Colonialism*. Ed. Jonathan White. Baltimore: Johns Hopkins University Press, 1993. 120–36.

——, 'Reading from Elsewhere: George Lamming and the Paradox of Exile', *The Tempest and Its Travels*. Eds Peter Hulme and William H. Sherman. London: Reaktion, 2000. 220–350.

Hunt, James D., *Gandhi in London*. Delhi: Promilla, 1993.

Ingersoll, Earl G. (ed.), *Putting the Questions Differently: Interviews with Doris Lessing 1964–1994*. London: Flamingo, 1996.

Innes, C. L., 'Wintering: Making a Home in Britain', Lee, *Other Britain* 21–34.

Isherwood, Christopher, *Ramakrishna and His Disciples*. 1965. Calcutta: Advaita Ashram, 1994.

Jacobs, J., *Wilhelm Meister und seine Bruder: Untersuchungen zum deutschen Bildungsroman*. Munich: Fink, 1972.

Jacobson, Dan, *The Beginners*. London: Weidenfeld and Nicholson, 1966.

——, *The Evidence of Love*. London: Weidenfeld and Nicholson, 1959, 1960.

——, 'No Return', *Alienation*. Ed. Timothy O'Keefe. London: Macgibbon and Kee, 1960. 13–22.

——, 'Trial and Error', 1973. *Through the Wilderness: Selected Stories*. Harmondsworth: Penguin, 1977.

Jaggar, Alison, *Feminist Politics and Human Nature*. Totowa, NJ: Rowman and Allanheld, 1983.

James, Winston, 'Migration, Racism and Identity Formation the Caribbean Experience in Britain', *Inside Babylon: The Caribbean Diaspora in Britain*. Eds Winston James and Clive Harris London: Verso, 1993. 221–87.

Jameson, Fredric, 'Third World Literature in the Era of Multinational Capitalism', *Social Text* 5.3 (1986): 65–88.

Jayawardena, Kumari, *The White Woman's Other Burden: Western Women and South Asia during British Rule*. New York & London: Routledge, 1995.

Jouve, Nicole Ward, 'Of mud and Other Matter – *The Children of Violence*', Taylor 75–134.

Kabir, *The Bijak of Kabir*. Trans. Linda Hess and Sukhdev Singh. Delhi: Motilal Banarsidass, 1986.

Kanaganayakam, Chelva, 'Exiles and Expatriates', *New National and Post-Colonial Literatures: An Introduction*. Ed. Bruce King. Oxford: Clarendon, 1996. 214–29.

Kaplan, Carey, 'Britain's Imperialist Past in Doris Lessing's Futurist Fiction', *Doris Lessing: The Alchemy of Survival*. Eds Carey Kaplan and Ellen Cronan Rose. Athens, Ohio: Ohio University Press, 1988. 149–58.

Kaplan, Sydney Janet, '"A Gigantic Mother" Katherine Mansfield's London', *Women Writers and the City*. Ed. Susan Merrill Squier. Knoxville: University of Tennessee Press, 1984.

Kavanagh, Paul, and Peter Kuch, (eds), *Conversations: Interviews with Australian Writers*. North Ryde: Angus and Robertson, 1991.

Kelley, Robin D. G., 'The Riddle of the Zoot: Malcolm Little and Black Cultural Politics during World War II', Stecopoulos and Uebel 231–52.

King, Russell J., 'Katherine Mansfield as an Expatriate Writer', *Journal of Commonwealth Literature* 8 (1973): 97–109.

Kipling, Rudyard, 'The Mother Hive', *Actions and Reactions*. 1909. London: Macmillan, 1951. 83–108.

Kureishi, Hanif, *The Buddha of Suburbia*. London: Faber, 1990.

——, 'London in Hanif Kureishi's Films: Hanif Kureishi in interview with Bart Moore-Gilbert', *Kunapipi* 21.2 (1999): 5–14.

L.M. [Pseudonym of Ida Baker], *Katherine Mansfield: The Memoirs of L.M.* London: Michael Joseph, 1971.

Lamming, George, 'Caribbean Novelist: A Conversation with George Lamming', by George E. Kent. *Black World* 22.5 (1973): 89–96.

——, *The Emigrants*. 1954. London: Allison and Busby, 1980.

——, *The Pleasures of Exile*. 1960. Foreword by Sandra Pouchet Paquet. Ann Arbor: University of Michigan Press, 1992.

——, *Water with Berries*. 1971. Trinidad: Longman Caribbean, 1973.

Langer, Peter, 'Sociology – Four Images of Organized Diversity: Bazaar, Jungle, Organism, and Machine', *Cities of the Mind: Images and Themes of the City in the Social Sciences*, eds Lloyd Rodwin and Robert M. Hollister. New York and London: Plenum, 1984. 97–117.

Lawrence, D. H, *The Cambridge Edition of the Letters and Works of D. H. Lawrence*. Gen. ed. James T. Boulton. 7 vols. Cambridge: Cambridge University Press, 1979–93.

Layton-Henry, Zig, 'Immigration and the Heath Government', *The Heath Government 1970–1974: A Reappraisal*. Eds Stuart Ball and Anthony Selden. London: Longman, 1996. 215–34.

Lee, A. Robert, 'Long Day's Journey: The Novels of Abdulrazak Gurnah', Lee, *Other Britain* 111–23.

——, (ed.), *Other Britain, Other British: Contemporary Multicultural Fiction*. London: Pluto, 1995.

Lehmann, John, 'A Note on this Book', Lehmann 7–12.

——, (ed.), *Coming to London*. London: Phoenix, 1957.

Leiss, William, 'Technology and Degeneration: The Sublime Machine', *Degeneration: The Dark Side of Progress*. Eds J. Edward Chamberlin and Sander L. Gilman. New York: Columbia University Press, 1985. 145–64.

Lessing, Doris, *Ben, in the World*. London: Flamingo, 2000.

——, 'England *versus* England', *A Man and Two Women*. 1963. London: Panther, 1965.

——, *The Fifth Child*. London: Cape, 1988.

——, *The Four-Gated City*. London: Macgibbon and Kee, 1969.

——, *The Golden Notebook*. New York: Simon, 1962.

——, *The Good Terrorist*. London: Cape, 1985.

——, *The Grass Is Singing*. 1950. London: Granada. 1980.

——, *In Pursuit of the English*. 1960. New York: Harper Perennial, 1996.

——, *London Observed*, Stories and Sketches. 1992. London: Flamingo, 1993.

——, *Love, Again*. London: Planningo, 1996.

——, 'The Lost Tribe of the Kalahari', *New Statesman* 15 Nov 1958: 700.

——, *Martha Quest*. 1964. Frogmore, St Albans: Granada, 1966.

——, 'Notes for a Case History', *A Man and Two Women*. 1963. London: Panther, 1965.

——, 'The Other Woman', *Five*. 1953. Harmondsworth: Penguin, 1960.

——, *This was the Old Chief's Country*. London: Michael Joseph, 1951.

——, *A Proper Marriage*. 1964. Frogmore, St Albans: Granada, 1966.

——, *A Small Personal Voice, Essays, Reviews, Interviews*. Ed. Paul Schuleter. 1974. London: Flamingo, 1994.

——, *Under My Skin: Volume One of My Autobiography, to 1949*. 1994. London: Harper Perennial, 1995.

——, *Walking in the Shade: Volume Two of My Autobiography 1949–1962*. London: HarperCollins, 1997.

Light, Alison, *Forever England: Femininity, Literature and Conservatism between the Wars*. London and NY: Routledge, 1991.

Lilley, Kate, 'The New Curiosity Shop: Marketing Genre and Feminity in *Miss Herbert (the Suburban Wife)*', *Southerly* 53.4 (1993): 5–12.

Lloyd, David, 'Arnold, Ferguson, Schiller: Aesthetic Culture and the Politics of Aesthetics', *Cultural Critique* 2 (1985–86): 157–69.

——, 'Race under Representation', *Oxford Literary Review* 13.1–2 (1991): 62–94.

Lurie, Alison, 'Bad Housekeeping', *New York Review* 19 Dec. 1985: 9–10.

Macaulay, Thomas Babington, 'Minute on Indian Education' [excerpt]. *The Post-Colonial Studies Reader*. Eds Bill Ashcroft, Gareth Griffiths and Helen Tiffin. London and New York: Routledge, 1995. 428–30.

——, 'Von Ranke', Rev. of *The Ecclesiastical and Political History of the Popes of Rome, during the Sixteenth and Seventeenth Centuries*, by Leopold Ranke. 1840.

Critical and Historical Essays in Two Volumes. Volume Two. Ed. A.J. Grieve. London: Dent, 1963. 38–72.

McClintock, Anne, *Imperial Leather: Race, Gender and Sexuality in the Colonial Contest.* New York: Routledge, 1995.

MacInnes, Colin, *City of Spades.* London: MacGibbon and Kee, 1957.

McLaine, Ian, *Ministry of Morale: Home Front Morale and to Ministry of Information in World War II.* London: Allen and William, 1979.

Mandeville, Bernard, 'The Grumbling Hive: or, Knaves Turn'd Honest', *The Fable of the Bees.* By Bernard Mandeville. Ed. Phillip Harth. Harmondsworth: Penguin, 1970. 61–75.

Mann, Thomas, 'Goethe as Representative of the Bourgeois Age', *Essays of Three Decades.* Trans. H. T. Lowe-Porter. New York: Knopf, 1965. 66–92.

Mansfield, Katherine, *The Collected Letters of Katherine Mansfield.* Ed. Vincent O'Sullivan and Margaret Scott. 4 vols. Oxford: Clarendon, 1984–96.

——, *The Katherine Mansfield Notebooks.* Ed. Margaret Scott. 2 vols. Canterbury: Lincoln University Press, 1997.

——, *The Stories of Katherine Mansfield.* Ed. Antony Alpers. Auckland: Oxford University Press, 1984.

Martini, Fritz, '*Bildungsroman* – Term and Theory', *Reflection and Action: Essays on the* Bildungsroman. Ed. J. Hardin. Columbia, SC: University of South Carolina Press, 1991. 1–25.

Maslen, Elizabeth, *Doris Lessing.* Writers and their Work. Plymouth: Northcote, 1994.

Mathews, Robin, *Canadian Literature, Surrender or Revolution.* Ed. Gail Dexter. Toronto: Steel Rail Educational Publishing, 1978.

Mee, Jon, 'After Midnight: The Indian Novel in English of the 80s and 90s', *Postcolonial Studies* 1.1(1998): 127–41.

Melville, Pauline, 'A Disguised Land', *Shape-Shifter: Stories.* London: Women's, 1990. 41–53.

Miles, Robert and Annie Phizacklea, *White Man's Country: Racism in British Politics.* London: Pluto, 1984.

Millon, T[heodore], 'Borderline Personality', *Encyclopedia of Psychology. Vol. 1.* 2nd edn. Ed. Raymond J. Corsini. New York: John Wiley, 1994.

Mishra, Pankaj, *The Romantics.* London: Picador, 2000.

Montefiore, Janet, 'Rudyard Kipling', *Makers of Modern Culture.* Ed. Justin Wintle. New York: Facts on File, 1981. 273–5.

Moretti, Franco, *The Way of the World: The* Bildungsroman *in European Culture.* London: Verso, 1987.

Morgan, Kenneth O., *Labour in Power 1945–1951.* Oxford: Clarendon, 1984.

Mulvaney, Rebekah Michele, *Rastafari and Reggae: A Dictionary and Sourcebook.* New York: Greenwood, 1990.

Murry, John Middleton, *Between Two Worlds.* London: Jonathan Cape, 1935.

——, 'John Middleton Murry', Lehmann, *Coming to London* 94–107.

——, *Katherine Mansfield and Other Literary Portraits.* London: Nevill, 1949.

Naik, M.K., *A History of Indian English Literature.* Delhi: Sahitya Academy, 1982.

Naipaul, V. S., *Among the Believers.* London: Deutsch, 1981.

——, *An Area of Darkness.* 1964. Harmondsworth: Penguin, 1968.

——, *A Bend in the River.* 1979. Harmondsworth: Penguin, 1980.

——, *Beyond Belief: Islamic Excursions Among the Converted Peoples*. 1998. London: Abacus, 1999.

——, 'Conrad's Darkness', *The Return of Eva Peron with The Killings in Trinidad*. New York: Knopf, 1980. 205–28.

——, *The Enigma of Arrival: A Novel*. Harmondsworth: Penguin, 1987.

——, *A Flag on the Island*. London: Deutsch, 1967.

——, *In a Free State*. 1971. Harmondsworth: Penguin, 1981.

——, *A House for Mr Biswas*. 1961. Harmondsworth: Penguin, 1985.

——, *India: A Million Mutinies Now*. London: Heinemann, 1990.

——, *The Loss of El Dorado: A History*. London: Deutsch, 1969.

——, 'Michael X', *The Return of Eva Peron with The Killings in Trinidad*. New York: Knopf, 1980. 1–92.

——, *The Middle Passage: Impressions of Five Societies – British, French* and *Dutch – in the West Indies and South America*. Harmondsworth: Penguin, 1989.

——, *Miguel Street*. 1959. London: Deutsch, 1966.

——, *The Mimic Men*. London: Deutsch, 1967.

——, *Mr Stone and the Knights Companion*. London: Deutsch, 1963.

——, *The Mystic Masseur*. London: Deutsch, 1957.

——, *The Overcrowded Baracoon*. New York: Knopf, 1973.

——, 'Prologue to An Autobiography', *Finding the Centre: 2 Narratives*. London: Deutsch, 1984. 15–86.

——, *The Suffrage of Elvira*. 1958. Harmondsworth: Penguin, 1978.

Nairn, Tom, *The Break-Up of Britain: Crisis and Neo- Nationalism*. London: New Left, 1977.

Nasta, Sushiela, 'Setting up Home in a City of Words: Sam Selvon's London Novels', Lee, *Other Britain* 48–68.

Nathan, Rhoda B. (ed.), *Critical Essays on Katherine Mansfield*. New York: Hall, 1993.

Nixon, Rob, *London Calling: V. S. Naipaul, Postcolonial Mandarin*. Oxford: Oxford University Press, 1992.

Nora, Pierre, 'Between Memory and History: *Les Lieux de Mémoire*', *Representations* 26 (Spring 1989): 7–25.

O'Brien, Susie, 'Serving a New World Order: Postcolonial Politics in Kasuo Ishiguro's *The Remains of the Day*', *Modern Fiction Studies* 42 (1996): 787–806.

O'Connor, Frank, 'An Author in Search of a Subject', *The Lonely Voice: A Study of the Short Story*. London: Macmillan, 1963. 128–42. Rpt in *Critical Essays on Katherine Mansfield*. Ed. Rhoda B. Nathan. New York: Hall, 1993. 174–82.

Ogunyemi, Chikwenye Okonjo, *Africa Wo/man Palava: The Nigerian Novel by Women*. Chicago: University of Chicago Press, 1996.

Oko, Emilia, 'The Female Estate – A Study of the Novels of Buchi Emecheta', *Feminism and Black Women's Creative Writing (Theory Practice and Criticism)*. Ed. Aduke Adebayo. Ibadan: AMD, 1996. 91–109.

Oppenheim, Janet, *'Shattered Nerves': Doctors, Patients, and Depression in Victorian England*. New York: Oxford University Press, 1991.

Orr, Bridget, ' "The Only Free People in the Empire" Gender Difference in Colonial Discourse', Tiffin and Lawson 152–68.

——, 'Reading with the Taint of the Pioneer: Katherine Mansfield', *Landfall: A New Zealand Quarterly* 43 (1989): 447–61.

Orrù, Marco, *Anomie: History and Meanings*. Boston: Allen and Unwin, 1987.

Orwell, George, *The Lion and the Unicorn: Socialism and the English Genius*. The Collected Essays, Journalism and Letters of George Orwell. Volume 2. Eds Sonia Orwell and Ian Angus. London: Secker and Warburg, 1968. 56–109.

Osborne, Arthur (ed.), *The Teachings of Bhagwan Sri Ramana Maharishi in His Own Words*. Tiruvannamalai : V. S. Ramanan, 1996.

O'Sullivan, Vincent, *Finding the Pattern, Solving the Problem: Katherine Mansfield the New Zealand European*. Wellington: Victoria University Press, 1989.

Palmer, Eustace, 'A powerful female Voice in the African Novel: Introducing the Novels of Buchi Emecheta', *New Literature Review* 11 (1982): 21–33.

Paris, Scott G., and Karen K. Wixson, 'The Development of Literacy: Access, Acquisition, and Instruction', *Literacy and Schooling*. Ed. David Bloome. Norwood: Ablex, 1987. 35–54.

Parry, Benita, 'David Dabydeen's *The Intended*' *Kunapipi* 13.3 (1991): 85–90.

Paul, Kathleen, *Whitewashing Britain: Race and Citizenship in the Postwar Era*. Ithaca: Cornell University Press, 1997.

Pesman, Ros, *Duty Free: Australian Women Abroad*. Melbourne: Oxford University Press, 1996.

Petersen, Kirsten Holst, 'Buchi Emecheta', *International Literature in English: Essays on the Major Writers*. Ed. Robert L. Ross. New York: Garland, 1991.

Phillips, Caryl, *Crossing the River*. London: Bloomsbury, 1993.

——, 'A Dream Deferred: Fifty Years of Caribbean Migration to Britain', *Kunapipi* 21.2 (1999): 106–18.

——, Preface. *Extravagant Strangers: A Literature of Belonging*. Ed. Phillips. x–xii.

——, *The Final Passage*. London: Faber and Faber, 1985.

——, 'Following On: The Legacy of Lamming and Selvon', *Wasafiri* 29 Spring 1999: 34–6.

——, 'Interview: "Crossing the River". Caryl Phillips talks to Maya Jaggi', *Wasafiri* 20 Autumn 1994: 25–9.

Piette, Adam, *Imagination at War: British Fiction and Poetry 1939–1945*. London: Macmillan, 1995.

Plomer, William, 'William Plomer'. Lehmann, *Coming to London*.

Poddar, Arabinda, *Renaissance in Bengal: Quests and Confrontations 1800–1860*. Simla: Institute of Advanced Studies, 1970.

Porter, Abioseh Michael, '*Second Class Citizen*: The Point of Departure for Understanding Buchi Emecheta's Major Fiction', *International Fiction Review* 15.2 (1988): 123–9.

Potkay, Adam, and Sandra Burr. 'Introduction', *Black Atlantic Writers of the Eighteenth Century: Living the New Exodus in England and the Americas*. Ed. Potkay and Burr. Basingstoke: Macmillan Press – Palgrave, 1995. 1–20.

Powell, J. Enoch, *Freedom and Reality*. Ed. John Wood. Kingswood: Paperfronts, 1969.

Pratt, Mary Louise, *Imperial Eyes: Travel Writing and Transculturation*. London: Routledge, 1992.

Prince, Mary, *The History of Mary Prince: A West Indian Slave Related by Herself*. 1831. Ed. Moira Ferguson. London: Pandora, 1987.

Pritchett, V. S., *London Perceived*. 1962. London: Hogarth, 1986.

——, Rev. of *Collected Stories of Katherine Mansfield*. *New Statesman and Nation* 2 February 1946: 86.

Procter, James, 'Descending the Stairwell: Dwelling Places and Doorways in Early Post-War Black British Writing', *Kunapipi* 20.1 (1998): 21–31.

Pybus, Rodney, '*Cotters' England*: In Appreciation', *Stand* 23.4 (1982): 40–7.

Pykett, Lyn, *Engendering Fictions: The English Novel in the Early Twentieth Century*. London: Edward Arnold, 1995.

Ragatz, Lowell Joseph, *The Fall of the Planter Class in the British Caribbean, 1763–1833: A Study in Social and Economic History*. New York: Century, 1928.

Raiskin, Judith, *Snow on the Cane Fields: Women's Writing and Creole Subjectivity*. Minneapolis: University of Minnesota Press, 1996.

Ramanujan, A. K., 'Talking to God in the Mother Tongue', *Manushi* 50–2 (1989): 9–14.

Ramraj, Victor J., 'Diasporas and Multiculturalism', *New National and Post-Colonial Literatures: An Introduction*. Ed. Bruce King. Oxford: Clarendon, 1996. 214–29.

Rauch, Angelika, 'The *Trauerspiel* of the Prostituted Body, or Woman as Allegory of Modernity', *Cultural Critique* 10 (1989): 77–88.

Raychaudhuri, Tapan, *Europe Reconsidered: Perceptions of the West in Nineteenth-Century Bengal*. Delhi: Oxford University Press, 1988.

Relich, Mario, 'Literary Subversion in David Dabydeen's *The Intended*', *Journal of West Indian Literature* 6.1 (July 1993): 45–57.

Rhys, Jean, *After Leaving Mr Mackenzie*. 1930. Harmondsworth: Penguin, 1971.

——, 'The Ant Civilisation. The Kingdom of the Human Ants'. British Library, London. ADD MS 57856, fs 151–2.

——, Black Exercise Book. Jean Rhys Papers. Department of Special Collections, McFarlin Library, University of Tulsa, Oklahoma.

——, 'Cowslips'. Jean Rhys Papers. Department of Special Collections, McFarlin Library, University of Tulsa, Oklahoma.

——, 'The Day They Burned the Books'. Rhys, *Tigers* [37]–43.

——, 'Essay on England'. Jean Rhys Papers. Department of Special Collections, McFarlin Library, University of Tulsa, Oklahoma.

——, *Good Morning, Midnight*. 1939. Harmondsworth: Penguin, 1969.

——, 'I Spy a Stranger'. *Wave Me Goodbye: Stories of the Second World War*. Ed. Anne Boston. London: Penguin, 1989. 114–27.

——, 'The Insect World' [1973]. Rhys, *Sleep* [157]–[72].

——, 'Let Them Call It Jazz' [1962]. Rhys, *Tigers* [44]–63.

——, *Letters 1931–66*. Eds Francis Wyndham and Diana Melly. 1984. Harmondsworth: Penguin, 1985.

——, 'New story'. Jean Rhys Papers. Department of Special Collections, McFarlin Library, University of Tulsa, Oklahoma.

——, Orange Notebook. Jean Rhys Papers. Department of Special Collections, McFarlin Library, University of Tulsa, Oklahoma.

——, 'Overture and Beginners Please' [1968]. Rhys *Sleep* [63]–[77].

——, 'Rapunzel, Rapunzel'. Rhys, *Sleep* [137]–[44].

——, *Sleep It Off Lady: Stories*. 1976. Harmondsworth: Penguin, 1979.

——, 'A Solid House'. Rhys, Tigers [112]–128.

——, 'Temps Perdi', *Tales of the Wide Caribbean*. Ed. Kenneth Ramchand. London: Heinemann, [1986]. 144–61.

——, 'Tigers Are Better-Looking'. Rhys, *Tigers* [64]–77.

——, *Tigers Are Better-Looking, With a selection from* The Left Bank. 1968. Harmondsworth: Penguin, 1972.

——, 'Till September Petronella'. Rhys, *Tigers* [10]–36.

——, 'Triple Sec' [1924]. Jean Rhys Papers. Department of Special Collections, McFarlin Library, University of Tulsa, Oklahoma.

——, *Voyage in the Dark*. 1934. Harmondsworth: Penguin, 1969.

——, '*Voyage in the Dark*. Part IV (Original Version)'. Ed. Nancy Hemond Brown. *The Gender of Modernism*. Ed. Bonnie Kime Scott. Bloomington: Indiana University Press, 1990. 381–9.

——, 'Who Knows What's Up in the Attic'. Rhys, *Sleep* [145]–[56].

——, *Wide Sargasso Sea*. 1966. Harmondsworth: Penguin, 1969.

Richards, Jeffrey, 'Popular imperialism and the image of the army in juvenile literature', *Popular Imperialism and the Military 1850–1950*. Ed. John M. MacKenzie. Manchester and New York: Manchester University Press, 1992. 80–108.

Riley, Denise, 'Some Peculiarities of Social Policy Concerning Women in Wartime and Postwar Britain', *Behind the Lines: Gender and the Two World Wars*. Eds Margaret Randolph Higonnet, Jane Jenson, Donya Michel and Margaret Collins Weitz. New Haven: Yale University Press, 1987. 260–71.

Riley, Joan, *The Unbelonging*. London: Women's Press, 1985.

Rody, Caroline, 'Burning Down the House: The Revisionary Paradigm of Jean Rhys's *Wide Sargasso Sea*', *Wide Sargasso Sea*. By Jean Rhys. Ed. Judith L. Raiskin. Norton Critical edn. New York: Norton, 1999. 217–25.

Rolland, Romain, *The Life of Ramakrishna*. 1929. Calcutta: Advaita Ashram, 1997.

——, *The Life of Vivekananda and the Universal Gospel*. 1931. Calcutta: Advaita Ashram, 1995.

Rosenbaum, S. P. (ed.), *The Bloomsbury Group: A Collection of Memoirs and Commentary*. Rev.edn. Toronto: Toronto University Press, 1995.

Rourke, Rebecca, 'Doris Lessing: exile and exception', Taylor 206–26.

Rowley, Hazel, *Christina Stead: A Biography*. Port Melbourne: William Heinemann Australia, 1993.

Roy, Arundhati, *The God of Small Things*. London: Flamingo, 1997.

Roy, Parama, *Indian Traffic: Identities in Question in Colonial and Postcolonial India*. Berkeley: University of California Press, 1988.

Rushdie, Salman, *The Ground Beneath Her Feet*. London: Cape, 1999.

——, *Imaginary Homelands: Essays and Criticism 1981–1991*. 1991. London: Granta in association with Penguin Books India, 1992.

——, *Midnight's Children*. 1981. London: Picador in association with Cape, 1982.

——, *The Moor's Last Sigh*. London: Cape, 1995.

——, *The Satanic Verses*. 1988. Dover: The Consortium, 1992.

——, *Shame*. London: Cape, 1983.

Sage, Lorna, *Doris Lessing*. London: Methuen, 1983.

——, *Women in the House of Fiction: Post-War Women Novelists*. London: Macmillan, 1992.

Said, Edward W., *Culture and Imperialism*. London: Chatto and Windus, 1993.

——, 'Intellectuals in the Post-Colonial World', *Salmagundi* 70–1 (1986): 44–64.

——, 'The Postcolonial Intellectual: A Discussion with Conor Cruise O'Brien, Edward Said & John Lukacs', *Salmagundi* 70–1 (1986): 65–81.

——, *The World, the Text, and the Critic*. Cambridge, MA: Harvard University Press, 1983.

Sammons, Jeffrey L., 'The *Bildungsroman* for Nonspecialists: An Attempt at Clarification', *Reflection and Action: Essays on the* Bildungsroman. Ed. James Hardin. Columbia: University of South Carolina Press, 1991. 26–45.

Savory, Elaine, *Jean Rhys*. Cambridge: Cambridge University Press, 1998.

Savory Fido, Elaine, 'The Politics of Colours and the Politics of Writing in the Fiction of Jean Rhys', *Jean Rhys Review* 4.2 (1991): 3–12.

Sayers, Dorothy L. (ed.), *The Comedy of Dante Alighieri the Florentine. Cantica 1 Hell 'L'Inferno'*. By Dante. Trans. Dorothy L. Sayers. 1949. Harmondsworth: Penguin, 1974.

Schaffner, Randolph P., *The Apprenticeship Novel: A Study of the* Bildungsroman *as a Regulative Type in Western Literature with a Focus on Three Classic Representatives by Goethe, Maugham and Mann.* German Studies in America 48. New York and Berne: Peter Lang, 1984.

Schreiner, Olive, *From Man to Man or Perhaps Only. . .* 1926. London: Virago, 1982.

——, *Woman and Labour.* London: Unwin, 1911.

Searle, Chris, 'Naipaulicity: a form of cultural imperialism', *Race & Class* 26. 2 (1984): 45–62.

Sedgwick, Eve Kosofsky, 'The Beast in the Closet: James and the Writing of Homosexual Panic', *Speaking of Gender*. Ed. Elaine Showalter. New York: Routledge, 1989. 243–68.

——, *Epistemology of the Closet.* Berkeley: University of California Press, 1990.

Selvon, Samuel, 'Finding West Indian Identity in London (1988)', *Kunapipi* 17.1 (1995): 58–61.

——, 'Interview with Sam Selvon', By Peter Nazareth. *World Literature Written in English 18* (1979): 420–37.

——, *The Housing Lark.* London: MacGibbon and Kee, 1965.

——, *The Lonely Londoners.* 1956. Burnt Mill, Harlow: Longman, 1979.

Sharpe, Jenny, *Allegories of Empire: The Figure of Woman in the Colonial Text.* Minneapolis: University of Minnesota Press, 1993.

Singer, June, *Boundaries of the Soul: The Practice of Jung's Psychology.* Rev. edn Sturminster Newton: Prism, 1994.

Spivak, Gayatri, *Outside in the Teaching Machine.* New York: Routledge, 1993.

Spear, Percival, *A History of India: From the Sixteenth-Century to the Twentieth Century.* Vol. 2. Harmondsworth: Penguin, 1965.

Springhall, John. ' "Healthy papers for manly boys": imperialism and race in the Harmsworths' halfpenny boys' papers of the 1890s and 1900s". *Imperialism and Juvenile Literature.* Ed. Jeffrey Richards Manchester: Manchester University Press, 1989.

Sri Aurobindo, *On Himself.* Pondicherry: Sri Aurobindo Ashram, 1972.

——, *The Upanishads: Texts, Translations and Commentaries.* Pondicherry: Sri Aurobindo Ashram, 1981.

Sri Ramakrishna, *Life of Sri Ramakrishna: Compiled from Various Authentic Sources.* Calcutta: Advaita Ashram, 1924.

Stallybrass, Peter and Allon White, *The Politics and Poetics of Transgression.* London: Methuen, 1986.

Stead, C. K., 'Katherine Mansfield: the Art of the 'Fiction', *In the Glass Case Essays on New Zealand Literature.* Auckland: Auckland University Press, 1981. 29–46.

Stead, Christina, 'Another View of the Homestead', *Ocean of Story: The Uncollected Stories of Christina Stead*. Ed. with an afterword by R. G. Geering. Ringwood: Viking Penguin Books, 1985. 513–20.

——, *The Beauties and Furies*. 1936. London: Virago, 1982.

——, *Cotters' England*. (*Dark Places of the Heart*, 1965) 1966. Sydney: Angus and Robertson, 1974.

——, *For Love Alone*. 1944. Sydney: Angus and Robertson, 1974.

——, *House of All Nations*. 1938. Sydney: Angus and Robertson, 1974.

——, *I'm Dying Laughing: The Humourist*. Edited and with a Preface by R.G. Geering. London: Virago, 1986.

——, 'Interview with Christina Stead' [1973]. By Joan Lidoff. *Aphra* 6.3–4 (1976): 39–64. Rpt in Joan Lidoff, *Christina Stead*. New York: Ungar, 1982. 180–220.

——, 'It is all a scramble for boodle'. Ed. Ron Geering. *Australian Book Review* 141 (1992): 22–4.

——, *The Man Who Loved Children*, 1940. Harmondsworth: Penguin, 1970.

——, *Miss Herbert (the Suburban Wife)*. New York: Random, 1976.

——, *Seven Poor Men of Sydney*. 1934. Sydney: Angus and Robertson, 1974.

——, *Talking into the Typewriter: Selected Letters* 1973–1983. Edited with preface and annotations by R. G. Geering. Pymble, Australia: Angus and Robertson, 1992.

——, *A Web of Friendship: Selected Letters* (1928–1973). Edited with preface and annotations by R. G. Geering. Pymble, Australia: Angus and Robertson, 1992.

——, 'A Writers's Friends', *Ocean of Story: The Uncollected Stories of Christina Stead*. Ed. with an afterword by R. G. Geering. Ringwood: Viking Penguin, 1985. 494–502.

Stecopoulos, Harry, and Michel Uebel (eds), *Race and the Subject of Masculinities*. Durham: Duke University Press, 1997.

Storr, Anthony, *Feet of Clay: A Study of Gurus*. London: Harper Collins, 1997.

Stow, Randolph, *The Girl Green as Elderflower*. London: Secker and Warburg, 1980.

Sturm, Terry, Afterword. Stead, *Cotters' England*. 353–8.

Suleri, Sara, *The Rhetoric of English India*. Chicago: University of Chicago Press, 1992.

Sunder Rajan, Rajeswari, *The Lie of the Land: English Literary Studies in India*. Delhi: Oxford University Press, 1993.

Taylor, Jenny (ed.), *Notebook/Memoirs/Archives: Reading and Rereading Doris Lessing*. Boston: Routledge and Kegan Paul, 1982.

Theroux, Paul, *Sir Vidia's Shadow: A Friendship Across Five Continents*. London: Hamilton, 1998.

Thomas, Sue, 'Conflicted Textual Affiliations: Jean Rhys's "The Insect World" and "Heat"', *A Talent(ed) Digger: Creations, Cameos and Essays in Honour of Anna Rutherford*. Eds Hena Maes-Jelinek, Gordon Collier, and Geoffrey V. Davis. Amsterdam: Rodopi, 1996. 287–94.

——, 'Jean Rhys, "Human Ants," and the Production of Expatriate Creole Identities', *Constructing British Identities: Texts, Sub-texts, and Contexts*. Eds Andrew Benjamin and Robert B. H. Goh. New York: Peter Lang, in press.

——, 'Modernity, voice and window-breaking: Jean Rhys's "Let Them Call It Jazz"'. Tiffin and Lawson 185–200.

——, *The Worlding of Jean Rhys*. Westport, CT and London: Greenwood, 1999.

Tiffin, Chris, and Alan Lawson (eds), *De-scribing Empire: Post-colonialism and Textuality*. London and New York: Routledge, 1994.

Tomalin, Claire, *Katherine Mansfield: A Secret Life*. London: Viking, 1987.

Viswanathan, Gauri, *Masks of Conquest: Literary Studies and British Rule in India*. London: Faber and Faber, 1989.

Walkowitz, Judith R., *City of Dreadful Delight: Narratives of Sexual Danger in Late-Victorian London*. London: Virago, 1992.

Wambu, Onyekachi, *Empire Windrush: Fifty Years of Writing about Black Britain*. London: Gollancz, 1998.

Washington, Peter, *Madam Blavatsky's Baboon: A History of the Mystics, Mediums, and Misfits Who Brought Spiritualism to America*. New York: Schocken, 1995.

White, Patrick, *The Living and the Dead*. 1941. London: Eyre Spottiswoode, 1962.

Whitehead, Ann, 'Christina Stead: An Interview', *Australian Literary Studies* 6 (1974): 230–48.

'Who' [Sarma, K. Lakshmana], *Maha Yoga, or The Upanishadic Lore in the Light of the Teachings of Bhagvan Sri Ramana*. Tiruvannamalai: V. S. Ramanan, 1996.

Williams, Chris, *Christina Stead: A Life of Letters*. Melbourne: McPhee Gribble, 1989.

Williams, Raymond, *The Country and the City*, St Albans: Paladin, 1975.

Woolf, Leonard, *Beginning Again, An Autobiography of the Years 1911–1915*. London: Hogarth, 1964.

——, *Growing: An Autobiography of the Years 1904–1911*. London, 1961.

Woolf, Virginia, *The Diary of Virginia Woolf. Volume 1: 1915–19*. Ed. Anne Oliver Bell. London: Hogarth, 1977.

Yelin, Louise, *From the Margins of Empire: Christina Stead, Doris Lessing, Nadine Gordimer*. Ithaca and London: Cornell University Press, 1998.

Yglesias, Helen, Rev. of *Miss Herbert (the Suburban Wife)*, by Christina Stead. *New York Review of Books* 13 June 1976: 4.

Yglesias, Jose, 'Marking off a chunk of England'. Rev. of *Dark Places of the Heart*, by Christina Stead. *Nation* 24 October 1966: 420–1.

Young, Lola, 'Missing persons: Fantasising black women in *Black Skin, White Masks*', *The Fact of Blackness: Frantz Fanon and Visual Representation*. Ed. Alan Read. London: Institute of Contemporary Arts, and Seattle: Bay, 1996.

Young, Robert J.C., *Colonial Desire: Hybridity in Theory, Culture and Race*. London: Routledge, 1995.

Zamyatin, Yevgeny, *The Islanders*. 1918. *Islanders and the Fishers of Men*. Trans. Sophie Fuller and Julian Sacchi. Edinburgh: Salamander, 1984.

Index

Main entries to individual writers are in **bold**. References to notes (e.g. 31 n6) are to the page (31) where the note (n6) is to be found at the end of the chapter.